Taylor
Taylor, Lorraine Andrews,
Leaving Time and Tennessee /
$24.95   on1028237457

Leaving Time and Tennessee

Lorraine Andrews Taylor

WESTBOW
PRESS®
A DIVISION OF THOMAS NELSON
& ZONDERVAN

Copyright © 2016 Lorraine Andrews Taylor.

All rights reserved. No part of this book may be used or reproduced by any means, graphic, electronic, or mechanical, including photocopying, recording, taping or by any information storage retrieval system without the written permission of the author except in the case of brief quotations embodied in critical articles and reviews.

This is a work of fiction. All of the characters, names, incidents, organizations, and dialogue in this novel are either the products of the author's imagination or are used fictitiously.

WestBow Press books may be ordered through booksellers or by contacting:

WestBow Press
A Division of Thomas Nelson & Zondervan
1663 Liberty Drive
Bloomington, IN 47403
www.westbowpress.com
1 (866) 928-1240

Because of the dynamic nature of the Internet, any web addresses or links contained in this book may have changed since publication and may no longer be valid. The views expressed in this work are solely those of the author and do not necessarily reflect the views of the publisher, and the publisher hereby disclaims any responsibility for them.

Any people depicted in stock imagery provided by Thinkstock are models, and such images are being used for illustrative purposes only.
Certain stock imagery © Thinkstock.

ISBN: 978-1-5127-5172-7 (sc)
ISBN: 978-1-5127-5173-4 (hc)
ISBN: 978-1-5127-5171-0 (e)

Library of Congress Control Number: 2016912328

Print information available on the last page.

WestBow Press rev. date: 09/19/2016

Human beings look separate because you see them walking about separately. But then we are so made that we can see only the present moment. If we could see the past, then of course it would look different. For there was a time when every man was part of his mother, and (earlier still) part of his father as well, and when they were part of his grandparents. If you could see humanity spread out in time, as God sees it, it would look like one single growing thing—rather like a very complicated tree. Every individual would appear connected with every other.

C.S. Lewis

CHAPTER 1

Distracted

At ten a.m. the fluffy white flakes swirled and tumbled down through the gray sky, crashing into the hard rusty surface over and over again. Minutes passed while the white pixies danced their way down only to become kamikazes giving their all for the mission at hand. By a quarter after, the graves of the fallen had transformed the dirty dumpster into a magnificent white castle. The gaping hole where the drawbridge should have been had taken in an occasional rogue pilot and by half past, the blinds had been drawn, and my mind was forced back into the classroom to learn how to tell time.

Years passed. The very old, long window at the end of the hall caught my eye. I had promised myself I would go to class even if I couldn't find my assignment, but I could see the trees swaying, gracefully inviting me to dance with them. A gentleman dressed in top hat and tails, an angelic creature, really, galloped past on a snow-white stallion. There must have been a dance on the Grand Lawn. Music was playing. I think it was Cole Porter. "Night and day you are the one, only you beneath the moon and under the sun…" It was unmistakably Fred Astaire. The wonderful way he phrased, "Whether near to me or far, no matter darling, where you are…" as he lowered Ginger, "I think of you." Maybe she would let me dance with him, just once. There was still half a song left to be sung, the whole longing part. The window was calling to me, telling me to go. It would be all right.

"Makenna...Makenna Manning? Has anyone seen Makenna Manning?" It wasn't the window calling at all, but Mrs. White screaming. I wondered if she was in the study with the lead pipe – like the game of Clue – ready to clobber me. Why couldn't I have stayed in the always calm Professor Plum's class?

"I saw her around the lockers trying to cram a bunch of papers back in. Looked like she might be there a while," one of my few, odd friends snorted while the class erupted.

I wanted to escape the jumble of busy work, though usually easier for me to keep up with than the treasonous vocabulary cards. They jumped from every nook and cranny encouraging me to skip class. Why couldn't we discuss and exchange ideas, like in Pa's day?

"Makenna, did you take your meds today?" I cringed, feeling the heat creep up my neck and onto my face, as I slid into my reserved seat at the front. How her tendency to blurt out students' private information didn't get her in any kind of trouble amazed me.

"No," I whispered. She didn't really want an answer. I hadn't taken them in months. Medication – any meds – made me feel like a hamster on a wheel, a mean, vicious hamster, at that. The few friends I had, albeit a little eccentric, could not tolerate my change in behavior. A machine, that's all I was, with every waking minute spent in some task relating to my future life, not able to relax or think my own thoughts. I didn't blame anyone for wanting me on a wonder drug, though. Expectations had become astronomical for every Jane and Johnny, and I couldn't hold up my end.

"Mak...Makenna," someone coughed my name. There was no point in turning around. I knew exactly who it was and what he wanted. Any time Mrs. White brought up the subject, the Pest begged me to sell him some. He could get it from half the school, yet he insisted on pestering me.

"Where is your assignment?" A shrill voice jarred me into reality.

"I'd be glad to give you a synopsis of the story aloud," I offered, knowing full well it was futile. A sigh of resignation wouldn't help matters, but one escaped nonetheless.

"That wasn't the assignment and you watch your attitude, young lady," said the now cranky voice. "How you think you will graduate is beyond me...little work done...can't get along with others..." I was considered difficult because I didn't memorize answers – those meaningless to me anyway – and despised group work. It wasn't an inability to get along but an aversion to explaining concepts to others who got grades for doing nothing.

"I did it...I have no idea what happened to it." That was the honest truth though she probably couldn't have read it anyway due to my atrocious handwriting, completing it in about three minutes. Visions of pulling a gum-laden assignment from a pocket in some 80's movie crept into my head while I attempted to stifle the laugh bubbling to the surface.

"Well, you can just miss the pep rally and do it again, in the library," whined Almira Gulch taking Toto, "if *you* really did it in the first place." My face reddened as she insinuated again that my mom had done it. "Oh, do I really have to miss the pep rally?" I countered, giving it the best shot I had at being sincere. Actually, that had been the best thing to happen all day.

"You heard me!" cried the transformed Wicked Witch.

"Yes, ma'am. I misplace things all the time, as you know. But I am not lying to you," I managed to reply as respectfully as I had been brought up to be.

Last class, in the middle of a quiz she charged in, and might as well have attacked Professor Plum – in the study with the wrench – for the petrified look on his face as she proceeded to belittle him for not paying attention. Trusting soul, he hadn't noticed all the roving eyes as he worked at his desk. For that very reason, I didn't have any answers marked, waiting until the last minute so others couldn't copy from me. I wouldn't have changed him though. Plum didn't care if you were the coach's or the custodian's kid. You didn't have to think about how to do well in his class, you just had to think.

The rest of the class filed out to the gym while I went to the Island of Misfit Toys. Through the library door, I stumbled and came face-to-face with the Pest, usually being worshipped in the gym.

"Come on Makenna, you know my parents will kill me if I don't make an A on White's test. You know how unfair it is." If he didn't stop whining I was liable to kick his shins, not my first thought but a nicer way to get him to move out of the way. "I have a game tonight and won't have time to really study."

"Test? Hmmm." I didn't remember we were having a test but that wasn't the point. "Aren't you in the running for valedictorian?" His pouty, pleading face probably worked with most girls but with me he had kicked it into high gear to no avail. "I am not giving you medication. I can see it now, you would be allergic, and I would be in alt school forever. NO."

Ducking into the bathroom before finding a seat at the back of the room, across from a large reproduction of a Van Gogh, I hid. I stared at the painting for some time having already rewritten the three minute assignment in two minutes, my senses prickled with the blobs of muddy yellow. Around and around, the tired brown strokes mixed with faded green leaving a frazzled background of washed out blue. The apathetic *Sunflowers* matched my disposition, and I knew they could have easily been painted on site.

"Well, here you are. Did the Absent Minded Professor really think she could hide from me?"

Why would he not leave me alone? I gave him the required dirty look, and he continued his obnoxious line of questioning.

"What if I told your parents you never took your medicine and threw it away?" The Pest smirked at me, thinking he had me over a barrel.

"Go ahead…matters not to me. Grandmother is the one who insisted and, for some reason, no one stands up to Grandmother."

"What a waste of money!" He countered, thinking somehow I might change my mind with that brilliant remark.

"As I said, matters not to me. I rather enjoy wasting her money, but you might consider I know more on you than you know on me."

The beady eyes and o-shaped mouth said it all. Red faced, he childishly stomped off. Leaving the library, I headed down the hallway to look out the window, once again, but this time Ginger had relented and I was in the fluffy, long white dress dancing with Fred. Sigh.

CHAPTER

What to Do?

No one knew what to do with me in school, and for a time it was decided I must be a behavior problem. My mother assured anyone who would listen that I behaved just fine at home, thank you very much. Then it was ADD or ADHD, maybe SPD with a little OCD, but LMNOP for all I cared. But, according to my father, love his heart, I was unique and should be left alone.

Grandmother, on the other hand, was horrified when I rambled on warning me against watching too many movies. When I reminded her I preferred movies from her era, she quickly changed the warning to "those horrible video games will give you nightmares," even though I rarely played them. She had preached global warming and the destruction of our planet my whole life, but that wasn't supposed to be scary.

In her quest for me to be "normal" I had been poked and prodded and was fine, finally, to be left alone with no true diagnosis, but her doctors thought drugs might help. Help what? No matter how expensive the test, Grandmother wouldn't settle for some minor explanation and told all her uppity friends I had epilepsy and took medication for seizures. Sheesh.

What was so bad about escaping the present when it didn't make sense, no matter how hard you tried? When a situation fit you like a square peg in a round hole? One minute I was actively engaged in life and the next, by necessity, staring off into space having some "wacky episode," as she termed them.

On one of her visits from New York, she cornered Dad in the den. I tried desperately to find something to occupy me in the kitchen so I didn't become part of the conversation. I considered making a pie but that was a no-no. After all, sugar was bad for you. Then I thought of making a pot of coffee for Dad, but we didn't have the right kind for her taste. I decided to quietly get a drink of water, out of the tap, without a filter. Didn't matter anyway, I was always the topic of conversation.

"Kenneth, you are going to have to do something about her. If nothing else, find a private school before it's too late, if there are any decent schools here." A backhanded insult at my mother's upbringing, she delighted in finding a way to make that point for the umpteenth time. Unfortunately, I couldn't debate her point because of my lack of stellar performance.

"Are you listening to me Kenneth?" Grandmother nagged. I shuddered as she poked and prodded my father whose only faults had something to do with her, usually giving in just to shut her up. It didn't seem possible he was her son.

"Mother, you know how Audra feels about that..." Dad agreed with Mom but Grandmother was a pit bull on steroids, and it was easier to blame my mom than to stand up to his mom.

"Yes, we all know how Audra feels about everything. It's always about Audra, never about you or your daughter. Blah, blah, blah, blah. BLLLLLLLAAAAAAAHHHHHHHH De Dahhhhhhhhhhhhhhhhhh."

My defense mechanism kicked in and I tried to tune them out. "Dah, de, dah, de dah she'll be fine once we take a few days off." My Dad's voice brought me back briefly. "We were thinking of popping over to Dollywood." Smiling, I thought of how he always said after Labor Day we could go back there because the Yankees had all gone home.

"Kenneth, you know I was thinking about this new doctor..." I had escaped, and in my mind we were waiting in line for the log ride. No, it's a roller coaster, The Tennessee Tornado.

"Mother, we are done with that, leave her alone."

Roller coasters weren't my favorite, but Dad loved them, and I loved watching his face as he screamed through every dip and curve. Afterwards, loving Southern customs the way he did, we would have to grab a turkey leg and listen to some gospel music.

"I just can't believe with all the advances in medicine..."

I could see us laughing and joking, ready for an exciting adventure. One of the hundred bored kids having to work summers decided to quit chatting with friends and locked the bar in place on my car, and then Mom and Dad's behind me. Children waved as we went by, smiling as if they knew us. The ice cream they probably threw a fit to get was melting and dripping down their arms. But still they continued to wave.

"It isn't yours to decide…"

It was a hot day. The wind felt good on my face as the ride began to speed up, smooth at first. The kids were still waving though I could barely see them. After the first curve they began to laugh – deafeningly loud the faster we went. Faster and faster the cars whipped, wailing and groaning as they made their way through the sharp curves.

"What are you thinking? If you don't get this straightened out, she is going to be…like this…her whole life!"

The wheels grated on the rails. EEEEEECCCHHHHEEEEEE. Why were those kids still laughing? Would this never end?

"And what is wrong with her being like this? Makenna, go outside. Everything is fine. Mother, you have to stop saying such things. I know you are concerned, but we are her parents."

Get me out of the curves, and I would be okay. It would be fun then. At that point the clack, clack, clack of the track moved up, up, up. It didn't help. The speed increased again.

"She is intelligent…much too intelligent to be wasting herself here. Don't you see she has these fantastic episodes because she needs stimulation?"

Before I saw what was coming, I was upside down. Over and over again, I found myself upside down seriously trying to calm down and think.

"She is fine. We are fine. Makenna, I said to go outside… now."

I said to myself everything would be fine. It was just a ride, but I was on and couldn't get off. It wouldn't stop.

"Fine? Fine? You call those grades she brought home last semester, fine? What about all those wonderful papers she wrote? What happened to those?"

What? Who let her read my papers? Papers flew off the ride and into the wind, snatched by a hawk circling above us looking for prey.

"Mother, I told you already. She lost them."

Faster and faster and faster. Noise, noise, noise. Screeching and howling then moaning and groaning.

"On purpose! I bet she lost those on purpose. There is something wrong with this whole situation. How do you think she will ever get into a decent college?"

The screeching of the wheels turned into horrible screaming. Plunging down the mountain with no control, we left the track, flying through the air, and crashing into the ravine.

"Mother, that's enough."

A dull roar in my head replaced screaming, and I looked around to get my bearings. No one else moved. As I counted my fingers and toes, something poured down my face. I felt a deep gash in the side of my head. Where were my parents?

"Oh my, what's wrong now? Tell Grandfather all about it." He had noticed tears streaming down my face. "Look, here's Grandmother."

Mangled trees didn't hide the destruction. Park visitors on the train saw us, and we saw their gawking faces. How did those kids get on that train? The sound of the whistle as the train went around the bend had more of an "I told you soooooooo" sound to it than a whoo-whoo. How did a harmless ride turn so ugly? Where were my parents?

"Audra Makenna Manning. Have you heard a thing I've said?" Grandmother's voice came at me with a dull thud-thud then a dizzy whirring in my head. I ran out the door to get a breath of fresh air as Mom's car was pulling in the driveway. The whirring slowly subsided, and my senses became my own again, relieved she hadn't been here to witness it all, whatever it was.

The chatter lessened as I tried to focus. Had all the chaos surrounding my life affected me so much I was cracking up? Was I the walking wounded, or had I actually become one of the zombies? Nothing like others my age, I dreamed of cohosting the old movie channel not the video music awards.

Mom patted my head and walked past me, knowing instinctively I was upset and who had upset me. Pondering over the chaos in my head made me crazier. Ultimately, I chastised myself because it had no meaning. It was a constant occupation, a coping mechanism for me to make some sense of the polar opposite families I came from and deal with why I was so different from everyone else. But this time, maybe it *was* all my wild imagination taking control.

CHAPTER

2008

A Saturday in mid-June, the summer had already started off with a bang. Two very important events had already happened – high school graduation and my nineteenth birthday.

I'd wager graduation from high school meant more to me than the average student. For some reason I could not comprehend, most of my classmates were in anguish they would not see the same kids they had seen for years, so much so they walked up and down the halls hugging and crying – even the jocks. Not me. Mostly what I had learned in school was how to take abuse, so I was thankful this stage of my life was over.

It was a great birthday, not spectacular by most kids' standards but for me it was more than awesome. If I lived to be a thousand I would never forget camping for days in the Cherokee National Forest next to the peaceful, shimmering lake of Indian Boundary. I canoed, and Pa fished while Mom and Dad rode their bikes on the Cherohala Skyway, "The Ride above the Clouds." We had successfully talked Pa into spending more time with us instead of rattling around at home alone after Ma died. Hiking and breathing in the air of the woods had brought him back more to his former self.

The Cherokee were caretakers of this land long before the English and, eventually, the Scots-Irish appeared in colonial times. Not long after the removal of the natives came further sorrow when brother fought brother and the land was taken hostage by the victors: northern timber and mining companies after the Civil War. After the destruction of the forest and family farms, the companies moved westward, leaving more poverty, desolation, and unemployment. Roads were later built during the Depression and slowly small towns and small businesses developed in the area. The Skyway, built years later, provided magnificent mile-high vistas. It had taken a long time, but somehow the land had survived and healed. Its inhabitants, past and present, told its story.

Here, south of the Smokies and just as beautiful, I felt and heard them. The presence of my ancestors, the ones I claimed, anyway, were a mixed bag of Cherokee, British, and possibly the Portuguese, depending on which theory of the mixed race Mulungeons you subscribed. The others were Scots-Irish, desperately wanting land of their own. Like the others, however they got it, they clung to it and fought for it. The trees whispered of struggles, man against man, while the creeks gurgled, sharing the joy of owning land and raising families.

In the evenings on our trip, we built a campfire making it easy to stuff ourselves on hot dogs, s'mores, and endless conversation. Dad often sang, causing the coyotes to howl and, in turn, Pa would pull out his harmonica, his eyes bright, dancing with memories, and play one of my favorites, "The Donkey Serenade," a tune played a lot in World War II. We sang, laughing then crying, tripping over the few words we knew, for the melody we had heard a gazillion times.

After the birthday, I wasn't sure what the future held, still in negotiations over what happened next. My crazy parents still believed in me, the loving people they were, but I could have said I wanted to be an astronaut, and they would believe I could somehow make it happen. Just had to put my mind to it is what my Pa said. Well, right then all I wanted to do was ride horses and forget all previous years.

Riding around Pa's farm on an old mare had been my life every summer I spent with Mom's folks. Early on, I found I liked to spend time with them allowing my parents to do their traveling thing, mostly on motorcycles. They didn't quite get it that I had rather be at Pa's on a horse than with them playing "Easy Rider." Occasionally, I could be convinced to jump off and jump in the creek to cool off, but I much preferred to stir up dust on an old wagon trail. Seeing how many crazy ways I could ride her without falling off was like kids with their feet on the handlebars of a bike, turned around pedaling backwards. It wasn't a shock to anyone but Grandmother when I gave up English riding and jumping lessons for trick riding and barrel racing.

Sharon and Hank, the owners of the barn, also performed at rodeos and anything having to do with horses. They had asked me to travel with them after graduation, but I hadn't definitely decided. With Pa getting older, I didn't want to miss my annual summer trip and, of course, there was the conflict with my other grandparents. No matter how much I loved my parents, I needed to get away, to stop being the source of arguments.

On that Saturday in mid-June, Mom and Dad were riding Deals Gap and I was packing for my summer trip to middle Tennessee to spend with Pa. The Tail of the Dragon is a favorite with motorcycle enthusiasts, a succession of curves and switchbacks – 318 curves to be exact over eleven miles, easily compared to the whole beast because it could eat you alive. Everything from Harleys to bullet bikes to semis traveled Hwy. 129 into North Carolina, a very challenging and exciting road to navigate.

The Dragon had attracted new businesses in addition to the couple of markets before you got to serious curves. A campground, restaurant, and souvenir shop beckoned those on the highway to stop off for a bite and a t-shirt. Around many curves, your picture would be snapped by photographers and later posted online in one of the newer ideas for making money off the mountains.

Mom and Dad had ridden so many places all over the United States that the Dragon was no biggie to them, sort of their home track. But in the last three years nine people had died. That wasn't surprising. Riders were constantly asking for a death sentence and, as a result, many were ticketed for speeding and improper passing. Orange and red stripes painted on the trees where others had died had no effect on riders who kept on coming.

It was a very impressive thing to say you had ridden the Dragon, especially to scooter trash. Every now and then a guy, I might or might not know, would come up to me and say, something to the effect of, "So you ride the Dragon?" Eye-rolling would ensue and I would reply with a sigh, "No, I ride *horses* in Cades Cove. My parents ride the Dragon." Where they got any of their information, I had no idea, but I answered the question having stupidly promised my family I would try a little harder to be sociable.

Occasionally Mom and Dad would ride through the Park and the Cove on the chance of seeing a bear. The beautiful valley, surrounded by mountains, had been a close-knit community at one time although it was now relegated to a tourist attraction. A glimpse of the once vibrant lives of the families through the now empty cabins nestled in the woods left a bad taste in my mouth. It protected the forests from further stripping but generations of hard work had still been taken by the National Park Service in the 1930's. Riding the trails for me was a time of respect and reverence for the families who gave up their homes so we could all vacation.

Other times, they rode on to Fontana Dam from the Dragon. Mom's folks would come for a visit in October, before cold weather set in, and follow them in the car. A beautiful trip in the fall, no matter what transportation you chose, the trees were so close to the road, arms crawling out of the dips and curves to hug you, while the vibrant yellows and pumpkin-orange leaves blew across the road as you wound along.

It wasn't as exciting a ride for the scooters when the road crowded with sightseers were there for the thrill of the scenery and not the mastery of the road. Sometimes convertibles whipped around the curves, the wind whipping their hair, with the sport bikes becoming impatient, just the same, passing on curves as we held our breath.

As the road slinked on to the dam, the area opened up, a curtain pulled back to reveal the stage – the trees blended together for a magnificent show alongside the brilliance of the lake. When we got to the dam, Pa was my own personal tour guide telling me how it was built during World War II to supply an additional source of electricity to "The Secret City" of Oak Ridge and the aluminum plant nearby.

In addition to the thousand farming families that had to leave the Oak Ridge area, a whole community existed here as well that had to give up their homes and way of life to build the dam. An amazing sacrifice and an amazing accomplishment, you couldn't look across the dam or down into the deep spill wells and not appreciate all the hard work and talent that went into making it. It created jobs for the locals and gave them a way to help in the war effort, yet I still couldn't help feeling sad because it was another ax chopping up the mountain way of life.

Fontana was gorgeous in the fall, but it could truly be said the colors of each season anywhere in the Smoky Mountains were just as astounding. Winter didn't bring in near as much tourist activity, but the views were just as moving. When snow and ice weren't covering it, the winding road of the Dragon was bright and open along Cat Tail Straight with thousands of bare trees sticking up out of the hills like toothpicks. Riders wore cold weather gear challenging the road, shifting right to left around Gravity Cavity, almost lying down yet refusing to give up.

When summer finally arrived, mostly teenagers to middle-aged were on the road. The heat of the day made the rocket boys roar back at the road until they reached that part of the road winding down similar to a funnel cloud. As their eyes adjusted to what appeared to be night, their bodies leaned and strained with each curve. Those thousands of toothpick trees were now wearing the glamorous shades of summer, in unison, making one magnificent green blanket. So dark and green, it could have been Sherwood Forest with Erroll Flynn, as Robin Hood, riding out of the woods at any minute.

On that particular Saturday in mid-June, when Mom and Dad were out taming that Dragon, instead of running into the Sheriff of Nottingham, a Sheriff's deputy knocked at my door. A tractor trailer had taken up both sides of the road going around a curve. My wonderful, crazy parents didn't have a chance.

CHAPTER 4

Sorrow

Tsk, tsk, tsk was all I heard for days after with someone there to tell me what I should think or feel or do. If I got out of anyone's sight for too long, someone had to come rein me back into reality like that was a kindness. Words were pronounced as lines in a drama, but seemed more a dark comedy. If I was to act a certain way, where was my script?

Grandmother just knew I was going to break down or space out to make her look bad as she was taking care of everything, all-knowing, all-seeing behind every door and answering every phone call. Wherever she showed up it was understood who was in control. Unlike the jovial Wizard of Oz, the air of authority her silvery bobbed hair and stately posture gave off made the Wicked Witch into an amateur. In her presence, many a scarecrow had been torched.

"We always hold our heads high, my dear," she said more than once. "It is our legacy." Then she added, "This unpleasantness will soon be over and you can continue the business of being a young woman with a very promising future." She thought the sun came up just to hear her crow.

That future always involved what she thought was correct and, if all else failed, name-dropped that her grandfather was Duke of Somewhere. After he passed away, the rest of the family moved back to New York City from England where Grandmother was born and raised in America. Inheriting wealth, they lived and travelled with the so-called intellectual and socially correct crowd, pretending to care about everyday people yet criticizing anyone who lived in the real world trying to make a decent living. Of course, it was their belief that they spent money correctly which really meant telling everyone else how they ought to spend theirs.

Grandmother could never understand I loved Tennessee as much as she loved New York. Both had strengths and weaknesses, but every Southerner, to her, was somehow responsible for every injustice that had happened to anyone. In her New York Times mind, they were not responsible for anything bad that happened anywhere – tolerant of the world just not us. I guess you could call it elitism, but we called it being a snob.

Grandfather gave the appearance of thinking for himself, wandering around with a drink in one hand and the other in his pocket, jingling change, but ultimately he always did what she wanted. Spinelessly, he made some lame excuse and then returned to his status of the Invisible Man.

"Your Grandmother wants what is best for you. She has made so many plans for your benefit, even taking into consideration the things you have been…involved in here. It will be a different world for you, one we both think will be so much better."

"Well, of course, Makenna. You will see." She had pronounced my sentence without a trial.

The doorbell rang, and she transformed into the Queen of Hearts, on it like a fly on a cow pile ready to "off heads" without missing a beat. This time, however, it was a gang of her friends. A million dollars would not have been enough to give for a picture of the expression on her face. Hypocrisy met hypocrisy, and the nasal pity party began.

"Oh my, I never expected for a minute all of you would travel *here*." Grandmother was actually crimson from the neck up.

"Nonsense! We came as soon as we heard. It's so horrible." So-called friend one said.

"Why on earth someone of their age and responsibilities would have…Kenneth should never have sold his business and moved here. Well, it's no matter now." So-called friend two added and continued, "We had no idea of the area. There was a pleasant airport and an assortment of hotels and restaurants." Between the speed of her words and the bile creeping up in the back of my throat, I had no time or ability to object to anything she said.

"Yes, I think we saw a mall of sorts but then the most unusual assortment of...structures. I know I saw horses, and, I'm not sure, but maybe cows? And goats! I saw goats. Another place, we had to stop for the geese to cross the road to a pond. Then there were several large homes in the middle of nowhere!" So-called friend three almost hyperventilated.

"Haven't you ever seen a cow before?" My voice cracking, I had recovered enough to wonder about this and managed to ask.

"Of course, we have zoos. And who might you be?"

"Makenna Manning, Kenneth was my father. This is Pa, Will Ross, my mother's father."

"How sad for you, my child." Uncertain if she meant about my father or Pa, he wasn't wearing his usual overalls but navy cotton pants and a plaid shirt. Evidently, they still weren't up to her standards. She had fallen out of the ugly tree and hit every branch on the way down, so she had no right to put on airs.

"Howdy there, Mizz Manning. Haven't seen you in a coon's age." Pa reached out to shake her hand and acknowledge the others, but they were scowling at him.

"How dare you use such an offensive term!" so-called friend two shrieked.

"What? Howdy?" Pa innocently replied. Knowing what they meant, he would not change his ways for anyone and didn't expect this representative of the PC police to either. It was still a free country, for now anyway.

"Raccoons live a long time, or so people used to think, and then some of us hicks just call each other that. It goes way back... nothing to do with what you're thinking." I refused to let them think badly of Pa. His speech was endearing with a down-to-earth way of looking at things. Sometimes he exaggerated, going out of his way to make people think he was a *stupid* hillbilly to get them to let down their guard and show their true nature, friend or foe. The latter was not a good choice. Nine times out of ten Pa would make *you* look foolish all with a smile and a wink.

Friend two noticed, out the front window, the Chilhowees and the Great Smoky Mountains behind them. "My, my, I didn't notice what a lovely view you have here. How is the real estate market?"

It went on and on for what seemed an eternity. Insults were disguised as condolences. We didn't know what kind of food was good. We didn't know what qualified as good entertainment. Our customs were stupid. We were prejudiced for wanting to even have our own customs. It was a tired rerun of many television and news programs where the only group perfectly fine to ridicule were white, Southern, Christians. Southerners tried, for the most part, to be friendly people, but it went against the grain being denigrated at the same time.

Today Pa chose to let all that go with Grandmother's friends. Rude remarks came from right and left, yet he stared past them as if they didn't exist. He listened politely to an hour long discussion over how their neighborhoods in New York were being taken over by businesses. Once upon a time, according to so-called friend one, "the restaurants and bars grew organically out of the fabric of the neighborhood, but now it was all marketing buzz or demographics." The worst, to them, was they had become tourist destinations instead of real communities. It never occurred to them, not once, that what they thought of in Tennessee as a real estate market and the national park had been someone's community, too.

While Grandmother was commiserating with her pals over the terrible thing that had happened to her, Pa had managed to slip out to the back porch where I found him and threw myself down at his feet, my head on his lap for a good cry. It was implied only her son had died and in vain. Adding insult to injury, she didn't realize I understood her deeper meaning being the terrible thing, to her, had happened when he married my mother. After that, they had already considered him dead.

"Mac, what 'xactly got you all riled up? Who you thinkin' 'bout? Mom and Dad, or them?" He stopped swaying in the oversized rocker to comfort me, patting my back then stroking my head.

"Both. It's just their attitude. Mom was a good person and doesn't deserve their sneers. Maybe they're right certain things are better but maybe not. I'm sure Grandmother would be thrilled if I moved up there and told her how she and her friends ought to act. She's too busy putting us all in the bad box."

"Why....whattya mean by that?"

"Pop, they think they are better than us and that clinging to our guns and religion is a bad thing."

"Pshaw…what do we care if'n they do think that? We should pity them on accounta' it ain't likely in these times that is gwanna change. But that ain't all is it? All this talk is hidin' somethin' else."

"No, it's just …" Not intending to share my morbidly intense daydream, I weaseled out, "I wanted to prove I could do something without worrying everyone. Now look what has happened."

"Mac, that's what young folk do…it was natural, it is natural to want to be on your own. You didn't cause any of this to happen."

"I can't put up with how they are treating us." The rocker creaked as I jumped away from it to the steps and finally to the yard.

"'Kenna, can't never did nuttin'…" He watched me pace with the patience of a saint as he began to sway again in the rocker, always sure and steady.

"Why couldn't they be like Dad? He didn't just love us, he loved it here. But he did say things would change and he didn't want that to happen."

"Naw, nobody wants change, but it happens ever'where, 'tether we want it or not. You 'member Ma's family moved North 'fore she was born lookin' for work. That's how it is sometimes…tryin' to survive."

"You know good and well that bunch inside aren't just trying to survive." I shuddered at the thought of them moving here. "It's the likes of them that bought land taken from the farmers when they built the dams. Instead of the government giving back what they didn't use they sold it for high-end subdivisions and mansions right on the lake." I was in rare form and kept right on preaching. "Don't they ever think about where those silos sticking up out of the water came from while they're whizzing golf balls over old family cemeteries?"

"Why you worried about them? Only two thangs certain, death and taxes, and you can't do nuttin' 'bout neither one." He conceded my point, but then continued to himself out loud, "Before air conditioning nobody came here that much."

A long time ago, a doctor in Florida helped malaria patients by using air conditioning, but he sure hadn't been a friend to the South since. I began to pace again, adding hand motions and any theatrics that would release the tension taking over my body.

Wishing for all the world I could go on a good hike, I thought about the last time at Clingman's Dome. Trails in the mountains were more of a back-to-nature trek but sometimes you just couldn't beat the paved half-mile trail leading to the observation tower and panoramic view of the Smokies. Along with everyone else huffing and puffing up the steep incline, I witnessed the dark, green spruce mixed together with the sticks of the Fraser firs, the results of the balsam wooly adelgid. From all the pollution around, the firs were my kinsmen, both of us stripped bare by non-native insects. The palm of my hand made a shallow tenor sound against my forehead as I tried, in vain, to smack some sense into it.

"'kenna, you know there's good and bad people ever'where. You jest can't lump ever'one into the same dough. You can't tell me that you ain't met nobody from other parts that wasn't a decent soul." His tone was serious with a touch of sweet, knowing what a mess I was right now.

I mumbled another maybe and then added, "Your grandparents didn't treat you as if you were a stock option." Fumbling for another chair to throw myself down in, I chose a rather hard, metal one that punched back from my weight.

"No, didn't know my grandparents. They died 'fore I was born. Folks didn't have that kind of money then. Not 'round here anyway. Scratched out a livin'. I wasn't raised on no stump…but you knew yer folks cared fer you then if you had food an' clothes, an' a roof over yer head. That's 'bout it."

I was too big and he too frail to sit on his lap and hang my arms around his neck as I had done on so many occasions. Again, I knelt beside him. "You know I try to treat others how I want to be treated but I get SO tired of the attitude."

"You ain't jest whistlin' Dixie. But jest like in any other time, you treat people decent and hope they return the favor. If they don't, then they don't, but you're the better person fer it."

"Well, I think people always try to claim the moral high ground, but it gets very confusing to me to know what that is."

"If'n we really wanted to, we could all blame Adam and Eve seein' that we could still be living in the Garden instead of fighting over what's left of it. But that's all nonsense…we're all sinners." He laughed, but I got his point. "We only have now. Take what you're given. It's no use livin' in what has already happened." He cleared his throat and shakily said, "You can't change thangs, no matter if you try. Forgive and live." I felt a tear splatter on my arm, but he turned his head when I looked up, always the man of strength.

Continuing to comfort me, he prayed for our strength, forgiveness of those who would trespass against us, and as his voice cracked, thanking God for me. Pa always found a way to correct me when I was wrong yet encourage me to do good, challenging me to find a way to use my talents for good. I told him I would be glad to if I knew what they were.

Later at the funeral home, the lull of low voices continued. Pa and I stood for hours as the line went on and on as we were hugged, cried on, and mostly left speechless. It was hard on me, but it was worse for Pa. Watching him grieve again while Grandmother and Grandfather seemed bored by the little people was beyond disgusting. It was an inconvenience for them to come south of the Mason-Dixon line even if it was their son's funeral.

Numbness set in. I couldn't feel my feet. Stepping on them didn't help. Pinching my arm just made red splotches. Pulling my hair should give me a headache, but it did nothing. Biting my lip brought no sense of feeling at all only blood. There was no difference when we sat down to listen to the preacher say a few words about my parents. I felt nothing. I heard nothing. Pa tried to bring me out of zombie land. We smiled and held hands, knowing it didn't matter how much you cried or were mad, it didn't bring them back. You had to accept it and thank God for the time you had with them.

Leaving the mountains was difficult, but there was nothing for me here now. The next day, I packed my things and went to live with Pa outside of Nashville.

July 1, 2008

TO: barngirl
FROM: NewYorkGrandmother

It was over two weeks ago when we last heard from you. Most girls your age would jump at the chance to live in the City. If you have time for equestrian interests, I'm sure we can secure riding time at the stables. We will get to the bottom of your episodes with new medicines available. We will certainly find a suitable tutor, as well. Please consider this a gift to your grandparents while you still have the opportunity. Of course, we will take care of all the legal considerations at that time. You will love it here! P.S. Is something wrong with your phone?

July 5, 2008

TO: NewYorkGrandmother
FROM: barngirl

My job at the barn has kept me very busy. I am still considering the offer to ride the rodeo circuit with my teacher. I've been doing very well lately. The only thing out of the ordinary for me is the urge to color my hair and get a tattoo.

Pa lives in a wonderful farm house on the land where Ma grew up. It's still a beautiful house and gives Pa something to tinker with while I'm out. You are welcome at our home for a visit any time.

Makenna

Lorraine Andrews Taylor

July 15, 2008

Dearest Makenna,

You cannot mean you are living in the house where your other grandmother grew up. It was not one of the most pleasant experiences of my life listening to her tell about her background at your parents' wedding reception. We cannot allow you to reduce yourself to squalor of that kind whether or not your other grandfather has considered this. Speaking of him, I am also concerned you will be living in a house with weapons. It is certainly unnecessary in this day and age. I must advise against it.

It appalls me you would consider a junior college! You must understand that the key to your social life is dependent on the school you attend. What could you be thinking?

We are still at the country house for the summer and, it would please us for you to visit here. I could plan a trip to England for your winter break.

Sincerely yours,
Grandmother

P.S. Did you change your email address? I had to send this regular mail when I could not reach you.

August 1, 2008

Grandmother,

Pa said you must be upset about losing your son to say such things. He understands loss very well.

We live in the main house. Plumbing was installed when it was built. I know you don't understand having to work hard to barely survive, inheriting your fortune as you did. Neither do I, but I looked up to Ma instead of down on her as you have.

It's hard for me to believe that you want me to go to the right school for my social standing. Whenever I decide to attend college, the local school will be just fine. In the next several months I will be travelling on the rodeo circuit, mostly in Oklahoma and Texas.

Pa has to constantly remind me there are good and bad people all over this country. What is most important is how we treat each other. Obviously, money does not buy happiness and formal education does not necessarily indicate intelligence. You might consider reading the Constitution. Thanks to Pa, I do know how to keep us from going hungry.

I loved my family very much. It makes me very unhappy to hear you criticize them or their way of life. It does not make me want to come and live with you. Please respect my decision.

Your granddaughter,
Makenna

CHAPTER 5

Growing Up

Nashville had grown. Like kudzu, it tended to swallow up everything living around it. Every few years a few more miles were gulped in every direction until it seemed you kept driving through traffic lights going north until you got to Kentucky. Not able to stop a freight train on a dime but chugging right ahead, acres of beautiful pasture land were bought up and by-passes put around all the communities. That was what happened to Pa's farm. It was still hard for me to drive down the middle of that gorgeous expanse of horse acreage on the new four-lane.

It was even harder to continue driving through the hills of the Ridge instead of around them to get to Ma's old stomping grounds. Parts of the old road were still there, although one of my favorite hills now resembled a Mohawk haircut gone wrong. I always heard her say they were supposed to straighten out that road ages ago, but the money always went to something else in a backroom deal. Who knows? Ma was always saying that sort of thing. It wasn't as twisted as the Dragon, but accidents did happen. Most people thought economics and safety made it a good idea to build the new road since truckers could transport goods quicker on a straight road. All for the greater good unless, of course, it was your ox getting gored. Several families had their houses moved and others completely moved away.

Many a summer afternoon sitting on an old stool next to the stove, I watched Ma cook supper and listened to her life stories, piecing them together. Now turning off onto the old road, twisting through hills and hollers, I could see the family stories as she told them. The winding, snaky paths led to rusty stills where dirty patrons, young and old men alike were hiding behind the bigger trees, in temporary shacks, chugging their hard earned money. One of the several sweaty slinked out towards home just before dark, the end of a week of toiling. Wailing an old tune and slurping the last of the corn likker from the jar, he crawled out of the holler and made his way slowly toward the railroad tracks on the wagon road. Stumbling over an old dirt fort, he found himself face down in the mud struggling to get up. Cussin' and fussin', wiping the dirt and leaves sticking to his face, he discovered an old minie ball. They were still around in the fields he ploughed, the creeks he waded through sixty years after the Civil War. As he steadied himself on two feet, he flung it at the Rebel ghosts, still fighting losing battles, haunting the tracks and eroding forts still there. His jar, long empty, had disappeared somewhere, and he was angry. The closer he got towards home, the angrier he became at the life he was trying to eke out of someone else's dirt, at the phantom's plight, at his own struggle of trying to provide for his large family. The small board house was in sight, and he cursed it being too small for everyone even though he had to have them all for any of them to eat. He sang twangier and cussed louder wanting them to know he was coming home, to get out of his way and away from this anger caused by life and moonshine.

 Having to stop at the bottom of the hill for the train to pass, I continued channeling Ma's stories and thought of him again, a much older man, slightly hunched over with a cane, standing at the depot that was, in my day, no longer there. World War II soldiers were getting on and off the train while he looked for someone, maybe his own sons, leaving for war. Maneuvers had been conducted there using the wooded areas so similar to regions in Europe where they would be sent. Monstrous tanks practiced in the back fields as trucks unloaded troops to set up tents and get in position. Jeeps honked at excited local girls waiting to ride into town on the train with a new Army beau. Lonely married women waited too, some for their husbands, some for bad news, and some for a good time with someone else. At the top of the hill looking down upon the depot was the estate he had sharecropped with his family for many years. It was good honest work in a very hard time, a way to survive until machines and government checks made it unnecessary though in his case too old.

It was just one story, a small part of the life and hard times of a community when people were so poor they didn't notice the Depression. Traces of it still existed. The once thriving rural community was a sleepy combination of old and new with a reluctance to completely change. There was no depot, general store, community center, or small houses for railroad attendants only old tobacco barns filled with junk, useless as the fields behind the house that were now subdivided, replaced with sprawling, more modern structures. The once proud white farmhouse, now a sad blue, looked down at other declining houses, trailers, and the overgrown area where the store had fallen with age and been removed.

When I settled in, friends and neighbors, some of the best people on earth, came to express their condolences bringing home-cooked meals and home-canned jars of vegetables or fruits. Despite their kind wishes, I felt the weight of the world on my shoulders for several days, pressing down so tight I couldn't breathe.

Hiking to the back of the old property lines, along fence rows and deer trails, I found more scraps of Ma's former life there as the youngest of ten children, mostly boys, working the farm for a place to live and some of the crops. The small childhood home now surrendered its old weathered boards to the vines where new growth encircled the broken rocks of the chimney and every piece of wood choked out its very existence. From the funny tale of a hard biscuit thrown breaking the window to the tragic fireplace death of a sister, her stories swirled in my head. My worries seemed inconsequential here.

Although I was happy Pa wanted to watch a movie after supper, thinking it might be a distraction, I struggled to choose between Jimmy Stewart and Ginger Rogers. When Pop chose Ginger in *The Major and the Minor*, it wasn't long before I was in that train station pretending to be twelve years old, wearing braids and a big hat, snatching a kid's balloon since I didn't have enough money for the ticket. There was no other choice. I couldn't make a go of it in New York.

Hmmph, Ginger should have called Grandmother. Before getting out of the train station, Grandmother would have her enrolled in the best private school, complete with uniform. Rats, was there nowhere I could go, real or pretend she didn't invade?

Not long after, I got a phone call from Sharon, my riding teacher, telling me they would be by in a couple of days to pick me up to go on the rodeo circuit. Pop had called telling her all about what he wanted to do for a couple months and that I was cramping his style. When I made him explain this later, his crinkling eyes tried to twinkle, as they often did with the hint of a joke, but only managed a wink. The sideways part of his sly grin was the only thing keeping us both from bawling. He knew I needed to get on with life, and I agreed on the condition that as soon as he was done sewing his wild oats – most likely allowing the widows in the community to bring him supper or play cards – he would let me come back.

"All righty Miss 'kenna, that's a deal." The tears flowed from both of us when he brought out a new trick-riding saddle replacing the one I always borrowed from Sharon and Hank.

"What are you thinking, silly, spending so much money on this saddle?" I asked incredulously.

"Oh I jest thought I'd begin spendin' your inheritance. You know 'nother big chunk'll be gone after I get passed around by all the fine ladies here. I'll have to take 'em out to supper and the VFW hall dance. That do cost money," he said with a twinkle-wink.

"Just as long as I don't come home to a big rock on one of those ladies' fingers. I get to inspect the troops before I agree to you being drafted." The thought of it sent me into a panic. After all, I was Pa's best girl!

"Ah, 'kenna, you don't have to worry none 'bout that. Jest a distraction until whatever happens happens."

CHAPTER

Horse sense

Sharon had just come off a month's "vacation" from working shows at state and county fairs in the Midwest and a few in the South. Her specialty was Roman riding while her husband Hank's was trick roping and riding. Even when they were off the road, they worked harder than anybody I knew, tending and training for upcoming shows.

Starting out in Oklahoma, the rodeo circuit was equal parts excitement and exhaustion. The day of the show, owners made sure of their place in line while those of us along for the ride groomed and readied the horses. Braiding manes and tacking became something you could do in your sleep if not for all the noise and commotion going on around you. Once the show began, I was relegated to the sidelines unless someone was needed to ride patterns with the Stars and Stripes to open and end.

With the weather cooperating, we booked a local ring for a few days practice before moving on to Texas. We started with some simple jumps over poles and then fences, Sharon insisted the practice would do her good, but it was obvious she didn't want to leave me alone. Mid-morning, Hank came around to give his opinions on just about everything, as usual.

"Wow, aren't you impressive? Think you girls might go fox-hunting later?" He wasn't fond of anything that smacked of English riding, a strictly Western guy. "I might be able to catch one out back. Though at your speed, it ought to be a weasel chase."

"Keep on talking, yeah, keep it up," I countered, sticking my tongue out at him. Competitions got a little cutthroat for my taste, but I did enjoy jumping. Treating me like a prize pony, however, made us both a little crazy.

"Well, just for you we'll switch to pole bending and barrel racing after lunch." Sharon grinned at him and added, "You finally decide to get up and join the rest of the world?" Chronic back problems kept him awake many nights. The horse world wasn't always kind to the body but that didn't stop the two of them from picking at each other. It's how they related.

"Early bird may get the worm, but the second mouse gets the cheese," he smirked. "We need to talk about the trailer tires. Can y'all take a break?"

"Of course, I need a little snack." Conversation about horses was fine but so far I had avoided any heart-to-hearts. Knocking some peanuts out of a tired old machine released frustration but tension remained as I tore out the back and down through the pasture that doubled as a parking lot, getting away from the inspection for just a little while.

While my speed wasn't quite up to par, Sharon decided to work on stunts with me the next day anyway. We headed to the barn where the mats for the horses would make the ground a bit softer if you fell. Again, I got the feeling it was really just an excuse to chat.

"You did great yesterday but I think we need to alternate riding and practicing tricks." She didn't look at me as we stretched.

"Oh?" I cleared my throat trying to get her to look at me. "Good idea, I need the practice ... the lower stunts are harder." I threw my right leg up on the outside boards of the stall using it as a barre.

"I would guess that's true of most people." Sharon was doing handstands on the outside of the stall opposite from me until stopping to push her hair back, casually adding, "Have you fallen off a horse lately?" Not missing a beat she continued her handstands.

"No." I paused. "You know my standing balance has always been better than upside down." We switched places, still not making eye contact. Wobbly with my handstands, I commented, "On a horse and on the ground, evidently."

"How did you sleep last night?" she asked, grabbing hold of the outside stall boards, practicing her stance.

"Fine. Why, am I cranky?" I stood on my right leg, flinging the left out behind me, trying to balance.

"Oh, no. You just seemed a little tired and disoriented after your walk yesterday. We were concerned." Grabbing a rope, she tied it tight to the stall to practice leaning and balance.

"Oh, that. You know, if everything seems to be going well, you have obviously overlooked something." Standing up from a back bend, I exhaled. In my latest episode, I had flown above it all as an eagle and later stupidly explained, "Eagles may soar but weasels don't get caught in jet engines." Half-smiling, I walked out to the ring hopeful she would let it go.

Riding backwards was first and hanging off the side after that. Since we hadn't practiced much before I moved, it was still pretty difficult to get my feet in the stirrups right. A couple of positions weren't too difficult: one leg in the stirrup with the other lifted behind me on the side and the stroud layout – leaning over while standing with both hands out. But the Suicide Drag, leaning over the opposite side with my arms flung out, was mighty scary. If your feet slip, your head is close to the ground and the horse's hooves. Not a pretty sight. After an hour of that, I was ready for a break.

"Makenna, when was the last time you've been out to eat or done anything with friends?" Hank demanded. We had decided to grab lunch at a local diner. Actually two of us decided and the third was drug along, but I had to admit it felt good. Well, it was good until I got the third degree.

"What difference does that make? UHHHHHHH!!!!" I threw myself down into the seat of the booth. Outside the window, I could see a gang of clowns and monkeys, along with gymnasts and unicyclists, walking down the street. I really detested clowns and monkeys but hoped my antics would get them to talk about something else…with no luck.

"Good grief girl, they're just clowns advertising the circus coming to town over the weekend. Now quit trying to change the subject and answer the question."

"I dunno." Mumbling, I hoped he would have mercy on me.

"Okay, they're gone. You are just too funny. As tough as you are, being afraid of them? I know you could probably take those clowns if you wanted to. They look a little soft to me. Don't you think Hank?" Sharon elbowed him, to lighten up.

"Oh, definitely. How many are there? Five or six? I'd say she could take at least four and a couple of those gorillas, too. Now answer the question." He didn't lighten up.

I let out a huge sigh and checked to be sure the circus freaks were gone. Thankfully, they were, but I'd rather deal with them than this subject.

"All right, all right. Maybe the end of June? That probably doesn't count. It was with my grandparents, and they aren't exactly friendly. I moved in with Pop right after that."

"I guess you haven't had a lot of time to find kids your age over there. When we get back I bet Pa has dates lined up for you." Sharon always tried to put a positive on everything even if it did sound like I was in the fifth grade hoping to get an invitation to the skating rink.

"Uh, no, that is definitely the last thing I want right now." Grimacing at Hank, I tried to find the right words. "I didn't want to leave Pop, that is until I realized he was grieving for me." Focusing on the bottle of Tabasco I was flipping around, I tried to stay calm.

"You're kidding. After all his loss, he can see the pain of others. That is one amazing man."

"That's Pa for you. He's heartbroken yet learned how to deal with it on some level. It's still pretty new to me, and he was constantly trying to find ways to fix it."

"I think he was also trying to get you to focus. The main thing is to keep the main thing the main thing."

"Well, Miss Sharon, aren't you just the motivational guru?" Hank grinned.

"Are you telling me the main thing is Pa or riding?" I asked.

"You have to figure out what the main thing is for yourself, but Pa would never want you to make it him. Besides, you never know, that ole rascal might be married when you get back!" Leave it to Hank to put that idea back in my head. It would probably be good for Pa to have someone to share things with besides a stubborn tomboy. But for now, I was not ready to share.

"Maybe, we can fix you up with some nice cowboy while we're out on the road. Hank knows several of the guys that will be in the Houston show."

"Oh, I'm sure that's what I need right now. Another disaster, all because I march to the beat of a different drum, as they say." I dumped some of the Tabasco on the eggs that had finally arrived.

"Well, we'll talk about it later. Maybe I have something that will cheer you up a bit. Did you know I'm working on a show for all three of us? As soon as you get the cobwebs dusted off, I want to begin the choreography. What do you say to that?" Sharon's face glowed with creativity.

"Are you serious? Any kind of particular theme or do you just want to make up double rider tricks? Wait, what kind of costumes are you thinking of? Please don't put me in a toga!" I sounded a bit too squeaky, the result when my brain worked faster than my mouth.

Sharon was a petite, blonde bombshell who always appeared to have stepped out of a salon even though she worked in some pretty dirty places. Imagine Barbara Eden in *I Dream of Jeannie* and you wouldn't be far off from the way she looked to the fact she owned a costume similar to a genie. One particular costume was particularly fitting for Roman riding – Cleopatra to Hank's Caesar. Unfortunately for her, that was the last time she talked him into dressing for a show, considering himself all cowboy wanting nothing to do with anything frilly or fancy. My sentiments matched his, in that regard, exactly.

"Okay, okay. I understand how much you despise dressing up. It's pretty obvious in the way you dress every day. I thought we would go with more of an Annie Oakley type of costume. You know skirts and short jackets with cowboy hats. Hank's even agreed to dress as Buffalo Bill. Isn't that cool?"

"Noooooo, instead we should do Roy Rogers and Dale Evans. Perfect roles for you guys! I could dress as Trigger. Ha!"

"Yeah, yeah. Very funny. You wait. Just for that I'll make sure Sharon gives you the girliest thing I've ever seen. You know, ruffles and stuff!" Hank loved to make light of how I had always been such a tomboy, hanging off monkey bars, no matter how I was dressed.

"Seriously, Mac. I was thinking something Western, but I wouldn't make it uncomfortable. It would really suit you and the show. I promise. You'll see."

The rodeo circuit was tough but challenging, working with the horses and hanging out with Sharon and Hank being the best part. The downside, of course, was being on the road. She tried to keep me focused, not allowing the past to sneak into the present and wreck my future, whatever that might be. Hank continued to be a match-maker with a John Wayne wanna-be here or a singing Gene Autry there. Sometimes I'd go, but it was usually a disaster. I was empty, going through the motions.

When it got really bad, I called Pa. "Lord, girl you would worry an ant. I am fine and getting fatter by the day. That widderlady Smith thinks I oughta get married. I keep telling her no. Miss Audra Jean was the love of my life. When I reminded her that you still live with me and what a pistol you are, she changed her tune."

It wasn't long before I drove myself crazy with the thought of it and went home to stay.

CHAPTER 7

School dazed

It hit the moment my eyes opened even though it had been over four years. Would there ever be a day I didn't think about what we had lost and my part in it? The only thing I knew to do was to get through another day.

The one bright spot besides living with Pa all the time now was working at a barn again. Up-scale horse lovers around Nashville either owned barns or boarded their horses at barns such as the Foster's. It didn't matter to me who owned them, all the horses were special. I could work there 24 hours a day and be perfectly satisfied. Mrs. Foster had to remind me more than once they couldn't pay me for that many hours.

Now community college was not my idea of a plan for the future, but my rodeo pals had decided to start a family, and Pa thought it would get me back around kids closer to my own age. After all we had been through together, he could have asked me to jump off the 109 bridge, and I probably would have. He always worried I hung out with him too much, and I reminded him I had a whole barn full of friends. But he was always right, I was either at the barn or with him.

"Pop, can't you ever let me get you breakfast for once?" I asked as I kissed his stubbly cheek and grabbed a mug of coffee. Always up at the crack of dawn, I could never beat him to cooking. My place was already set with our usual oatmeal, toast and fried egg. We always ate the same thing every morning, never tiring of it.

"Aw, Mac, you know that I don't mind. 'Sides I figured you might wanna take some extra time gittin' ready fer school. You know, brush your hair, and put on a dress, maybe some lipstick…" Calling me Mac tickled me as much as him patting my head and tousling my mid-length, shaggy hair.

"You mean like Claudette Colbert? I don't think a gold lame would work today." We had just watched *Midnight* with Don Ameche. She flits all over Paris in the pouring rain, wearing a gold lame evening dress, looking for a job as a singer transported by a handsome taxi driver. Gorgeous, of course, even soaking wet. "So what are you up to today?"

"I b'lieve there's still a mess of okra in the garden. Maybe a few squash…always plenty of cucumbers. If I can find Ma's recipe I might make some of them pickles you like so much."

"Wow, I'm impressed. Don't wear yourself out though. I don't know what I have to do at the barn, but I'll come back and help you. Maybe a little hot for you to be out."

Suds flew all over the counter as he began to wash the breakfast dishes. Not the neatest housekeeper but determined to stay busy. "Don't you worry none 'bout me. I'll be fine."

But the fact was I had worried about him, all the time! How could one person go through so much and still be so upbeat about everything – and all before the recent tragedies. Adding insult to injury he watched the freedom he had fought for taken away daily and our Constitution shredded, wondering if those years of war had all been for nothing. Now he was stuck with me. How much worse could it get?

"After supper you wanna watch one of them Marx Brothers movies?"

"That would be great. I gotta run Pop. See you later. I love you." A revolving door, I ran out and quickly back in to give him another hug and kiss. He deserved everything nice in the world and never asked for anything.

"I love you Mac girl." He tousled my hair again as I turned to leave.

Every day for the last several weeks, I stuffed my feet into the always dirty boots on the back porch and jumped into the old white truck. It smelled of good times, before death and sadness, with worn seats perfect for the jeans I wore most of the time. Still in pretty good shape for a 1971 Ford Ranger, the engine had been rebuilt some time ago, but other than a tire or the oil I wouldn't let anything else get changed. As long as it got me where I was going I was happy.

Driving into town on the old road, I noticed the change in the trees. It had been a dry summer with another month, or more, before leaves would begin to change colors here with the first cool nights. That is, if they didn't drop off first leaving us without the usually gorgeous show between the hills where the even older roads and paths, still visible, used to be wagon trails.

My favorite, as a child, was around the next turn where a beautiful, blue star had once graced the hillside at Christmas and beamed in the night sky, warming many hearts, old and young alike. The light blue "star of wonder, star of light" represented the star wise men and shepherds had followed now replaced with a huge, blue and white water tower. Looking similar to something from the *War of the Worlds,* I snapped my head quickly to avoid seeing the monster.

For no particular reason, I felt anxious to see the beginnings of reds and oranges of the sugar and water maples. Other times and other places brought me suddenly out of the hills of middle Tennessee into the mountains, to Foothills Parkway and Look Rock or Happy Valley, places we loved to hike and camp when the colors were at peak. Jumping the Parkway my mind instantly intersected with the Dragon. Happy times replaced by the ugly, my brain kept hitting on them leaping up like a mother bear growling with the nightmare, over and over despite my best efforts to concentrate on the good times. Time was supposed to heal all wounds but time was falling down on the job.

Leaning over, I switched on the radio to the big band channel, praying for something to transport me to different times. Glen Miller tunes always calmed me down except when I watched the movie about him with Jimmy Stewart and June Allyson. He died at the end during the War. Most of my favorite singers were gone, too…

"Stop it! Stop being so morbid, you idiot!" I screamed at myself.

"A love song, my darling, a Moonlight Serenade."

Ah, how nice that would be to have someone sing you a song in the moonlight and mean it. Dick Haymes would fit that bill. Hmmm, blonde hair, blue eyes. Why were all my favorite stars dead? I was born in the wrong time, period.

"Shut up and calm down." I breathed in to the music and out with the memories. Imagining how it would be dancing to that tune, I hummed the woodwind parts. As my broad-shouldered partner, maybe Robert Mitchum, and I stepped across the floor, the mirror ball flashed echoing the excitement of all the dancers. Surprised, everyone stopped to applaud the clarinets and saxophones as they stood to play, making the unique sound Glen Miller worked so hard to find. My mind stayed in the 1940's until I was jerked into reality in the school parking lot fighting for a space.

School wasn't too bad. Not that I would want to be caught saying that out loud. I'd had such a chip on my shoulder with the whole idea of it I was pleasantly surprised how laid back it was. Of course, I was older now, but there didn't seem to be any enormous consequences for being yourself. No one beat you over the head about anything. There wasn't a social hierarchy where you bought your friends. I found I could actually breathe in this atmosphere. Some of the kids in my classes might not have enjoyed the discussions I had with the professors, but they didn't particularly care either. It was so different.

My first two classes went pretty fast finding myself in history before I knew it listening to a teacher as old as Methuselah. Although his voice was a little raspy, he fascinated me with his knowledge of so much local history - the early settlers and their adversities and later, famous Tennesseans. When he lectured, it was a challenge to keep from drifting off in my world. This time I was the central character in history instead of a classic movie, one of the adventurous men and women coming of age in some kind of unfortunate circumstance, striking out as much to find themselves as to forget. Probably not a good idea for my grade, but sometimes I got so wrapped up in Methuselah's stories I forgot to take notes.

On one particular day when most of the students were asleep or busily clicking away on their phones, I was enthralled with a lecture about Sergeant Alvin York, a Jamestown native, who had fought his demons and found God. Drafted into World War I, his faith was tested until he realized why freedom was so important and fought to keep it, receiving medals for bravery and skill with a rifle – a survival skill learned on the farm.

The professor posed the question, "Was he right to go ahead and fight after first claiming to be a conscientious objector? What would you have done if you considered yourself a conscientious objector?"

Waiting for an answer, he got none. They either didn't want to think or didn't know how, having been given busy work most of their educational lives, now refusing to participate in something that couldn't be copied or bought online.

Evidently, he saw the wheels turning in my head though I was actually thinking about Gary Cooper in *The Sergeant Alvin York Story*. My love of history and movies had collided. To be completely honest, Gary Cooper could have played the tree in *White Christmas* and stolen the show.

"Yes, Miss Manning?" he prodded.

Stumbling around with my answer I finally said, "I've always thought it was a little presumptuous of us to say what someone in the past should have done or what we would have done. I mean, it's always easier in hindsight, you know 20/20. We can look at it with our 2000 eyes. They looked at it with the experience from their time as we would with our time. What was acceptable in their time period? What were they born with? How could we possibly know what it was like for them to make their choices any more than they could know if they came to our time period and had to make choices now?" Someone from the back yawned loudly. I stopped, somewhat frustrated.

"Would you please cover your mouth, sir?" Mr. Methusaleh shook his head at the very idea of having to teach manners at this age. "Continue Miss Manning...please, go on."

"I know I haven't answered the question exactly. Hopefully I'm not committing the very act I'm trying to point out but every age is critical of those past and I find that a bit egotistical because, in my opinion, some of the things we do today are comparable and even far worse and will, possibly, have far worse consequences." I gulped and added, "But as far as Sergeant York is concerned, I will add, my Pa always said turkey hunting was a good skill to have."

The few paying attention laughed, and I thought Mr. Methusaleh would probably throw me out. Scanning the room for a dissenting argument, or any comment at all, he found the students around the room still snoring or texting. Sighing, he stacked his papers, and said, "I tend to agree with you Miss Manning." Picking up the rest of his books and papers, he walked to the door, scanned the room again, and left.

Okay, so now I was on the same wave length as a teacher and a really old one at that. What was happening to me?

CHAPTER 8

A lot of Manure

Driving by the gorgeous, very old-school barn where I worked was such a kick and had to be for anyone fond of horses. Several others in the area as well had been part of a master plan of steeplechase races in the roaring 20's when everyone was still riding high on the stock market before ultimately hitting rock bottom because of the Depression. The traditional stone structure, accented with white wood trim and matching fences, was holding its own while others had been leveled or transformed into club houses for new neighborhoods.

Long before those barns were thought of Andrew Jackson bought, sold, and raced thoroughbreds in the area. As in his day, the beauty of the horses paled only in comparison to the lay of the land. Gently rolling hills enhanced the appearance of any structure, house or barn, even the old tobacco barn barely visible at the back of adjacent property – the kind seen throughout the South painted with some version of "See Rock City."

"See that barn?" Mom pointed, "We couldn't go there. But the house, oh that house, was wonderful." Whenever we drove by on the way to Nashville, on a rise overlooking the companion barn, a rock house stood comfortably, encircled by the shade of several oaks and maples. Her hands fluttered with emphasis, leaving the steering wheel for a second before grasping again. "Bay windows, hard wood floors with rugs thrown all around, an upstairs, and plantation shutters with so much character. It brought you into its story." The wistful excitement in her voice built.

"I could imagine the horse racing set in certain rooms long ago." She flipped her soft brown hair back over her shoulder, as I had seen her do a million times, describing a time with a friend. "We played *Gone with the Wind* with our Barbie dolls. She had homemade long dresses for hers. We had seen the movie several times by then – goodness, by the time I was a teen I think I had seen it at least twenty times at the theater or drive-in – read the book, too. My doll had long dark hair similar to Vivien Leigh so she had to be Scarlett. My friend was so mad but her doll resembled Melanie, anyway. I don't know why she cared. Scarlett didn't get Ashley as a Barbie either. There was only one Ken!" Giggling at her silly story, Mom flashed a smile and reached over, poking me in the ribs as payback. Memories overflowed onto my cheeks.

Pulling in and around to the back, I noticed Drew's SUV was there. His parents owned the stables, but he didn't ride unless you counted the mechanical bull when he was drunk as a skunk. I thought he might have actually been watering, standing across the ring at the gate to the stalls with a hose pipe wrapped around his arms.

"Hey Makenna, you doing all right…" With anyone else that would have been a question.

"Yes siree," I answered anyway, continuing to walk to the stalls, "I'm doing just fine." Maybe if I ignored him he would just go away.

"Wait a minute there. Why are you in such a hurry?" Throwing down the hose pipe, he trotted along behind me. "My parents have gone to get a load of hay and they won't be back for a long time. You never did answer me about going out sometime," his words matched his slower I'm-trying-to-talk-you-into-something style.

"That was a hundred years ago. What are you doing here anyway, isn't it time for you to go back to school? I started back today." I turned and pointed at the still-running hose pipe.

Quickly turning back to shut it off, not missing a beat, he conceitedly said, "Oh, I was there last week for a, uh, fraternity deal but classes don't start 'til next week."

"Folks that sew wild oats had better pray for a crop failure," I recited under my breath, from one of a hundred kitchen trivets and printed sayings hung on the walls of Pa's house. Then wiping the drops of sweat from my forehead, I checked the board for any feeding changes.

"Plenty of time for us to have some fun," he challenged, winking at me, though I didn't turn around to see. I didn't have to, his modus operandi hadn't changed much, but I did try to pretend he didn't mean what he just said.

"Drew, don't be a jerk. I don't want to date right now. I'm trying to figure out which direction my life is going and I don't want any… complications." Walking past him to the feed bags, I was relieved to hear water splashing once again into troughs, but it didn't stop the conversation. He insisted on hollering across at me.

"I don't think I've ever been called a complication before. I didn't ask you to marry me, just go out with me." Flies buzzed around his head, knowing better than to land on his poisonous sweat.

"Good thing dude. I hope I could find someone a little more interesting than you to spend my life with." Dust coated my throat, punishing me for that nasty comment.

"Ooh burn." He thought a moment before adding, "You do go out don't ya… or have you gone over to the other side?"

"Oh very funny. That's so you. It's easier for you to think that than the fact I'm selective. Now can I please just finish feeding? I need to turn some horses out and muck their stalls." I wasn't going to go into the number of dates in my history, which were few and far between and lately, nonexistent.

"Yeah, yeah. Oh by the way, I think I know someone who knows you," with a slur and another wink.

"Who would that be?" I was afraid to ask but I knew he wasn't going to quit.

"Didn't you go to school with Joe…uh…uh….what's his name? He's in my frat. What a character! He'll try just about anything. Has a really good-looking girlfriend too." You could see it in his eyes. I felt the color drain out of my face as he took a step forward and put his arm against the barn door just over my head. From that posture, he thought he knew exactly what kind of relationship I had. What exactly did Joe tell him?

"Yeah, I went to school with a guy named Joe. We didn't really run in the same circles though. See ya, Drew." Trying not to lose it, I walked away. Pa had talked to me on more than one occasion about keeping my cool when others around you were ugly.

It was all I could do to get into the stall where he couldn't see me. Hot, angry tears welled up to explode. Emotional outbursts were not something I was proud of or easily controlled. If I was happy, I teared up. If something was funny, I laughed until I cried. If I was angry, I bawled while I slammed doors or whatever was around. If I was sad, I wept buckets, and in the last few years I had filled up my share.

Coughing and spitting, I pushed myself to put the harness on Sally, the sorrel quarter horse, grabbing her by the reins and walking out to the pasture, away from my tormentor. I had let him get to me and I hated it. My walls were not as strong as they used to be, tested too many times of late, and now, strolling down high school memory lane was part of a bigger unavoidable everything.

Closing the gate behind me, I thought of senior year, beginning as any other year in school for me. Yuck with a capital Y. Somewhere around October I noticed this kid in one of my classes staring at me. It was not a drooling, ogling stare but more of the laid-back, I'd-be-chewing-on-a-piece-of-straw-if-I-had one, slow and easy stare. New around school, I thought he looked older than a senior, and as most new kids do, at least for a while, ran with the popular crowd.

Slowly walking down the beaten path back to the barn I remembered how he would continue to stare at me, not looking away, even when I would look directly at him. Soon after, he started talking to me, a joke here and there. Every day it got easier to talk and I actually looked forward to seeing him, coming out of a class there he would be, a *Rebel without a Cause* staring at me and waiting, eventually asking me several times to wait for him in the parking lot after school.

I stopped, briefly, outside the barn to spray off the trough and thought of those next few weeks getting to know Joe. When he was with me, he was different, saying funny things, using cheesy expressions. It was such an ego boost when his friends couldn't figure out why he would spend time with me, the social pariah, instead of them.

The wheelbarrow in the hallway waited for me. Grabbing the shovel and rake, I pushed to the first stall stopping to flick my hair out of my collar. Once, I remembered him gazing intently and asked me why I cut it, causing me to instantly look down and stumble over my words. "I haven't had l-long hair since middle school when it was c-constantly pulled out by some jealous girls that couldn't grow their own… I'm a barn kind of girl anyway. Who wants to waste time on hair?"

The shovel smacked the floor as I scooped and tossed, the exertion bringing color to my cheeks, as I thought about the feel of his hand on my hot cheek, turning my head and trying to avoid what I thought was coming. Never angry or impatient, most of the time grinning or chuckling, he picked me up, threw me over his shoulder, and took off running.

My wheelbarrow full, I pushed it out into the hallway, turning back to rake what was left. Back and forth, smoothing out the remnants of old straw, I saw the orchid corsage, such a sentimental gesture, as he nervously cleared his throat and asked if I liked him. Before I could answer, he rambled on about how much fun he had had the last few weeks and how he didn't want it to end as he escorted me to his big black vintage 1940 Ford Deluxe.

The conversation continued in my head as I spread the fresh straw, how I tried to fill the awkward silence. "Wow, you know, I didn't know anybody else drove an old jalopy besides me. What…maybe about thirty years older than my truck? It must be pretty expensive…to keep up, I mean." It hadn't been completely restored but it ran pretty good for such an old car. I rubbed my hand along the exterior, impressed by its age. "Nah, found it in my cousin's old barn, and he didn't want it anymore. Just took a few parts out of some old junk yard cars to fix." He opened the door for me to get in, sliding onto the bench seat affording much more room than modern cars. Couldn't get more retro than this, I thought, as I buried my nose in the whitish-pink bloom on my wrist.

I needed more straw. I went to get it and thought about how he started the engine, revving it up to prove its worth and squealing the tires as we pulled out. Flying down the road, windows down, the oldies channel blared as Joe began to sing along, "I only have eyes for you, dear," then stopped and said, "I like this song, do wop shoo bop. This is pretty nifty but the girl singer was way sultry." His words were a mix of times, something we had in common. I asked him if he meant Peggy Lee. "Yeah, you know her? She's da bomb."

Distracted, I stood in the stall holding the straw thinking I hadn't asked him where we were going and probably should have. Soon we were at the lake access dancing, as he continued to sing what had long ago ended on the radio, "You are here, so am I..." Holding me close, whispering in my ear, he asked me to be his *only* girl, forever.

On to the next stall, I started all over, scooping and tossing, trying not to recollect but seeing myself in a movie desperately needing the director to yell "Cut!" and end this big, romantic cliché stuff. Ridiculously way over the top, and weird for him, I think I mumbled yes anyway. He kissed me, and I stopped thinking about that. I, Makenna Manning, was in tremendous like with this boy. Okay, maybe love. Whatever, it was wonderful. I barely noticed the surprise on his face when he broke into a gorgeous smile, again, from ear to ear all sparkly. He could have been in a commercial for toothpaste.

Raking and smoothing, scratching a bug bite that wouldn't stop itching, I remembered. "Is that your first kiss???" he asked incredulously, searching my face trying to gauge my reaction. He ran his hands through his hair excitedly and licked his lips, as if he were about to tear into a juicy steak.

Tossing the new straw, I coughed from the dust. "Ye-epp." I cleared my throat, nervously, and tried to continue. "Unless you count a very brief but nerdy game of spin-the-bottle in middle school." My voice came out a bit squeaky as I tried to convey the truth.

The wheelbarrow was heavy with manure but I pushed it on anyway. "I knew it. The connection is there. You would love me first. I would be the first." His voice was sweet with a hint of smug and hard to listen to with that lazy stare. Without realizing how quickly things were moving, we were in the car again, the fragrance of the flower and the taste of his lips making it hard to think. What did he say about a connection? My senses were drugged, and I was slow to respond. The first, love me, first, I would be first? I don't know, what did he say?

Heavier and heavier the manure weighed down the wheels, and it was harder and harder to push, but my memories wouldn't stop. Pulling me closer, his rambling didn't stop. Something about how he would win out. Overwhelmed by the moment, I had not thought of the emphasis on *only* girl or the implications of being Joe's girl at all. "I knew it, I knew it," he kept saying.

Out at the pile, I heaved the smelly contents out of the wheelbarrow, going back for more. His voice soured, now mostly smug. Orchids meant love. Did he say he loved me? The only girl forever – was that a proposal? But there was no ring. Did I even want a ring?

Wiping my forehead, I felt the heat of the sun and the stench of the manure. "What are you talking about Joe?" It was pretty dark, and I realized the moon had gone behind the clouds as he continued to plant kisses, through my words.

A slight breeze brought relief while I pushed the clanking wheelbarrow back into the barn. "Hmm? Oh, never mind. It's all good." He brushed off my question and continued his quest, pulling me much too close, tugging at my clothes. He wasn't trying to make it to bases but trying to steal, skip and go all the way to home.

At the next stall, clanking and chunking, faster and faster, I shoveled noisily. "Wait! Oh Joe! Stop it! I'm sorry, I'm truly sorry." Shockingly alert, I was also very scared and pushed him away. "What's wrong? What did you do?" He was finally listening but not moving away as I continued to hold him back with all my strength.

Raking and smoothing, I tried to catch my breath thinking of how spineless I was. "Nothing, yet. I…you misunderstood. Let's go. Please, let's go." My arms quivered. "Really? I misunderstood? Let's go?" The moon reappeared, and in the semi-dark I could see the bright red of his face, not from the moment but anger. "That's all you've got?" "No, I mean, I want to be your girl, yes. But the other…" He sat back to listen then foolishly tried again putting his arm behind my head, pulling me back to him. I had no choice, as I saw it, and slapped his face hard.

Still breathing hard, I threw down new straw knowing I should have started with the face slap and ended with a knee for good measure. "Was that really necessary?" He asked, rubbing his jaw as he started the car, pulling out fast, tearing up the grass until we got on the blacktop where the tires squealed again. "Why yes, I thought so. You weren't listening to me." I scooted over to the other side of the car and looked out the window, not wanting him to see me brushing the indignant tears away.

Dumping the last wheelbarrow full, I put everything away and shuffled back up the path. There was no other conversation only the rattling of the car speeding down the road. When we got home, Mom and Dad were sitting on the porch, thankfully sparing me from a replay. In fact, it was never mentioned again, by either of us.

Kicking absently at a new, but angry fire ant mound along the path reminded me of his betrayal. I took a minute to rest at the gate, leaning my head on the post, throbbing with the memory of how callous he had been, texting me we should break up. He actually said it must not be our destiny after all. Say what? Had he been watching *Back to the Future*? George McFly's goof "I'm your density" would have made more sense than Joe's explanation. It was over, and I felt like a penny waiting for change.

Collapsing to the ground, the memory of the air being let out of my happy balloon should have dulled by now. I tried to pretend it was no big deal. That he had *not* grabbed the heart out of my chest and stomped on it. Every day he was with a different girl, finally dawning on me he wanted me to be his only girl not forever but for that night. The romance had only been a tool.

Sympathetic drops on my cheeks recalled the red hot tears spitting from my eyes as I ran down the hallway and threw my books into my locker. The locker door didn't survive. It couldn't absorb all my anger and betrayal any more than I could stop crying.

It still hurt and Drew had picked at the scab. Joe had mistaken me for someone else, I supposed, a girl who needed to feel special to someone at any cost. No matter how badly I felt for that girl, it was still hard to sit on the sidelines with that kind of competition.

Sniveling and snorting, I pushed myself up off the ground. Carelessly wiping at my nose, I had to admit to myself the whole thing ended so abruptly I never really knew for sure what killed it. Strangely enough, any time I saw him after that he would stare at me for a bit then walk away. When my parents died, he came to the funeral by himself, never saying anything to me but standing in the back staring at me the whole time.

After an afternoon of mucking stalls, I knew Joe and Drew were a lot more manure than manure even was. I returned the horses to their stalls, found Drew had finally gone, and took my favorite thoroughbred, Quasar, a beautiful grayish-white Adonis of a horse, out for a ride. Owned by Drew's parents, he was a special horse making you feel as special to get to brush him, let alone ride him. We walked together down the back lane where at some point I threw myself on him and took off through the back pasture, the wind on my face, blowing my hair in every direction.

The creek was coming up quickly. I needed to slow down. Quasar loved to jump as much as I did and would go over the fence in a heartbeat but without permission I thought better of it. I pulled him up and veered off to the left down by the back fence to land owned by Drew's grandparents posted ABSOLUTELY NO TRESPASSING. Pa said their land had an old graveyard and some other kind of historical significance I couldn't remember, my mind still cluttered with old wounds. I rode on.

Quasar's tail swished, flicking me and the flies at the same time, alerting me of the odd place we had stopped in the middle of the pasture. How long we had ridden or stopped there, I couldn't say. It had gotten late and Pa would be worried about me even though he probably wouldn't mention it. I squeezed my thighs into the horse and headed back to the barn.

Rattling down the road in my old truck, Glenn Miller reached out to me again on the way home, this time *Serenade in Blue*.

CHAPTER 9

Beans and Cornbread

There were few things more comforting than sitting on a big back porch shelling beans. The slight breeze brought the heat down a bit. Pa had been to the garden, as promised, and was now slurping his late afternoon coffee with one teaspoon of sugar.

"How'd your classes go today?" Dead-tired and still he asked about me.

"Oh fine. My history class was quite interesting. Mr. Methuselah is really something." I knew Pa would get a kick out of that, and I considered it my job to come up with something to make him laugh.

"So what do ya' call me behind my back if he is Methuselah?" He crossed his legs and kicked my chair.

"Saint Pop, of course." Actually, his cheeks were rosy and his eyes were twinkly making him more Saint Nicholas though he didn't have an ounce of fat on him. "It also occurred to me today how much you remind me of Gary Cooper. Did you realize that you're that cute?"

"All right, girlie, if I'm Gary Cooper then you must be Barbara Stanwyck." Wickedly grinning, he pulled the old tractor company cap off his head, scratched it, and flipped it back on.

"Ooh, I'll take that! Gorgeous, head-strong, spit-fire, a real take charge kind of girl. Why Pa, how you do flatter me." Spoken in my best fake Southern Belle voice – the one Hollywood thinks everyone in the South speaks.

"Pa, what happened to the world? When did everybody just stop caring?" I pinched the top of a bean, pulling the string down not letting my eyes catch his.

"I knew you's up to somethin' with all that pretty talk." He winked and patted my arm. "What makes ya' thank they ever did?"

"Oh you know, how once upon a time in your day, guys were good to girls. I think it was called respect. You know, in that movie about the nun on the island with the GI in World War Two." I snapped the bean into sections and threw them hard into the bowl. "How are you ever supposed to find the right person?" Surprised by my own question, I didn't know I was looking.

"Well, that's Hollywood. But, I see what you're gittin' at. You can't say that ev'rybody was – jest like you can't say now everybody ain't." He slurped a hot mouthful and gulped it down. "It's not only 'bout findin' the right person, it's 'bout becoming the right person, don't ya know." Squinting, I shook my head. It made no sense to me.

"It seems such a shame good and bad can't find each other instead of each getting mixed up with the other. It would make everything so much simpler if we could just pair off at a square dance." He laughed deeply, wheezed and then slapped his leg.

"You mean fairy tales, where you match up with someone and live happily ever after." Another slurp, he wiped his mouth with the back of his hand. "That's kid stuff that you ought to leave behind when you become an adult. Life ain't like that 'tall. You work on you…somebody'll come along good like that too…you'll know it."

"Ha! Just so much left to chance." I had confused myself, wondering where this conversation was going.

"Not 'xactly, 'kenna. From the beginning of time folks has always wanted to do what they shouldn't. Adam and Eve wanted what *they* wanted. Made life harder than it had to be. The same is true in every age. Not just mine or yours. People want to do what *they* want to do, not realizin' that they jest hurt themselves and…" He dropped his voice, "sometimes the people they love the most.

"I love sittin' here with ya' but I know ya' won't be 'round forever. You shouldn't. You'll meet somebody, sometime or 'nother, and will want to live with him somewhere. I want ya' to know that I will be happy…if it's for one year or fifty." He gazed at me so hard as if he was trying to put all those words in my head, to make me believe them.

"I don't know Pop. Sometimes I think my heart can't take losing anyone else. Even though I want what you had with Ma, I don't think I could have it and give it up. I'm not strong enough."

"Dying is jest part of livin'. We have to give everyone up 'ventually. One day we can live together forever. So we need to be thankful for the days we have. Who said anything 'bout being strong? Right now, we are livin' with the cards we've been dealt. We are doing jest fine! Live thankfully all the time…God will take care of us now 'n later. Now, we need to get supper on the table. By the way, you goin' huntin' with me Saturday?"

"Hmm, I'll go with you if you want me to… so I'm sure to know how….in case the stock market crashes again, or more likely, the country spends itself into oblivion, and we have to scrounge for food. But you do realize pan-fried grasshoppers or toasted crickets would work in a pinch. Just pull the legs and wings off if you don't like them crunchy." I elbowed him, guessing I had him with that remark, but I was wrong.

"That's Ma's girl. You weren't named Audra for nothing." He patted my head and I followed him into the kitchen to put the beans on the stove. "You're thinking I never ate a bug, hhmph. June bugs is pretty tasty cooked over a fire," grinning, I didn't know whether to believe him or not.

"Thank goodness, no squirrel, or bugs, tonight just the original vegetarian meal of green beans, cornbread, okra, fried corn, boiled new potatoes and sliced tomatoes."

"Hey missy, we were happy to get a squirrel or rabbit back when I was growin' up. Beans get a little old if you eat 'em every night."

I couldn't imagine eating that way unless I had to. But I could imagine Pa doing lots of things as a kid such as chores before school, carrying water and firewood first thing in the morning. I could see him in the barn slinging waves of bright reddish-gold hair out of his eyes while sitting on a stool milking or running down the road to school, breaking a limb off a hickory tree and swishing flies, or stopping to skip a rock in a creek. There he was, freckle-faced, squirming in his seat, trying his best to finish up the endless rows of perfect numbers and letters or ciphering in front of the class before he could dart out back to share his cold tater or biscuit from his lunch bucket with someone less fortunate. Miles back home again, maybe in snow or rain, he fed the chickens and gathered eggs. He worked the tobacco in the fields and barns, his back peeling and sun-burned while he hoped not to miss too much school and have to repeat a grade.

After supper, we pulled out the Scrabble board and set it up on the card table in front of the television. Every now and again I would beat Pa but it wasn't likely. He was a pretty smart old guy and could spell too, whether he talked that way or not. It was a win-win for me enjoying the time with him, listening to him laugh at Harpo chasing girls, dropping all that silverware out of his trench coat and being amazed at Chico playing the piano with his index finger. When Pa let out a kind of "he, he, heeeeeee" I couldn't do anything but laugh with him. What else were you going to do when Groucho said, "With a hey nonnie nonnie and a hot cha-cha?"

After a couple of hours, I knew he needed to go to bed. He would sit up until he fell asleep in his chair if I didn't claim to be worn out. Getting up, I pulled the last of the curtains shut and turned off the lights. "Pop, I just can't play anymore. Today was hard. I'd better turn in or I won't have any gas for tomorrow."

"You're right sweetie." He yawned and pushed himself out of his recliner. "You oughta pray about it. It'll do you good. Of course, y' know I'm always here for you if you wanna talk some more about it. G'night." He fluffed my hair and gave me a kiss.

Twelve o'clock came and I was still thinking about what Pa said. If it was anyone else, I would think he meant a boy was going to save me, the knight in shining armor, but Pa didn't mean that. Pa had a lot of hard times and heartache but a lot of love. He wanted that for me.

Two o'clock came and I slung the book across the room and began to pray mighty hard. I didn't know what to pray for but I asked God to help me sort it all out and do whatever would be helpful to Pa. Whatever is in the cards for me, I needed to be strong for him.

Dick Haymes woke me at five o'clock singing *It Might as Well Be Spring*. Bleary eyed and miserable, I pulled on my jeans, rolled up my sleeves, and stumbled into another day.

CHAPTER 10

Mockingbirds and Such-like

Local history was the focus in class today, fact or fiction? A man who supposedly disappeared in 1880 not too far from the school had been discussed as far back as when Mr. Methusaleh had been in college, and we were continuing that tradition with an on-line version.

Lots of people believed it until the last decade when computer research made it easier for people to discount the story as nothing more than a story made up by a traveling salesman who could have also been invented. Either story intrigued me. Out walking in your field one day and the earth just swallowed you up, tasty as a chicken leg. What made people believe it for so long?

Seemed as though I remembered Mom telling me this story in a different place. It would be funnier now since that farm had several stores on it now. Wouldn't it be crazy if you were shopping in the produce aisle and all of a sudden you disappeared? Where would you go? Would you have seen David Lang, the man from the other incident? Was he in another dimension or some kind of prism as the villains in Superman II were? Could the grocery be haunted because of the energy caused by this giant vacuum cleaner that swallowed up people?

What would be the motivation of the salesman besides entertainment? Could he be involved with an early Vaudeville show and practiced on people as the Marx Brothers did when they first started out? Would he have knocked on your door and told this outrageous story? Or was he an Eddie Albert salesman type from the musical *Oklahoma*? Would he have sold you the elixir of Egypt and told you a story as you went into the trance as Shirley Jones did? Was it all a sales gimmick?

Mr. Methusaleh didn't really get into this aspect of the history. I made a note to ask him more about it at the next class with questions I had from the previous reading assignments. Then when I got to class I just fell into a trance as he told us these stories. Maybe he was pumping elixir of Egypt through the air ducts.

Throwing my book bag into the truck, I headed for the barn. On the seat, half out of a ragged tear stuck a small envelope with "Mac" shakily written in Pa's ornate cursive, the kind they taught in the one room schoolhouse. I must have been half-asleep this morning, not seeing another of his sweet little notes containing money. Always afraid I would get caught out somewhere hungry, he insisted on pulling dollars from an old jug he called his boyhood savings. "Don't b'lieve I'll need this in heaven," he would quip. Folding it small, I stuffed it into my jeans pocket for later, gripping the steering wheel hard with my left hand. Dark angry clouds rolled while the wind nearly blew me off the road, looking to pour down any minute. It was doubtful I would get the stalls done before it let loose, and I sighed, preferring not to play in the mud tonight.

The radio, still on the AM station, ached with the Johnny Mercer tune, *Blues in the Night*. From Nashville, Dinah Shore's version was cool with the sass of Johnny's Savannah.

> Mark my word the mockingbird
> Will sing the saddest kind of song
> He knows things are wrong and he's right

What had happened to me? Not a fan of mockingbirds, having had more than one swoop down to peck me while I was taking sheets down off the clothesline, and here I was agreeing with this one. On the outside, I felt strong and in control but play a really old tune, and suddenly I was nostalgic for a time not even my own.

When I pulled off the highway into the pasture road, my teeth clinched together at the sight of Drew's SUV again. What was his problem? Maybe he was here to see his parents for money and not pester me. He didn't seem to know how to make it, but he could sure spend it.

"Well if it isn't the High and Mighty Makenna Manning finally gracing us with her presence." Ugh, he even talked slime.

"Drew, haven't you ever heard silence is golden…duct tape is silver?" He rolled his eyes, my attempt at humor falling flat. I walked around him, sideways from a sudden gust. What I would have given to have had a riding crop about then. I didn't use them on horses, but wouldn't it come in handy about now?

Hoping I'd have time to give Quasar a little exercise before it began to storm, I tied him up in the arena. Drew looked confused over my last comment and continued to follow me around.

"Hey, the parentals wanted me to tell you that they are gone for the evening and to please close up when you get done with the watering and feeding tonight. I could help you so we could get done faster. Maybe we could go get some sushi or something." His sudden camaraderie was laughable.

"Yuck, you mean bait? No thanks, I can take care of it. Can't you find an old buddy to go hang out with about now?" I'd finished brushing and started to pick his hooves without looking up.

"Sure, I'll go ring up Joe and maybe we could all talk about the good old days. It's a shame you don't go to school with us. I'm already a little sad about graduating in the spring so I might decide to take a light load and stay a little longer."

"Oh, I didn't know they offered a major in "revelry and such-like." So far he had not taken the hint to leave. Wishful thinking had me saddle up Quasar in case I could ride.

"What exactly does that mean? Sometimes you sound so old I don't know why I bother with you."

"I'm sure I don't know but I'd be fine if you did stop bothering me." As I turned the corner of the stalls, a loud, booming clap of thunder made me jump a foot off the ground and right into Drew, still tagging right behind me.

"What's the matter Makenna? You afraid of a little storm?" One arm around me, he was so close I could feel his breath on my face. Not good, he smelled of whiskey. Didn't even know the boy touched the hard stuff. Frat boys tended to get wasted on massive amounts of beer.

"No, I'm not afraid of a little or a big storm. I wasn't expecting it is all." I maneuvered past him and continued down the stalls filling the buckets with feed. It would have taken a lot less time if chatter box would hit the road.

Rats… the hose I needed to clean out the water trough was outside forcing me to the other end of the barn to grab my coat and hat. It was raining so hard I didn't want to get totally soaked when there was still so much to do. As I came back through the arena, Drew was doubled over laughing.

"Can't you get your entertainment elsewhere?" By this point, I'm a little more than annoyed at his attention to me.

"You look like a hobo ready to catch a train in that getup, a very wet hobo." He continued pointing and laughing, tears streaming down his face.

"Well, if I was planning on winning a beauty contest I would have dressed for the occasion." Unfortunately, my rain gear was at home and all I had here was a worn out old barn coat several sizes too big belonging to Pa some years ago. I'm sure I looked very attractive, but as usual I did not care.

I hadn't ever noticed how broad Drew's shoulders were but here they were being paraded around in front of me, much closer than I would have liked, in a tight wife-beater tee, not his usual style at all. Not that I thought he was attractive. His personality made him one of the ugliest men alive in my estimation though I was forced to maintain a certain level of civility with him.

"Ooh, Sugar, you checkin' me out? I've waited a long time to get a sign from you."

"Well as Groucho would say, "Time flies like an arrow. Fruit flies like a banana." What I really wanted to say would get me fired.

"What? Ha, ha. Ah, come on girlie girl. Quit putting it off." He punched me lightly on the shoulder in a playfully sickening manner.

"Oh, please. Don't be ridiculous. I've got to finish cleaning in this century if you don't mind." I walked on past him to the hallway and hooked up the hose pipe. He leaned against the stall, staring at me. Again, I was a t-bone about to be devoured, and the last time that happened it hadn't ended well.

"What is it?" I turned to face him impatiently as I continued hosing out the troughs and filling them up.

"You are real nice to look at Makenna. You could stand to grow your hair out and dress like a girl sometimes, you know, show a little skin. You do make me wonder what's under all that clothing." His voice was slurred, maybe a visit to the dentist with a fat lip from a shot. Probably a shot of Jack Daniels now that I thought about it, walking closer with every slurred sound.

"That isn't a very nice thing to say Drew. Your mommy wouldn't like that. Why don't you just go on home now, like a good boy?" As he sauntered over closer, I held up the hose pipe, "I have a brain and I'm not afraid to use it," I joked but he continued, forcing me to let him have it with the hose pipe on full blast. Thoroughly disgusted, I turned the hose off after he pretended to take a shower then grabbed a bucket hoping I could tend to my work enough to get out the door. No such luck.

"Whoever said I was a good boy? Or you were a good girl for that matter?"

"Drew, I swear, you touch me and I'll knock you into the middle of next week lookin' both ways for Sunday!"

"Stop jawing and…Makenna." He grabbed me with one swoop and I shrieked like a squeaky toy stepped on. Over and over, he kept repeating my name. Trying his best to turn my head to his, the wide brim of my hat tied under my chin, kept smacking him in the face. With a grunt, he gave up on that and tugged at my coat. Sensing his frustration and with all the energy I could muster, shoved my knee squarely in the family jewels. He staggered back just far enough for me to get a head start.

Fumbling to find my keys with no luck, the only sure way I knew to get away from him at this point was on horseback. Quasar, hitched to the wall of the arena where I had saddled him, stomped and snorted when I clumsily grabbed the reins and threw myself upon him. Drew, stumbling across the arena after me, coughed and sputtered some insane nonsense.

"Wait, you don't understand. I'm in to you…really…Makenna!" Hunched over, grabbing his stomach with one hand and the edge of my saddle with the other, his face was scrunched up from pain, but his begging had no effect on me.

"You've got to be kidding me. Get out of my way!" I squarely planted my boot in his face and galloped away from him, out of the barn, into the pouring rain.

CHAPTER 11

Pause

Drew was on Satan, the meanest, fastest horse in the stable, but it was doubtful he could catch up to me, let alone stay on him. Anger exploded in me, like a demon attacking, and I couldn't stop. All the hurt from every bad joke, snide comment, failed relationship, and, now, the attempted assault released into my veins, pulsing and throbbing then crashing into the sides of Quasar while I hung on and kept riding and riding and riding. And thinking and thinking and thinking of what he did and said.

Across the back pasture, far from the barely visible pea-brained form of my pursuer, we flew through the pelting rain, darts at a board, stinging my naked face. The worn hat and coat protected the rest of my body though drenched as if in a tub. I couldn't remember being this wet fully clothed. Before I had time to panic or scream or try to stop him, which would have done more harm than good, Quasar was sailing over the back fence, an unbelievable jump, without losing any speed. Hopefully, I would live to tell about it. However, my job would be lost with their favorite horse out in the rain, and they certainly wouldn't believe what their precious son had tried. I was a goner either way.

The rain got even heavier, and we raced through the trees to what I thought was more pasture. A rocky area was just ahead. We definitely needed to slow down. The closer we got the more perilous the situation. It was futile to pull up. He wouldn't stop, and if he did it was likely I would nose-dive into the rocks, a bug on a windshield without the guts to do it again. Some kind of force had taken over. Neither of us would make it at this pace. A bright jag of lightning split the sky and immediately boomed back, lighting a fuse to Quasar and though I hadn't thought that possible, made him run even faster, soaring through the air. I knew we were going to die. He would break a leg. I would crack my head wide open. In my mind, at that moment, there were no other options.

Now jumps were an oddity to me. I didn't care for the cut-throat show competitions, but I did enjoy jumping with a cooperative horse every now and again. As I recall, you went over quickly and there you were, just as we did with the back fence. But this was unlike any jump ever. The lightning had charged the air into a cocoon of sorts encasing us in its fiery inside. Several high pitched tones rattled my ears, but I didn't dare let go to cover them. Instead, a scream from deep in my soul hung in the air an incredibly long time – almost as if someone had pushed the pause button, gotten up for snacks and then to the bathroom before finishing the movie.

Incredibly, somehow, we landed on the other side of the rocks with a sound similar to a sizz-boom spinner on the Fourth of July, depositing us on the ground barely missing the old white oak. Quasar landed and slowed to a trot then stopped, breathing as hard as I was – so hard I didn't think we would ever catch our breath. The snorting and blowing noises and the occasional jerk from the horse echoed my own coughing and hacking, hanging over his side in exhaustion. I checked my ears for blood, certain my ear drums had shattered, but there was none.

Turning back to investigate what exactly we had jumped, I found there weren't any rocks. It was crater-like, a hole scooped out of the ground, with some dead trees fallen around the edges. Had we made that? One side was higher than the other, quite large yet shallow. There was a much younger tree at the place where I thought we had jumped. The scorched grass and other vegetation left a giant grill pit, one upon further inspection had been used before, but it was not wet or muddy at all.

"Wait, when did it stop raining? I'm not complaining but it stopped so quickly!" Muttering to myself, we turned around several times trying to get a bearing on which way to go. Sweating profusely, my coat was dry when I went to unbutton it, but the heat of the sun was not enough to dry it that fast. However, that fireball without a heat shield we jumped over on certainly was. Somehow my clothes were intact, not even singed, and neither of us had burns though we must have been hit by lightning. How else to describe the feeling of being stung all over by fire ants?

"Let's get over to the big house and make some phone calls, Quasar." Slowly, still trying to shake off the irritable, down-right ugly feeling from Drew and whatever else that was, we walked through a bare field to where I figured the house would be. There was no evidence of the tobacco I thought they continued to grow here long after others had quit. Guess I misunderstood, not surprising at all lately, for a whole host of subjects I didn't quite get. We had gone some ways when we came upon a creek.

"Okay, well this works." Jumping down, my legs were jelly, and I had to grab on to the saddle to keep from falling. I let him get a quick drink out of the clear, clean stream, and then decided it would be nice to get one myself.

"I thought they kept cows around here somewhere, too. The water wouldn't be that clean if they did. Oh well, maybe one sip won't kill me." The water quenched my thirst and reminded me Mom would be fussing at me if she knew I was drinking out of a creek, and she would be right. Oh, how I would love to hear her fuss at me again.

We rested a few moments listening to the bubble and trickle of the water while I said a quick prayer exchanging the meanness I felt all over for peace and calm from above. Wishing I had been to their house before so I could get my bearings, I looked around for some clue but found none. Instead, we trudged on with things rattling around in my head. Too bad I didn't have my phone or wear a watch.

The sun was bright. Squinting, I didn't see a house anywhere. Off in the distance, coming from the woods, someone was riding. Who was it? Drew's grandparents were much too old, and they didn't keep horses. Had they let that part of their land get away from them or leave it for trail riding? Wow, they were riding pretty fast, for trails, in my direction. As he got closer, he slowed a bit, enough to scream in my direction.

"Yo, there, make haste. Chickamaugas close behind. Follow me if you desire to live. Tarry no longer!!!!!"

The dude had on some kind of Daniel Boone outfit and rode a gorgeous paint. He wasn't lying though. In the distance, I could see several others on horseback in pursuit, complete with feathers. "Okay," I said to myself, "I'll play along." Maybe I could find my way out if I joined the crowd but it seemed to me I was going back the same way. If I could get them all to stop maybe I could ask directions.

"SSSSSSSIIIIIIIZZZZZZZ"

"What??????" My neck turned with the vibration, and I loudly cried out. Was a giant bug of some kind trying to make a meal out of the side of my head?

"SSSIIZZZ, SSIIZZ, SSSIIZZ" The sounds continued, and I realized those were arrows and frantically reacted as they whizzed past. I had no idea why but whatever was going on, I wasn't staying around to argue with them. These guys definitely had a law-suit coming their way. Shooting arrows on this property and at unarmed citizens was against the law. If they were after a deer, bow-hunting didn't start until late October, so they now had three strikes against them.

With every whiz, Quasar propelled us forward, faster still even though he had already had one tremendous work-out earlier. As we neared the area where I jumped, the throng decided to abruptly stop and ride back in the other direction. Daniel Boone had slowed down to a stop.

"I am glad to encounter thee, my friend. Your presence has been desired for some time. Gabriel Christian, your servant. It is odd, but I felt you might arrive today. I trust you are no messenger of evil tidings?" He extended his hand as we trotted along next to each other. Since I had no idea who this was, I mock saluted him. He frowned at me as if I had slapped him, yanking his hand back.

"Sorry, you caught me by surprise. I don't know how to address Daniel Boone. Are they gonna do that again?" I laughed a little nervous half-laugh and pointed toward the retreating Indians. This was so weird.

"Daniel Boone? He is not of our party. His wayfaring of late is said to be through the mountains. May I make your acquaintance, sir?" The inflection in his voice made a sing-song quality – some type of English accent and very fast.

"Ohhhhhh! It's a reenactment…I didn't realize." Wait, what did he say? "Sir??? I'm Makenna Manning. I work over at the Foster's and got a little turned around…it is a perfect place, I must say. I had no idea they owned so much land!" I whistled with amazement.

"What "Foster's" has claimed this land? 'Tis an impossibility. I know not where you heard this idle tale. 'Tis the third journey to this situation. Our station lies along the way on yon creek and for some weeks. We know not where would be agreeable for a permanent position." He seemed a little more upset as his accent became a little thicker and harder to understand.

"Okay, okay. Calm down. Maybe I got turned around in the storm, and I'm not on the Foster property anymore. Can you tell me how to get there?" Normally, my apprehension of strangers would have kicked in, but even though he was acting oddly, I felt no danger. I smiled at him hoping he would be a little friendlier, then thought twice realizing that was probably not a good idea after what happened with Drew when I tried to be nice. I'd have to get the emotion out of my voice and sound tough just to be on the safe side.

He squinted at me as if he was trying to identify something under a microscope. How long had he been practicing with that language? He was definitely hard core. I'd have to play along until he got tired and told me how to get back.

"I wish not to inquire into the details afore we arrive. I will ask an especial account to the others. You speak of a storm. Only fair weather have I seen for many days. It is exceedingly dry here. Are your provisions then lost in the storm?"

"Provisions? No, you see I wasn't planning on riding for long. I was involved in an ...unpleasant altercation and decided to ride away from it. I just got turned around in the storm."

"Saw you savages in your travels as well? They seem not to have tarried here in some time. We have encountered burial grounds but none of settlements. They hunt the same as we and distrust our intentions as we distrust theirs. What think you?" I shrugged trying to think of what to say.

It seemed like forever we had been riding. The sun was setting behind us, and I was concerned about where we were going. I had already fought off one overly anxious male today and didn't want to do it again. Especially, if there were others. Riding through these woods with the largest poplars I had ever seen and around patches of cane twice as tall as Pa, I couldn't figure out why we hadn't passed any houses or hit a main road yet. We should have passed over another part of the new four-lane somewhere in this direction or maybe the state highway.   "Look Mr. Christian. All I know is I rode through a storm, ended up on the other side of that crater place, and then I ran into you guys playing cowboys and Indians. I guess you could say I tussled with one savage but that was several hours ago now, I guess. I don't really know. I'm so confused. I just really need to let my grandfather know where I am. My horse needs a rest and rubdown. Do you have a phone on you I could use?"

"Others? I know not any. We sought a fur trader, an acquaintance of ours to join us. It is not unusual I would assume so with your mount. The gentleman of whom I speak has wealth as well. Phone… I know not of what you speak." Again, he stared intently at me. It made me uncomfortable, and I looked away. When I felt him finally look away, I peeked back from under my hat at his similar floppy hat, reminding me of a beaver.

"Okay, I'll go to your camp, but they will know I'm missing and come looking for me. If you try anything bad you won't get away with it." I tried to sound stern.

"Bad, you say? You will, then, pardon me if I was mistaken. I thought you were the acquaintance set to join us. We mean no harm." He sounded genuinely sorry.

"Okay, what year are we in? Oops, sorry. I guess you want to stay in character."

"Yes, yes, you must have been long hunting and therefore extremely fatigued. It is August in the year of our Lord 1772."

"Hmmm. Okay. Well I'll have to think about that for a minute if I have a part to play." As usual I didn't know my lines.

We rode along in silence, confusion keeping me quiet. Winding in and out of large walnut trees, the dirt paths we followed were obviously made by animals running through over and over, keeping the vegetation to a minimum. Ma had shown me animal paths through the woods to her place and then some had become wagon trails, and then later roads, but this was unlike anything we had seen in her neck of the woods and less than ten miles from there I would guess.

When we reached a creek we turned north and rode parallel with it. Was it the same I drank out of earlier but further north? If so, it had cut a much larger area in the land. A campfire and some lanterns flickered ahead. Breathing a sigh of relief, I knew it was getting awfully dark and nobody seemed to have brought a flashlight.

"Who comes hither among the beasts and dangers of the wilderness?" The words sounded more menacing than the tone of voice.

"Talk of the devil and he will come!" This guy had a sense of humor, and I chuckled lightly.

"Don't tell me, Davy Crockett and Sam Houston?" I laughed while Daniel Boone glanced quizzically in my direction. Guess he didn't have a sense of humor after all.

We dismounted and were joined by a group of men dressed similar to Daniel Boone – long shirts tied at the waist, leggings, and moccasins – but different lengths and styles, if you could call it that, for each. Coarse material of the shirts made the seams crude and the leggings awkward. All were shaking my hand and patting me on the back as if they expected me. Another larger group was off in the distance at another campfire.

"I have not the person we expected. Kenneth Manning here appeared within the sound of an ambushment, out of the thicket by the accursed place."

He gave a knowing glance to the others. The man who seemed to be in charge introduced himself and some of the others so quickly I caught only a few of the names. Wait, did he call me Kenneth?

"Greetings Kenneth Manning. Pay no mind to Mr. Christian with the beard. He thinks himself a French woodsman…coureurs de bois." Grabbing hold of it and laughing loudly, Daniel Boone smacked his hand away, playfully shoving him back.

"What news have you?" demanded another of the men, evidently impatient with the horseplay and stepped forward.

This was one rough looking bunch. Whomever Gabriel Christian was, had a beard, the rest five o'clock shadow, playing early explorers in perfect character. Reminding me of how my dad looked in high school with shoulder length dark hair and fringed suede from the 70's, I would hope he bathed more frequently.

"This boy has been separated from his grandfather in a storm and without arms. He desires a phone. Do you have such he might use? I am unfamiliar with that weaponry." Christian arched his brows trying desperately to stay in character while I tried desperately not to laugh. They were so serious about it all.

"I am glad you are in health. God keep him, if he was wise to find shelter in a cave or a tree. We have encountered Chickamaugas. Upon our arrival in May, they had but little interest. They have decided to attack of late. We had been some distance and upon return our camp was plundered. We have only recently recovered and rebuilt our lean-to." The others nodded in a concerned way as the head guy spoke.

"Vee know not ter "phone" but vee vill share ter rifle and ter teer, understant 'til you fint your supplies. Put you may as vell pring us some goot fortune." Another acknowledged the look and kindly added whatever help he could give me. I didn't know what to say, but I did know how to shoot.

"We were most fortunate they are still superstitious and turned back at the barren area. We found safety there." Christian turned to them, walking over to a small fire.

"Okay, guys. I'm sorry if I messed up your...game? But it is really late and I need to get back. Can we just talk on the level here?" They turned back at my pleading, looking at me very strangely. I'd progressed from something under the microscope to something from *Lost in Space*. They turned to each other again and spoke in low voices.

I wasn't sure what to do at this point but I did know Quasar needed some attention. We walked over to the creek and got a drink. I fidgeted with his saddle trying to overhear what the men were talking about. It seemed Daniel Boone was relating parts of my conversation to them but not telling it exactly right. He seemed to think *I* must be crazy! Not good times crazy, mentally ill crazy. This had to be a joke.

"Believe you this boy's account?" one man asked Christian.

"I know not what to make of it. He is very odd. He may have the fever though I have not seen him purge. Some talk out of their heads with strange words when they are ill. London is not the only place for the sickness and the evils surrounding it, I see." Christian's voice took a strange tone. It was a language I recognized, tragedy and death.

Something was not right here. Since I couldn't get them to stop and help me, maybe I'd be the sick boy, a jab at my vanity but not a stretch the way I looked in these clothes. They seemed surprised when I walked over and interrupted their conversation.

"Ummm guys, I'm not feeling very well. I'm going to lie down under this tree for a while and catch some zzzz's." I practically threw myself down on the ground at an angle where I could watch their reactions.

They definitely thought something was wrong with me. Daniel Boone stared in my direction while the others mumbled something and sat down. I waited for him to leave but he sat down not far from me.

Someone said matter-of-factly, "Were we not preparing to leave soon?"

Another voice, vaguely, a German accent said, "Ja, not much powder left. Vee shoult break camp and leaf ter home."

"How many pelts have we now since the thievish skulks made off with them?" There was definite anger in that voice although it did no good to cry over spilt milk.

"Not as many as we need... we must try to recover them. With the warmness of days the buffalo are thin and not good for much meat. Leave soon, maybe a week or so, and we will be in Virginny before winter."

Two voices sounded similar, a sort of looser English accent, not cockney though I couldn't exactly place it. Christian's was thicker and much quicker while another's was a jumble of English and German.

When it was quiet I pretended to snore hoping he would believe I was asleep and leave but no luck. The others went to the small shelter but he began to hum, then playing some kind of flute, so soothing it could have been something Pa played on the harmonica. Sleep was taking over and all thoughts of escape to find Pa gave way to exhaustion.

CHAPTER 12

You Snooze, You Lose

"A quarter hour since the sun arose and still he sleeps. We need not delay with our supplies low and need of furs to trade. The others left some time ago."

"Even so. He may be worse upon awakening. Go you ahead. If all is well, we shall not tarry long. If he is not well, I will make him comfortable and leave on my own. Take you the pack horses for the kill."

"I hope for your sake he will arouse absent the madness. Gabriel, God speed."

"Thou sayest well. God speed."

Who was talking? My head was thick with a roar and somewhere off in the background an old movie was playing with an English actor... Laurence Olivier, no, maybe Leslie Howard. I wasn't sure, but Pa never watched anything except the news in the morning before he went out. Ugh, was I sore! Sitting up and stretching was painful and rubbing my eyes brought into focus a strange man sitting not far from me.

"Ayyyyyy, who are you?" I jumped up and took a few steps back tripping over my feet and falling down again.

"Do you not remember yesterday?" Pausing, he covered his mouth to laugh where he thought I couldn't see. "Your way was lost in a storm apart from your grandfather. The savages gave chase afore we came here. Gabriel Christian is my name. The others have not long gone. Are you in health today?" He steadied me and then guided me over to a low fire.

"Uhhhhh, I think I'm okay. Seriously, you're keeping up this charade today? I can't take this anymore. You have to let me call my Pa. Let me go home." I shrugged his arm off of me.

"Young Manning, I do not know of what you speak. You are free to leave but it is not wise to journey alone unfamiliar as you are. Where is your home and of what length were your journeys?" His voice was soft and kind as if he was talking to a child. Oh right, he thought I was a young boy. He poured something into a cup, offering it to me with a question in his expression.

It didn't taste like any coffee I'd ever had. I was about to ask him what on earth he had given me when I began to recognize where I was. Although pretty far away from the hills, it was the creek running along the road coming out of the holler. The cut of the creek and the shade of grass I remembered distinctly from when I was a child going with Pa to dig up ferns or gather mint out of the smaller streams weaving in and out of the hills. How green and mossy the grass was next to the creek, as if someone had sliced a chunk out of the earth, filled it with water, and iced the banks with mashed up green Fruit Loops. As green as the grass was, the earth under it was a dark brown rich, fertile, easy-to-grow-a-garden-brown, nothing to the red clay of my home in East Tennessee.

"Would you mind telling me again where we are and how you got here? I'm a little confused this morning. Please forgive me." My voice was shaky but I didn't know how to make it stop.

"We are some miles from the Cumberland River where we arrived. We have encamped at this station from May of this year, seventeen hundred seventy-two. Virginia is our home place. If you are still unwell, permit me to help you lie down." He seemed as nervous as I was though I couldn't imagine why.

"No, no. I need to find my grandfather though I have no idea where he might be." I continued to drink the very strong liquid not caring what it was at that point. He offered me some type of meat but I didn't think I could stomach that.

"You are not well, then? Do you know what kind of illness you suffer from?"

"Ugh, not really sick just a little tired from all the confusion of being lost. I'm sure you can understand that." Oh, I finally got it. He thought I might have something contagious and didn't really want to be around me. Did I remember him saying something about the sickness last night or was that a dream?

Where were the houses close to this creek? Mom had a school friend living up the road only there was no road, but a path made from the horses and whatever animals had tracked through here. The steeple of the white church on the left over the rise should be visible but there wasn't one there. Where were all the landmarks? All I saw were trees, the creek, and this very strange campsite. It was as if I were here before anything was built. My head was swimming from turning this over and over in my head.

"I am pleased to hear it. I have had my share of sickness and do not desire its presence again. You should eat...we need to leave soon and may encounter your grandfather on hunt. Our supplies are low and are little to trade with due to the scoundrels plundering our camp some time ago." He was up walking toward his horse. "If you remain with us again, might I suggest you sleep closer to our protection?" He pointed toward the lean-to where skins had been thrown back to reveal a gun resting upon two sets of forked sticks stuck in the ground. "It is primed and at the ready in case of attack."

"Of course...could you give me a few minutes to...compose myself?" Not waiting for an answer, I quickly darted behind a large hickory tree. Like old times when hunting with Pa, you either had to hold it or go behind a tree, except this time I was with a group of men who played pioneer so it wasn't a good idea to hold it. Afterwards, I attempted to wash my face in the creek but not going very well I dunked my whole head. As the water dripped around me, realization slowly sank in. Was this some kind of cruel cosmic joke on me? I pretended I had let go of the past, of that hideous relationship, and the death of my parents, but I hadn't really, so I was sent way, way back? *Time Passages* played in my head as randomly as the occurrence I was now facing.

Gabriel Christian really dressed and acted like Daniel Boone. Not Fess Parker in the old television series. There was nothing of the modern day here unlike reenactors I had known bringing their cell phones or parking their cars close by. This was the way the real men dressed with crude seams because they were handmade buckskin shirts. The others couldn't be Davy Crockett and Sam Houston. They weren't alive in... did he say...1772? These men were the first settlers of this area, the real long hunters! I recognized a few names yesterday, but I thought they had picked them. Gabriel Christian, the one I called Daniel Boone, did not sound familiar. Who was he? The lean-to, with propped up pieces of wood and some skins thrown over the top, was a pop-up camper holding their supplies, built with the trees in the area.

As I shook my head all over the place much like a wet dog would, I felt eyes on me. Looking out from under my dripping hair, I noticed Christian had walked his horse closer to Quasar and alternately checked me out and then the saddle. He felt the leather and ran his hands around the horn and down around the girth. Sure, he was surprised at my Western saddle since they weren't made that way for another fifty years. His was similar to the English saddle I used for jumping with the exception of the flatness of the seat. Maybe he fox hunted, no… just hunted…anything.

Looking up, he stared as if I were mentally ill or an alien. I *was* an alien to him, from a foreign land called the twenty-first century. And now, it was more the ridiculous girl stare I got from Drew. Grabbing my hat, I shoved it on top of my wet hair, uselessly. That wasn't going to fix anything because I was wearing jeans with a zipper and a long sleeve tee with sleeves much too long I frequently rolled up. Not the way a lady would dress in the eighteenth century. Not well endowed by any means, my clothing was clinging to me from the water and not modest by these standards, much too form-fitting. Although according to the scum from my day, I didn't show enough body and skin.

Not sure what to do at this point, being in the company of adventurous, thrill-seeking, hunters who had been away from their homes for months, I would definitely be in trouble in my time and most likely here as well. Maybe he didn't get a good look, and I could continue the deception. Yesterday he thought I was a sick boy. Should I try that again? Grabbing the huge coat, I ran behind the tree again and pretended to be sick.

"Bleh, bleh, bleh" and other assorted gagging and spitting sounds as I got back into the huge coat. Waiting for his reaction, I noticed Quasar grazing and rushed over to check on him, knowing there was a good chance he could get colic from the change in his diet.

"You should stay if you are unwell. We return at sunset if we are separated." His words had the hint of I-want-to-get-very-far-away-from-you. But he still had that stare. I was back under the microscope. No matter how much this creeped me out, I had to stay with him. What would happen to me if I was left alone?

"No, no, no. I am much better now. Just very upset over everything that has happened. I'm ready to go." I mounted Quasar, gave him a hug, and whispered to go. What a sentimental thing to do! I had to be more careful. What could I say? My best friends had always been horses and Pa.

As we rode, the long-forgotten note in my pocket rubbed my upper thigh with the motion of the horse. With the light of day, I longed to read it knowing any message from Pa, no matter how far away, would bring me some comfort, but I didn't dare. It would only bring questions that I didn't have the answers to give.

Pa must be sick with worry by now. Surely, Drew admitted having seen me. No, he wouldn't. But they would have been looking all around the barn anyway, and maybe they would accuse him of foul play. They wouldn't find me anywhere unless they rode through a storm and ended up here. What were the chances of that happening again? That couldn't be all there was to getting here.

Trying to keep up with Daniel Boone and think this through was not easy. Was there some significance to yesterday's date that sent me here? What was the date anyway? August uhm, the eighth, no, the ninth. Oh, I couldn't remember. It didn't really matter as I had no way of looking up anything. Didn't bring my phone and, even if I had, it isn't likely a signal could travel across time.

How did I get here? I didn't have a DeLorean that could reach 88 mph using gigawatts at just the right time. I didn't have a time machine or a super computer or a cyborg. I wasn't involved in a government project. No one put a curse on me that I was aware of. I didn't switch places with anyone or jump off a bridge. No one hit me on the head. No special stones to touch. There was no atomic explosion or hypnosis. If Superman had pushed the earth back, I wouldn't be traveling alone. That about covered the plot of any movie I had ever seen with time travel.

The only thing I knew was I rode really fast in the rain, jumped the Foster's fence, rode faster, and got buzzed nearly piercing my ear drums as we reached the rocks next to that dip in the hill. The closest scenario was the parking lot at the shopping mall in *Back to the Future*, but instead of Libyans I had Drew Foster chasing me. The problem with that is I didn't have any plutonium. I didn't have any answers either.

CHAPTER 13

Oh, Give me a Home

When we left the camp area, we traveled southeast, I think. With the light of a new, or old…well, a different day, I was able to experience the abundance of the trees towering over us, the towering cane crowding in on us, and the irritating, sameness of chiggers and seed ticks digging into me. As we traveled in and out of wide and narrow paths, I tried in vain to keep from scratching.

At an opening in the woods, he jumped down, cautiously looking around reached down next to a cedar and plucked up a plant.

"It would be advisable to rub this on the bites before illness sets in… wrap skins around the lower legs." Back on his horse, he maneuvered into the woods and continued as if nothing at all had transpired. Not in a position to argue, I quickly removed my jacket and took him up on his suggestion.

We rode in silence for some time. Unsure what he was thinking or where he was going, I didn't know what to say. Every time I opened my mouth I risked saying something that might make me appear crazier to him than I already was.

"Where is your family? You ask for your grandfather, but where are your children?" He looked back over his shoulder to speak to me. I felt the note rubbing my leg again.

"My children? I don't have any children. I'm not married." It was easier looking at his back.

"What is Quasar?" He looked back again.

"My horse."

"What meaning, in what language do you speak?" He stopped and turned in his saddle and looked at me. I slipped my jacket back on buttoning it up to the top.

"Oh, it's kind of a nonsense word I guess you could say." Yeah, I could see me telling him it was a star around a black hole or better yet, an old television or even a military satellite. Maybe he would understand a character from a comic book or a wrestler? How about laser tag? Mrs. Foster was amused by the word and the horse. That was all there was to it.

"Your clothing is unusual. Is it not warm for such a day as this?" He was still turned looking at me.

"Do you think so? They do their job." I turned my head so he couldn't see how hard I was evading his questions. He was right, the sweat popped up on my forehead, but I didn't dare do more than unbutton my coat not wanting to expose my t-shirt and jeans again.

"Where are your children and the rest of your family?" To keep him on defense instead of risking his questions to me, I began to ask questions.

"I am, at present, unmarried. My cousins in Virginia were so kind as to allow me board until I get my claim. The remainder of my family passed." His chin stuck up with that last part, and I felt the difficulty he had talking about it. His horse took over, slowly stepping over roots and around fallen trees.

"In Virginia, is that where they died?" I had to keep asking questions.

"No, London…much sickness. My parents and sister died as a result." His voice caught in his throat for a moment, and then he continued. "I left almost ten years ago now for the colonies…to live with cousins."

"And you, young Manning, you must be younger than I first supposed – your voice still a bit high. Where is the remainder of your family? How did you arrive here, by river or over land?"

Gasping in surprise I shrieked, "I know this place!!!!!"

It had been some time that we had ridden on narrow trails through the woods when we suddenly came upon a flat open area, much like the area near the crater. From this clearing and the northerly direction of the ridge, the familiar cedar trees sprang up for several miles along where Pa's old farm was and where the new highway *would* be except these cedars were huge with the first branches beginning taller than most trees I had ever seen. Although saved by the land from that line of questioning, I had brought the alien stare back with my stupid comment.

"Hist! Do not proceed into the clearing until we ascertain whether the savages are about. We do not want to be part of their bounty." Continuing to stare, he grabbed my reins and almost jerked me off my horse.

"Oh, sorry, I didn't think about that." I regained my composure and followed him carefully around the edge of the clearing. "It seems there's been a fire here." The ground was burned but not charred as much as the crater.

"Yes, the Indians are exceedingly clever to encourage the buffalo in this way." His mouth twisted up at one side. Was that supposed to be a joke?

"Oh give me a home, where the buffalo roam…" I unsuccessfully joked back not really thinking we would see any.

As we dismounted and took the horses into the cover of woods, he gave me another curious look and took off, back to the clearing, continuing to stay close to the trees, with me clumsily following. He stared across the open range at specks, from our distance.

"Tell me, what companions had you on the journey, whence you came afore? We may have common acquaintances." Interrogation time again.

Once again I was saved from his pointed questioning when the ground began to shake. I was sure it was an earthquake until a herd of buffalo – BUFFALO!!!! – ran across the clearing not too far from us. The stampede from *How the West was Won* was pretty impressive but nothing like seeing them in person. Massive, most were at least 6 feet, about the height of Daniel Boone, and Pa, come to think of it, with heads and shoulders huge compared to their narrow hips. They weren't quite as wooly as I remembered from pictures but, of course, it was summer. A hundred or more were running as if someone was holding fire to their backside. Not looking to either side they ran towards the other side of the clearing. They were not slow. As they ran towards woods they had trampled before, I opened my mouth and said a very stupid thing.

"Buffalo! I bet they are headed toward the salt lick near the Springs and probably came from the other one towards Nashville. Wow, aren't they amazing? Not many of them left. All we need is George Peppard and Henry Fonda!"

In a matter of minutes, Daniel Boone had shot several times and was screaming for me to stay back before I got trampled, pushing me to the ground and crawling behind the trees. When one fell, the others abruptly changed course tied together by an invisible force. I'd read somewhere they could turn faster than a horse, but I didn't believe it until now as they came back toward us, running around the kill along the way. We waited behind trees until they changed course again and were a safe distance away.

I wondered why we didn't move then, but I decided to keep my mouth shut having maxed-out stupid. Christian was eyeing the clearing and all the woods around, listening for any unwelcome sounds, whatever had caused the stampede. After what seemed to be a half hour, we headed out to the downed buffalo.

Another item to add onto the huge list I was grateful to Pa for was taking me hunting with him. Even though I had only seen him field dress deer and wild turkeys, it helped me to understand the process and get over it. What this man was able to do to that buffalo so rapidly was beyond confounding.

"Quick boy, lend a hand." Skinning it down the back, despite the gnats that had descended, and cutting out the top meat, his long fingers though toughened by hard work moved over and through the animal. "It is not much…they are thin but good for tallow and the marrow bones, and yes, the skin."

"Do you want to put it on these?" I grabbed a deerskin and a kind of rope from off his horse.

Throwing the meat on the skins, he then continued to cut the front legs and the shoulder blades. Quickly and skillfully he took care of it without the aid of any of the machines a butcher at a grocery store would have. Continuing into the ribs and organs, he saved every bit and wrapped it in a different skin. Finally, he bundled up all the full ones with the rope. What kind of rope it was, animal ligament or bark, I couldn't tell but it held tight.

"Make haste. To cover!" And he was on his horse, back into the woods on the trail before I could hardly mount Quasar. When I caught up with him he had stopped dead still, with a somewhere between I'm-listening-for-Indians face and an uh-oh-I-want-to-talk face. In case it was the latter, I hoped to head it off.

"Would it be possible to go back to the area where you found me yesterday?" It was still difficult to keep my voice low enough to sound something like an adolescent boy experiencing voice change.

"We needs must to camp…by the Lord, tomorrow," he answered tersely then got off his horse and walked it. I followed suit, walking on some ways when he changed his mind again and stopped. This time he gave me an ear full.

"Are there then others that come and kill the buffalo that are your acquaintances?"

"Not any that I know. Why do you ask that?"

"Why do you pretend to know not of what you said? You knew of the salt licks and made mention of a Henry and George."

"I'm not pretending. I just didn't remember."

"Well, then?"

"Henry and George? Those are just actors in a movie, uh, I mean play. It was probably a book as well but I didn't read it, I prefer the…, uh, play."

"Where would one see a play in the colonies?"

What could I say or do to make him stop this line of questioning? One of the oldest tricks in the book, I looked up at the sky behind him with a puzzled expression on my face causing him to turn and look, then look back at me. Since that worked, I continued to stare into the sky causing him to look once more and then at me again. Steam could have come out of his ears so it didn't really work all that well.

"Of course, you think me a simpleton. There is much you say that lacks sense and of much you are silent as the grave. I presume that was your first buffalo kill. You have not journeyed as you say but you comprehend our position. I will not press to reveal your true nature and state of affairs as long as you make additions to the camp and our expedition. Try you not anything bad as well."

CHAPTER 14

Shindig

By the time we got back to camp, I realized I hadn't eaten anything since the day before. My legs were getting weak. How did I go about asking for food when I didn't know what they had? The envelope money in my pocket would do no good. I should probably eat anything and ask questions later, but I didn't.

"Uh, is there anything to eat here? I didn't feel well yesterday and was afraid to eat."

"Dried meat is in yon cover. Take only one portion for we have rationed what we need for present. The meat from today will provide nourishment upon their return." He was tending to his horse and laying out the buffalo.

The food situation was questionable for me but not good at all for Quasar. It could be fatal to feed a horse something he was unaccustomed to. Pasture grass would be okay but some of the undergrowth might not be. Covertly, I lead him to a safer area in search of greens.

It was August in Tennessee and no matter what time period, it was hot. The coat was light, but I didn't need it. Christian was wearing a long thin shirt and leather britches, pretty sweaty as well but I was sure he wasn't as hot as I was. It would be a huge problem if I took the coat off so I suffered in silence, satisfied with washing my face and hands in the creek and drinking some of it as well.

After a bit, I wandered over to the lean-to and hunted for some of the meat. They had a lot more before the Indians plundered the camp, I understood, but it appeared they had recovered most of it. Under some skins, there were several small containers of what I assumed was gun powder and lead for the bullets. If this was all they had, they were definitely low on supplies. Another contained molds, files and flint. Hanging on one of the poles, a couple of smaller steel traps made my ankles hurt just to look at them. A few pots and crude utensils made of bones and wood nearby probably got the job done as well as anything you could buy. I found a couple of haversacks. One had a block of something that was probably salt and another had hunks of meat in it. As I bit off some I decided it was probably deer meat and much thicker than jerky. It was good, but I think I could have eaten one of those wooden spoons and it would have tasted divine at this point. While I ate, I inspected all the different supplies they had, out of curiosity.

"Young Manning, please come give a hand."

What did he want from me now? Stepping out from the lean-to, Daniel Boone was still hard at work taking care of the remains of the buffalo. He had already cut most of the meat in strips and was soaking it in brine.

"For what are you searching? You placed your hands on everything and smelled it as well," he stated matter-of-factly.

"What did you need help with?" Ignoring his statement, I watched him build a small fire.

With an extremely condescending tone in his voice, he asked "What skills have you?"

"I can do lots of things. " Careful in my phrasing, whatever I said had to be something he would understand or, again, I risked raising his suspicions even more.

"Think you so?" This time it was more of an arrogant tone. But who's to know with the way he phrased things with that British accent. Cary Grant meets Hugh Grant, kind of.

"Yes, I do think so. I am very good with horses. I can shoot. I can cook although I am better with vegetables than meat."

"What mean you, 'Very good with horses'?"

"What I said."

"What…you can ride one? Who cannot do that?"

"You would be surprised."

"Enlighten me then. Tell me in what manner people conduct themselves where you live for I feel certain it is far different than any of us are accustomed."

"What makes you say that?"

"Are you not aware you ignore all questions enabling me to gain knowledge of your former whereabouts?"

"Really?" I shrugged my shoulders trying to continue what he had accused me of.

"Yes... real-ly." He wasn't comfortable with the word. "We have been most forthcoming of our intentions and you might as well be a thief for all the information we have ascertained." He walked into the lean-to and came back with one of the haversacks.

"I thought you weren't going to press about my "true nature" though I will tell you honestly I am not a thief. You still haven't said what it is you want help with."

"Get more hickory for the fire...if chopping wood is a skill you possess." The sarcasm in his voice was not hidden but changed to alarm. "Hist! Someone approaches."

Suddenly, a commotion came from the other side of the camp causing the horses to rare and whinny. He grabbed his rifle and got behind some trees motioning for me to do the same. I chose to crawl not having a weapon of any kind.

"Young Manning, you would do well to move faster lest you not see the morrow," he whispered as loudly as he dared.

"Very funny hotshot. I don't have a rifle, remember. I assumed you would give me cover." Any action movie I had ever seen, no matter what time period, had this scene.

"Had I understood your words, I might have complied with your wishes." He looked sideways at me while combing the area for the cause.

The sounds of gunshot and screaming sent a chill down my back. Daniel Boone took off running from tree to tree around the edge, trying to get in on the action. I lost sight of him, and it wasn't long before I heard scuffling and grunting.

All I could do was hug my tree and stay out of the action. The horses had become quiet. I heard nothing but a small breeze rustling the leaves. There was nothing I could do besides pray Gabriel Christian wasn't outnumbered. I had been extremely fortunate to come upon him before the Natives. Now, what would happen to me if he was killed? I had to think about something else. As in, how I got here and how I would get back.

The more I thought, it must have happened at the area where I noticed I was wet, then dry. What was special about that place? One of the men mentioned the Indians were superstitious. It was kind of bowl-like. Maybe an opening to a huge rabbit hole? That would make me Alice and someone on this side murdered time.

Maybe it was a giant portal you jumped through. Great. I never was very good with Portals, or any other game system for that matter but it would be very helpful right now if I had a blue and orange portal here. It would even be comforting to hear the sarcastic voice of the defeated machine guiding you through the testing area right now. Talk about similarities. I was in the middle of a huge test I was about to fail. Question One: Where was the portal? Answer: I didn't see a portal or anything different for that matter. Just taking a ride through a field. The same way that guy was walking in the field and disappeared. Question Two: How did it send you through time? Answer: Maybe the lightning? Didn't matter how it happened, I just needed to figure out a way to get back. Question Three…

"MMMPH!!!" A hand clamped down on my mouth and I tried unsuccessfully to scream. Out of reflex, I began to fight to get the hand off my mouth. Didn't work, this guy was strong.

"HOLD! It is Christian. I know not if there are other savages. We need to stay calm until our men have scouted the area." His mouth was so close I could feel breath on my face, his hand still over my mouth. After a few minutes, I pulled it away, roughly.

"That was ridiculous." I grumbled, averting my eyes.

"Shush. A low voice only."

"You must be the Mad Hatter. You didn't have to get all up in my business like that. I understand danger."

"What *is* your business? Danger is evidently not for you had loud conversation to yourself. We will stay here until the others arrive with good tidings."

"Tidings of comfort and joy, I suppose." I said this with a smirk but obviously he did not get it. I tried again.

"A joke. God Rest Ye Merry Gentleman?" It fell flat. He still didn't find the humor.

A couple of whistles were heard off in the distance – an all clear. Christian jumped up and motioned to go with him back to the camp and the rest of the group. They had returned with their earlier kill, busy preparing it with the salt and water mixture. Ours was done and ready to be put on the fire to dry.

"If you would be so kind as to tend the horses…" Again, he said this sarcastically, but I pretended not to notice.

Quasar had been in the thick of it, but so far he hadn't gotten hold of anything bad for him or been shot. He'd had a rough time of it but had been a real trooper. The other horses weren't injured from the scuffle either, but they badly needed other attention. Picking their hooves, brushing, and listening to the conversation of others, I made myself useful.

"Vee tidn't see any others. It voult have been better if vee had shot tem." The man wiped his brow and stared at the ground with a look of resignation. They would have to deal with them again.

"I had the white man but he ran away with the savages." Daniel Boone postured as if he were talking about a fish that got away.

"Wait, there was a white man with the Indians? I thought you said it was Chickamauguas. Where do they settle?" I blurted out. If there was a white man, why wasn't he with our group?

"It was not your grandfather. We have seen these men before. They are Chickamauguas, but they also have some Cherokee and a few white men. The best we can figure they are criminals trying to steal others claims and whatever else they can. We believe them to be the group that raided our camp. They don't settle. There are reports of them in the upper settlement near the Gap as well as to the south." It was the leader who was very patient in explaining. He did not realize I wouldn't have thought of Pa.

Christian was not so patient. His tone reminded me of a lawyer, one Lionel Barrymore played in *A Free Soul* with Leslie Howard and Clark Gable. Oh, that I was at home in front of the television with either Howard or Gable. Either one would do just fine.

"Did not you encounter any of these rogue bands in your travels?" He challenged, but I ignored him.

"That's a relief. My grandfather is not a young man. I am confident we'll find him tomorrow and finish our trip. Where is it you all are headed?" The others hadn't picked up on my evasions yet but Boone did.

"Back to Virginia for supplies and respite. Eventually we will file claims and decide accordingly." Again, the leader answered so politely.

"Ja, ter make merry mit ter girls!" The German dude had a different idea.

"Not just any girl. I know not whether my lass still awaits me. Praise be to God if she does for she is a prize above all. She could have her pick of men and knows not when I'll return. But she did promise whether in trickery or true to be mine. Aye, a saucy girl to be sure." His description was the coquette at a country dance.

"Vie you vant to marry I vill never understand. Tere are many vill not neet tat – at least teel ter babes become many and vant a vill ven you die!! Ja, Ja!!" He teased, laughing loudly and elbowing.

"Who wanted not marriage? The man eloped!" They all laughed at his truth. "Your beloved's father had not a rifle the likes of yours!" He picked up the other's rifle and pretended to chase him.

"Our London frient hat his choice of ter females. In Virginny, every girl in ter town grins and vinks at ter varmint not to mention ter cousin batting her eyes." Stopping the chase, he pointed at Daniel Boone who didn't seem to care much for the teasing.

Boone was the ladies' man? How could girls see him with all that hair smashed down under his hat and the beard hiding his face? He certainly didn't have much personality.

"The women in London were either gentry or harlots. Both were of a sickly nature. Besides, my good man, you are long married. What care you what I choose?" Christian became Mr. Matter-of-fact again. "Gentlemen, we have a fine hump tonight, on the morrow the tongue, and that was most of the beast I brought down this day that was fine."

Turning to work with supper again, he had taken a page out of my book attempting to change the subject. Even though several made noise to indicate they enjoyed a good buffalo tongue, the air remained a bit heavy, lightened only by the German who walked over and patted Christian on the back.

"Gabreel, your cousin is a fine voman as vell. She vill make a fine lady of ter house."

He didn't look up, replying sarcastically in a low voice, "We will have much use for powdered wigs here. I am sure savages will appreciate the finery."

"Powder without lavender or cornstarch?" asked another.

"You must begin to grow them and make ready for your bride." Others chimed in but then snickered. "When is the happy day?" I detected equal sarcasm in the question, but did he mean marriage?

"Uncle says upon my return." The death sentence didn't change his busying about the "kitchen." He had prepared some kind of bread. Corn pone maybe?

"What's wrong with her? Doesn't know how to cook?" I popped off.

"Ah, she is a beautiful lady…clad in the finest of clothing and much respected in town." Another had been silent for some time but piped up like an ad man.

"She is able to command an estate and embroider cushions. She might cease to glance at her reflection to play upon the harpsichord." Daniel Boone commented and then rolled his eyes. Maybe he would rather have all his teeth pulled?

"Oh, I get it. She's not the pioneer type. I thought most men wanted good looks… I mean, I understand…we want a girl that looks good and can take care of the children." I was failing miserably at being a dude.

"You say true! She is beautiful, yes. Betters often assume they are every person's choice. But the marriage must be of my choosing. I am not ungrateful but my uncle's family does not live the kind of life for which I left London."

At first I had a hard time feeling sorry for Daniel Boone, wanting a good-looking girl and someone that would do everything. Then I thought about how much work it was without electricity and machines. He would need someone useful to start a family with. What did he mean by "betters?" Before I could figure out a way to ask, he had given us each a portion.

"Young Manning, you miss your family no doubt." Christian actually offered a kind word to me as we sat around the fire to eat.

"I want more than anything for Pa to know I'm okay. He is all the family I have. Well, that I acknowledge anyway." I had been thinking of the note but now had to look away quickly, the abominable tears were beginning to flow. "I'm not very hungry," I mumbled then stumbled off to find my friend the enormous hickory tree, hiding for a few minutes behind it contemplating how I could take a bath. My clothes could stand up on their own. If I asked anything about a bath that would be a dead giveaway I was not a young boy.

Half-asleep, the men were lying around the fire enjoying the aroma of buffalo tongue roasting in the bed of embers while I ventured far enough to wash off, a possible bath as Ma would say, "Wash down as far as possible, wash up as far as possible, then wash possible a little bit." Just pulling off my boots and putting my feet in the water was a treat. Pa's old bandana made a decent wash rag. The sticky mess of hair was driving me mad, and I dunked my head again. Finally, I felt a little refreshed and put everything back together. I didn't dare leave off the stinky, sweaty hat. Checking on Quasar, I heard more of a conversation about me.

"Will you ride with Manning again tomorrow?" the leader asked.

"Best to return to the barren area where I first saw him. Maybe some clue will appear as to the whereabouts of his grandfather," growled Christian.

"What shall we do if he is not found? We cannot allow this boy to continue with us. He has no claim here." I couldn't quite make out who said that.

"Aye. I will take responsibility if necessary," said Christian impatiently.

"What is your meaning? Wilst thou share yours for I am certain no other here will share?" Unintelligible voice again.

"That will not be necessary. If need be we will separate from you and continue on a search. Young Manning may return to Virginia with me if he has no other desire." Wow, more kind words from Mr. Boone.

"That is not advisable. We should start our journey soon, afore the winter season. We know not what will come at this place. If we separate we may not have provisions enough for both." The voice was muffled.

"I know not where the youth gets his information, he did not say. But earlier when we came upon the herd this morn, he stated knowledge, as if fact, of several salt licks in different directions. When I questioned him of his knowledge of such places, he answered in the usual manner. His answers are confused and he speaks a language I do not comprehend."

"Even so. If he stated as fact, then he has been to those licks. Is it possible his group is responsible for all the dried bones found there and the smaller herds we have now found?" More mumbling then, "I cannot believe it! He is not forthcoming with information. We must question him and find who gave them leave to explore. You will go with him then?

"Shall we see what tomorrow may bring forth?" Christian ended the conversation abruptly when I came back closer to sit down. There was no way I was going to sleep with them in the shelter, savages or not. My plan was not to say goodnight or anything bringing on more questions but to sit within distance of them and pretend to fall asleep there.

The group had gone in conversation from me to girls again, something about a comely maiden and plucky lass. While they were trying to decide, again, what kind of girl was their favorite, I took the wet rag and tied it around my head. Stretching out on the ground, I covered my face with the foul smelling wide-brimmed hat. Their conversation was quite amusing with a lot of good natured ribbing. Guffawing and giggling, I heard "What then?" and "Eh, now." Several low whispers and pshaws. One broke out in song.

"Girls and boys come out to play,
The moon doth shine as bright as day;
Leave your supper and leave your sleep,
And come to your playfellows down the street."

Christian began to play the flute and the others clapped and whistled along. I gave up on sleep and sat up to watch this craziness. Unfortunately, I was detected and they called for me to come over and join them threatening to dunk me head-to-toe in the creek if I didn't. Reluctantly pulling on my hat and shuffling over to the party, I plopped down on the outside ring of the group.

"Come with a whoop, come with a call,
Come with goodwill or not at all.
Up the ladder and down the wall,
A half-penny roll will serve us all."

Once more they sang the ditty and decided to dance some type of jig. I hadn't seen any liquor around so I was a little surprised at their liveliness. Guess they all just needed to let off a little steam. The pressures of survival, I suppose.

"Hey, what kind of flute is that?" I asked after they had exhausted themselves and fallen around the campfire once more.

"Not a very good one but whittled when first I arrived in the colonies and happenstance separated our belongings. My guitar was taken by those scoundrels who stole our furs as well. They do not play but the white men would recognize the instrument as something worth trade." Funny, I expected Daniel Boone to be a washboard or jug-blowing kind of musician.

"A guitar? Cool. Where did you learn to play?"

"My father was a musician. He taught my sister as well to play many instruments."

"Where did he play?"

"He would on occasion play the fiddle or harpsichord at an assembly or a respectable inn."

"Did *you* play at dances too?"

"Yes, it was income our family was in need of."

"Why didn't you do that in Virginia instead of coming out here?"

"Young Manning, I might question you as well. Why are you here? Who is your benefactor? How do you know of salt licks?"

"Uhhhh, you really should be a musician."

"That may be so. You must answer the questions I asked of you." Christian's voice had suddenly taken a very stern tone. Almost as if Grandmother was telling me what I must do to be an acceptable member of society.

Another of the party who had been quiet jumped out at me rather loudly as well. "It would be advisable to do so Young Manning. There is much strange in your manner of speech and dress. If we should trust you to continue as a member of our party, you must be forthcoming."

The conversation had interested me so much, I was a sitting duck blindsided with all those questions. I wanted to tell them all I had no idea why I was here, and I certainly didn't want to be. I was a freak of time and I supposed nature as well.

"I don't want to talk about it. It's all been so horrible. You would never understand, not in a million years!!!" Screaming at them felt good but all it did was make them stare harder. My crying machine was cranked up to full blast as I ran away from them up the creek and past some trees. Sweat was pouring off of me. I couldn't take it anymore. Off came the huge coat and hat. My boots and socks were off and thrown in the pile of clothes I'd just discarded, the pants next. The mossy ground felt cool on my face. All I could do was cry and cry and cry.

Somehow in the fog that was my brain, I heard the voice of Christian demanding they leave me alone.

CHAPTER 15

Under Cover

THUD!!! Right next to my ear. THUD!! Another sound made me bolt upright out of a dead sleep. Hissing, it was definitely hissing.

"AAAAHHHHEEEE!!! Where did that come from?" With a repeat of yesterday morning's wakeup, jumping back, tripping over my feet, this time trying to get away from a huge copperhead. Even though it had two knives sticking out of it, I still wanted no part of it.

"It is a better idea in the wild to sleep where all has been cleared. You are fortunate I returned at this time. Had you awoken on your own, well, you might not have awoken at all." Daniel Boone was all mountain man this morning as he grabbed the knives out of the snake and wiped them off on the grass. He stuck them back in a pouch slung around his hips and gathered the snake up, tossing it over to the camp for a later snack, I guessed.

Evidently, I had rolled around in my sleep and was partly under some bushes.

"Thanks." My head was throbbing. Why was I holding my coat?

"Is there evidence of a bite or any other malady of the face?"

"Is that your polite way of saying my face looks all puffy this morning?" I wrapped the coat around me and shuffled over to the creek.

"Yes, it is very swollen." He sounded alarmed as if he just saw something from a horror house.

"I'm okay. It does this whenever…I'm sure it looks like somebody punched me in the eyes." Oh great, my hair was sticking up all over the place with grass in it.

"The others left at dawn. I took the liberty to cover you when first I awoke – before they saw." His voice was very harsh and the meaning clear. Yet, he walked back to the campfire and brought me a cup of that same something.

What, was I naked? No, I had on my very long t-shirt and underclothes. But not appropriate in this time for someone he knew was a girl. Where did we go from here?

"Thanks. It was a little hot last night. I'm not as used to the heat as I used to be. My parents used to take me camping some and my Pa would let me camp on his farm. It's been a while since I've done any of that. It's been a while since I've done anything fun, come to mention it." I paused a moment to gulp the concoction. "This isn't bad. I guess you'll drink anything if you're thirsty, too. Where did they all go?" When all else failed, I ran my mouth even though my head screamed stop. They were not in sync.

It seemed hard for him to keep up with my ranting though he didn't question it. "I accompanied them to the area of the buffalo from yesterday. They have divided to return to the salt licks of which you spoke in search of the herd." Nonchalantly, he spoke trying to gauge my reaction, no doubt.

"What was the big deal I knew of the salt licks?" They already knew so that shouldn't affect the future.

Before he answered, I asked if I could dress and then we would talk. He agreed. I took my time because I had no idea what to say to him.

Quasar needed some tending to as well. I used the makeshift tools they had carved out of wood to pick his hooves. He got a drink, and I tied him to a different tree to graze. If I'd had a brush I would have taken care of his mane. Instead, I combed my fingers through it and wiped him down with my dry bandana. I hugged him tight and buried my face in his mane. He was my only friend.

"You are gentle yet with your horse. You have had him long?" Not as gruff but not exactly kind either, very matter-of-fact.

"No, he doesn't belong to me. He belongs to the people I work for. I love them all, the horses, I mean. Well, except for the one that threw me once and I just liked him."

"You are a servant? Or did you steal this horse?" Curiosity became outrage.

"No, I take care of their horses. We were out riding, just as I told you when you saw me. We were lost in a storm." He sensed the desperation in my voice and let it drop.

"At present your face has better color. Nourishment might aid recovery as well." He handed me a plate of something similar to yesterday. Beggars couldn't be choosers therefore, while sitting on a stump I inhaled the food. In a few minutes, I was done and trying to find the words to explain this ridiculous situation I was in.

"Look, I can't tell you everything. It's not that I don't want to. You won't believe me. You will think I'm crazy and probably leave me out here in the middle of nowhere. I'm pretty resourceful, but I can't do this alone. So please just give me some time to find a way to tell you what has happened to me."

"Badly treated by someone, then?" His back was turned while he cleared the food from the area.

"That's part of it but probably not what you think. I do need to find Pa and go home. I want to go home so badly. It's a very long way off where I live." I paused to take a breath. "You have been very good to me. What you did last night… was very decent of you." My voice was so low he could barely hear me.

"More than you deserve, I would wager." He turned and spoke directly to me. "All would be more confused, and we need not make them aware as you will soon be gone."

"You don't know anything about what I deserve." I stood and spit the words back at him.

"Plainly you choose not to explain any little thing. At the least, you have not made your profession known. You should be so kind to let it remain so." Stepping closer to me his voice was higher.

"My profession…what's wrong with taking care of horses?" Incredulously, I stepped closer. "Wait, are you accusing me of being a hooker, uh, prostitute?"

"Can you not tell me where your family is? Why you clothe yourself in such a manner? I do not condemn you but rather advise 'to go and sin no more.'"

"These are all the clothes I have right now, but trust me, I am not like that. If I didn't depend on you to survive right now, I would beat you to a pulp." I stopped to rephrase that. Probably couldn't do more than break my own bones on him. "Er…I would try anyway. My parents died in an accident over a year ago. I live with my Pa. My other grandparents live in New York and I have nothing to do with them. So there." By this point, I was up in his face hurling the words at him with all the frustration of the previous evening but none of the tears. I had none left. But I did manage, in a huff, to go wash my face again.

It made sense why he thought that of me. Women just didn't dress anything like this then. Not even pants so I couldn't blame him for thinking with the brain of his time. When I returned, he seemed different. Maybe my words had gotten through to him.

"I am sorry for your loss. It may be painful for some time. But it is good you have resources when women do not at such times." He stared off as if he was in another place, speaking from experience.

"I understand why you thought that way. Eventually, I will be able to explain all this. It's just too difficult. It would be great if we could keep this between you and me. It's hard enough as it is."

"You are strong…similar to my sister when she was …I will ready the horses." Something else was bothering him but he chose not to tell me. Another time I guess … he was already across the camp.

CHAPTER 16

Twenty Questions

We left the camp behind us late in the morning, another hot day. Who knew what the day would bring, but it was nice to have the burden of my identity lifted, sort of.

"The barren land may offer some clue. We must be watchful, however, for that dirty band may appear at any moment."

"Sounds like a plan."

"What is your real name?"

"Makenna Manning. The name I gave you when we met, named after my father."

"It has the sound of Kenneth and you are dressed as a Kenneth."

"Women sometimes dress this way where I am from."

"And may I ask where would that be?"

"You wouldn't know the place if I told you."

"Speak the name and I will tell you."

"I could take you there and you wouldn't recognize the place."

"You know not that to be true."

"Yes, I do."

"Nay, you cannot comprehend what is another's mind."

"Trust me. I am positive of this. Are we close yet? I don't see anything that looks familiar." That was an understatement.

"It became dark when last we were here."

Daniel Boone continued to ask questions, and I evaded them. He wanted to know, and he wanted to know now. How could I possibly explain this without him running away from me? The Native Americans might have given crazy people a pass, but I was pretty sure these dudes would run screaming from me. Then what would I do?

As we rode, I tried to formulate a plan. What would I say when I tried to explain why Pa wasn't there or no clues for his whereabouts? Maybe if I rode on the other side of the crater I could figure out a reason for what happened, or if I rode fast enough through the crater I could go through a portal to my time again. It couldn't hurt to try.

Christian alternated between being gruff and seeming to understand. I'm sure he was just frustrated at not knowing the whole story, but he would just have to be frustrated. There was nothing else I could do right now. Besides, if I was successful, he would figure it out when I disappeared.

As we rode up to the area, it seemed like a month in retrospect yet only a few days had transpired. Someone had said the Chickamauga always turned back here, but I had no intention of doing so.

"You spoke of the Indians being superstitious about this area. That's what saved me or something like that. What did you mean?" We got off our horses and walked around a bit supposedly looking for clues to find Pa.

"Many traders speak of what was told them. They questioned why none settled here as they do east and south. The Indians told of a blinding flash from the heavens burying itself in the earth where it burned and smoked for weeks. The tribes pondered the meaning of such a thing. After weeks their shamans concluded it was a sign they should leave the area and move their villages away from the Cumberland. Whether that is true, we know not. They do hunt in the area, but not close to the burnt ground. We saw none until the last journey."

"Oh, I thought it was a 'bloody ground' because so many different groups of Indians fought over it they declared it only a hunting ground." Pausing for his reaction, something else occurred to me. "So there is something *abnormal* about that spot! Why didn't I think of that…the meteor crater in Arizona? But with those weird noises maybe instead it was aliens. Or Roswell! Don't you know those Indians freaked if they saw those little weird guys from *ET* or *Close Encounters*? Or maybe it was just a bad thunderstorm. But no, it wouldn't smoke for weeks from a storm. It had to be a spaceship or an asteroid."

In the excitement of the moment, I had let my thoughts run away out loud again. Not only was I talking to myself but about things that would do exactly what I didn't want. I would appear batty at best. It was a huge mistake.

"What say you?" he gasped. "You are mad! It is the jubilee of the devils! What the savages fear, I know not but it has infected you as well. Your illness is grave, I fear." He had stepped back in fear of the earth and of me.

"This is part of what I can't tell you. See, you already think I'm mad, and I haven't even told you anything. I was talking to myself trying to figure some things out. Just wait a minute. Please don't leave me. I need to try something."

Quasar and I rode around the area while Christian cautiously watched me. Like old times warming up for Sharon and Hank, I tried to build up some speed in an effort to "jump through" the crater. From where I came out, I tried again but it didn't work. Going around to the back of the spot didn't work either. In fact, running into the burned area had made Quasar skittish, wanting nothing to do with this. It wasn't smoking, but it was still warm. The next several attempts resulted in almost being thrown or running in a complete circle away from the area. This land had some mean juju for sure.

Frustrated, I rode back over to Christian who had watched my spectacle as if I were a June bug on its back – wanting to help but unable to quit watching to see if it turned itself over.

"Madam, are you quite yourself? Whomever that might be?"

"Look, it makes me really angry I can't just ride away from you and go back home. I haven't figured out how to do that yet. When I have, believe you me, I will be as far away from you as I can. You have been incredibly patient considering what I've put you through. But something tells me you are a real jerk around regular everyday people."

"A jerk? What mean you? If upset I think you mad, should I think different than your deeds have shown?"

"I find it interesting you were almost nice to me when you thought I was a boy. But now you know I'm a girl, you act like I'm the plague through no fault of my own. I am not insane, eccentric maybe, but not crazy." Again I had to prove I was not a nutjob – déjà vu to the max.

"Is it not enough I will keep that knowledge to myself? Any change in manner was due to the effort to ascertain *what* you are. Female, male, harlot, lunatic, thief, liar…"

"Ha! I always thought you frontier chaps were all gracious gentlemen around ladies and rough and ready in the woods. Didn't your mama teach you any manners?"

"Speak you of manners? My mother died of a terrible illness! We are gentlemen around ladies. Where are the ladies here? I see none."

"Why you…" Just as I was going to let him have it, he shushed me in a tone frightening me. All I heard was the chattering of a squirrel and some birds but, of course, that could be the signal of the returning Chickamauguas.

"Hold…we must not tarry at this place. Let us return before we bring the devil himself down upon us."

I thought we would be safer to stay, but I agreed because I had nothing else. At least, he was allowing the crazy person to go with him.

CHAPTER 17

Onward

The days went by with a lot of activity, everyday rituals becoming less unusual to me. What was unusual to me was I hadn't gone anywhere in my head. I mean, my thoughts were all centered on the here and now, not some far off dream world. Concentration was essential if I was going to survive this.

Strangely enough, Daniel Boone chose to keep my secret. Taking a page from my book, he headed off any comments the others made that were suspicious. He even showed me how to prepare the meat and skins from our different hunting trips. Until I was somewhere where I could grow a garden, it was mostly meat to eat. I did find some poke, but much too late in the year to risk fixing it. It had to be picked in early spring, or it was too hard to wash the poison out of it. I had to settle with dandelion greens, very good with deer meat, sautéed in the same pan or fresh. Later, I dried the leaves and made some tea that was quite soothing. The frontier guys brought wild blackberries along with the smaller catch they had trapped helping to mix up our diet.

More importantly, he did not leave me alone. Barely talking to me, he never let me out of his sight except for the personals. Rubbing my fingers over the small envelope in my pocket, I gave up trying to look at its contents, figuring it was the same as the others with some money and a jotted "Love you, Pa." Still, I could use a letter from back home.

It was back to business, hunting and preparing whatever we killed then the next day spent in making additional supplies in case we separated. A few times, we rode out to the "barren area" as they referred to it, scouting for Chickamauga. When we slowed, I rode up alongside and asked Christian why they left.

"Hunting as we are. We should remain watchful."

"It's hard not to when you could be tomahawked at any second. By the way, are you ever going to explain what happened to your sister?"

"Again I say, from disease most likely typhoid."

"You said I was strong, as your sister before she had to do something. You didn't finish. It was a couple of weeks ago but I haven't forgotten."

His reluctance gave way to a long stifled need to talk about it.

"After our parents died, we endeavored to maintain the hosiery business below our upstairs quarters. Of much we were not aware, credits given to the poor, accounts at other businesses. We were of music not business and some time it took to make good with everyone. There was little once our debts were settled and I, having no other choice, procured positions at assemblies. It would have been natural for her to do the same were it not proper for ladies. But she would have means every now and again. Said she had sold something of our mother's. It was much later she confided, after she was very ill, a well-to-do man had taken her to dine without a chaperone. You understand, then," his voice was low, barely audible "there was no want… from her favors, I suppose. Half-mad with anger and sorrow, I designed to end it all somehow…a duel, maybe…but then…the both were dying. What would it profit to shoot him? I hear her yet, weeping, begging forgiveness."

By this time we had reached the area. I dismounted and pulled up some dandelions for Quasar. I wished now I had not asked, knowing it had been horrible. As he looked to see my reaction, he was startled by it. Words wouldn't come but, as usual, my tears did.

"Don't mind me. I wear my heart on my sleeve… really inconvenient sometimes." Wiping them away, I tried to get the subject back on him. "That must have been very hard for you to cope with all by yourself."

"Your lot in life should not be as hers. You have chosen to remain silent for whatever reason. I try, out of respect for my sister, to resist casting judgment for the actions I have seen. For that reason, I continue to seek your grandfather until we leave."

"You've come here for me?" I hadn't realized.

"Of course, it would be nigh a miracle at this point if we found anyone here, a camp perchance, but at least a message. I refuse to believe anyone would leave a woman, of any sort, here to fend alone. Our return journey to Virginia will begin in a few days." As he eyed the skies he added, "We hope for fair weather to begin. You may do as you wish, accompany us or go your own way. If you choose Virginia, I will help you once we arrive but no further."

Stamping and huffing, Quasar still didn't like to ride through the area. I couldn't understand why it wouldn't take me back home not that the method mattered at this point – ruby red slippers, magic dust, or a bad dream and I could awaken.

"Well, what other amusement might we partake in today?" he said sarcastically, one of the three manners of speaking he reserved for me: gruff, low, or sarcastic.

"Oh, I dunno. How about riding back to camp or riding back to camp?"

"I believe riding back to camp would be the most satisfactory."

CHAPTER 18

Star Light, Star Bright

The mood around the campfire that night was somber. Something seemed wrong, but I couldn't exactly put my finger on what it was. Since Christian had made the effort to keep my secret, I had tried to keep to myself as much as possible, away from them and their conversation. Unless someone directly asked me a question, I didn't talk, but that didn't mean I couldn't hear.

"Tomorrow, vee vill divite our supplies so tat we might travel separately."

"Are we not all on our way to Virginia?"

"Yes, Gabreel vee are. You may choose to share your claim but vee do not only because vee vill start families. You are straddling ter fence. If vee return to Virginia togeter it may be tat vay."

"You fear Young Manning wants your land? He has no interest in a claim. From the first, he has desired only to find his family. I have offered help once we arrive in Virginia considering he is unable to locate his grandfather."

"Another reason, we go as two groups. I want nothing that will give pause to marry." Another spoke while staring across the fire at me. If she were a jealous creature, then he must know I'm a girl. Why didn't he confront me?

At that point, Christian let the subject drop. Obviously the others knew about me as well. They would hash out the arrangements later without asking my opinion. I was fortunate to be allowed to travel with them. My face felt hot, and I needed to hug my only friend.

"What on earth are we going to do, Quasar? We need to stay here, but we won't survive on our own. What can we possibly do on our own in Virginia? I will have to keep up this ridiculous charade forced on me in order to get any kind of job that won't label me a harlot. Can you believe that? Me, a harlot. I've only had one steady boyfriend in my life, and we know how that ended up."

"Young Manning, see here." I jumped and turned.

"My name is Makenna."

Daniel Boone was standing behind me pointing to the sky where a fantastic meteor shower was taking place. It probably would have gone unnoticed in my time because of the lights, but out here in the open space it was amazing.

"Wow. What an amazing display of God's creation."

"You are not afraid, then?"

"Why should I be afraid?"

"There are those who believe it is a judgment on the sinful man."

"That won't happen until the end of the age, and it's not here, not yet anyway, until then…" I was about to say what goes around comes around and thought better of it. Maybe something not so modern sounding, "ummm… for every action there is an equal and opposite reaction, so to speak."

"You have studied Sir Isaac Newton?"

"Science is not my forte by any means but I've studied a bit." Straining to see, it was over. "I bet we'll see more soon. At this time of year, they can occur any time."

"You speak as a scientist," he turned to me with that stare.

"No, definitely not. History and literature were my favorite subjects in school… not fond of school at all though. Actually, that is an understatement."

"I will not ask *where* you attended because I doubt you would tell me. May I ask what kind of institution you attended?"

"Ha! I called it an institution too, paid for with people's taxes and certain subjects you had to study. Then you went to college…I'm in my first year though I doubt I will continue. Not everyone is cut out for it. Horse riding is my talent."

"You spoke of that earlier. I grant you sit in the saddle well for a female but how is that a course of study?"

"I took lessons to learn to ride. Later I learned tricks to do on horseback. If the time ever comes when I can explain I will. You wouldn't understand at all."

He suddenly became angry. "What think you I have no mind to understand? A common female should say such to me!"

"Whoa, dude. I meant no disrespect… hey, what do you mean by a *common* female?"

"Explain yourself first."

"I swear you could make a preacher cuss." Let it go Makenna, I thought to myself, he didn't understand. "It's just there is so much that is different about your way of life and mine you wouldn't have a frame of reference for what I would tell you."

"You say true." He thought a minute and then added, "I will say this with as little offense as possible, a lady does not ask to be called by her Christian name until a more personal acquaintance has been formed, an understanding. A common female dresses in clothes not lady-like and gives occasion to wonder her…motives. The clothes you wear are questionable, however, I did overhear you to say there had been only one suitor. Therefore, I will assume your motives pure until proven otherwise."

"That's mighty nice of you. I didn't choose to dress in this particular way for the occasion of being lost. Where I am from and the work I do, I am appropriately dressed, except for this coat and hat that are beyond tacky. By the way, I believe it has always been a faux pas to eavesdrop." I glared at him, and he glared back.

We looked at the sky in silence for a few more moments waiting for the show to continue. My anger subsided after reasoning with myself about current customs.

"I'm not sure about these yahoos, uh, savages that have been trying to attack us but some Native Am….uh, Indians believe the meteor showers are a sacred sign, as well. They have some kind of spiritual importance. That and white bison."

"Which was important, the meteor or the bison?"

"Both, I believe. It seems to be a foretelling of coming events – peace in times of war or the birth of a great leader, something like that." I hesitated a minute. "Christian, you do believe me when I tell you I don't want any of this land?"

"Yes, I do believe that. You must understand they are very anxious to start their families in a place where they are beholden to none."

"So, is Virginia that restricting?"

"It has become so. The English taxes on all of the colonies continue to be oppressive. Of late, it has become violent with sinking of ships and what else I do not know. War is an expensive proposition."

"Do you think there will be war?" Of course, I knew the answer to that question.

"I speak of all the wars that have already taken place on the backs of citizens and the many taxes."

"So you aren't in a hurry to start a family then?"

"Owning my own land is attractive otherwise I would not have ventured so far from London and Virginia. After settling our debts, there was little left. My prospects were few – enlist and continue to fight the French or Scots I had no quarrel with, or come to the colonies. It will be on my terms, though. Not on the custom or fashion of the day."

"Well said. I couldn't agree with you more." He seemed uncomfortable that I agreed with him.

Even without the meteor shower, the stars were amazing. I looked for one to wish upon, wishing I was home, watching some old movie. The last scene from *Now, Voyager*, one of my favorite Bette Davis films, began to play in my head, "Let's not ask for the moon, we have the stars." The familiar low voice jolted me from my wish.

"The showers have become less and I am in need of rest for tomorrow. We will hunt once more and assure our supplies are sufficient for whatever the group decides." He began to walk away.

"Hey, Daniel Boone."

It had gotten darker so I could not read his expression.

"Why do you insist on calling me by that name?"

"It suits you. Thanks for helping me."

"Do not become accustomed to it, horse girl. You know not of what will befall you in Virginia."

CHAPTER 19

Crazy

Tomorrow would be our last day at the station. One last check of all the traps and horses would put us in good order. Not knowing how long we would be gone, I grabbed a bag of jerky and attached it to my saddle before Christian and I rode out one final time to the crater. This might be my last chance to go back home the way I came.

"It all feels so hopeless…trying to find Pa, you know."

"I would not say such. When we begin our journey we may come upon others who might have seen him in their travels. At any of the stops along the river we may stop and check."

"Okay, but I don't think that will be necessary if I haven't found him yet."

He looked at me to find my hidden meaning knowing I spoke truth somehow just not all of it.

"Have you thought of what you might do in Virginia?"

"You mean whether I'm going to be a girl or boy? Look, I never pretended to be a boy. You guys just assumed from a misunderstanding of my name. That and I looked pretty rough after…after riding for so long."

"Well, yes there is that consideration. It will make a difference how I introduce you and explain why you are with me."

"To your girl? I wondered if you really felt as the others or if you wanted to use me as an excuse to get out of that situation."

"An excuse? I do not need an excuse to do what I should not or want not to do."

"Okay, whatever you say Boone. What do you think would be the easiest and...safest, if you understand my meaning?"

"If you choose to continue the charade, I might find employment for you at any stable. Your safety is your own to procure. It would be yours to find suitable lodging."

"Why? Couldn't I just stay with your cousins?"

"No, it could cause complications if any were to detect your secret. It is better you find your own place to stay."

"Okay, so what happens if I decide to be a girl?"

"I believe it would be more difficult. We must find suitable clothing and explain where I happened upon you. You would then be obliged to stay with my relatives until you found a suitor."

"Are you serious? I would have to get married? That's not likely to happen unless I have a bath pretty soon." For the record, Daniel Boone smelled just as rank.

"Yes, it is much the same here as in England. A single woman, much like my sister, has to be very careful whom she chooses as companions. You may not live alone as a single person or risk being considered of little reputation. You could not be presented as a servant or there would be conversation concerning ..."

"Concerning our relationship? You have a point. I'll have to think about that then. It doesn't sound like a lot of fun to be a girl there. It could be interesting though. What kind of story would I have? What on earth would you be doing with a female? Wouldn't your cousin just love that? She probably wouldn't care considering I haven't cleaned up in so long. She definitely wouldn't have anything to be jealous of."

At that statement, Daniel Boone made some kind of hhmphing noise. "It is all very bothersome."

"You're telling me."

We took a turn through a dense growth of cane along an open area near another branch of the creek then walked for some time on deer trails along the side of a hill. Even though it was much cooler in the trees, my hair was sticking to my neck. Since the cat was out of the bag, I wore the hat only in the blazing sun but continued to wear my coat out of respect for the morays of the day.

After another half hour or so, it began to rain, cool and gentle. Across the horizon slender reeds waved along the creek bank, and our attention was soon diverted by a small group of buffalo, maybe five, standing opposite. In front of the group, and a small distance in between, stood a magnificent white one.

All these weeks of hunting gave me an even higher respect and this particular, almost mythical creature, stood with an air of majesty. Few had ever seen them, yet here I was standing within a football field length of him. Something suddenly spooked them at the same time the sky opened up, pouring. As one huge creature with a central brain, they ran straight at us led by the Royal White One.

"Stay with me horse girl." Christian yelled and took off, not back into the wooded area, but around them, towards the crater.

"What are we doing? Are you crazy?" I screamed. About that time I saw the cause in the distance and knew we had no choice. My voice might as well have been a whisper in the middle of the open field competing with the thundering of hooves and the crash of thunder.

Quasar was right with him, matching speed, darting and zigzagging across the opening trying to stay ahead of the mad herd now behind us and away from the fierce throng of natives coming toward us. Faster and faster, spurred on by the buzz and snap of the electricity filling the air, the blinding light of the bolt encompassed us both.

CHAPTER 20

We're not in Kansas Anymore

The thud of the horses' hooves on the dry ground jolted me back into reality. If Daniel Boone wasn't right in front of me, I would think I was going mad. This couldn't have happened again! The high-pitched tone still rang in my ears, and millions of yellow jackets left their stingers in me, or so it felt. Sunny and hot, I dreaded what I immediately knew to be true. It must be another time. Was it the right time? We were smack dab in the middle of a field, somewhat grown over, and surrounded by a make-do fence where it appeared cows might have once grazed. A sort of shed and trough were to one side where none existed only a few minutes ago. Not far from it sat a small singed, clapboard house with a dirt road running in front of what I guessed had been a yard, now a combination of weeds and muddy ruts. There was no sign of the white bison only a rather thin, yet very angry, black bull ready to charge us.

"Look out! Go, run fast!" I screamed at my traveling companion to no avail. The dazed state hung on until his horse rared up throwing him to the ground. Sensing the bull almost on him, he rolled out of the way and jumped to his feet chasing his horse toward the back as fast as he could. The terrified horse made it on pure adrenalin with his owner right behind him. Quasar made the jump with ease, and as soon as we cleared the excuse for a fence, Boone scrambled to regain his horse.

"From where did that mad animal come? It has ceased to rain and is completely dry! See here, my clothes are dry!" He swallowed and gasped for air, turning slowly, checking his clothes, rubbing his skin, and trying to get bees off that were not there, taking in the surroundings yet continuing to rant. "We must have ridden through a hornet's nest for I feel a hundred stings." Amazed that his skin was unblemished he raved on. "Across yon meadow there sits a house, a rather sad one, but a house and there an outer structure, for the cattle I would suppose! Only a moment ago, they were not there. We traveled through...they were *not* there. How is that possible?"

The angry bull circled back, snorting and collecting himself, but obviously bothered by the smoking pit. Grabbing the reins from my stunned companion, I tried to get us hidden. It wasn't an easy task. My companion was useless in this state, and there wasn't much of a place to take cover.

"Will you please calm down and try to help me out here?" I screamed an equally useless question.

He completely ignored my question. "Are you not confused? You are remarkably still while I rave as a lunatic! You understand this which is why you do not speak?"

"Lunatic is right. I'm not talking because I can't get a word in edgewise. How about you tell me what you think happened?" Forcing both horses behind the mound of dirt, rocks, and rope serving for a fence was not remarkably still in my estimation.

"How am I to possibly know what this sudden change of scene can mean? Understand you this?"

"Yes, unfortunately I do. Do you have any idea why I would know?"

"By the Lord, girl, you do speak in such a strange manner and now we are to engage in some kind of game where I know not the rules!"

"Welcome to my life, Daniel Boone."

"Are you much given to madness? I am my own man, unless, that is, you fancy the name horse girl."

"My, my, what a surprise. You don't want to be treated like someone you're not. Ever since you found out I am a girl you have treated me like someone I'm not. You couldn't possibly understand what I know, or the way I act because I'm from another time. But you will *not* assume...that I have no morals."

"What nonsense do you speak?" He muttered to himself and then screamed out, "Of that which you speak, makes no sense…what mean you… from another time?"

Not far behind us a shot rang out, a not so gentle reminder we were rehashing something totally unimportant at this very uncertain time. Immediately, we both ducked behind the fence and some puny bushes, getting entangled in each other and our horses, thinking we were the target. However, while we had been arguing with all the ability our lungs would provide, possessed by an irritable force we couldn't explain, the bull had circled around toward the front and met his doom.

"Ye thaur, hauld oan a minute. Ye burned doon mah barn an' th' fences th' lest time ye cam ben haur. Ye got most ay mah herd 'en. Wa dornt ye gang sooth? Lit it be their turn." The older man limped out into the front yard, unarmed, to survey the damage that had been done to the bull, now on the ground dead.

"How is it that the Scots are here? I knew of them in the Carolinas but few ventured west!" Christian was dumbfounded by the man but unconcerned with our circumstances.

"Shhhhhh," I grabbed his arm and thrust my hand over his mouth. It was my turn to shut him up before we were discovered. Of course, he didn't care for this and shrugged me off but didn't speak again for some time.

"Well, what a fine suggestion you have sir, but our men in Nashville have dibs on that area." A small group of soldiers clad in blue coats sniggered behind their officer. "You didn't lose the house. You should be grateful."

"Thought you would have learned your lesson the last time and taught that bull some manners. Guess we'll just have dinner with that lovely daughter of yours and decide whether we will report this to General Paine." Another spoke with authority although he had none.

They dismounted and tied their horses to the shed while the old man tried to explain they had little to eat themselves. They, again, thought what he said funny, their raucous laughter hanging cruelly in the air.

"You Secesh made this bed, now you have to lie in it," another said, evidently feeling the need to sound important as well.

It was fortunate for us they had not heard us arguing. Although their going inside was probably bad for the inhabitants, it gave us enough time to get away. This was not good, not good at all.

"We just got a huge break," I whispered and motioned for him to lead his horse on. He was, understandably, stunned from what we had witnessed, but I was still perturbed with his conceit. Weakly, he began to whisper back, aware there might be some kind of danger.

"What you spoke, before…what mean you?"

"Just what I said. Now put two and two together smart man and tell me where we are."

"We are in the Cumberland River area…not far from our station."

"Where did the houses come from?"

"I know not. We have not seen any settlements nor were we aware any were in the area, even when we found you."

"Found me? Wouldn't it make better sense to say I just appeared? Out of nowhere? Because that is exactly what happened. I just happen to know where nowhere is."

"You insist on confusing me with all your talk. "Where nowhere is" what meaning does that have?"

"What year do you think we are in?"

"Think we are in? I *know* it is the year seventeen hundred seventy-two."

"Where I come from it is the year two thousand twelve and this appears to be the 1860's."

Daniel Boone was staring a totally different stare. Then slowly, his eyes made obvious what his brain did not want to comprehend. I had thrown way too much information at him at once, but I hadn't known how else to put it. How do you tell someone they just skipped almost 100 years in one leap? He finally opened his mouth shrieking at me, almost to the point where I was afraid. It would have frightened me yesterday but that was before we landed in the middle of The War for Southern Independence, incorrectly known as the Civil War. I had much bigger fears now.

"You are an absolute lunatic! What kind of mind invents such a preposterous thought? How would that even be possible?"

"Would you please hush? You are putting us in danger every time you open your big mouth," I warned.

"Would that I understood…" he muttered to himself.

We came upon an odd tree line, ragged bushes and vines winding around mutilated trunks with bent limbs and hanging branches. The mangled flora didn't provide much shade but gave us adequate cover to ride behind for a bit.

"By the way, what's with that word lunatic? If you will stay calm, I will try my best to explain what I know." With a swallow and a sigh, I wondered out loud where to start. "I guess H.G. Wells and Jules Verne are still later, so you wouldn't even have the thought of fantastic things happening like this."

His expression was one of horror and intense curiosity. The length and shagginess of his hair forced down by his hat only added to the protrusion of his eyes, boring holes into me trying to understand what I was saying. The more I spoke, the more his expression hardened. Fear of the unknown was quite understandable.

"You are daft, no unhinged…" He growled the accusations at me.

"I'm as freaked out by this as you are. I didn't really believe in time travel. Thought it was just a plot to some fantastic story for entertainment – that I totally enjoyed – but not so much now. Now, I'm a believer and not enjoying this one little bit."

"You imagine the impossible." Sucking in his anger, he finally began to listen as I recalled the day we met. It was my turn. I continued to ramble, and he continued to listen.

"I don't know why if this has to happen, I can't end up in the 1940's where I could possibly function. But no!!!!" I muttered to myself, "I don't get it. We jumped over that crater I came through on… Did I come through on an orange portal and then we go out a different direction on it, into a blue one? Maybe a meteor created the crater and gave it some kind of portal power. What *does* give this area its power?"

Several thoughts occurred to me at once and I continued mumbling on to myself until I realized Boone had stopped listening. He looked as if his head might blow off, turning his body to the right and left and then almost completely around in the saddle. The scenery was not to be ignored. We rode on in shocked silence.

Instead of thick forests with animal trails, there were occasional clumps of bushes or an odd sapling along the deeply rutted road. Where once an open field, cultivated by the Native Americans or stampeded by hundreds of buffalo, small deserted farms stood, every field long stripped of vegetation. Houses stared back at us through shattered windows. Larger brick farmhouses showed signs of struggle and defeat with charred chimneys and overgrown gardens. The occasional stone fence, built by the Irish a dozen years ago, lined the front along the road but there wasn't a fence rail to be seen. Hundreds of acres of countryside had been ravaged. Desolation was everywhere.

Dark clouds rumbled in the distance or were those cannons? I didn't mention my suspicions aloud. My mind was jumbled and headed for a short circuit. History lessons were colliding with my new reality.

"The sun sets soon and we have need of cover. It appears we might choose among many shelters," he said grimly.

A small stone house, once a cottage, sat back from the road surrounded by large crepe myrtles. The beauty of the heavy white flowers against the dilapidated structure made me want to scream HOW DARE YOU, NATURE, going on about your business as if nothing had happened here! The intoxicating scent of the flowering lilacs, despite the destruction surrounding them, brought to mind my sweet Pa, who would remind me to be thankful they were large enough cover to hide our horses in the smaller rock outbuilding in the back.

It was modest to begin with, only a couple of windows, though broken, along with the doors. Although small, the once comfortable home didn't give its intruders much to work with, but it was obvious it had been plundered anyway. Whatever was left was strewed, broken, or burned. If this was what had happened to my beloved Tennessee, I couldn't imagine how the Shenandoah Valley must look…or Georgia and South Carolina.

"Sherman described war accurately, I'd say. Of course, he and his bunch caused a lot of it," I said angrily.

The frontier man stood, his mouth hanging open in disgust. When he finally closed it and looked at me again he said very quietly, "What war?"

CHAPTER 21

The Importance of Jerky

As the rain poured outside, we sat in the dimly lit room, what I supposed was the main room, awaiting the dark. I tried to imagine the family that had lived there and what transpired to make them leave.

"Man, I'm glad I grabbed that bag." I offered him a piece of the dried meat.

"From what time are you?" He stared past me.

"I told you."

"I would not have inquired of you if I did not want the information again." He snatched the food from my hand. What a smarty pants he was even when in shock.

"2012. The year two thousand twelve."

He processed that for a moment and then asked in a very low voice, "Were we not seeking your Grandfather? But hold, you knew he would not be there! We rode through the barren area... not seeking your Pa at all!"

"Are you serious? Out of all I've told you and what we've seen, this is all you've got? You think I lied to you about looking for Pa? I *was* looking for my Pa...looking for a way to get back to him. I thought maybe a certain time of day would work or a direction. Even rain but it never stormed while we were there, until today. I thought maybe it had to be storming on the other side for me to get across, but I just couldn't figure it out. But you know, both times it storms and then we cross into sunshine." His face was still red from anger at what he thought was a lie. "If I had told you this in 1772, you would have chased me out of camp. I don't think I would have survived on my own."

"You did not tell me for fear of being thought mad?" Still angry, he remained quiet for some time. "I cannot place blame," he whispered, though the anger was still there.

"You know, I thought about that meteor shower last night, when it happened. Some Native Americans believe it is a foretelling of something to happen."

"Native Americans?"

"Indians. Some of my ancestors were Cherokee but, honestly, who can say who was here first and what group. They fought as much as anybody else over land and stuff. I do agree Columbus was a bit confused about where he was when he called them that." Christian had no clue what I was jabbering about, as usual. "Why did you follow that bison anyway?"

"My first thought was how unusual and to hunt it. But only a brief moment, for then that band of savages came, driving the buffalo towards us, with no other choice but to possibly run them into each other."

"They're supposed to be some kind of spiritual sign. Not sure what either has to do with time travel. Are they some kind of impetus? You know… a journey to learn some kind of life lesson. I've learned some valuable lessons but uncertain about anything else."

"What lessons do you speak of learning from 1772?" He spit at me with heavy sarcasm.

"To appreciate certain creature comforts a little more – indoor plumbing for one," I spat back.

"I know not of what you speak but I hope you will now explain things to me I wanted to know before." His fist was clenched but he was not quite as loud.

"Like I said before, you could be a little more civil towards me if you want information."

He processed that for a minute and said in the same hateful tone, "Pardon my offense. What would you have me do? Beg at your feet?"

"That works. But I think first we need to figure out how we are going to survive here until we can find a way to move on. The thing I had to come to grips with before is I might never leave 1772 and what I would do to survive."

Our conversation seemed to have reached an impasse. My head was pounding, trying to come up with some solution to our predicament. Daniel Boone was useless because he was still in shock. I knew he still didn't fully believe. If I weren't here he would believe quicker. He thought I was pulling some kind of prank on him. Oh, that I had that kind of power.

"If those soldiers weren't around and if I knew..." angrily, I tried to think of something but it was useless, "and if I had wheels, I'd be a wagon."

"I do not comprehend how any of these events could be so." Sometimes his way of speaking really grated on my nerves.

"Why don't you just say you don't know how in the world any of this could have happened, huh?" I screamed this at him for no good reason. It didn't seem to faze him so I continued. "At any other time, this would be intruding on private property."

"Private property! This land is part of my claim, of this I am sure!"

"Well, I hate to tell you Daniel Boone, this *was* to be part of your claim. All your friends built forts on their claim. Along with a lot of other people and so on and so on and here we are."

"Surely you could not have forgotten my name in all these trials of late?" Sarcastically he looked at me sideways until he realized what I had said. "How do you know these things?"

"Well, I lived here!" Unbelievably he needed more proof. "Duh...I can read and my grandparents are from this area... in Tennessee...in the United States...of America." He didn't get it.

"What country are you speaking of...the British Empire?"

"Uh no, the United States of America...what the colonies became... the Revolutionary War was fought not long after your friends go back to Virginia. Weren't they in the militia?"

"By heaven! One would have expected that. The taxation...and they would not allow any say...."

"I thought it was hard on the English people having to pay for the protection of the colonies," playing devil's advocate, I threw that at him.

"I would imagine it to be difficult but liberty would absolve them of that responsibility. Exactly whose side would you be on madam?"

"Since it happened well over two hundred years ago for me, I hardly think it matters."

"My compatriots did well, did they?"

"Yes, but I don't want to tell you any more specifics in case we figure out a way to get back to our times. I don't want to do anything that messes up the future. Let's leave this at a need to know basis."

He didn't seem to understand and became frustrated again.

"Look, if I tell you what happens to any of them…what if you go back and tell them something that makes them change their minds? You never know how much that could influence my time. I don't want to be responsible for that. I also want to be born."

"This war, at present, you spoke of earlier is not that war?"

"Unfortunately, no, but there are similarities…unequal taxation for one." I imagined William Holden explaining the government to Judy Holliday in *Born Yesterday*. Of course, he wasn't eating a Popsicle or wearing high-heels.

The man's face fell with the realization of how careful we needed to be. His voice was low. "Well, horse girl, what will become of us?"

"How do you think I know? I was trying to figure that out before we time warped again…" Distractedly, I half hummed the last part and then realized how ridiculous that was in relation to what was going on. As you might expect, he stared at me like I had two heads and rightly so. Was I going mad…again?

CHAPTER 22

Power Grab

The next morning, my head was still dull from trying to teach *The Civil War for Dummies*. My goal last night had been to explain the high points but it wasn't long until I realized it had turned into the long version.

"Evidently you changed your position concerning what I, ah, need to know," he had smirked.

"I don't know how long it will take us to find a way out of this craziness. You may need to know what's going on to survive," I countered.

"By all means then, carry on." Frustration was evident in his sarcasm.

"Look, it wasn't really a civil war because the South tried to secede peacefully and have their own country – like we did against the English. Truthfully, it was the War of Hypocrisy, on both sides, getting into the war. You know…a rich man's war but a poor man's fight. Generals from the Union and Confederate countries even became friends later commiserating over their respective governments being stubborn about all the issues, you know, leaving the people to fight it out."

That was the last thing I remembered saying before I fell into a fitful sleep, curling up in one corner with my saddle and Daniel Boone in the other. Now that the dawn had arrived, I needed to get my head clear. The remains of the door groaned as he went out into the uncertainty. My neck was quite stiff when I stood to stretch out the night's pains and think through things. If the Union were already occupying middle Tennessee then it was at least a year or two in. Not knowing if we would ever leave this time period, we had to figure out what to do. My thoughts were to stay safe, first and foremost, and then try to get out of the war zone, maybe out west somewhere.

He had been outside for some time when I went to check on Quasar. The sky was beginning to lighten though heavy dark clouds remained all around. The rain from the night before had made the ground squishy as I neared the shed.

"Good morning, you guys! Did you sleep well with all the commotion?" Quasar snorted and stomped with anticipation. "Hey Daniel Boone's horse! I've never heard him call you anything so I'm going to name you Traveller. I think that is very appropriate to the situation. Quasar, meet your dining companion Traveller." I led him around the back. While they munched on the few patches of wet grass, I wondered where the frontier man was.

It was mid-morning, though still very dark, when I knew he wasn't coming back leaving me to wander around in a daze trying to think what to do. This area must have been one of the first stops in burning and pillaging with bushes, lilacs and crepe myrtle beginning to grow back. Some distance behind the rock shed, what was left of bee gums sat adjacent to the remains of a small orchard. They had both been burned to ensure not even a bee remained to make honey to feed one starving person. But wild blackberry vines tangled up in scrub along the back were heavy, and I picked them clean. They were a delicious break from the usual and worth every chigger I would probably get.

Lucky for me, since I didn't trust any water not directly out of the ground, when tracking further I found a spring not too far back from the vines. Water was as easily ruined in war as anything else. After filling our containers and helping myself, I helped the horses. That was the only bit of luck I would have for when I crept around to the front, it was just in time to see a group of Union soldiers pushing and taunting Christian. Trying to stay hidden in the bushes, I felt sick over his capture.

They had his long rifle and were having a fine time ridiculing it and his dress. He said nothing. In fact, he acted as if he couldn't hear, his face bright red from the humiliation, but he wasn't stupid enough to let his anger get him into more trouble. It was a smart choice. His English accent might cause them to think he was a spy or at least lead to more questioning where now they only thought him a deaf and dumb hillbilly.

After they played with his rifle for a bit, they threw it on the ground having no need of an antique with their sharp new Spencer rifles. Then roping him, mounted their horses, and poked him to run with them or be drug behind. Helplessly, I looked around, but there was nothing I could do at that moment but angrily wipe the tears from my face and mouth. As soon as they were gone, I picked up his rifle and stared at it, trying to absorb what had happened.

I wanted to scream and cry with the realization I was alone, again, in a strange time and during the bleakest years for the South. This was my home state, and I abhorred what I saw all around me. This wasn't a battlefield — Shiloh or Murfreesboro or even Missionary Ridge. This wasn't showing slave owners the error of their ways when the majority of the citizens had no dog in that fight, only getting into the war to protect the homes they had worked so hard for from invasion. This was the little community of my ancestors and what they feared most had happened anyway. The ugly boot of the federal government had stomped on it and used its soldiers in a power grab.

CHAPTER 23

Information, Please

Crying didn't help a thing, but the flood of tears wouldn't stop and continued later after I read it. All alone, in my despair, I had pulled out the envelope pushed deep into my pants and finally saw what Pa had placed on my truck seat that morning, now, in the future. Folded inside a letter, an old, faded twenty dollar bill was stuck to a note that read, "Hope this helps, wherever you are. Love you, Pa." I wasn't sure at this point if he should have sent Confederate money, or whether it was already worthless.

The rest of that day and several more I rambled miserably around the small house, watching it rain and waiting for him to come back although highly unlikely. Beyond my misery, out there somewhere was a man in prison, or worse, and I didn't know what to do despite having read the old, yellowed, letter that explained, sort of, how I got here and, maybe, what I should do next. Part of me sulked and declared it was my life to live, and I would choose how I wanted to live it. The other part knew no matter how angry I was at the presumptuous nature of the letter something worse might happen if I didn't attempt to follow that particular course of action. I decided it didn't matter what I wanted to do, at this point anyway.

If I had learned nothing else in my life and different times, when things changed you had to move with them or get run over. That was precisely what motivated me to get the horses and ride on the day the sun finally came out. I had to know what had happened to him even if it meant something happening to me. Gabriel Christian had protected my identity and stayed with me in his strange time and now, no matter how difficult he was, I was going to do what I could to help him, if he was still alive.

It was awkward bringing Traveller with me, yet I didn't want to leave him alone with the obvious chance of being stolen or ending up as dinner for man or beast. Back went the hat on my head, stuffing my hair into it, trying to be a very young boy if I could get away with it. I retraced our path around the few bushes and trees that were left and rode miles down the road.

The same pasture of the deceased bull was up ahead. Coming in the back way, I didn't have to move the makeshift fence since it was gone and so were all the animals, including the remains of the bull, barely held in only a few days ago. I tied the horses up to the back of the house, checked the saddlebags for what little feed I had found for them, and carefully, came to the front door.

"Sir? Sir? I'm not looking for food, and I'm not the enemy. I just need to talk to you a minute." With a loud whisper, I tapped lightly watching out all around me in case I had missed another band of foragers.

The old man slowly opened the warped door to peer out. My heart broke at the site of his battered face, a swollen, purpled eye, and puffy lips.

"Och aye? Whit is it?" His gravelly voice gave way to a wheeze.

"Could I please come in? I'm afraid of being seen. Do you want some jerky?" I held out a medium piece which was quickly jerked from my hand and devoured, all but a couple of bites. The man hardly noticed that I had pushed the door open and come in. The room was small and sparsely furnished with only a small chair and bench.

"Whit is it," he paused to clear his throat, "'at ye want wi' me loon?" A young girl, maybe a teen, cautiously eyed me from an even smaller room.

"My name is Kenneth Manning, pleased to meet you sir." I held out my hand to shake his but he repeated his demand. Coughing nervously, I continued, "Only to leave one of my horses here with you. Back in a few days – I'll get him then. His name is Traveller."

"General Lee's horse?" The girl squealed excitedly.

"No, but that's where I got the name. The man who owns him was taken by the same group that shot your bull."

"How do you know he's alive?" She came into the room to stand next to the older man, whom I presumed was her grandfather.

"Leoia, gie back in th' other room." He growled and handed her the jerky.

"Sir, I mean no harm." I took a step back trying to make them comfortable. "It'll be difficult enough to find him without gettin' my horse stolen. I couldn't leave him tied up where we'd been stayin' in case, well, you know, I didn't come back. If I'm not back in a week he's yours."

"Hoo dae ye ken abit mah bull an' whit ur ye daein' haur? Ah ne'er saw ye afair."

"We were here yesterday, until we saw the soldiers and had to run back that-a-way." Pointing towards the back, I tried to think of something plausible. "We rode in from the east and it was a rough way to get here, figured on going west."

"You cannae be it an' abit ur ye will be snatched up loch a hawk efter field mice. Ye will nae make it, Ah teel ye, an' he will nae lest haur. They awreddy took everythin'. But if ye want tae lae 'at cuddie haur it's nane ay mah concern. Ah dornt hae anything' tae feed it an' barely onie girse but whit Ah dae hae he is welcome tae. Anybody got somethin' tae dae wi' General Lee ooght tae be okay, Ah figure."

"Cuddie?" I had no idea what he was talking about surprised to still hear such a strong accent.

"He means your horse," the girl interjected.

"Oh... mighty obliged to you. I'm a hopin' that since they been here lately they'll be done over here fer a spell," trying to sound Pa-like so as not to arouse more suspicion.

"That'd be a miracle. Seems since they got Colonel Morgan last month up to Ohio that Paine's been worse than usual, if'n that's possible..." The girl's voice was soft, without the thick accent of the older man, appearing frail as well when she stepped out into view.

"That scoundrel in charge of the Federals...he'll grab anybody for no good reason and hang 'em," I added. The old man nodded his head mumbling "aye" while rubbing the back of his neck. From what Pa had told me, Paine was cut from the same cloth as Sherman.

"He's mighty fond of other people's belongings too. I heard tell that he goes out for Rebels and sometimes comes back with furniture." Pushing the hair out of her eyes, round with the absurdity of what she had said, acknowledging that in war the bizarre was more than likely true. "Everything cost so much before the war. Bet that's why he takes it, to teach us a lesson 'cause we stopped buying from the Yankees." She was pretty wise to it all whether she had formal education or not.

After a while they felt comfortable with me, offering me a dipper of water. "Sir, I'm pleased to make your acquaintance," I said, trying my best to shake hands in a manly manner not like a limp fish, "and yours too, Miss Leoia. Have you lived here long?"

John Sloan, although educated as most Scots were, had struggled with hunger and the English most of his young life. Landlords had exchanged the people for sheep to graze the open lands, pushing them to the sea to scratch out a living from the kelp. The old eyes turned misty as they gazed off in the distance, seeing the crags and lochs of his native land after all the years. After a moment, he regained his composure and related how, at thirteen, his family had sent him to Wilmington after the turn of the century as a "servant" with his wages to be sent home. After extremely cramped conditions and little food or water on the boat, things didn't improve once he arrived. It didn't take him long to know there would be no freedom, for the master considered him disposable. Time and again he saw it happen to others around him, tacking extra years on for this or that, sick and broken until they died, struggling to fulfill their contract. He knew he had to make a break.

A large community of Scots lived up the Cape Fear River, having made their way over years before, and offered refuge then supplies for the first leg of his journey. The guilt of not sending the promised money home ate at him, but he was forced for many years to live hidden in the mountains, helping out a farmer here or there, living off the land. Wanderlust and desire for his own land took over, and he continued here, meeting his wife, and working hard for his family.

It was quiet for a bit. Then, with his voice low and cracking, he added how his wife had died not long after the war began. Things hadn't seemed right since. His story over, I cleared my throat to say something, but everything seemed lame in comparison to what he had been through and still had ahead of him.

"My Pa's family came over from North Carolina, too, from Ulster. But that was a hundred years ago." It felt very weird to say that. "And they lived several places before making this their home."

"Och aye, we ur a roamin' sort. Hud Ah nae mit mah sweetheart, Ah wood still be roamin' noo. Whaur is yer Pa?"

"I don't know. So much time has passed since I saw him. I'm afeared I have lost him in the struggle." That was the gospel truth.

Before he asked any more about my background, I asked more about his. Leoia's mother had died in childbirth years ago prompting his son and child to live with them. When his son enlisted to protect what little they had, Mr. Sloan had promised to take care of her.

"It was a sham th' way he died…up thaur in Kentucky…it rained stoaner an' those flintlocks jist didne wark. But th' yankees' guns surely did. Aw their guns got dreich tay but they kept oan firin'…th' flintlock muskets jist wooldnae wark." Shaking his head from the sheer waste of it all, he struggled to cope.

"We've been sold a bill of goods on both sides, but they think it's their duty to teach us all a lesson." He was listening to me intently, grunting "aye" occasionally in agreement. "But it's our homes being invaded…in the name of freedom and liberty, no less."

Hearing his story had made me angry, but at the same time, I understood the manipulation by the federal government – in history and my own time. It was possible my father's ancestors, whom I didn't know too much about, nor had I wanted to until now, had no idea what was really happening here. Had they lost family as well doing what they were told was right to keep the country together? "Somewhere up North mothers are grievin' too." Still in thought, I hadn't realized it came out of my mouth.

"Ye frae th' moontains, ye main be a Federal talkin' loch 'at. Those puir sons ay a Yankee mammy, ye say," he raised his voice at me angrily and spat, "killed mah son."

"I'm so sorry for your loss, but I'm not a traitor to my state."

"What's gonnae oan ower thaur whaur ye come frae an' wa' are nae ye fightin?"

"Well, a lot of people are fightin' but they're using the war as an excuse to end old feuds." The mountain people of Tennessee and North Carolina were in a constant struggle with the regular armies and also with those not signing up, whether they were guerrillas or home guard. "Then you have the Cherokees joined up with the Thomas' Legion fightin' with the Rebels to keep what they have left of their lands. Federals never gave 'em cause to trust 'em." Not having answered his question exactly, I paused for his reaction and then added, "I got out of there and came lookin' for Pa."

Leoia, silent through all of our conversation, suddenly piped up. "Are you with that group of Federals from over east that terrorizes the contrabands?" She turned to her grandfather and added, "Pappy, you remember Paine's blue coats talking about them… the time they made me cook the last of our chickens?" He nodded. "None of them liked the black folk, but they said those soldiers from east of the state believed they worked as hard as the Negroes and were just as poor and weren't going to fight for the rich Rebels to keep them." She paused to wipe at her runny nose then continued. "Paine's men agreed 'cause they looked down on both of them anyways and laughed thinking that was real funny. Bet those blues would change their minds now knowing Yankees are taking their belongings the same as ours." Shrugging her shoulders at the irony, they both looked at me for a reply.

"No, honestly, I'm not a soldier of any kind. I just hate loss of any life." They had no idea how much.

Sighing, he gave me the basics of his parents' struggle with the English and famine, reminding me that he knew about death and suffering as well. He had been in bondage and knew it happened everywhere, to every race, and was no proponent of it. However, it had also been a struggle to get his own place, and nobody was going to take it without a fight.

Tired didn't begin to describe the lines etched on his face, the deep creases between the brows and the sides of the swollen frown. Squinting to see him, we all realized the room had darkened, and there was no evidence of candles or oil for the lamp. He said we would talk more in the morning if I wanted to bed down there for the night.

The next morning, over some kind of hot drink, we talked about the town and where Christian most likely would be. Without a map, this was the next best thing. Of all my questions, he asked the worst one.

"Hoo dae ye ken we will nae eat your cuddie?"

I took two small pieces of the food out for myself and gave him the bag.

CHAPTER 24

The Bonnie Blue Flag

Of course, I had no idea how I was going to get Christian released from wherever he was. It wasn't long until the decision was made for me. About ten men rode up out of nowhere and overtook me.

"C'mon boy, 'less you want to be captured by Paine's men on the prowl. We're headed up to the Tunnels to see what we can do!" An older, yet burly man shouted at me as they slowed to a trot. They were all a pretty untidy bunch with scraggly beards and filthy, ripped remnants of the butternut uniform that was underneath much newer blue overcoats. Short on food, as their mostly gaunt appearance indicated, they were not lacking in enthusiasm. Although I couldn't identify them, they must be better than the others not having shot me on sight.

The desolate area north of town made it difficult to approach the railroad without being seen. Riding west then turning back north allowed us to reach the ridge and be somewhat hidden by the hills, riding over the same terrain where I had camped along the creek with the frontiersmen, days ago. The mossy banks, trampled and muddy, outlined part of small farms, all burned and deserted.

Winding paths through the hills that would later be well-known for their passage to stills were not easy to travel. Quasar obeyed dutifully although it was hard for him. Trees had been axed or fallen in storms, decaying in the vines and brush entangling our way. Often we had to lead instead of ride, and I was acutely aware of the possibility of stepping on rattlers and copperheads prevalent in the area.

As we trudged along, the men began to laugh about acquiring the overcoats some time ago when the infamous Morgan was still around, raiding the countryside and capturing guards placed there to protect the railroad from Louisville to Nashville. They particularly enjoyed telling the story of blocking the tunnel with a captured locomotive, burning a whole section of trestlework.

When that got old they began to chant something of a game to keep their minds on the task ahead. Some of it rhymed and was about people and places I had never heard of. Then someone called out "John Morgan's got your mule" and they broke out into song.

> Come on, come on, come on, old man,
> And don't be made a fool;
> I'll tell you the truth as best I can:
> "John Morgan's got your Mule!"

The good-natured ribbing lasted for some time as they sang it over and over. Then, from giddy to somber, the mood changed when a soldier sang the usual rallying song in a much slower almost wistful fashion.

> Hurrah! Hurrah! For Southern rights hurrah!
> Hurrah for the Bonnie Blue Flag
> That bears a single star.
>
> We are a band of brothers
>   And native to the soil,
> Fighting for the property
>   We gained by honest toil;
> And when our rights were threatened,
>   The cry rose near and far–
> "Hurrah for the Bonnie Blue Flag
>   That bears a single star!"

After singing about each of the Confederate states as a solo, the others repeated the chorus many times. Nobody had one of those flags but instead an original flag, the real "stars and bars," edged in red and white stripes with the circle of stars displaying the obvious reason for changing. It was much too similar to the U.S. flag. Another had the battle flag of the Army of Northern Virginia known as the "Southern Cross", the Cross of St. Andrew paying homage to so many of Scottish heritage. The flags had seen better days though tattered and torn, mended many times, most likely obtained from one who had proudly died carrying it. In their voices you could hear a genuine, sincere love of their land and all the flags represented– the sweat of their brow and hours of toil they or their ancestors had purchased that land with.

I wanted to grab them and tell them to quit now that people would still argue years from now over the causes of the war and who had the moral high ground. Neither side could honestly claim that. But these poor rag-tag soldiers felt their rights had been usurped and were determined to make that statement with their lives. The sad fact was they would have even fewer when Reconstruction came and with it more invasion and theft causing war weary men, no matter how wounded, if they even survived, continuing to fight to protect their own. My heart ached for not only what these men on the fringes were trying to do but how they would be misrepresented in the future. From the flag they carried and any way they tried to protect their loved ones, it would eventually be twisted many times into something different and used politically, again and again. I knew how it ended and it wasn't pretty. But, of course, I could say nothing.

At dark, we made camp at the base of another section of hills. An odd assortment of food was passed around. Tins of beans, bits of hard bread, and an odd piece of fruit were all from plunder of one kind or another. I slept fitfully on the hard ground when finally day began again. Slow to start, it was hours until we emerged from the sparse undergrowth to find a fortification, sure to be equipped with guns, on the hill overlooking the area between the tunnels. The same tunnels they had participated in blocking for a time. The same tunnels teenagers had hiked over and dared each other to run through for years to come. The same overlook where couples in my time sat to watch the train or occasionally throw a rock, asking for it from Homeland Security. It would be suicide, now, to try anything since there was no cover. Trees had been chopped down in every direction leaving no place to hide. The group opted to divide and conquer, leaving the tunnels altogether.

"Men, we have to do better than yesterday. Let's make Morgan proud!" shouted the leader, riding off south with part of the group as we rode north. I never saw him again, but it wasn't long before I heard the destruction when the train came barreling down the tracks past us, and then screeching and howling to stop. The ground shook with the blast. Smoke and flames shot up into the sky at the deafening crash.

"That torpedo threw that train to kingdom come...Yee-ahhhh-ooo!!" screamed a ghost of a man without an arm.

"Ain't seen nothing like 'at since Perr'ville...Yee-ahhhh-ooo-ahh-oooo!!" wailed another as he turned round on his horse showing half of a missing leg.

Sending a chill down my spine, it was the Rebel yell and only someone who had been in battle would know how to give it the proper sound. These men had been to war and back and were now trying to do what they could to keep their home unoccupied. The Union command was quickly alerted to be after those who would not submit to what the Federals thought was the rightful authority.

They were everywhere with gunfire at our backs and coming up on our sides – so many hornets whose nest had been disturbed. But Quasar was made for this kind of riding and was as fast as the bullets whizzing past our ears, charging ahead leaving the rest in his dust. I never looked back riding on until all was quiet except for the panting of my horse and the bass drum in my chest.

The sun was lower now as I continued north some distance from the railroad, trying my best to ride along tree lines or behind bushes. Continued destruction made that almost impossible, so I vowed to stop at the first place I found, empty or not. It was a larger house, though it would not qualify as a plantation by any means, and must have been used by the Federals, since no part of it was burned. Big clumps of blooms from the lilacs hung over one side of the porch and bluish hydrangeas trimmed the other side. No one appeared to be inside when I rode around to the back. I was tired and hoped I wasn't being foolish, but I didn't really know what else I could do. Quasar helped himself to the water trough while I tried to formulate a plan.

Since he seemed okay, I walked some distance away from the house and tied him to one of the few older trees I had seen behind a trellis of wisteria. It didn't take long for me to figure out, once inside the house, the enemy was still in the area and would probably be back soon. In a mad dash for food, I noticed a vase of flowers and a handkerchief, and I knew an officer must have brought his wife. While I munched on an apple I stuffed my bag with bread and more fruit and went in search of clothes. I knew, now, what I was going to do.

Before the sun set I had a plan. I tied the new provisions onto Quasar and rode off in search of water. The clean-up was going to take some effort.

CHAPTER 25

Fox on the Run

The sun had set when I finally reached town. Cautiously, I had ridden south, a more direct route, but not by the railroad. Because of the terrain and surrounding devastation, I had to weave in and out around stumps, ruts, and the leftovers of foraging parties. I didn't want to ride right up on the square but instead, gambling, I rode to the Federal fort, just inside town, where a young man stood watch. Just as I arrived, he motioned me back to allow several to exit, and I knew immediately the infamous General Eleazer Paine. Charles Manson psycho eyes, under the unruly ghost-white mop of hair, stared in my direction at some wagons.

After I finished choking, I pulled the rag of a handkerchief away from my face, safe from dust and evil. Hot and sticky, I tried to gracefully dismount, but the skirt of my dress caught in the saddle. In trying to get free and keep the rest of the dress down over my jeans, my foot turned in the stirrup. I was falling off before I realized what was happening.

"Whoa, careful miss," the young private said in a rather stuffy tone as he caught me and helped me to my feet. "What a shame you have to ride that way." I couldn't decide if that was meant sarcastically.

I hadn't been here long enough to figure out the nuances of the southern accent of this day, yet I knew it was different than mine. The stereotype southern belle accent irked me having never heard anybody in my lifetime that truly had one, but I didn't have a choice.

"I'm mighty obliged to you sir." What came out of my mouth was a cross between Scarlett O'Hara and the Hee Haw Hunnies. "I know, but my side saddle was taken…"

"You're not from around here," he said, trying to place me. I nervously rubbed my horse to divert attention, and then wished I hadn't.

"What a beauty," he said, patting Quasar. I knew I had to get his attention, or he would confiscate him. It had never worked for me to cry to get my way so I had to try something else.

"Why thank you. How kind of you to say so." Speaking softly, I attempted to look longingly into his eyes from under the ruffle of the large bonnet I had been fortunate to confiscate. I paused, sorry I had to throw Georgia under the bus, "My brother and I are from Georgia, up to visit some family. He was taken by your friends the other day, and I wondered if you might know where he is."

"If he was arrested, then he would be inside or maybe still at General Paine's headquarters." I must have been useless at that approach, too, as I watched him open Quasar's mouth to check his teeth.

"Oh, I don't think he was arrested. You see, they probably didn't realize he is truly ill, I mean, he can't hear or speak." I took his hands and tried to turn his attention away from my horse. "Your men have been nothing but kind to my family, and it was silly of my brother to run off. But how do you tell someone that can't hear to wait for you?" I chuckled lightly for effect.

"Yes, I know who you mean now. They brought him in about the same time as some Rebels trying to sneak into town to see family. General Paine nearly had him hanged then and there with the others, but one of the officer's wives insisted on saving him to watch with her lady friends."

"Wa-atch?" The one syllable word became two, trying to decipher his meaning.

"Oh, yes. They have a fine game of it. The prisoner, on a slow horse, gets turned loose and then the others chase him on fresh horses. The ladies think it's quite funny that he's chased, like a fox." I felt sick. The private had no qualms relating this to anyone much less a visitor to the town, or so he thought.

"Hysterical, I'm sure," I said under my breath and added louder, "I'm sure it was all a big misunderstanding. Why Yankees would never do such a thing." I smiled sweetly.

"Well, he didn't know what to do with him so he sent him to the hospital…at the church. But I think it's only until the lady returns." The young man smiled back at me briefly and turned to eye Quasar's backside, considering whether he was going to take the horse or me.

"Oh, that's wonderful. Thank you ever so much. I wondered if you would mind looking the other way while I mount my horse. It's not very graceful and I would be so embarrassed…"

"Let me help," Eagerly, he stepped up to assist.

"All right, then, if you insist." I could have been in the saddle and on my way, but I did not want to alert him to the fact I had on clothes underneath and, more importantly, the ease I could get in the saddle on my own, dress or no dress. Clumsily, I grabbed the pommel and held my dress with the other hand. There was enough skirt to the dress to completely cover me.

"Who was it exactly you were visiting?" he remembered to ask.

"Bye now." I pretended not to hear him and trotted away thanking my lucky stars he couldn't make up his mind between the two of us, so we both got away.

Gas lights lit up the area around the square. I could see them as I crossed the railroad tracks, but I had to go quite a ways around to find a low place to cross the creek. It ended up to my advantage to be able to come up behind the church and tie up out of view. Someone was firing a gun nearby, and I cautiously peered around the building to see what was going on.

It was the occupying soldiers having a bit of fun at the expense of the court house, not at all the building I was familiar with. From my vantage point, the brick Federal style had evenly spaced windows with little ornamentation, excepting the object of attention at this moment. Wagers were being made who could hit the finial atop the dome without knocking out the windows in the cupola below. Even though the church where I stood was a couple of blocks from the town square, the boisterous event had brought out many to the streets enabling me to slip inside the front door without notice.

One of several nurses tending wounded patients looked up as I walked into the room.

"Yes, what is it you want?" Her rather pinched tone, though not rude, was straight to the point. She continued tending her patient.

"Well, you see ma'am, my brother was brought here…"

"This is a Union hospital. Rebels are not brought here."

"I understand but the gentleman at Fort Thomas said he was brought here." I had walked over to her at this point and whispered, "He can't hear or speak and I've come for him, if that's all right."

"You cannot turn loose a prisoner, no matter the affliction." Another nurse made it her business to interrupt. I wanted to tell her to sneeze, and maybe it would clear up the tone making her sound so stopped up.

"No, it's quite all right. I'm sure General Paine would not treat someone of his misfortune in such a way. I will get him for you." I begged to differ from what I had heard, but I wasn't going to argue since she was being decent. All eyes were boring a hole in me when she left the room.

The room was full of the wounded. Some had legs amputated, others arms. Bandages around the eyes would not heal the wounds or the memories of the bloody battle that took one soldier's sight.

The closing door jarred me back to the room and a different set of eyes, those I had never paid much attention to before now. Although still mostly hidden by the mass of facial hair, gratitude and surprise radiated across the room and smacked me upside the head. My arms reached out to him as I crossed the room.

I refrained from speaking to him but kissed his cheek as any dutiful sister would. "Thank you ever so much for your kindness towards my brother. We won't trouble you further." I led him out but remained silent knowing that was the only way to continue the charade.

"Wait… " My stomach turned over twice, needlessly. The nurse had scribbled a note giving us permission to pass if we were stopped for any reason. I smiled at her kindness over the persistent objections of the others.

"You've been ever so kind." I said in my best faux-belle.

Outside, the shenanigans had turned deadly as the soldiers wounded the courthouse and the citizens alike with the beginning of executions, suggesting Paine's return had not been fortunate for so many. As we retraced the steps I had made earlier, neither of us spoke until we reached Quasar and then only in whispers.

"I'll ride behind you and maybe this monster of a dress will cover his hind quarters." I heard a faint chuckle at my description of the dress. As soon as we got a good distance away I explained how I happened upon the clothes, and he had escaped being a fox.

"Not five minutes more and I would be as the others on their cots or perhaps in the grave. Your timely arrival rescued me from the wrath of the General and morbid curiosity of others, to be sure."

"You have no idea what a smart move you made, acting that way. That general could give Sherman a run for his money."

"Sherman... you spoke of him earlier..."

"A Union general hated by his side until he burned and pillaged with the best of them...or looked the other way while his men did it...and then of course he was loved." Pa's face flashed in my mind, his stubbly cheek and the way he gummed it when he didn't have his teeth in. "My Pa always said anyone can lead men to do the worst in their hearts, but it takes a master to lead men to act on the good. I wish I knew what year it is. Sherman might be in Nashville getting ready to trash Atlanta and on to the sea..."

"Ah. It is 1863 though I cannot believe I am saying such. Are we not fortunate it is the warmest time of the year?" He removed his hat, swatted a mosquito, and wiped sweat out of his eyes.

"Yes, we are indeed," I mumbled, itching from the sweat trickling down my back then feeling remorse at my lack of gratitude. "1863, no, it's sometime yet before that happens," I said somewhat distracted. "Almost two more years of this war left. How will we survive?" Scratching through the layers, I couldn't imagine how hot I would be if I had worn all the petticoats that were supposed to go under the rather plain slate blue dress I was wearing.

"My rescue...it was greatly appreciated though I was intrigued by your method...not acquainted with this fashion of dress in my traveling companion." Humor then turned to sadness. "My own sister could not have done better." He cleared his throat and stared ahead.

"Don't mention it. You weren't too bad yourself Daniel Boone." I poked his shoulder playfully trying to lighten the mood.

We rode on quietly for some time through the dark. Occasionally, a howl could be heard, but I doubted if even coyotes ventured out in these times where anything was fair game to eat. The moon went in and out behind the clouds alerting us to be on the lookout for others. The wind picked up causing us to choke on the dust blowing into our path from the uncultivated fields. Off in the distance, lightning streaked the sky.

Smaller lights appeared just ahead causing us concern until we realized we had ridden onto a plantation. Light shone from the slave houses where chatter and singing could be heard. Even though they were working for wages at this stage of the war, in this occupied area, they weren't likely to be out and about as a target for anyone, Union, Confederate, or guerillas. Despite how Grandmother falsely accused me, I prayed things could be different for them now and in the future instead of their descendants continuing to be used by her crowd for another 150 years.

"Events I witnessed these several days are much different than your explanation." He turned his head to make sure I heard what he said. "Conversations I overheard are not consistent."

"History is said to have been written by the victors. What was different?"

"It appears, until recently, the Major was a having a most difficult time in battle. The Rebels, I believe they called them, excelled on the battlefield and in Indian-style fighting from behind trees and with munitions. He was most irritated at the incompetence of his men though I suspect he was to blame."

"So what else is new?"

"Evidently, you are not shocked." He paused to collect his thoughts and chose his words carefully. "Instead of drawing up new plans and drilling his men in attack, he sent them for citizens of the town…it was disgraceful."

"Ah, the glory of war," I snarked and sighed similar to someone about to take a deep breath to go under water, my chest heavy from the constant weight of apprehension.

"And you are not to blame for slavery of this time or mine, no matter what your Grandmother infers, any more than I am to blame for English who persist in kidnapping the poor off our streets and selling them into slavery…along with the Scots, Irish, and Africans."

"Ah, so you know about them too. Maybe that's the reason we are here...maybe somehow we can change things. If I had realized it when we were here in the 1770's maybe we could have done something to stop it– north and south. Now that we are in it, I want to stop this maniac here and then Sherman. We'll have to figure out the rest along the way."

Our conversation was forced to an end as we changed our course and continued toward the farm, thunder booming all around us. We recognized the sad house and shed in the streaks of lightning.

"Perhaps we should ask your friend for a roof over our heads tonight." Agreeing, I pointed to the back where I had left Traveller, thankful he was in the same place I had left him earlier, only now there were two others beside him. The enemy was here, evident from blood curdling screams, and I could only imagine what acts were being committed against my friends.

Racking my brain for a plan to end the madness inside and at the same time quietly trying to make our exchange, it was all for naught when a stray soldier came around the corner of the shack, dragging Leoia with him. She had either fainted or been hit over the head, oblivious to his intentions as he then dropped her and reached for his gun, unsuccessfully. Christian, as quick as was humanly possible rode up and kicked him in the face, causing him to fall backwards. Detected by the others looking to share in whatever plans the first soldier had, we tried to ride away dodging the gunfire ringing out from the porch and behind the house as the soldiers shouted at us to stop at once. I thought I had been clever untying their horses, slapping them to go on, but it didn't make any difference for soon we had to circle back to avoid the rest of their group approaching from town.

"Make haste! Follow me!" Christian bellowed.

The rain had begun to pour making it even harder for the horses' hooves to grip the ground. We flew by the original soldiers, again, whizzing bullets in all directions. By the signaling of the others, the gang behind us was slowed briefly and we took advantage charging ahead, driven by the perilous situation, pelted by the torrential rain. Following him in the dark onto the branch of the road much less traveled, coupled with the blinding rain there was no way we could continue to hold the lead. With no advance warning, in the brightness of a lightning bolt, the road had ended in a pile of rocks, unfortunately, with nowhere to go.

CHAPTER 26

Reach Out in the Darkness

The pitch black darkness invaded every pore, so dark I could barely see my hands gripping the reins. Quasar rode up close to Traveller, following the swish of his tail. For what seemed an eternity, we rode quietly, well, as quietly as we could, in the depth of old leaves and fallen branches trying to ascertain whether we had brought our pursuers with us. We had been suspended in time, fried in mid-air, and now it was pretty obvious we had been thrown, once again, into another dimension. My best guess was we had circled back and found the crater, now grown over, in the night of another time.

Christian stopped, clumsily dismounted and suggested we sit awhile until it got light. It wouldn't do for one of the horses to become lame trying to navigate the unfamiliar.

"I might be able to think clearer if I wasn't so hungry." My stomach growled the appropriate sound to prove my point. A piece of jerky was placed under my nose in the next instant.

"Hey, where did you get that?" I asked quickly before practically swallowing it whole.

"We were readying ourselves for Virginia had that mishap, and now this, not occurred." A familiar sadness in his voice, he handed me some more of the deer meat we had prepared, so long ago, from his saddle bag. "Think you the only one to prepare ahead?"

"It doesn't sound as if we brought our friends along. They would have made all kinds of noise by now..." Leaning against the tree where Quasar was tied, I slid to the ground exhausted not caring if I ripped the ridiculous dress now providing a cover from the ground. In seconds, I found myself slipping away to meet the darkness.

Blowing and chewing sounds woke me much later. Quasar was grazing around the tree bumping his face into my ear trying to get to a choice vine. Feeling to pat him, I couldn't quite focus. My eyes were gritty, but it didn't do much good to rub them. Remembering how we got here, I tried to get up, fighting both the helter-skelter dress and bones that felt older than Pa's. The thought of him put an idea in my head. Was it possible we had come back to my time?

Christian noticed my struggle from the spring where he was filling up his leather pouch. Why did he always wait for me to wake up instead of waking me up? He could have just yelled at me. I felt embarrassed at the state I was in but knew all I had to help was water. Dragging all the layers with me, I tugged the bonnet off my head and tried to splash my face downstream.

"Brrr." The air was brisk and the cold water, even though it woke me up, chilled my already weary bones.

"I suspect it is early spring." The budding trees around us agreed with his assessment, though said in a rather odd tone of voice.

"Probably blackberry winter. It is definitely chilly out. Did you sleep at all? You look a little pale."

"A bit. Here is the remainder...a bit tough." He walked down and handed me the last chunk of what we had prepared.

"Sorry to sleep so late, if it is late. It's hard to tell the time through all these clouds." I chewed the meat just fine.

"I suspect afternoon. There is a smallish house in that direction. I saw the smoke from it earlier." He paused a minute. "Is it always the same...the method of travel? My skin felt as fire but not a hair is burned."

"Well, the first time, I was alone and I thought it was never going to end...being suspended in that way. The burning seemed more intense this time." I rubbed at my arm and discovered dried blood. "What on earth?" Not really surprised by it at all right above my left elbow, I must have been grazed by a bullet. It would have been more surprising if we had come out of the melee unscathed. He watched me as I inspected and washed the inch long wound while I continued talking. "Of course, I don't understand how it happens at all but I *really* don't get how we came together." The cold water felt good, numbing the site.

"The storm and the ground...the charge from the storm blackened the ground initially, in my age, and when we arrived staring into the face of the bull, but last night it was quite dark I recall only vines and bushes, the way unfamiliar." He threw up his hands in frustration. "Is there much pain?" he asked, pointing to my arm.

"No, it's fine." I said dismissing the wound, knowing I had a tetanus shot not too long ago. "I agree the storm sets off some sort of charge making our horses crazy but what about the thing that encloses us? Did you notice the sound? Each time, I thought my head might explode or my ear drums shatter but there is no blood, well, except for this, or hearing loss. It feels as if the devil himself invades your body and I can only get away from it by praying mightily."

Nodding in agreement, "My apologies we were not able to stop the Yankees. You might have been successful had you not come for me."

"I knew that wasn't likely to happen just wishful thinking I guess." To the bottom of my soul, I felt the wasted opportunity and had tried not to think of it since it wasn't his fault. Being more upset than I let on, I bit my lip and changed the subject. "What was he like?" I asked.

"Pardon?"

"Major Paine. Pretty vicious character, huh?"

He leaned down and yanked a tall weed out of the ground, tearing it into small pieces and pausing to throw each piece in a different direction as he spoke. "A very imposing figure, the face of a boy though covered with dark beard yet the hair of an old man, white as snow. The citizens were treated as soldiers – no protection for them at all – and the soldiers as wild beasts. Never did they acknowledge they were the aggressors and felt no mercy should be shown."

I reminded him of Ft. Sumter and how the South was considered to blame. In the true form of a rebellious colonist, he objected to the terms of the agreement and the heavy handedness of the government. He said that didn't excuse the behavior toward the citizens he had seen. Several were shot along the tracks or hung on the spot without any kind of trial or questioning. In attending to other matters, Paine became aware of the death of a young child and for no other reason than pure evil, the mother was forbidden to attend to it.

"Well, you're preaching to the choir here. At least he ends up having charges brought against him for his behavior though it wasn't more than a slap on the wrist...but Sherman...thought of as a hero." I humphed to myself. "Another thing I have never understood is Lincoln. He didn't provide any way to care for those emancipated slaves and often they were mistreated by the very soldiers who were supposedly fighting to free them. A lot of them died. And why didn't he stop Sherman from all the bad things he did? Or Payne? He was also a friend of his, came from the same state. Why didn't he stop him?" After some time, we both shook our heads in disbelief and left it behind. We could talk about it all day, but it wouldn't change anything that happened.

"If it's all the same to you, I am going to change back into my boy clothes. Not only is this dress impractical out here, it leaves something to be desired in the comfort zone." I didn't wait for his answer but trudged over behind Quasar and untangled the mess of wadded clothes in my bag and replaced it with dress and bonnet. It took some doing but I managed to stuff it all in. When I had finished, I tugged down the old hat and pulled the worn jacket close around me feeling the letter, once again, pushed deep into my pocket for safe-keeping. Should I mention it to him? He might have a different perspective on its contents and outcome. No, at this point, it would make things awkward and more uncertain than they were. I resolved to keep it hidden for now.

We kept cover in the brush until we found the road. The best bet seemed to be to follow it toward what I thought was town. But which direction was a bit uncertain. Just as uncertain was the war. Was it over or had it even started? I rode up even with him.

We passed an old, for my time, two-story whitish brick house seeming familiar, though bricks were missing and one side appeared ready to fall down at any moment. Although it sat some distance from us on the side of a hill, I was curious about what looked to be earthquake bolts shaped as stars on the front of the house. The only earthquake I knew about was the New Madrid that formed Reelfoot Lake putting us at least to 1820. It occurred in the western part of the state though middle Tennessee had felt it. Or was this destruction caused by the war? Were we going back or ahead?

Thinking of something to bring us out of the funk I offered, "I bet at one time that was as elegant as Buckingham Palace."

"A palace? No, but more than was here only this morn." Pausing, he added, "I knew of a Buckingham House in London…"

"It's where the Queen of England lives. Queen Victoria was the first to live there. I think she would be queen now. Queen Elizabeth, mmm, the second, I believe, is in my time."

He looked very annoyed but said nothing. It must have been frustrating for someone to tell you the history of your country in advance, especially when they said they weren't going to. We rode on in silence, stopping only to let the horses drink from a creek or graze.

We ran into the creek again as it wound around the hill and beside the road. I knew this was not my time, I could feel it, and looked to Christian for his reaction to the general scenery. There was none. Still missing my phone, I guessed we had been traveling about an hour. The sun had finally decided to come out warming my achy bones. Signs of late spring were detectable in the rows of pastel iris or crisp white snow ball bushes often outlining a shadow of what had been there in a past time. The last yellow clumps of buttercups – what most people, Grandmother was sure to point out, called daffodils – had crumbled and spilled over to rest on the mounds of browned-tinged green stems.

Running into a larger dirt road, we took it. Every couple of miles we noticed a structure: farm house, shack, the occasional older brick house, or the lone chimney standing guard over a still desolate area. All of them looked worn and barely standing but inhabited. Other than the difference in vegetation it was not much different than yesterday in 1863. The occasional rock fence marked the road and gave me another clue to our whereabouts and time, but I still didn't know for sure. Maybe, we had turned in the wrong direction.

"We must locate some suitable camp for tonight and rest. We have no supplies and know not when, or if, we shall return to our rightful times… we must gather provisions."

"Thank the Lord! He speaks!"

"Prefer you I babble like yon creek? Your labor is not without thanks. Would that I could conduct us! I know not the way since there now is a way. When all was but forest and bush, I made way as I chose. Now I must needs follow for I know not…any little thing." He seemed to be in a trance of some sort.

"Oh, I get it. You have to be in charge. If I'm ever in England, I'll call you up and you can show me how to get around. Okay?" I didn't understand what had happened to the civil person I was beginning to know. Whatever the reason for the change, I was not reacting well to it.

With a huge sigh, he responded. "Who could find fault with such? Is it so changed in your time men, or women, suffer knowledge of naught with pleasure?"

"Hmmm. Everybody is stupid at one time or another. Interesting you can't understand me but I can understand you. Guess I wouldn't understand anyone from 2050. I don't like to feel out of control either so you got me there." Tired and in a brain fog, I conceded.

"Let us then push on to find camp," he said wearily.

This part of the road ran along fence rows and around the water in a zig-zag manner in some places. Not many straight stretches of road here so it wasn't too difficult to find a secluded place to camp. The trees, either young or shattered old trunks, followed another branch of the creek. We walked our horses along an older animal trail looking for any sign of farming.

"Hey Christian, it has to be after the war! Look at the fences and the farm house along those hills." Off in the distance sat a house, not new but not burned out, surrounded by young trees and hugged by a tidy fence. I never thought I would be so happy to see a rail fence in my life. "Wonder how old the…are you feeling well? Christian, are you okay?"

He looked at me but didn't really see me and slumped over onto Traveler.

CHAPTER 27

The Kindness of Strangers

After the initial panic wore off, I launched into action gathering dry brush, covering it with the enormous dress, and feeling quite happy it was good for something. Placing his saddle against a row of trees, along with the dry bed, gave him a place to rest while I worked at getting his fever down. The wet cloth I put on his forehead quickly turned hot, and I flipped it over to blot around his neck and chest. He mumbled something I couldn't understand, and then something I could, "Don't leave me," repeating it several times in his fevered anxiety.

The words, chilling and desperate, ran down my back and up again. Had he read the letter? I assured him I was there and was trying to help him, but my words seemed empty to such a plea. Cool water was all I had to offer him, first to drink and then to dab his hot brow with. Repeating the procedure hadn't brought the fever down or reassured him of my presence. He continued to moan. Before long it would be dark and much colder. In a low voice, I told him I was near but needed to build a fire.

Finding and gathering wood and leaves wasn't the hard part. Finding dry ones was, forcing me to alternate pulling broken limbs out of trees and changing the hot rag on Christian's head. After digging a small pit, I filled it with leaves and pine needles, topping it with a frame of sticks then using the flint and knife in his saddle bag to get a spark to light the tinder. Gradually, I added larger sticks. In between the creek and the tree row, the fire radiated an even heat keeping the patient from cooling down too quickly on either side while I continued to work on his fever.

It seemed forever before his temperature cooled to give me a bit of breathing room. Standing to stretch and wiping my hands on my already filthy clothes reminded me how badly the horses must feel. I was pretty sure we wouldn't be attacked by Indians now, and there was no evidence of any kind of war so I took Quasar's saddle off and saw to the rest of his needs the best I could. Then I did my best for Traveller as well and tied them up for the night.

Now dark, our small fire would not last long. Christian's small hatchet would help me collect more if I couldn't find enough on the ground. All these thoughts about the fire when there were so many other things we still had to consider. Where would we go? How would we eat? But most importantly, how to get him better when I didn't even know what was wrong? I gathered until I was exhausted and could gather no more.

Cooling his cloth again, I propped myself up on my saddle, enjoying the warmth, and continued to think. I needed a plan but trying to hash out a plan was the plan for now. My mind was headed in the right direction anyway.

"So what do we do now? I would suggest trying to get back but it didn't work for me in 1772 or 1863, it was all out of my control," I said to the starry sky.

"When will we be catapulted again?" I asked myself.

"We don't know," I said pessimistically to no one in particular, "but this isn't our last stop according to the way things look." I pulled the worn envelope from deep in my pockets again and touched Pa's writing. How could the contents of the letter be true? This unshaven, ornery, headstrong man lying here couldn't be what it said. Already he had saved my life, and I had saved his. We hadn't had the chance to change the ugliness we just came from but how did either of us make a difference in the years ahead?

Christian responded with a sound not unlike someone having been to the dentist, the sound of a fat lip. I shoved the envelope back in its hiding place once more.

"Shhh, I'm here. I'm not leaving you." In helping him get a drink of water, I noticed the swelling around the jawline, pushing on the pudginess behind the ears and into the cheeks.

"Oh Mr. Christian…you have the mumps!"

With a yelp, he tried to get up, but then realized it was useless and gave up. I continued to cool his fever most of the night, keeping him hydrated, praying the spring water would last until I could find more. The fire crackled and popped with each new branch I threw on, and as I stared hard into the flames I saw my parents, loving and happy, at that birthday celebration so long ago. The sound of Pa's harmonica was so real I hummed along with "Donkey Serenade," choking with emotion.

Christian was some better next morning though the swelling was evident, and he wasn't able to say much. He did point at his jaws and my eyes, letting me know I didn't look any better than he did. It was a warmer day and with his fever gone, he sat up against his saddle and the tree, watching me tend the horses. Remembering the apples in my bag, I snagged one, trying to munch on it secretly. I knew he couldn't eat it even if I mushed it up, and the clean water was running low. Somehow, I would need to get him some soft food soon. I waited until I saw him doze off again and went off on a mission.

"Excuse me ma'am." The small, slightly hunched gray haired lady watched every movement I had made from the moment I rode up the long path and jumped off Quasar. She continued to watch as she threw corn out to her chickens from her apron pocket. "We wuz passing through and my friend over yonder got sick. Hope you'ins don't mind we camped there last night. I believe he's got the mumps 'n he can't eat nothin' we got." I pointed down to the creek bank at the bottom of the hill.

She never said a word but slowly turned and made her way past the clucking hens onto the porch. The boards sighed then squeaked as she made her way inside the old board house. A few minutes later, carrying a rifle and something wrapped up in a piece of cloth, she said in a wary voice, "You can fill up your pouch outta that bucket…if'n you come back tomorrow I might have a bit more to spare, long as you don't cause no trouble." Her kindness mixed with caution must have been a product of the times, whatever time it was. Not wanting to alarm her, I decided it was best not to ask.

"Thank you, kindly, ma'am."

Christian rolled the soft bread around in his mouth and washed it down. He managed to eat a few bites before wrapping it up to lean back on the saddle while I told him about our new friend.

"That is the...second time you have...come to my aid. I am thankful but am not...comfortable in the position of invalid." He whispered the words taking several minutes to finish.

"I believe you came to mine several times. It happens to everyone. Don't worry about it."

"Did she not think your speech strange?"

"Naw, I threw in a little of Pa's talk and it wuz jest fine."

When he awoke much later in the day, I walked him around the creek bed. He was weak but, stubbornly, didn't allow much help from me. We finally agreed I would stand nearby while he washed up a bit and took care of other essentials.

"You know, you aren't a very good patient, now that you can talk more." For lack of anything better to say I thought of when he was better. "What do you think we should do next?"

"Now it appears all danger from war is over, I am impatient to continue." He slurred his words a bit and stopped to swallow. "It seems we have no power to return from whence we came. It was for land I journeyed to the Cumberland," he took a deep breath, "and if there is any to claim, then that is what I intend." Again, he swallowed. "What you will is of your own making." He could have hit me upside the head with a two-by-four, and I wouldn't have been as surprised. I understood his willingness but was rather surprised at the abrupt manner of his last statement.

"I know that! Maybe you haven't realized though if we call attention to ourselves it could get ugly." I was defensive and confused.

"Unpleasant to look at?"

"You could say that. Unpleasant anyway. You thought I was mad when I tried to fit in, both times. Imagine my fate among the other men if I had let it be known how I got there!"

"Continue then as a young boy and say little. Some farmer will surely employ you to care for his horses. Or wear the dress and entertain as such."

"As such?" I let the comment go. If he still thought of me that way, how could I change his opinion? "And what will you do? You don't think your lack of knowledge of the present day will be a problem?"

"No, I will take my own advice and say little until I am confident of the surroundings."

"I don't get you. Earlier you didn't know what would become of US! Now you are basically telling me to get lost. I don't particularly want to hang out with you either, but I know it won't be pleasant for me in any time before 1940ish to dress like a boy. They probably won't bat an eye for your proper talk and weird ways because you can smash their mouths and get away with it. I can smash a few mouths myself but when the cat is out of the bag it could be worse than being trapped with a couple of creeps from high school."

At this point, he was done washing and had returned to watch me stoke the fire and settle in. Staring at me with no comprehension of what I had said, I wasn't sure I knew what I had said. I meant I didn't want to be left alone, but for some reason I felt very weak to say that. Besides, whether or not I liked it, somehow our future was linked.

"Whatever in heaven's name you spoke then is no doubt a result of vexation?" Swallow, breath. "Is there no other way you might speak of your trials so I may understand?"

With that speech, I lost it. I began to laugh. I laughed some more. I tried not to laugh and laughed harder.

"What…?" His eyebrows raised in concern until his brain got the message.

"Sor…sor…sorry. Pa would say I'm wound tight as fishin' line. I just needed a little release, you know, I just needed a good laugh. You definitely provided the comic relief!" And I started to laugh again.

"You laugh at me? You are daft!" Swallow, deep breath, swallow. "Your speech is of a madman not any kind of breeding or refinement such as a lady would have."

"Oh, so we're back to that are we? I'm not a lady. Let me let you in on a little secret. I'm more of a lady in my day than a lot of married women. Maybe of this day too. I don't know. I'll have to find out what day we're in before I can really comment."

"Let us then wait and see what the morrow brings. I am weary of your strangeness."

With that he turned over and went to sleep.

CHAPTER 28

Man or Myth

The aroma of chicken permeated the air wrapping its scent around my mind and dragging it through the foggy veil of sleep to a summer Saturday afternoon in my childhood. Dad, grilling and lounging on the deck, every now and then, jumped up to flip the juicy hunks of meat and pour on more of the sweet barbecue sauce. Mom danced around to an oldies station, mixing up a delicious concoction that would later be poured into a frozen container and, ta-da, turned into ice cream. "It's a lot more work to turn the crank and add rock salt to the old freezer. Don't you think it's just as good?" They were having a great time. All I had to do was reach out and hug them close to me.

"Makenna. Makenna. Awaken…you need nourishment." The sound was way off, maybe the bottom of a well, but insistent. "You are in need of food and we should go." Through a fog, I managed to pry my eyes open and sit up.

"You dream of your family often." It was a statement not a question.

How many nights had I talked in my sleep?

"Yes, I do. It was a wonderful dream of cooking out and laughing with them. I loved them so much. So did Pa." While I was talking he handed me some mystery meat cooked on a stick. I was hungry, and he cooked it. That was good enough for me right now, at this place.

"It is still early but I have seen no movement other than this adequate catch." The faint pink of the sky and the noisy outdoors, with birds and bugs equally loud, announced the new day. He must have been up for some time.

"Wow, you must be feeling a lot better. Wait, how did you eat this?"

"I did not. There was plenty of the bread from before. I hope you did not mind I ate the rest."

"Of course not but you shouldn't have gone to the trouble." I couldn't figure him out lately. Yesterday he is eager to split up, and today he cooks me breakfast.

"I will rest until you are ready." He was leaning up against the tree having already put the saddle back on Traveller and thrown the dress across Quasar.

"Is it not peculiar how we travel…in time…to different seasons as well?" He had pulled a small limb and was using it for a toothbrush. I had many conversations with Pa while brushing my teeth but this felt too weird.

"I would say time traveling itself is peculiar but, yeah, I find it odd. It was August in 2014 then September 1772, briefly August 1863…then we left. Now it looks to be spring…and a little warmer today, thank goodness. I've been fortunate not to land in Valley Forge in 1777." I continued to eat but he kept on brushing and looking at me, waiting for me to keep talking. Exasperated, he spit whatever he had got out of his teeth.

"You cannot say whatever you please and proceed to the next subject with nary a hint of explanation." You would have thought I had committed a mortal sin, yet I knew how he felt to be left in the dark. But really, he didn't have to be so bossy britches.

"Valley Forge is in Pennsylvania where George Washington spent a winter during the Revolutionary War, the one I told you about against England. Lots of snow, lots of deaths. He didn't die then, though. He became the first President."

"Would he be Colonel Washington from Virginia?" His anger subsided, perking up at the familiar name.

"You sound as if you know him." Of course, he could have known him, but it seemed so unlikely in the course of this bizarre conversation. Done with his teeth, he was now attempting to comb through his hair with his fingers.

"He is an acquaintance of my uncle not to mention the brave military might of the French and Indian War. I was introduced to Mr. Washington at a country dance. He is very light-footed." Christian spoke of the dance as if it had happened yesterday. He was in multiple times trying to reconcile what he knew to be true, where he actually was now, and where he had been yesterday. "On another occasion, at the horse races… he is known as an excellent horseman, to ride and to train. My uncle owns and breeds some fine quarter horses. I assisted him at the racetrack. Mr. Washington was there on occasion but I did not have reason to speak with him. " He noticed my skepticism. "You doubt what I say?"

"No, not at all…" Before I could ask him about the dance or Washington's horses, he changed the subject to a more serious note.

"What say you of locating the town?"

"Okay. Once we get there, we need to find out the date so we don't make any major blunders. Hopefully, I can find somewhere decent to sleep and get real food. What do you think?"

"As I told you before, I intend to claim land, so I must find the authority to aid in that endeavor."

"Seriously, all of it has been claimed. You will have to see about buying it from someone who already has it. In that case, you and I both will need jobs to get what we need, that is, unless you are independently wealthy and have been holding out on me."

"No, unfortunately I have what you see. Can it be I finally understand your meaning?!"

"Dude, awesome!"

He shook his head, confounded, and pulled his hat low on his face to snooze.

I, on the other hand, went to the creek for another "possible" bath. The water was still cool, but I could tolerate it better than being dirty. My reflection in the water was pretty scary looking, and I realized I had no cause to get up on my high horse. Was that why he was trying to get away now?

"Hey, friend. S'up? You and Traveller getting along okay?" I nuzzled my head into his mane and tried to comb through it, again, with my fingers.

"Traveller? Do you find it necessary to rename everyone?" Christian's voice came from behind me. "Do not you want to know his authentic name?" I ignored him.

"That's an appropriate name, isn't it Trav? So, do you guys chat much, about girls or what's good to eat out on the old trail, that kind of stuff?"

"You will wait a great length to hear an answer to that question." I detected a smile in his voice but by the time I turned to see it, he was gone.

"I'm ready to go when you are…she said to the back of his horse as he rode away."

CHAPTER 29

Everything has an End

After briefly stopping at the house on the hill, we retraced our path to the main road. Such a kind-hearted woman allowing us to fill up our canteen and packing a small box of food, she could see Christian was still swollen and cautioned him to rest soon. By now it was probably seven or eight in the morning. We were back to Pa's old farm where the four-lane went through, not too far from town. Somehow we had come in from a different direction having gone further northwest than I thought.

"Were it not for these roads, I would think this is where we found many buffalo." In every direction, he turned trying to get his bearings.

"You're right," I responded, pointing the directions of the hills, also reminding him where the salt licks were. It would have taken a major earth quake and not just erosion to change the landscape. In one day, some areas had grown up that had been demolished and others cleared that had been tough to get through. It still looked bad either way.

"When we were here, I slipped up about the salt licks. I was in shock when we rode out of the trees, looking at my Pa's old farm, well, where it will be. Pa doesn't live there now, I mean in my time. He sold it not long before my ma died and then rented a smaller place up along the ridge, about six or seven miles from here, where I lived with him. I think my relatives on Mom's side must still live in another county." I paused for a minute, so he could soak in what I had said. "You wouldn't believe how this looks in my time. Imagine this muddy riveted road hard as rock but flat. There are four of them running alongside of each other to the state line. Two going north and two going south towards Nashville. The capitol of Tennessee, our state, is Nashville."

Concerned about his understanding of what had happened, I tried to think of ways to say things that wouldn't totally shock him, having travelled twice in so few days. But it was too hard for me. In explaining this area to him, nostalgia or grief, whatever you want to call it, washed over me, and I couldn't help it. The tears came non-stop though I tried in vain to hide them. My shaking shoulders gave me away.

"Good heavens, Miss Manning, what is the matter?" He jerked his horse around and rode up next to me.

"Never mind. Don't worry about it. It's just all coming down on me again. Being away from Pa... I can go for a while and be pretty up about things, thinking I am going to find a way back. But here we are, right here, where I should be able to go to my house and reach out and touch him. I know he isn't there. The house wouldn't even be there yet, and it's a really old house!" I jumped off Quasar and led him, trying to hide the sobs that just kept coming.

"Is there nothing I might do for your distress?" He actually sounded sincere.

"Other than finding a rabbit hole in the space-time, uhh, uhh, whatever they call that on Star Trek, uhh, continuum. I just want to go home." Sniffing and snorting loudly, I paused. "Wait, why did you call me Miss Manning?" I stopped in the middle of the road.

"Is that not your name?"

"Yes, but I have never heard you call me anything but Makenna or Young Manning or horse girl. Why the change?"

"Well, I have come to the conclusion our very different eras and customs gave me an incorrect impression of you. After our conversation last evening, I must apologize for my previous actions. I used much too familiar a term for someone I do not know well."

"You mean you no longer think I should entertain?" I said spitefully.

"Heaven forbid I should apologize to you for anything! Besides, I have no interest in your affairs."

"Well, that was a nice way to put that." The feeling was mutual but he said it in such a harsh manner. "I'm sorry. Really. It's hard for us both to understand what we mean. I was truly trying to say I appreciate you no longer think of me as a fallen woman. Is that how you would put it?"

"No... but I detect your meaning." That was enough for me and I remained silent the rest of the way.

Occupation by the federal troops, as much as I hated it, saved the town instead of being burned to the ground as so many were. A few of the larger residences along the road looked the same. Christian pointed at the church where he had been held. Muddy ruts indented the road with the increased traffic – certainly not traffic jams with honking car horns and spewing exhaust – rather from the repetition of many wheels and hooves. Dirt also blew about the bleating sheep and goats herded by some young boys anxious to be through town and on to some mischief. Many wagons were cloistered further along at the courthouse, but my attention was diverted as we passed one whose driver and passengers gave us a double-take. Even though they were dressed in what I would describe as working clothes, Gabriel Christian still resembled Daniel Boone, and I probably looked like something off the bottom of his shoe.

"It may not have been a good idea to ride through town. People don't know what to make of the way we're dressed."

"The way we are dressed? Did we not look the same when here last?"

"Yes, I know but everybody looked rough or strange in some way during the war. We fit in better then, well, except for having to run to stay alive."

"Look at the tightness of the clothing on those men. Can they not breathe?"

About that time, a woman in a long dark dress, snugly fit in the bodice and lower front yet fluffy in the back with several overskirts, stepped out of a store front to adjust a sign. Christian almost broke his neck looking at her as we rode by. The stare was mutual. Clean and well-dressed looking at unwashed and unusual, the way I looked at exhibits at the Knoxville Zoo.

The court house was the same, cubed two-story brick building we had seen earlier although it had more of a Victorian feel to it now since the tall drum-shaped windows of the cupola had been replaced with a squared overlay. The silver alloy finial still sat atop proudly though it and the dome were still dented by the target practice of the Federal soldiers. The large windows on each floor seemed tired in comparison to the addition. They circled the structure interrupted only by the occasional door to meet the main entrance facing south.

"Shall we tie here and make our claim?" He dismounted and began despite asking my opinion.

"You can't do that! I told you this land is probably already owned. I'm not sure exactly the year but it's long past claim time. You'll have to buy it from someone." I stayed on Quasar.

"That may be so. It does no harm to question. I care not if they think ill of me." Shrugging his shoulders and tromping off, he turned to hear my next remark but didn't stop.

"It wouldn't be ill of you. It would be that you ARE ill, in more ways than one."

"Not a concern." And in he walked with me scrambling to catch up.

It was a fascinating place with wide hallways and high ceilings. The scuffed and rather dusty hardwood floors must have been impossible to clean. How would you when everyone in here just walked off the dirt road? Large brass spittoons sat at every corner though it looked as if lots of people missed or didn't even try to hit them. Tobacco juice was everywhere, and nobody seemed bothered by it.

The registrar of deeds seemed a good place to start. Walking to the second floor, our feet stuck to the steps while they groaned and creaked at each point of contact. It wouldn't take much to set this place on fire. Not only was there a lot of wood but a primitive gas light fixture hung at the top of the stairs. Entering the office, a couple of oil lamps sat on each end of the counter though not lit due to the time and brightness of day.

A tall, thin gentleman stood behind a window with bars. Looking past him, I honed in on the large daily calendar: Tuesday, May 11, 1886. I tried to think of anything remarkable about that year that might be helpful in conversation, but I drew a blank. My fixation on the calendar was interrupted by his equally piercing stare. As bugs under a microscope, he looked at us, all the while fiddling with one side of his very bushy moustache. Christian approached the window, speaking to him in a friendly manner.

"Yes, good day sir." Swallow, breath. "I am come to inquire what the state of land claims are in this area."

"Beggin' your pardon, sir?"

"Are there any lands that have not claims against them?"

"Claims? There is land in the area you might purchase if that is what you mean. I personally know of a nice farm up for sale by a gentleman owning the shoe store across the street. You might stop in there and inquire. By the way, sir, your jaws are a bit swollen. I hope it isn't contagious."

I could tell Christian wanted to discuss the matter more, and that would be disastrous. Thanking the clerk in the lowest voice I could muster, I elbowed him out the door. It surprised me he didn't put up a fight after all.

"I told you so, I told you so, I told you so. You almost got his suspicions up. There's no telling what people will do. We need to take a look-see before we go charging in to take care of matters."

"Methods differ in securing the same ends. Could it be possible I might make arrangements without your assistance?" I knew he didn't feel well but anger trumped illness as the words punched me in the gut. "If that is difficult for you, I apologize. But I must have opportunity to consider…"

"Look, I thought we could be of use to each other since I do know something of this time period and you don't." I had lost patience with his changing mood. First he's angry, and then he's sorry but not really.

"Possibly, but you must give me leave to consider. Our situations are not similar." Rubbing his neck and pacing back and forth, he was obviously uncomfortable, and I was frustrated.

"You're right. I had no right to assume we would be better traveling together. Take care of yourself and try not to get yourself killed. I plan on getting a job around here first, so I can eat, then trying to find that spot to go home on. It was very nice to have met you. I appreciate everything you did for me in your time, especially not letting the others know I'm a girl."

He stood there in the street with his swollen jaws, surprised, yet not objecting.

Since everything has an end, except a sausage having two, I jumped on Quasar and rode north.

CHAPTER 30

The Jig's up

I didn't gallop off, but I sure didn't poke either. Not having a plan other than wanting to go home, I thought about trying to find kin folk in Ma's old neighborhood.

None of the buildings looked familiar to me in this direction, those Pa talked about from his childhood or even Mom's. The old silent film theater wasn't there yet – not until 1913 – or the buggy shop, just vacant lots and an occasional odd frame house doubling for a shop. Just before town creek, a huge wagon parked in front of a wheel repair shop was loaded down with an odd assortment of things, mostly strawberries, and something that might have been asparagus or broccoli yesterday, a few pots, and bottles of some unidentifiable liquid. Several people milled around while a young salesman loudly hawked his wares. There was a familiar way about him, dressed similar to Rhett Butler or Colonel Sanders with a light striped shirt, the collar higher up on the neck and the jacket buttoned up barely showing the tie, the cliché of a southern gentleman.

"Yes sirree, this is the best medicine you can buy for what ails you. Everything you got, this mixture is for it. You have pain in the stomach, drink this, and it will leave immediately. You will be dancin' a jig before night! Does your head hurt? My, my just swallow this down, and your troubles will be over!! Now, how many bottles do you want my young friend?" He took his straw hat off and pointed it at the crowd.

As he turned to my direction, I nearly fell off my horse from my pounding heart and scalding face. What were the odds that I would know this person or at least the great-great-grandfather of someone from my time? I wanted to scream at him, kick him, and make him as generally miserable as he had made me over a hundred years from now.

Although I was still on horseback at the back of the crowd, he singled me out as more people gathered and now turned to look at me.

"Uh, sorry there. I don't have any money, just here looking for a job." I tried to get away, but he was too quick.

"Oh, that's no problem. If I tell you where you might find work, will you come back and buy a bottle? I believe that is more than a fair trade. Don't you my good people?" Lots of yeps and uh-huhs from the crowd.

"Really? That's all I have to do to get a job is buy some of that from you?"

"The quality of my product speaks for itself but often times people need just a little help. That's what I'm here to do, my friends, help those in need."

Evidently, I didn't look familiar to him because he didn't treat me any differently than anyone else in the crowd. Everyone was money.

Before I had the chance to get down and talk to him, he was surrounded by people, barely having a dime to their name, shoving money at him. Over to the side, I tied Quasar to a tree and got a better look at his wares and the Morgan horses he used to pull the wagon. When the crowd cleared, he sauntered over to speak.

"Hello there young ...sir." He reached out his hand to shake mine, pausing before the sir. The sir was comforting for my cover but did little for my vanity.

"Hello. Now what is this about you getting me a job?" I tried to lower my voice a little. It cracked but that was okay, fitting in with adolescent boys.

"Oh yes, yes. Do you have a name?"

"Umm, Kenneth Manning."

"Nice to meet you...Kenneth... Joseph Mulholland. Do my horses pass your inspection?" I pointed out some problems with one's foot although he was clearly disinterested. "Not from around here are you?"

"No, Joseph, I'm not." It couldn't possibly be him. But it was the same oval face and crystal blue eyes, dark blonde hair. Once again, picture James Dean and you would be close. His name was Joseph Mulholland *not* Joe Mulhatten. "Now what about that job?"

"The gentleman that does the hiring has been very good to me. I don't want to give him anybody's name that plans on running off."

"If I say I'll stay for a set amount of time, then I'll stay. What kind of job is it and for how long?"

"See this wagon load here? The strawberries come from up above the ridge. It's been a plentiful year and he needs pickers. Can you do that?"

"Sure. I've picked strawberries many a time." Coincidentally, with Ma and she picked when she was a girl in the same area he spoke of. Wow.

"All day?"

"No, but I'm a hard worker and I need the money, so I will. I also need a place to stay and some clothes."

"Yes, I reckon you do. That isn't part of the deal. Just pick the berries and get your money at the end of the day according to how many you pick. But I might be able to help you if you help me."

"What do you mean? I don't go in for any funny stuff."

"Funny stuff? Oh. I need someone to help me sell some of this medicine. You know, set it up and take the money while I sell. You would need a dress."

"Okay, uh, wait. A dress? What are you talking about?"

"Well, Miss. You may be able to fool a lot of people wearing those clothes and acting like a boy but you can't fool me. I could tell the way you sit a horse and…well, never you mind. Here's the deal. I find you a respectable place to live and get you some clothes. You'd work pert' near all day in the patch, 'til he calls it a day, and then if it's early enough I pick you up to work until dark, every Saturday too. Is that a deal?"

"That sounds a little too good to be true. I said no funny stuff."

"Look, I know plenty of girls. I need somebody that isn't afraid of hard work. From the looks of you, I'd say you're used to it." The heat on my neck moved around to my face, infuriating me even more. First he bragged, and then he insulted my appearance. I should want to punch him out. What was my problem? I didn't know what he had, maybe Love Potion #9, but it made me weak. Just as before. I looked down and kicked dirt trying to recover. Finally, I cleared my throat and took a deep breath.

"You know, you look about my age."

"I thought women didn't talk about their age."

"I'm not. We're talking about your age. You're pretty young to have this set-up."

"Why do you say that? Most everyone works by the time they are able to carry a bucket. I just don't care to carry a bucket. Selling is better suited to my talents." He winked and my head felt light.

"You mean, taking people. By the way, are you from around here? You sound a lot like me." Okay, I gave him the perfect opportunity to spill his guts, but he did the classic answer a question with a question to cover himself. It was one he had already asked. For now, I would have to believe he really didn't know me.

"Not from around here, are you?"

"Well, not exactly." I gave up and got on with it "Okay, when do I start?"

"I'd say tomorrow. Let me pack up, and you can follow me. By the way, what's the real name?"

"Makenna Manning. Audra Makenna Manning" I added hoping it would ring a bell. It didn't.

"Well, which is it? Makenna or Audra?"

"Makenna is fine. Don't forget to get that one's foot looked at."

He shrugged and began to carefully pack the bottles of elixir, without the same regard for the vegetables. It seemed to irritate him when people came to buy the last of the strawberries instead of the medicine, if that's what it really was.

When all was packed, he turned the wagon, passing the footbridge and rode parallel with the creek. Chugging and gurgling as the water hit the dirt, it was a lot bigger than I remembered. Maybe it had been a rainy spring since it didn't lack much overflowing its banks. Pa said the National Guard used to help people out when it flooded in his day, before they reworked it with drains.

After crossing, we rode faster, at an easier pace for me. The sooner I started the sooner I could figure out this area and, in my mind, possibly find a way back to Pa, to be in the right place at the right time. But Mulholland had plucked at a different set of heart strings, first love ones, making me unsure what I should do.

God's creation was an amazing thing. After all man had done to the land, it was recovering. Vast expanses burned by the Indians gradually turned into woods or cane fields of the settlers then, in turn, became a wartime desert with only rotting stumps remaining. The decayed wood caused the ground to be fertile once more. Although what man had built was still in sad shape, the land was being used for crops or cattle and the young growing forests encouraged hunting.

Parts of the winding road seemed familiar, an animal path here or a wagon trail there, but no matter where we were the air was thick with the scent of honeysuckle. We rode on for about fifteen minutes when he had to slow down and then to a stop, our wheels stuck in the thick brown soup of a deep rut. Evidently, this part of the road was traveled a lot by farmers and muddy potholes were everywhere. Getting out to push the wagon, I stood transfixed in a flashback of bullets and sweat, chased by the soldiers not far from where the guerillas had blown up the tracks.

"Are you gonna stand there gaping at the mud hole or help me get it out?" His words startled me into action.

By the time we reached our destination, it was mid-afternoon. Mulholland pulled up to a two-story board farm house and went inside while I wandered around in amazement knowing the dress in my saddle bag was taken from this very house. Though standing, it needed paint, whitewash, or whatever they used now and some roof repair, several shingles having come loose. I expected to see John Boy since it was similar to the Walton's farmhouse, made cheerful with the same lilac and bluish bushes, though barely blooming, and velvety, violet irises around the front porch I had seen before. In a manner of minutes, a short, rather thin, yet pleasant looking woman came out, wiping her hands on an apron long as the skirt she was wearing.

"Well, I declare. What a beauty! Joseph, take him around back to the shed. Let me have a look at you. Yes, yes. She is a dirty little thing but wearing something on her feet so I guess she is fine." She proceeded to look close into my eyes and then inspected my hair, my clothes, and even looked down my throat. My horse didn't even get that treatment!

"I know how it is to be travelling for such a long time and have to make do. But I'm sure you understand. So many people have worms and every kind of thing. Got used to inspecting after that ole war…don't want none of that ever again. You just come in here with me and we'll get you all fixed up in no time. Oh, but where are my manners? Lacey Hodges, Widder Lacey is what most folk call me. My house ain't full so sometimes I let respectable folk stay. Joseph here tells me that you are and he ain't lied to me yet. It's only Tuesday but I guess we can see to gettin' you a bath so as you'll be ... presentable. Goin' to start at the patch tomorrow are you? I know John Robert will be mighty glad to get the extra help. The rain made those berries take off and he's got to get them outta the mud before it rains again and ruins them. Now, you just come here with me Miss Manning. It is Manning, isn't it?"

I could swear I had just met a smaller version of Aunt Eller from *Oklahoma* with a voice sweet as Aunt Bea of Mayberry. She herded me into a small, yet functional kitchen where she put on several pots of water to boil on a large black iron stove. According to Miss Lacey, I was lucky she still had a fire going and hadn't begun the task of cleaning out the ashes and polishing the stove. She hardly took a breath all the way to a smaller back room. I didn't seem to have a choice but I didn't want one. I wanted that bath!

"Now you will be just fine in here. Everybody should be out for a few more hours. Usually drag in here just at supper time. Can't say as I blame them as busy as they are. They will be so excited to have another woman besides me to talk to. Maybe your being here will stop some of the gossip about me being a widder lady here with these men, even with a preacher being here, though it is for just a short time, people will talk. Here, I thought you might be thirsty so I brought the bucket in here."

"I'm sure you won't be single much longer unless you choose to be. How many men are there?" I picked the dipper out of the bucket and drank like there was no tomorrow hoping no one around here had anything catching.

"Oh, don't you just have the loveliest voice? So soft, no wonder you couldn't fool anyone into thinkin' you were a boy. Now, don't you worry none about that. Sometimes we have to do things to protect ourselves, now don't we? Oh, let's see now. There's Brother Watson who is the travelling preacher man, of course, and Mr. Mulholland who you know and then you."

"Mr. Mulholland, the kid– uh, young man – that brought me here, he lives here?"

"Oh yes. John Robert, that would be Mr. Monroe, hired him when he first came here last year. What a way that young man has with words. Brother Watson said he would be an excellent minister but Joseph would have none of that. He wanted to help John Robert out since he had been so good to him. He sells some produce as well as that elixir that he makes. It's very good. Have you had any of it?"

"No, I haven't. I'm sure it works for what ails you though. He isn't from here then?"

"Oh no. It's quite tragic. His parents died in some mishap in Nashville a couple of years ago. Afterward, Joseph just picked up and came up here to get out of that sick city. Any big city is that way I hear tell. Why Memphis almost fell apart after yellow jack some years ago. People just can't live on top of each other and not be sick. No sir, they just can't. Well, anyway, John Robert hired him and he is such a hard worker. He does go to Nashville on occasion to see some of his relatives or visit some pretty girls. He is quite the ladies' man. I believe he may have a couple of girls in town that are mighty sweet on him." Nothing new here, I thought, fascinated as I watched and listened to her continue to talk.

"And then he does travel some to sell his elixir. Why all these crates are his bottles. He uses these tables to mix it all together. He keeps me supplied for free for using this room and my wood stove." Only a few were similar to the ones I saw on his truck. I made a mental note to grab one to doctor my wound, pretty sure it had some amount of alcohol in it.

If I had asked the right questions, I'm sure I could have found out the history of the whole state. Of all the places for me to have landed, this had quite a bit of potential to help me get my bearings. At this point, I didn't care about that stupid letter, but if something of significance turned up pertaining to it, so be it.

She poured the glorious, hot water into a sort of barrel that had been flattened on one end – not exactly what I would call a tub – in the corner sitting behind all the stacked crates.

"I would say to keep this to ourselves, having a bath in the middle of the week, but men don't tend to want to take a bath when they should!"

After I finished taking what I will always remember to be the best bath of my life, I wrapped up in a blanket, careful to grab my dirty things since I had no clue how to explain my underwear. Surprised by my request to wash my own things out later, she didn't press but continued chatting endlessly about where she got the blanket and the clothes I could wear.

Miss Lacey showed me to my room, plain with hardwood floors and a rag rug. A dresser with a small bowl and pitcher was on one end and the wonderful bed was on the other. Nothing special but a plain headboard and footboard held together with a larger plank covered with a feather mattress, cotton sheet, and a pieced quilt. Still, I wanted to crawl in there and then. Next to the bed was some kind of pitcher with a lid.

"We take care of our personals ourselves. The pump is in the back for your washin' up pitcher and empty your jar on back from there, in the outhouse. When you want to take a bath, you need to make sure no one else is planning on it. Saturday afternoon gets pretty busy around here."

Realizing the ceramic pitcher next to the bed was a slop jar, I nodded. When Ma used to tell me about using them or an outhouse it grossed me out, but after being outside for so long it seemed a luxury.

A large trunk sat at the end of the bed containing clothes that once belonged to a cousin of Miss Lacey's. There were a couple of camisoles and long underwear pants, bloomers I guess, made out of light cotton, along with a nightgown. A long skirt and long sleeved blouse in a darker fabric with something I would describe as a skirt slip were in the bottom with a darker dress that looked similar to the one the lady I saw in town was wearing. I examined them as she spoke.

"Yessiree, this right here is why I won't marry again until I'm at least fifty. So many precious women die having babies. I'm sure you know someone. Sometimes a relative will take 'em and love 'em and it works itself out, but not always." Shuddering with some memory she didn't choose to share, she added, "I won't question what the Almighty does but I don't have to like it."

The image of Leoia and her grandfather came to me. I wished that advances in medicine had made everything better since women rarely died in childbirth in my time. Instead children, without choices, were hurt by divorce, live-ins, anger, addictions, neglect, and abortion. I resolved to ask God, later in my prayers, to help adults choose what is best for children as I now considered it an honor to wear the clothes of someone who had given so much for a child.

"Now, I'll just leave you to your dressin'. Oh, there may be a few more things in that dresser there you might could use. If'n you need anything at all, just holler, hear?" The stairs creaked and then all was quiet.

Though I thought it silly to wear all these layers, I needed to fit in, for now anyway. Slipping on the camisole and bloomers, I realized

I needed to do something about my hair before I finished the task of getting dressed. It had grown so fast, past my shoulders, while dunking it in a creek and cramming it in a hat. The result had been a tangled mess but the soap and vinegar helped immensely in taming it. In the dresser, I found a comb along with some large hair pins, a wide brimmed hat, gloves, and a plain shawl. As I tried to get it through my wet hair, I thought about the woman who wore these clothes. Did her child live? Had there been other children? Was her husband hardened by death or heartbroken?

Christian had gone through this, too, and was still upset, particularly about his sister. I would even venture he had built an emotional wall to keep hurt away having experienced too much. Maybe that was the reason he could be a real jerk, sometimes.

As I dressed, a slight pang went through me knowing we had death in common. Kindred sad spirits, I supposed, yet for these times it wasn't uncommon. Though I tried to ignore it, we were linked through the letter. Maybe I resented it, and with all my previous pain I was also a jerk. Was that the reason he wanted me gone? Was I that annoying? The breeze fluttered the curtains and released a much needed breath of fresh air into the stuffy room but didn't seem to help my clouded brain. He had been my protector, and I had been his rescuer. Whatever I was, I wasn't anymore.

CHAPTER 31

They're here

The silver poplars swayed in the breeze, their leaves alternating green then silver, green then silver, on and on. The gentle motion mesmerized me until I could no longer see, my hair blown across my face. Pushing the strands out of the way, I saw it was just those creepy kids eating ice cream again. I followed them up a hill, wanting some ice cream, past the carousel where a man told jokes with a hand puppet. Everyone laughed while they got on the train. I followed, sitting across from them. There was no ice cream here. When the train whistle blew, the kids jumped off. But I couldn't get my legs to move. They were stuck to the seat.

The train chugged hard up the hill, groaning and moaning, whistling and spluttering. I heard myself saying over and over, "I will be fine, I will be fine." The kids were still laughing, and I knew I was wrong. When we got up to the top, it ran faster and faster down the hills through the curves of the track and into a tunnel, but it was in the wrong place. Yet we continued to speed, clearing it not at the bottom but really high on top of a mountain, heading straight down. I screamed over and over but no sound came out. This had happened before! It was too fast. We were rounding a curve now. The train would fly off the track and into…"

"Miss Manning?" A tap at the door gave way to a sweet voice. "Miss Manning, are you okay? Do you need help?" Tapping changed to loud knocking. "Supper is ready. Can you hear me, Miss Manning?"

I rubbed my eyes viciously trying to figure out where I was and who was talking to me. Wasn't I at Dollywood? No, I was in the window. Startled, I moved back into the room.

"Oh, I'm so sorry Miss Lacey, must have dozed off. I'll be right there to help you."

"Not to worry. Come as soon as you get ready. The gentlemen are anxious to see you."

The dining room, just large enough for the table and hutch behind it, was located between the parlor and kitchen. Everyone was already seated. Joseph was next to me and jumped up to pull out my chair.

"My, aren't you just the prettiest thing? Look what a little soap and water will do! Don't you agree Mr. Mulholland?"

"Absolutely, Mizz Lacey." His hands brushed my back as he slid my chair in. Electricity sparked and frustrated me.

"Oh, forgive me Brother Watson, this is Miss Manning." Miss Lacey continued her introductions. "John Robert, here is your new worker," looking at me then speaking to me, "Mr. Monroe just stopped by for a bite to eat." I tried not to stare at the empty, loose sleeve.

He tipped his head in my direction and mumbled what I think was "Glad to have the extra help."

"So very pleased to meet you ma'am. Glad to see you're all right. Thought you were about to fall out the window." Preacher Watson had salt-and-pepper colored thick hair and was stocky, about as round as he was tall. Though very pleasant, speaking in a sing-song manner, I got the idea there wasn't much that got past him.

"Oh, thanks for your concern, just trying to get a little air," I replied then bowed my head with the others while he lead the prayer.

"Our Father which art in heaven, in whom we live, move, and have our continued being, we want to thank you for this day and all its many blessings. Especially now we thank you for this food, bless it to the nourishment of our bodies and our bodies in your service. We also want to thank you for this time of fellowship. Bless us and keep us in your care this day. In Jesus name we pray, Amen"

Immediately, I felt a kinship to the dishes on the table with everyone staring at me. I couldn't blame them. Looking like a boy, hanging out the window, and now trying to be a girl was a stretch for anyone. Feminine was a very unusual look for me anyway, but anything was better than the way I had looked for the last couple of months. Or would that be couple of hundred years? As the dishes were passed around, I about fainted from the aroma of the food not having eaten since the meat-on-a-stick Christian rounded up this morning.

Miss Lacey was an excellent cook, no doubt about that. Her cooking reminded me of Ma's Sunday dinners – a huge black skillet full of fried chicken or pork chops. Another iron skillet would have fresh corn cut off and simmering in fresh churned butter with salt. Green beans and whole new potatoes boiled in a big metal pot with ham hock added for extra seasoning. Biscuits were light with lard, baked high and mouthwatering in a pan.

While I was savoring every bite, the group was preparing for the kill. Mulholland was up first.

"We never discussed who your companion was, Miss Manning," he said smacking his lips a bit from the mouthful he had just swallowed.

"You're right, we didn't. " I stuffed the tender chicken and crunchy skin in my mouth.

"I may be mistaken but it seemed there was a rather unsavory character lurking. He didn't leave until we rode away," he looked down for a moment to sop up the milky gravy with a biscuit.

"Really? Why did you think he was with me?" Turnip greens with just the right amount of bacon drippings rolled around in my mouth.

"He watched you closely for some time. I thought he might be with Buffalo Bill's show. Some came through here a couple of years ago. He definitely fit the bill. Pass the butter please." He eyed me carefully, skillfully buttering another biscuit at the same time.

"You're a very observant person, Mr. Mulholland. Thanks for keeping an eye out." Mmmm, the biscuits melted in your mouth with the velvety smoothness from the lard. I definitely loved lard.

He knew I had not answered his questions but asked my own. I didn't know who he was for sure, but I should probably be the one keeping an eye out. No one could have an identical twin in another time, could they? Miss Lacey jumped right in this conversation.

"You really thought this gentleman was with that show? What did he look like? I might have seen him." Miss Lacey's eyes were so big they might end up in the gravy bowl.

"He had on deerskin and his hair was long, maybe on the trail for a long time. Rode a paint with some kind of odd saddle. I've heard those in the show have a lot of unusual equipment being about Buffalo Bill's dealings out west and all. He could be ahead of the others to hire for a show. I don't know where they're playing now." I detected a hint of wistfulness in Joseph's voice.

"Is that something you would be interested in doing?" It was a subject having nothing to do with how I got here, so I jumped right in.

"Of course. I do ride pretty fast and could possibly sell my elixir on the side if they allowed it."

"Are you kidding? When I heard you selling that elixir I thought you could have easily been on …" I caught myself before I finished with a shopping network.

"What's that? I didn't catch the rest of what you said."

"Oh, never mind. You wouldn't know…this person. Miss Lacey, this is a very delicious meal."

"I am pleased…never saw anybody eat so fast in all my borned days. Who can put away some strawberry shortcake?"

I was stuffed, but I asked for a small piece. The shortcake was a sweet biscuit topped with the naturally sweet small strawberries picked that day.

"Miss Manning, I don't believe you said where you came from. I know Mr. Mulholland met you in town but surely you weren't alone." The preacher started out in a louder tone causing everyone to look up.

All I could hear was the clock ticking in the parlor and the staring faces, waiting for an answer I couldn't give. How much would they accept?

"Well, I am from East Tennessee. Like Mr. Mulholland, I lost my parents in an accident a few years back and since then I've been travelling with friends, but I have relatives in the area. I decided I would start fresh here."

"What relatives?" He continued to press.

"Oh some cousins…in Nashville…" Yep, just not born yet.

"You need to be more careful, Miss Manning. Riding alone from Nashville? Mr. Mulholland must have come along at just the right time. Why, I bet that other man noticed you were travelling alone."

"My goodness, you all would worry a mouse out of its hole. Why don't we talk about those shingles on the roof? They aren't going to fix themselves you know."

"Thank you Miss Lacey. If you don't mind, I'm very tired and need to rest. I'm sure I will have a long day tomorrow. But first I need to check on my horse."

"Oh, don't worry. I took care of him earlier. That's an interesting saddle you have there." Talk about being under the microscope. I kept up with the Preacher, but the Salesman was taking double turns.

"So, did you think I was with the show, too?" Maybe he would catch my tone and leave it alone.

"No, but with a horse and saddle like yours, someone could be. How do you ride?"

"I ride very well, thank you. You will see tomorrow. Now if you will excuse me." I was out of my chair and up the stairs before he could ask me anything else.

CHAPTER 32

Pickin' and Grinnin'

The next day continued to be a challenge to try to fit in. There wasn't anything new about that, not since that stormy day at the Foster's where I began my time travel. The long skirt, blouse, and sun bonnet were to be my uniform for the next however many days I remained here. Miss Lacey was a gem to slip a cold biscuit wrapped in a clean rag in my hand as I headed out to get Quasar. I hadn't thought about lunch while I was chowing down on the eggs she had fixed us for breakfast.

The large fields of ripe strawberries were a welcome sight after two miles on horseback over rutted, muddy wagon roads. Mr. Monroe walked slightly off-balance without the use of one arm, pointing to the baskets, showing where I should begin. Today, he grunted like one of his pigs instead of speaking as the owner of this farm.

Thankfully, it was mid-May meaning hot weather shouldn't be here for another couple of weeks. If things went smoothly, I could get enough pay by then to keep eating and begin searching for my way home. Picking strawberries took patience and diligence with stooping and squatting hard on the back and knees. I muttered to them to shut up. They would soon get accustomed to the new positions.

By lunch, I had "picked enough to stay on," Mr. Monroe grunted. The "pickin's" from the morning were loaded on several wagons and carted off in different directions. Joseph's wagon was loaded last as Mr. Monroe called it quits for the day, having other duties on the farm to take care of. Mulholland informed me, as he set off to other farmers to add to his wares, I could rest and have supper with the others but tomorrow would start double shifts. Exhausted, I rode back.

True as promised, after we rode back to Miss Lacey's the next day, I had a brief chance to clean up, change, and rework my sticky mess of hair back into its bun. Mulholland had finished making his rounds and was cleaned up as well. Setting off again in the wagon, I was uncomfortable leaving Quasar behind and confused whether I was infuriated or infatuated with Joseph. Either way I hoped he knew I had a pretty good right hook.

Selling elixir was a curious job. Customers bought this stuff up and didn't a bit more know what was in it than I did. But Joseph Mulholland could sell water to a drowning man with a pleasantly empathetic way about him that made everyone believe he really felt their pain. That same personality had made me think I was special to him, once upon a time.

We sold all over town, maximizing profits. Once we set up close to the Opera House demonstrating to everyone Mulholland could fit right in with the variety show playing. When this kid was in action, to my amazement, nothing stopped him. We sold right up to the first show on a Friday, something to do with the fact the bottles had gotten a little larger and the elixir tonight was called Dr. Mulholland's Tonic.

On another occasion, we set up at a general store not too far from the lick where one of the long hunters was afraid to get off his horse because the buffalo were so plentiful. Although the owner tried to run us off Mr. Salesman talked his way right out of that one, actually getting the man to stock his elixir selling it for more than our price.

After that, Mulholland realized he could sell to a larger area and forget about the street corner business and farmer trade, concentrating only on his elixir and tonic. Before long he suggested we sell in Nashville, and we could make sure my cousins knew I was okay. Another excuse to have his nose in my business, but I said I would think about that.

Our hours were quite long and I was dead tired. With the earnings I made from the farm work and being "Mr. Mulholland's personal assistant," I was soon able to buy a more suitable pair of shoes. On a trip to town, Mr. Salesman noticed my clothes though I thought that was a little personal. Like everything else, he thought he could talk you into his way of thinking.

"You know Makenna, I may call you Makenna?" Of course, he had called me that from the beginning and intended to continue to do so. "If we travel to larger stores in Nashville, you are going to have to dress as my assistant instead of a farm girl."

"Thank you so much for pointing that out in your not so subtle manner. If you are agreeable to buying the dress, as long as it is modest, then I will agree to wear it. That is, if I don't have to pay for it."

"Of course, I wouldn't dream of asking you to do that. How about we stop in here and see what they have?"

It was the shop and lady we saw the first day we rode in. Dressed to the nines, she obviously knew Mulholland, crossing the room with a broad smile and a flirt on her lips.

"Joseph Mulholland! Where have you been keeping yourself? You haven't been in here in at least a month. My father was asking me the other day if you had seen the new suits."

"Now, you know that my business is just a-booming." Was he mocking her drawl? "Why, I've come in here to buy my assistant, Miss Manning, appropriate clothing for the position she has risen to."

Normally, I would have been insulted by his tone, but I was distracted by the well-dressed Scarlett and the piercing deadly stare I was receiving from her. She might as well have vaporized me with a laser beam like GORT from *The Day the Earth Stood Still*.

"Of course…how do you do?" Her tone was very chilly as she swished her many skirts toward the women's side of the store all the while sticking her nose up in the air. Maybe she really spoke that way, but it was so hard to believe.

"Mutual, I'm sure." I couldn't resist answering as the chorus girl from *White Christmas*.

Miss Conceited ran around behind Mulholland batting her eyes and being silly. If she were an inch taller she'd be round. Although barking up the right tree, she was the wrong type for he was a fan of tall slim girls, or so I thought. But she was a woman, with all the right curves, and he did appreciate those.

Within about a half hour, another lady who most likely did the bulk of the work had taken my measurements and told me when my dress and accessories would be ready. Everything taken care of, I could rid myself of this awkward situation.

Nauseating me with their goodbyes, giddy from flirting, Mulholland ran directly into the man coming in as we were leaving. Genuine apologies came from both, but the English gentleman stopped short and turned. I would not have recognized him if I hadn't heard his voice.

Trying to place the connection, he stared at me with eyes warm and sincere not squinted slits from constant caution. Coffee and cream in color and comfort, they beckoned and made you want to follow. Before, his face had been a scrubby mess of dark beard and tangled hair, cut shorter now past his ears with no trace of swelling. His loose fitting shirt smoothed into form fitting britches tucked into high slim riding boots. The way he carried his hat brought to mind someone going to play polo with one of the Princes of England instead of walking into this very inconsequential clothing store. Guess I couldn't call him Daniel Boone anymore.

Looking on, I pretended not to know him, shoving Mulholland out the door.

"Why are you in such a hurry?" Mulholland was confused, turning it over in his head where he had seen him.

"A little put out with the southern belle thing," I mumbled, the best excuse I could come up with in a pinch.

It was early afternoon, so the street was still somewhat busy as we continued to walk away from the shop, crossing the street to get to the wagon but to no avail. Out of the corner of my eye, Gabriel Christian appeared suddenly catching up, grabbing my arm.

"Miss Manning, I cannot ... you are clothed in a dress! uh, and, uh, your hair is up, uh... I cannot stand by and witness your, uh, debauchery. I know not what to make of this." A powder keg, his reddened face led me to expect his head would blow off at any moment. Instead, he let go of my arm and pointed a warning finger at Mulholland. "You sir, if indeed you are a sir, should not take advantage of a lady in a much confused state." Then, he put his fist in the very stunned face of my companion.

"Joseph, oh no, are you okay? Mr. Christian, what do you think you're doing?" I screamed at him with disbelief but secretly delighted in the fact I had a champion, even if it wasn't warranted. How many times had I wanted to do the exact same thing, to punch Joe out? "Where did you get those...and you cut your hair!" I managed to squeak back.

"This scoundrel has given cause for idle chatter. He refers to you by your Christian name and buys you expensive clothing. The ladies in the shop spoke of your character in an unworthy manner. Deny it not, for I heard it with mine own ears."

All I could say in reply was "Oh."

The shock of being punched first nor the handkerchief did little to stop the blood pouring from Mr. Salesman's nose. I suspect he usually got the first punch in any fight and probably won out of sheer determination.

"You knew him! I knew you did yet you denied it!" He directed his anger toward me grabbing my arm and dragging me toward the wagon all the while trying to keep his nose covered. "We have to get out of here, or it will be the last bottle of anything I ever sell." Note to self, if I ever wanted to hurt him, hit him in the pocketbook. "I'll deal with you later." He slung the words at Christian.

Standing in the middle of the road, flabbergasted, he watched us drive away. Why had he punched him? Why had I let myself be drug off? What had he overheard? Was I pond scum? Did it really matter? What would I call him now that he didn't look like Daniel Boone?

The wagon was going just a little too fast for my taste. If we had been carrying elixir, it would have all been broken in the first minute. Not bleeding as bad now, he growled something to the effect of "Nobody gets one over on Joseph Mulholland," and then "He has one bigger than that coming to him, talking like he was right off the Mayflower."

Well, not that ship, but I didn't know which one. There were a *lot* of things I didn't know about him.

CHAPTER 33

Volleyball

"I saw him at the racetrack. Didn't know him until you called his name and then I put two and two together. What does he know about riding?"

"What does who know about riding?"

"Quit acting like you don't know what I'm talking about. The jigs up Makenna. That's the guy that was in town with you, when I met you."

"Would you please slow down before my teeth fall out?"

"All right. Now tell me. That was the guy, the one who looked like Davy Crockett."

"No, closer to Daniel Boone."

"And?"

"And he must think you are a little improper with me, but I think that is the fault of your friends in the store. Evidently, they were talking about "my character in an unworthy manner." Wow, the way that man turned a phrase. What was I going to call him now? Who did he remind me of?

"I don't get it. He comes into town in deerskin duds, shows up at the racetrack as a trainer, and speaks the King's English. And he knows you."

"So, if I go on this Nashville trip, may I take Miss Lacey with me?"

"Really, you're going to go? That's great. I'll have to make some plans for where we'll stay. I know, the Maxwell House Hotel. I should be able to afford that now. I'll probably look into some of the stores down on the waterfront since they have a wide variety of shops. You won't believe how many different kinds of people you will run into in one block. Why, when I was there last year I stayed at, uh, with some friends that lived over a shop. In that one building, people were black and white and from other countries, worked on the river, and owned shops. You wouldn't believe all the hubbub. They couldn't understand each other and it didn't take much to start a fight. Gee whiz, it was great."

I had lit the fuse to a fire cracker, and he was off in some other land. I didn't want to stop him while he was on a roll and bring the subject back to Christian but what did he just say?

"Gee whiz??? Did you just say that? You know you really don't talk like anyone around here. Especially when you are with me."

"Hey, wait a minute. You changed the subject. What about that guy? Who is he and why were you two traveling together?"

"You sure have done a lot to be so young."

"You keep changing the subject. You called him Mr. Christian. What's the story?"

"Gee whiz, gee…where have I heard that? On tv…Leave It to Beaver…Wally says it all the time! Where would you have heard that?"

"What are you talking about? Did you just say tv?"

"No, I said you don't talk like anybody else."

"I could say the same for you."

"Yeah, and about that. I thought you grew up in Nashville."

"So?"

"You talk about Nashville as if you're a tourist."

"Who is Mr. Christian?"

We continued to dance around each other for some time. Several times I thought I had him admitting something I knew to be impossible – that he was Joe from my time. He had the same name. He looked like him. How did he get here? Does he know how to get back? I don't know how to ask him without being committed to an asylum if I'm wrong. I was pretty sure there was one in Nashville now.

"Okay, do we still work together? If so, there are some things I would rather not explain to you, and I have a feeling you are hiding a great deal about your past. Something you don't want me to know."

"Probably."

"Whatever. You didn't answer my question."

"I've lost count. Which question are you talking about now?"

"May I bring Miss Lacey? I'm not going with you without a chaperone."

"What? I'm harmless."

"Not really worried about you. I think I could take you if I had to but I don't care for all the gossip and rumor stuff that goes on in a town. Believe it or not, I want to be respectable. That matters to me no matter where I live."

The wheels in his head were turning hard. He hadn't considered my reputation. It seemed odd since Gabriel Christian mentioned it often. Thankfully, society still dictated it not just religion. If you wanted to function in society, you had to play by the rules. Joseph Mulholland either didn't know the rules or didn't care to play by them. That bothered me.

By the time we got to Miss Lacey's we were talked out. He still hadn't answered my question. So I asked again.

"One last time. May I ask Miss Lacey to go with us?"

"Sure. Who's going to take care of the boarders?"

"I don't know but I bet she could get someone. She deserves a vacation."

"A vacation? Who says that?"

"The two of us, I suspect."

Tired of dealing with him, I jumped off the wagon to run inside knowing the truth had to come out. I turned and added, "We need to talk...later."

CHAPTER 34

Persuasion

Supper was a bit later that night, being Friday, with everyone, including Miss Lacey, worn out. She had been so good to me the least I could do was set the table and carry in the food though she argued with me about helping her since I paid for my board. A mother to me in such a short time, I naturally wanted to help and reminded her how much quicker the dishes would get done if she quit balking. It was pleasant in her kitchen where there was always a good story, and she laughed at her own jokes.

Preacher Watson reminded us all we could sit in the parlor for a good while since the train had brought new oil on the last stop enabling them to use a new lamp instead of candles. I thanked him, but I preferred to sit on the porch to enjoy the beautiful evening. The peaceful setting of the sun was ruined when Joseph came outside and sat down beside me on the swing. My head didn't want to take another round with him until I figured out what to say and how to say it. Thankfully, he helped me out.

"Miss Lacey, I need to take a trip to Nashville to promote my business. Miss Manning here needs to come along but that wouldn't be proper without a chaperone. Would you consider coming with us?"

"Why, Joseph, what a wonderful thing to ask me! I would love to but I don't know…that roof needs fixin' and who would look after the chickens and the horses?"

"With us gone, it would just be the preacher. All he would need is his meals, and I'm sure some of the ladies in the community might help out a bit. You and I both know how those other ladies fight over him. He could probably take care of the other things too…I'll make it worth his while."

"Well, all right then, if he is agreeable then I certainly am. When were you thinking of going?"

"In another couple of weeks when berry season is about tapped out… can't take Miss Manning away from her commitment from Mr. Monroe."

"You are right about that. I believe I'll go in and talk to him since it's my place. He's studying his sermon in the parlor."

After she left, I tried, to no avail, avoiding his piercing stare. Those eyes, crystal clear, shined directly into my soul trying to change my mind about him. Caught in his gaze, a song jumped into my head seguing into Dad singing along with the radio.

"Better get ready gonna see the light

Love, love is the answer and that's all right."

With every creak of the swing, my heart ached for those innocent times, days that had seemed rocky but in comparison to now were void of any real problems. Dad was kind, often at his own expense, doing most anything to please – taking me for ice cream, taking long rides with Mom, joking with Pa, caving to Grandmother, and trying his best to find something in common with his father. Feeling a hand reach up and land on the back of the swing jolted me back to Joseph. I decided to spill my guts.

"You and I aren't from around here. We aren't even from this time. Don't say anything. Let me finish." I sat up and tried to turn so his arm wasn't quite so close.

When I finished telling him how I travelled, how I met Gabriel Christian and how we came here and then split up, he didn't seem surprised except for the year. He thought anyone coming from my time would be wearing some kind of space gear.

"Do you want to commit me now?" My mouth was dry, and I was worn out.

"No. I suspected as much. When I saw you riding down the hill in town, I knew immediately. That's why I picked you out and offered you a job. I thought he was with you, but I couldn't figure out why he didn't follow us so I left it alone. There are others you know, they don't stay long and they come in different ways. I picked one out when I was storytelling on a corner one day. I made some money that way for a while. My talent for talk seems to keep the suspicion off me. That and the fact that I'm more conscience of what I say in public. With you, I knew from the beginning I could say what I wanted."

"Will you tell me how you got here…and how old you really are?"

"I've been here almost two years, but my age…that's for me to know. I grew up in this area, around these hills. Mammy died when I was about ten and after that Pappy put me to work in the family business runnin' 'shine. She wouldn't have allowed it… There were stills all over the holler just like now. Why do you think I got in the elixir business? I could use it as a cover to sell moonshine with Mr. Monroe. I know how to do that.

Anyway, I was taking some into town one night and when I pulled out on the river road, the revenuers saw me. They had tailed me earlier so I thought they were on to us. Pappy kept saying nah they didn't, it'll be all right, just go on. They put on their sirens so I had to at least try to outrun them. I turned down every little crooked road I knew trying to get them off my tail. It was hard to see 'cause it was storming bad. I was doing pretty good until lightning hit me, I swear it did, caused me to miss a curve and end up in a bank, thrown from the car. I cut my head pretty bad but I didn't want to get caught so I jumped up and ran. The next thing I knew it had stopped raining and I tripped on a stump. I'll never forget it. The sky was filled with stars, lots of shooting stars. I lay there for the longest time just watching them until I fell asleep. When I woke up the next morning, I couldn't find my car and you can figure out the rest."

"You don't remember after the lightning, how you were transported?" I couldn't believe his experience was different.

"What difference does it make?"

"Did you notice the ground the next morning?"

"What do you mean? There was ground and grass." He was stalling, afraid to tell me something.

"Look, you can tell me. I'm not going to think you're weird. We already know we time travel. What could a few more details hurt?" I grabbed his hands hoping to sway him that way, but I soon regretted it.

"Okay, after the lightning, when I was thrown from the car, this round thing, I think it was a spaceship, wrapped around me. It was fiery hot inside with loud, high-pitched sounds. When it let me go, I ran trying to get whatever was stinging me off. I didn't know whether it was an alien invasion or what. Then I tripped."

"Well, I don't have to ask what time you're from. You've seen *War of the Worlds* or *This Island Earth*, or both." I wouldn't have described our experience that way, but if I was from the fifties I probably would. He volunteered the rest of the information including the crater and the smoking pit but the prickling feeling I had to force from him. Finally admitting it hurt all over for days, he still didn't feel quite right for a long time, the same irritable at-war-with-yourself feeling that Gabriel and I had experienced.

"What year exactly are you from?"

"It was 1955. Gee whiz, I don't know what Leave It to Beaver is but we were too poor for a t.v." He was kidding then and sounded so juvenile.

"This is incredible. Where do we go from here?"

"I don't know but I'm glad you're here."

He leaned in to kiss me just as Miss Lacey came back out on the porch. Jumping up to escape the situation, I almost fell onto her. She thought I was trying to hug her, so she gave me a happy bear hug.

"Oh my, I'm so excited! Preacher Man said go on. Now, I have to get together some clothes that will be decent for the trip."

"We can help each other since I know where to shop now," I said sarcastically, elbowing Joseph. Grabbing his hand, I shook it goodnight, talking with Miss Lacey all the way up the stairs.

As I put on my gown and got in bed, I thought of the episode I had my first day here, running into Christian today, and finding out about Joe – the one who still loved the old 40's coupe from his moonshine runnin' days. He traveled to get to my time but from what time? Who knew how many times you could travel? My head was muddled enough without the long, low rumbling heard off in the distance. Lightning struck. No wind fluttered the curtains. No rain pelted the house. It was all electricity. The air was thick and the sheets stuck to me. Pulled to the window to watch, sleep was out of the picture. Over and over it struck, illuminating the trees and outbuildings giving them life, rising up ghostly in appearance as the sky brightened again and again, like someone taking a picture with a flash bulb on an old Brownie camera. Boom, boom, the clash continued, a conflict of wills, finally becoming a whisper when darkness took over and the sky finally cried.

It was late when I finally dozed off. For the first time in a very long time, I dreamed when most people do. Everything was a Monet painting, blurred and hazy. Through the mist I could see him standing there in white, long dark hair, Zeus-like. His deep voice, though calm, spoke another language. Yet, I understood every word when he told me Pa was with everyone else dear to me, all in heaven, supremely happy.

Softly, he gently stroked my hair, assuring me everything would be okay lifting my sorrow. Four snowy white figures, radiant in God's love shone before me. The voice whispered in my ear that I was safe and protected. The eyes were not blue and piercing only warm and caring, searching mine. Then strong arms enveloped me, soothing me deeper into sleep.

CHAPTER 35

For Old Times Sake

It was Saturday morning and the retail business was buzzing here as it would be in anyone's time. We were on our way to town to sell Mr. Monroe's produce but mostly their elixir and tonic. Even though I had a hard time getting that dream out of my head, conversation was easy because I didn't have to be so guarded.

"I can't believe how everything looks. I don't know exactly how to describe it...uneven. Parts of town look new, possibly thriving and others, particularly out here...the countryside looks... beat down."

"It was a war zone you know."

"Uh-yes, I noticed but it's been more than twenty years."

"Why does that surprise you? More destruction was caused from tearing up and stealing than actual combat. There was plenty of that, too, though. I think Virginia is the only state that had more battles than Tennessee."

"How did the town fare so well?"

"Well Miss Lacey said the town was occupied by the Federals early on and made deals with the high fallutin' and the sympathizers so it didn't fare as badly as country folk did. Yankees just took what they wanted and anything that would burn went in campfires. Then afterwards, industry and firewood kept robbing nature. It won't grow back, like it was, for a long time."

"What about Mr. Monroe...his arm?"

"At Franklin, that's about all he will say." Oh, my heart went out to him and the bullet-ridden Carter House, south of Nashville, where the family hid in their basement while all forms of hand-to-hand combat took place on their front porch and yard. Ultimately, the family waded two and three deep through dead bodies, searching to find their own wounded son, who later died in their home then a hospital. More were killed in five hours than two days at Shiloh wiping out the Army of Tennessee.

"Yeah, I get it. Pa didn't talk much about World War II." When he did talk, it was sketchy but I understood, now, the trauma of losing loved ones and seeing the effects of innocent people being starved not only in concentration camps.

"John Robert did say when it all ended, reconstruction was just more destruction. Debt and taxes were run sky-high by rascals only interested in getting even." Shaking his head he added, "But of course their favorite way was stirring up trouble between ex-slaves and poor whites while the former owners were making deals with the devils. Still happening…." He shook his head and I took that to mean in his time, too.

"Economically and emotionally," I added. "I guess I'm used to seeing things torn down and replaced with new in a matter of weeks, as if the other way of life didn't need to exist anymore."

"War is different than just rebuilding and making things modern. Ways of living and surviving are changed… people trying to figure out how to hang on. " Not having seen the war, the effects had still made a definite impression on him. "People here had only their own backs and a lot fewer of them, especially farmers. Two mules and a plow can't do the work of three mules and two plows, if you even had a plow or a mule. Most I talked to lost their land or part of it, anyway…couldn't get help… and nobody would give you a nickel of credit. Oh sure, carpetbaggers would buy what you had, but you wouldn't have enough to start over. And it's not much better these days."

Seeing how little progress had been made in twenty years explained so much about the future and Grandmother. Her ancestors had always thought anyone outside of New England had no progress or ambition, and she repeated the fallacy. It wasn't a question of ambition but the continual task, no matter how hard you worked, of making something out of nothing. Land had often been stolen by the government and later resold to enterprising Yankees. Ordinary people had little before and less than nothing after.

"Nashville isn't so bad because it was occupied early, too. Lots of people on both sides made money there. You know...where there's a will there's a way."

"Contrary to public opinion, the South didn't have a patent on bad." I thought aloud.

"No definitely not, in any time you have to figure out a way to survive...and thrive." Dollar signs in his eyes brought to mind the sound of an old timey cash register, cha-ching. If he had been there I daresay he would have been on either or both sides depending on where the opportunities for dollars were – a Union government spy or a blockade running Rhett Butler. Not one of those, like Ma's uncle, who were so poor they swapped sides because they were starving and barefoot. It wouldn't have done any good to desert. There wasn't any food at home either.

"Well, you would have survived...you definitely know how to make money. Didn't you have any relatives in that war?"

"Yep, an old uncle that lived with us. Why are you looking at me like that?"

"How can you be so casual about it?"

"Not casual, matter-of-fact, can't do anything about it."

"But you could think of an angle for a time you aren't even in."

"You never know. Didn't think I would be here either. If I've learned nothing else, you have to figure out how to survive and thrive," repeating what he had said earlier, what he must have said many times.

"Well, that's true. It's bad enough to have to see the effects of a war let alone be in one." The thought of what might have happened had we not been slammed forward made me shiver.

"Somebody walk across your grave?"

"Huh, I wouldn't even know what time and where the grave would be." We half-snickered at the reality of that.

"Tell me about him, your uncle, I mean."

"Uncle Hiram? Well, let's see. He wouldn't talk about it much. Dad said he joined up late because he was real young, and I do remember he had a hole in his jaw where a bullet had gone through. His beard was real scruffy and mostly covered it.

"Better to stay out of his way. He drank a lot, they all drank, and he was real old. You never knew if he was going to be happy and crying or mean. Anyway, that's how the family business got started. They were trying to eke a living out of nothing. The taxes were bad for everyday stuff before the war and sky-high after. You got a whole lot more money for 'shine than selling the corn outright." He paused then added, "You think that's a bad thing to do, do you? Not everybody has advantages…"

"Why do you say that?"

"Well, I figured you thought my family way of making money was beneath you, the way you just sat there all high and mighty."

"High and mighty? Give me a break. Who can say what any of us would do if we were about to starve? Those people went through war. Doesn't it bother you now though, how it might affect the people you sell it to? I mean, the families?"

He sat silently. I stopped thinking about war or moonshine and instead about Pa and my dream. He was in heaven. Tears splatted on my skirt before I realized it. Stupid emotions.

"It's okay Makenna. You don't have to worry about me or them." I had surprised him, and he put his arm around me, squeezing me to make me feel better.

"No, I'm not crying about that. I just thought of Pa…about where he is."

"Tell me about your family. You know all about mine now."

The day passed quickly talking about relatives, laughing about my cousins in Nashville, and selling plenty of elixir and more of the tonic but little of the produce. We worked well together, yet I hoped I wasn't sending him mixed signals because I definitely had not forgotten the way he acted around the shop lady. He, in turn, had not forgotten how I had acted around Christian the same day. The difference was that I knew now that Joe, or Joseph, had no part in my life in any time and, I knew, possibly, who might. I dared to suggest, as we were packing up, to go by the horse farm where Gabriel Christian worked.

"Why on earth would you want to talk to that no-good? Have you forgotten that I owe him a sock in the jaw?"

"He's not a no-good. Hot-head yes. He may actually be able to help us get home. If we all put our heads together I'm pretty sure we could figure something out." That was the best excuse I could come up with to get him out there.

"I could care less. You are probably the only one who wants to go back."

"You don't? I thought you said earlier…"

"No, I just meant if it happened like last time…not by my choice. No, I don't want to go, not really. What have I got to go back for? My sot of a Dad? I don't think so."

"You have to go. It could change too many things if you don't." Mostly the chain of events that brought me to the 1700's, I suddenly realized.

"Why should I care about other times?" He had me there. I couldn't tell him what I knew. Instead, I changed the subject.

"I haven't forgotten that your friend started this and Mr. Christian was decent enough to defend me. Besides you really don't want to see me in the middle of a fist fight do you? I can hold my own."

"I don't doubt you can. But I have an investment in you and your clothes. I have to keep an eye on you." He gave me that wink as if he was the quarterback and I was the head cheerleader.

"Why do you think you need me to go on this trip to Nashville? Evidently, you were doing fine before I got here."

Nonchalantly, he said, "We're taking it to the next level. Businessmen will talk to me, but they will be interested in you."

"You mean you're going to use me?" I asked incredulously.

"Not like that. Just dangle you. You will hook them for me." Wow, my life's dream to be a minner, as Pa would say.

"I don't do that kind of thing. You know that by now. Besides, I don't know why you think I'll be able to hook anything."

"You've already hooked me baby," he said, staring deeply into my eyes. If he had the sophistication of David Niven, the original Pink Panther, it might have worked, but with our past, his delivery of that line reminded me instead of Pee Wee Herman. I had to turn my head not to laugh in his face.

CHAPTER 36

Moths

It was a grand estate and, of course, a plantation at one time. The two-story red brick house stared at us through multiple windows and stately white columns. The last time I had been here was on the back of Quasar hanging on to Christian. Now he worked here. We pulled in the side entrance and around to the stables in the back. A beautiful view, no matter where you stood, of the many acres, the distant lake, the horses, and, oh, Gabriel. There were several rings fenced for exercising and training the horses, nothing but thoroughbreds. In the middle of the furthest ring with a lunge line and whip, he stood, popping it on the ground encouraging the horse to continue on line in a circle, in full command.

"Wait here." I commanded Joseph doubting he would obey. Squeezing my hand, he must have thought I was going to tell Christian there was something between us.

"Is there anything you can't do?" I called out across the field. He didn't seem surprised to see me, as if he knew I would come.

"Might I inquire why that would interest you?" He glanced over but continued working with the horse. I leaned against the fence.

"You seem to know how to do a lot of things despite not knowing anything about this time."

"Think me not capable of existing here? The less one speaks the more others imagine." It was a kinder, gentler way of saying it is better to be thought a fool than open your mouth and remove all doubt.

"I did have a reason for coming to see you."

"I cannot imagine…"

"For one, why did you punch Joseph out? For another, are you interested in going back to your time?" Making it up as I went along, I had no idea what else to say.

"Ah, Joseph, is it? May I ask to what these questions tend?"

"I just want everything out in the open so there isn't any confusion."

When he stopped and brought the horse over to me, I finally realized who he reminded me of. No one. Not in my time or any other. From the beginning, I had noticed the way he carried himself and the way he rode a horse when he hunted, but I was too amused by the whole Daniel Boone thing and miffed by his behavior toward me I didn't notice *him*. It wasn't just his looks or his scent as he worked with the horses but seemingly, a magnet drawing me to him, a sensory overload. How silly of me, it was nothing. We had been through a lot together and had a connection. That was it. Why couldn't I get my breath? I thought only the girls that wore corsets had trouble breathing.

"That… is… a… beautiful horse." Finally, I got it out and began to breathe again.

"Yes. The owner purchased him in England. The particulars of the transaction caused much mirth."

"I bet." I didn't care about the particulars when my brain was so foggy. "Where's Traveller?" I asked, beginning to get my senses back.

"In yon pasture. Would there be any reason they would admire that name you call my horse? It has been the topic of conversation on more than one occasion. I seem to have found favor with many gentlemen by that fact alone."

"So you still call him that…too bad you can't google it."

"Pardon me, but you are continuing to do that, which I despise."

"What of the assortment of 'that, which I despise' would that be?"

"Leaving me to understand words that are very peculiar… words you insist upon saying."

"Oh, but mirth isn't peculiar?"

"Nay…"

"I hate to tell you no one uses mirth OR nay anymore so quit giving me grief about what I say."

"Makenna, could you wrap it up please? We have other places I would rather be." Joseph was mopping his head from the heat, but it was probably more from irritation with me for talking to Gabriel.

"Sir, if you wish to address Miss Manning you should call her thus… unless there is an understanding…and of that I would fain disbelief."

"Could you both just take a chill pill?" I was nowhere near to explaining what I came to tell him, distracted by our somewhat friendly conversation. I wasn't sure if we had ever had one and now I was really aggravated to be interrupted.

They both answered, at the same time, "What now?" with completely different meanings.

"Never mind. I'm coming." I turned back and continued my conversation. "I have something to tell you but now isn't the time. He didn't want to bring me today anyway. Is there some place we could meet later?"

"Had we not shared time together alone, I would refuse, but it is without point at this time."

"You're right. It doesn't matter now. Could you come over tomorrow afternoon? I think he has to take care of some business that doesn't involve me then."

"I cannot imagine what is of such an important nature."

Agreeing, I gave him directions and found his knowledge of the area surprising. A quick learner, it must have perturbed him when I suggested being of help to him in the area. It wouldn't have hurt him to let me help a little.

Meanwhile, Joseph was sighing and tapping his feet in the wagon. Pretending to attend to something, he jumped out and brought a bottle of tonic back to the front seat with him. It hadn't occurred to me, until then, he might have inherited his family's habit as well as the business.

All the way back to Miss Lacey's, I couldn't help but think how reluctant Gabriel was to talk to me when I was so drawn to him, all of a sudden. I felt like a moth drawn to a flame while the flame was trying to run away. I was such an idiot. Why didn't I just leave him alone?

CHAPTER 37

Blessed be the Name

A polite, mild-mannered gentleman, the preacher's transformation was one of shock and awe when he stepped into the pulpit the following morning to speak of card playing, dancing, and the evils of moonshine, rubbing the sides of the podium as if to rev up his engines. The little frame church vibrated with every syllable that came out of his mouth. Alternately wetting his fingers and flipping pages to prove his point, he continued on, quoting Deuteronomy trying to make a connection with the decency of women.

Holding up his Bible and shaking it fiercely to get additional power from Heaven, I surmised, he screamed women should never dress in anything even resembling men's clothing. As he brought it down, he thumped it with his fist for extra emphasis. Several times he drew out a handkerchief and mopped the sweat off his forehead as several women around me looked confused since they had never even considered doing that. I thought the wrath of the Almighty had fallen down upon my head and mine alone until he added liars, cheats, fornicators, adulterers, and murderers.

Where did that loud voice come from? I had never known him to raise his voice at anyone, much less, a whole room. Without any kind of device to project his voice, Preacher Watson had to shout. Telling someone in a normal voice God loved them and wanted them to live with

Him was comforting yet to hear it screamed took on another meaning. In this time, it worked. In mine, it sent people running.

The drama wasn't quite over, continuing when we stood to sing, begging and pleading for sinners to come down front and confess their sins. "No-bo-dy should go to hell. God created hell for Satan and his demons not for you and me. He wants us in Heaven with him, Jesus sitting on His right hand...no sorrow, no sickness! Won't it be wonderful there? You need a risen Savior. He died and rose for you. Right this very minute, repent of your sins and cast off that old life! You may not think your sins are known, but oh yes, they are known by the One that it matters the most, God our heavenly father." He began singing, just as loudly, with the rest of the congregation.

"Tho' your sins be as scarlet, They shall be as white as snow."

Several men and women ran down front crying, begging for prayer and forgiveness. The preacher kept up the pressure by singing along to the next verse even louder.

"Hear the voice that entreats you: Oh, return ye unto God!"

A younger woman, visibly shaken, ran, wanting to be baptized yet I didn't see anywhere that could happen, the church small and very plain. Again, he spoke to the church. "This precious soul has requested to be buried with her Lord and Saviour in baptism. But first..."

He turned to the woman, who seemed more of a girl, her cheeks bright red with nervousness and eyes wet with tears.

"Do you believe, with all your heart, that Jesus Christ is the son of the living God?"

"Yes, I d-do."

"I know you do and the angels in Heaven are rejoicing with this confession."

Another round of prayers was uttered and we all headed out and around to the back where at the bottom of the hill was a small pond. The woman had stayed behind a few minutes to change her clothes into several layers of something resembling white bed sheets. As she made her way down the hill, the group continued singing.

When she passed, I noticed her cheeks had deepened to purple with streaks spreading down her neck and then hidden with the covering. Trying not to be lost on judgment day and in front of everyone was too much. I expected her to pass out any moment from nervous exhaustion and wanted her to know that she was getting salvation but God's love and mercy as well. When I reached out and patted her arm to comfort her, I received a warm smile of relief in return.

By the time she reached the pond, Preacher Watson was already standing in the water. "Based on the confession of your faith, I now baptize you in the name of the Father, the Son, and the Holy Ghost." He covered her mouth and nose with a handkerchief and dunked her backwards under the water. As she came up out of the water, everyone was singing, this time a little faster.

"He'll forgive your transgressions, And remember them no more..."

After all the screaming and sweating, it had become a joyful experience. The young woman was all smiles as she was helped from the water and immediately covered with a blanket where the rash had begun to fade. She was hugged, congratulated, prayed over and then the group began to sing again.

"Blest be the tie that binds our hearts in Christian love."

When I looked around at the tight-knit group of people that's what I saw. They loved this girl so much they wanted the best for her, communion with His people and the final Reward, not ending with this life of misery. Aside from their communion with Christ, their connection with each other was, indeed, a support group. Most of these people went to town infrequently making the church body a gathering place to get away from isolation, a place of comfort if someone died, and a place to get help if your family was sick. In a rough patch, you had someone to turn to and keep you on the straight and narrow.

The church wasn't but a mile from Miss Lacey's. We walked, passing several others along the way, offering friendly conversation about the morning's events, excited about the new convert and how they could help her. Joseph pretended to listen to Preacher Watson who was very giddy with his success this morning. Surely he knew about the tonic business, yet they walked together without a care in the world.

I saw him across the field sitting on the swing. Recognizing us he stood tall, dressed in a light-colored suit and pleasant demeanor. Had he been to church? Why did he come so early? Had the others noticed? Needing to head this off, I started talking just as we got close enough he could hear what the story was going to be.

"Well, my goodness Joseph. There is the English gentleman we met in town the other day. I guess he took you up on your offer to stop by." I glanced back at Joseph and could see red creeping up from his collar to the top of his head. "Miss Lacey, Preacher Watson this is Mr. Gabriel Christian." They all shook hands.

"Please forgive me Madam for taking the liberty of arriving earlier than was planned." He leaned over in a slight bow. You could see Miss Lacey's head swim. She had been put in a trance.

"Why, it's not a problem at all for me young man. I fried a mighty big chicken this mornin' and we'd be pleased for you to join us for lunch." She touched the back of her hair, checking for any strays.

"Oh, I'm sure he doesn't have time for that. He was stopping by to say hello and see this part of the county." Joseph was not happy at all.

"You say true, Mr. Mulholland. Still, our plans must not prevent us from the wishes of this lady." He turned to Miss Lacey. "It would be very much appreciated." She smiled and went inside with the preacher.

"Well then. Why don't we take a look around here while they get the food on the table?" Joseph inquired in such a way he was probably up to something and I guessed it meant Gabriel wouldn't be staying for lunch.

"Joseph, would you mind to turn Quasar into the pasture? He deserves a Sunday break and the weather is so fine." Spoiling whatever his plans were, I smiled sweetly at them both.

He shot me a dirty look while Gabriel tipped his hat at me. I couldn't believe how different he looked from when I first met him. For that matter, he didn't exactly have the same disposition either.

From the porch I could hear them walking away, cursing each other. I chuckled.

"If Makenna didn't think you could somehow help her, I would tell you where to go and maybe help you get there." Joseph dug his heels into the ground, taking long strides.

"Every man to the devil in his own way," replied Gabriel.

CHAPTER 38

Stay or go?

Miss Lacey never ceased to amaze me. She had put out a spread in no time, most prepared before church including frying the chicken, which involved not only wringing its neck but plucking the feathers. The guys had a good nose and returned just as we put everything on the table. With impeccable manners, Gabriel hung his hat and then seated the ladies. I hadn't paid much attention to the others' habits but in comparison we were all lacking. From the way he described it, I doubted he had learned etiquette from his upbringing, more likely his uncle's family in Virginia.

Preacher Watson had become the curious cat again. As soon as we had filled our plates, he beat me to managing the conversation. He wanted to know all about his past. Gabriel seemed very relaxed and answered them all, telling most of the real story switching some of the dates. He also said he had learned of several large horse plantations, instead of land claims, and wanted to work with some of the great horses acquired from his native England. What a smooth move! No one questioned his formal language since they hadn't ever heard his accent before and just assumed everyone still spoke that way.

While he continued with the inquisition, I could feel Joseph's eyes on me trying to get my attention, but I refused to play. I needed to talk to Gabriel, and he was not going to stop me.

"Joseph, please give my regards to Mr. Monroe this afternoon." I turned to Gabriel and commented, "My hours have become a lot less since the strawberries are gone. He is very kind to let me continue working there at all." Before Joseph could answer I added, "Mr. Christian, I would be very glad to show you around the place. I sent you off on an errand of my own and I know you didn't see the lovely flowers or the creek at the back of the pasture."

"Certainly, Miss Manning." The tone in his voice was totally opposite from the day at the Courthouse. Instead, it was kind and gentlemanly.

"Would the two of you like to come as well?" Please say no, please say no, my mind pleaded.

"How nice of you, Makenna, but we enjoy our Sunday afternoons under that tree out back. Would you mind to bring some of the flowers for the table?" Miss Lacey coyly answered, not giving my intentions away.

"No, not at all," I cooed back.

"Well, that will be lovely. Y'all go on ahead and I'll have a nice cold drink ready when you're done." Miss Lacey gave me a look that in my time would be "Spill your guts, girlfriend."

I smiled at Joseph sending the message to give up and go on. He decided to surrender and leave but not without squeezing my shoulders as he walked by.

We walked across the pasture at a leisurely pace. Despite my best efforts, I found myself drawn like a paper clip to a magnet. Why, why, why? He glanced over at me, and I prayed he thought it was the heat making my face pink.

Once we reached the fence row, there were plenty of shade trees to cool us. The yellow-orange daylilies were clumped along the trees and in the fence row inviting me. I picked slowly, relaxing, beginning to enjoy the day.

"Is there a particular reason you did not wish Mr. Mulholland to accompany us?" He stood watching me.

"Yes, both of you tend to lose your temper easily, and I wouldn't have a chance to explain things to you without Joseph trying to talk over me."

"You have an understanding with him then?" He had taken off his hat, running it around and around between his thumb and index fingers.

"No. Not exactly." He looked at me in disbelief. "Would you please give me a chance to explain?" One by one, I picked the lilies, lifting each one to my nose, hoping for a scent but barely finding any.

"I would by no means suspend any pleasure of yours." Dropping the hat, he picked it up and flipped it, up and down, behind his back.

"Who said I enjoyed this?" I paused for a sneeze and continued my task.

"Were it certain you did not then I might as well leave." His warm gaze sucked me in, and I stared back a little too long.

"You are really confusing me." Forgetting I couldn't run my hands through my hair, I knocked the comb out, causing it to fall past my shoulders in a heap, no longer shaggy. It was a nervous habit to begin with and frustrating to wear it pinned up.

"How long...your hair is," he said absentmindedly as he again, dropped his hat, picking up the tortoise shell comb instead, turning it over in his hand. Questioning the color of my face as I snatched it from his hand, he reached to pick up his hat. Laying the clump of flowers on the ground, I hastily rearranged my hair trying to hide my embarrassment.

"Yeah, nobody wears it short here. There are some things about this time that are so restricting. I miss not being able to wear jeans although I believe the preacher directed a lot of his sermon at me this morning. In my time, I'm made fun of, umm, ridiculed for being ...reserved." I resumed the flower picking.

"My sincerest apologies. I understood different customs between countries in my day. I am only now learning the enormous change of customs in different times." He resumed fiddling with his hat.

"The dating and marriage customs here suit me much better. You aren't thought of as a weirdo if you tell someone to keep their hands to themselves." I had no idea why I told him that. The corners of his mouth turned up as he looked at me with an expression of amusement then one of deep thought.

"Weirdo?" He dropped his hat again, reminding me of Jimmy Stewart in a scene in *Mr. Smith Goes to Washington.* What would he have to be nervous about?

"Strange, weird, odd, a pariah. Anyway, when you and I parted ways at the courthouse, I saw Joseph at the wagon and immediately recognized him from my time. He doesn't know this yet, but he was my boyfriend, the only suitor."

"Ah, that explains your connection then." Slowly pacing instead of fooling with his hat tipped me off he wasn't too happy about this topic.

"He hasn't gone to my time yet. 1950 was his home and not a happy place for him. I wanted to explain this to you because he doesn't want to go anywhere else…and he has to." I didn't want to explain that I wouldn't be here with him if Drew hadn't made me so angry over Joe.

"That would explain his similar language to your own." He contemplated what I said for a bit and then turned to me. "I care not for the man, but why is it necessary?"

"He broke my heart that's why." He didn't comment so I added again, "Unfortunately, it has to happen." Why did he not catch that I want to be here with him?

"Then you have an understanding between you." His eyes were unusually harsh and dark as a hickory nut.

"No we don't. I can't deny old feelings, but this Joseph hasn't broken my heart yet. I suspect he would here if given the chance." I continued to pick the daylilies handing them to him to hold. "It has to happen in my time…it has to." Did I have to spell it out?

Gabriel was silent for a moment and then suddenly burst out.

"He is careless with your reputation. That is why I hit him. It is cowardly when men are the cause of a woman's ruin."

"Huh," I grunted in amazement. "I've wanted to do that for a long time. I also know why you feel that way with your sister's situation."

"Why did he purchase clothes for you?"

"Because I work with him and I'm going to Nashville to help him set up his business in shops there." He squinted angrily at me. "Miss Lacey is coming with me. I told him I wouldn't go unless I had a chaperone. I don't want people here to think badly of me. I do care about such things."

"Why would the lady in the shop speak in such an unkind way of you?"

"Jealous, maybe? She's in love with him. I could tell it by the way she looked at me. He loves that attention, and her father has money."

"In what manner will you persuade him to leave then?"

"I don't know…I don't even know if he will go straight to my time. We know it's possible to travel more than once since we have. Joseph has seen others. It irks me to have to say this but if I try to go, I don't want to go alone. Who knows where we would end up? I wouldn't ask you to help if you aren't planning on leaving. Do you want to go back to your time?"

"What do you mean if? Why do you ask if you do not intend to go?"

"I was sure I wanted to until I had this dream... Pa was in heaven with my parents. It doesn't really matter where I go if he isn't alive." Between the dream and the letter, I was pretty sure he wouldn't be there even if I could get back.

"I know nothing other than my desire for my own land. Why should it matter whether I stay or go? Mr. Mulholland would be with you." An awkward silence followed, my hopes dashed. "Is your wound healing properly?" He held the flowers in one hand, motioning to my arm, almost touching me then thinking better of it.

"Yes, it's fine. There's a springhouse in the back pasture along the other tree line. Let's go get a drink." In embarrassment, I ran ahead of him though it was further than I thought to the trees on the other side. Stopping midway through to pick some of the wild daisies, he caught up to me.

"Would it be helpful to show Mulholland what we remember and compare to his position, if we were able to locate it?" Gabriel asked, finally, back to the original subject.

"That's what I've been thinking to be sure. When do you think we could try?"

"We return from Williamsburg on Friday. Saturday would be the first day I might ask leave."

"You'll be gone all week. Oh... We are leaving for Nashville next week." Another awkward silence.

"Might you leave some flowers for the rest of the world?" His eyebrows arched with humor.

"Well, I believe daisies must be the friendliest flower in any age. So I've got to take some of these back as well." How would I explain the quote from another favorite movie when I would then have to explain email? Walking over to the cover of shade, I decided to let that one go. It was just too difficult to go there. Plopping down on the ground to rest, I caught him staring at me, shaking his head. "What?"

"You must try to act a lady even if those of your time don't. You will have your skirt soiled and if I guess correctly, those are not the clothes you wear for the fields."

"Good grief! I forgot again." I jumped up and brushed the dust off. "You must know I am considered a tomboy in my time. Mind you, I like boys, but sometimes I act a little too much like them. I never had to act all dainty around my Pa." In speaking of him, I must have known he was gone for some time, sensing a pleasant memory instead of a dull ache, the one I carried around for so long for my parents.

He found the thought of me trying to be dainty rather amusing since most of the girls he had been around were very much preoccupied with the way they looked. I tried a little harder when getting a drink from the creek but inevitably gave up, splashing my face instead.

"Do you miss your girl in Virginia very much?" I glanced over at him, water dripping off me.

"Of what girl do you speak?"

"The one the guys were giving you a hard time about. Back at camp. Was she a cousin maybe?"

"Yes, a cousin. No… I …. What prompted your thoughts of her?"

"Well, there's something funny about that relationship. And you hesitated."

He looked at me for a moment, shrugged his shoulders, grabbed part of the flowers, and walked ahead of me back across the pasture. I had obviously brought up a sore subject.

CHAPTER 39

Fisticuffs

It was a shame things had gotten all weird having had somewhat of a friendly conversation, meaning we weren't screaming or insulting each other. Wonder what else I was missing about the Virginia girl? Didn't really matter at this point. By the time we got back to the yard, Miss Lacey met us.

"My, my you got some lovely flowers here enough for the table and parlor. Let me take 'em." She ran inside to put them in water, having already poured us a glass of tea, while we all sat down to cool off. It didn't help Joseph much.

"I suppose y'all had a nice conversation," he pouted, glaring.

"Lovely. It was rather a warm walk but the spring back there was mighty refreshing," I said bringing back the southern belle. I wasn't sure what he was trying to suggest, but two can play at that game.

"Very funny." Joseph was not laughing and neither was anyone else since they didn't get I was poking back at him about the girl in the shop who sounded just like that.

Preacher Watson excused himself mumbling something about being much too hot out even in the shade. Gabriel decided to tell all.

"Miss Manning and I may be interested in returning to our own time. I understand you are not. We would consider it a favor if you would accompany us to compare the passages that we travelled upon."

"Us? Makenna and you are an "us" now? Good lord Makenna, you might have had the decency to tell me." Joseph's face had gone pale, his fists balled up. Any minute, I expected someone to be slugged, most likely me.

"Ho there lad, are you much given to misunderstandings? Indeed, I meant only we may want to travel. There is no connection between Miss Manning and myself other than that which has happened by chance. If we should find the way to travel, there is no way to know what time we would arrive in, or if we would arrive together. We have, as of yet, neither deciphered the reasoning for to travel nor the method." Gabriel's words brought equal feelings of disappointment and confusion over me.

"Joseph, please say you'll come. I know you want to stay here, but I feel the need to at least try to go home. I need your help." Truthfully, I only wanted him to leave.

Abruptly he stood pulling me up and to the side of the porch where he thought Christian couldn't hear. He gazed into my eyes so hard I was unable to look down, taking my breath as well. If he hadn't held my hands, I would have hit the ground.

"Makenna, I don't want you to leave. Things are good here between us. My business is doing well, and after our trip it will be even better. Why, we'll probably be the toast of Nashville! You want to stay. I know you want to stay." He continued the intense gaze into mine.

"I don't know Joe…" I wanted to say "Sure, you go I'll stay here with Gabriel." Why, oh why, couldn't it be that easy?

"His name is not Joe." Gabriel had appeared and was now trying to get my attention for some reason.

"Leave her alone. She can call me what she wants…She knows what she wants." Joseph shoved Gabriel out of the way, away from me.

"You? I think not." He shoved him back.

Preacher Watson came out of the door at just the right time, finding the two men brawling in the yard, punching, kicking, shoving, and screaming. Miss Lacey, right behind him screaming equally as loud, "Young men, I said young men! You stop that this instant, y'hear? Preacher man, help me break this up!"

Christian stopped when he heard her voice. Joseph decided to get one more hit in, but Christian ducked out of the way leaving Joseph reeling from the force of his own punch, sprawling on the lawn.

"Goodness lands, girl. Now you have two gentlemen fighting over you! What to do, what to do!"

"Miss Lacey, it's not like that. They had a disagreement about business, that's all. Now Joseph, you go inside and get cleaned up while I walk Mr. Christian here to his horse. Don't argue with me." I turned to Christian. "Let's get Traveller."

"Is he a relation to the real Traveller?" Preacher Watson perked up.

"What *real* Traveller?" Fatigue with a hint of curiosity got the best of Gabriel.

"Why, General Lee's horse! What generation is he?" the preacher asked in surprise.

"Pardon? I have always travelled. It seemed a good name for that which I do a lot of." Smiling, I walked past Gabriel and muttered, "Good save."

Gabriel shook his hand and made his goodbyes to Miss Lacey. The disappointed Preacher followed the others inside as we walked where Traveller was tied up.

"Well, now you know where the name came from."

"You will have to explain more fully so I know better how to answer."

"I will. Another time though. Now, what are we going to do to get Joseph to go with us?" "Were you aware he had such ability over you?"

"No, I mean, what did he do?"

"He persuaded you to stay here. Until I pushed him away and spoke to you, you were calling him Joe."

"No, not really. I already told him I was going to Nashville *with* Miss Lacey. What happens later depends on finding the passages. That stare... it was the same kind of gaze Joe used to give me, you know, *deja vu*."

"What response did he receive?"

"What are you insinuating?"

"You alone know the answer. Had you seen the change at that moment, it would give you pause." He had no clue who I was really thinking about.

"So, we're back to that again are we, Daniel Boone? No, he did not have that kind of power over me. If you must know, he broke it off for precisely that reason. I really don't see what difference it makes to you anyway, what kind of girl I am. I'm not your sister."

"Forgive me. My intentions are not to cause you pain. I cannot understand you or the time from which you belong." He seemed genuinely concerned. Wiping my forehead with the back of my hand, I nervously pushed the hair out of my eyes, once again knocking the comb, but this time I retrieved it.

"Well, I don't really know where I belong anymore." Clumsily arranging it I barked, "Since he won't come with us, we'll go without him and think about the rest later. Saturday, then?"

"Yes, Saturday." He barked back.

CHAPTER 40

Nashville

Little did I realize Joseph had, not only, figured out but sabotaged our plans. Our trip to Nashville was in another week but unknowingly Miss Lacey spilled the beans and the trip had been moved up to tomorrow, causing me to miss my meeting with Christian. Of course, I had no way of notifying him of the change of plans. There was a switchboard at the drugstore in town enabling limited phone service but not out here, not for many years.

It was a ridiculous ploy. I had wanted Joseph to meet with us in the first place. Had it not stormed soon after she told me I would have been on the road to inform Christian but battering wind and rain continued overnight. I had hopes the bad weather would delay our trip but no such luck. By morning the sky was clear, and the only evidence was the muddy roads and a few downed trees.

Preacher Watson took us in the wagon to the train depot. In the 1930's, a slender, young Ma waited there to ride into town and might have glanced back up to the beautiful house she walked past every day, the house we would all live in eventually. Though beautiful in its heyday, the years were not kind and on this day it had not even been built. While we waited, I noticed the hills dotted with the occasional cabin and along the tracks, the houses of railroad workers.

According to Mr. Mulholland, it was a waste of time to ride into town to meet the boat when we could get on the train and go all the way into the city. It hadn't occurred to me steamboats actually made several stops in the area along the Cumberland River and ferries ran a service. Evidently, the river was still the thriving place our German friend spoke of during my first time travel. They had transported furs and bear meat on crudely made boats and canoes and steered them down the river to Natchez. In this time, according to Miss Lacey, it was used by one of the largest industries in the area – timber. Mules would haul the timber, the most popular being walnut and cherry, to the river where logs were lashed together into a raft floating down river to the many sawmills lining the river opposite the main wharf.

The train trip wasn't horrible, but it wasn't a walk in the park either. Even though we had sense enough to go early, so the heat wouldn't be as oppressive as it would be later, the dress and bustle were still hot and confining. We sat pretty close to the front to avoid the ash and cinder that flew when riding on a steam locomotive.

Joseph kept grinning at me and trying to get me to look at him. Was he trying to melt my heart or brainwash my head? The scenery from the window made it easier to ignore him. Continually, I was stunned by what wasn't there yet and what was. When we crossed the railroad bridge into the city, I noticed the stone piers supporting the railroad tracks. In this day, it had the capability of opening to allow steamboat stacks of the riverboats to pass through. Thankfully, Miss Lacey kept up a lively conversation, worried from the leak in the roof, providing cover for my amazement. By the time we reached the station, I was frazzled, to say the least, at another place of change.

We pulled into a very crowded smaller station. Before we got off I could already taste the soot and dirt from smoke of incoming and outgoing trains. The bustle of lots of passengers in way too small a space was evident from the slow movement of the crowd and the murmurs of "Excuse me, Madam" or "Excuse me, Sir." Occasionally, someone would rudely push their way through feigning their importance, leaving behind them the appalled faces of those unaccustomed to bad manners. According to a conversation I overheard between the conductor and another passenger, the usual station for the L&N had burned earlier, and they were forced to come here. When I expressed my surprise, I remembered to hold it down.

"Joseph, where is Union Station? This is horrible!"

"I agree but Union Station is in the discussion phase still. Lots of politics and maneuvering still before it gets built. Luckily, this station isn't far from our hotel."

"What are y'all whispering about? We haven't been in Nashville five minutes and already you've got your heads together! You'll have two whole weeks to court, isn't it exciting?"

I was rather angry by that remark, but I had to remember how good she had been to come with me, so I could avoid that kind of thing.

"Wait, what do you mean two whole weeks? I thought it was a week and I might be home by Saturday."

"I know you did but my business will take much longer. Stop worrying. I'm sure you will see him soon enough." Jealousy did not agree with him, too much the little kid told he couldn't have the toy he wanted. "Makenna, you will love Nashville now. People are so…agreeable."

"I didn't say I didn't like it before. You mean they are easier to persuade this time around?"

"Oh, that's right dear. You have cousins here. We will just have to look them up. Do you know where they are staying?" Miss Lacey was obviously confused from our conversation, choosing to address what made sense.

"No, not exactly. I'm sure I'll run into them if we are staying two weeks though." How on earth could he afford two weeks at the Maxwell House Hotel and the clothes he said I'd need? Tonic and elixir, probably just the tonic, must have sold better than I realized.

We needed to get to the hotel, but no one relished the idea of joining the maddening throng. Much to my surprise, Joseph had spoken with the conductor and arranged a carriage to meet us. As soon as we stepped off the train we were escorted by a group of men, and I oddly thought of James Brown and his hundred bodyguards. It was obvious to me Joseph Mulholland could snap his fingers and arrange almost anything. I'd never seen anything to compare. Joe certainly didn't have that ability. Or did he?

Miss Lacey reminded me of a trip to New York with Dad when I saw skyscrapers for the first time. My whole body hung out of the car window to stare at the buildings in disbelief as she was doing now. I was amazed at the regression. Mud and dirt, mixed with manure, were everywhere. A maze of electric poles with tangled lines and archways for stoplights added to the chaos. She was speechless with the delight of new invention, a few years since she had been able to come to the city, marveling at each new thing and pointing several out to me. My surprise was sincere but for a different reason than she intended, of course.

Arriving at the Maxwell House, we both stared at the stately Corinthian columns holding up the handsome five story building. We were cautioned not to use the front entrance, part of what was called the "Men's Quarter," and taken around the side to the women's entrance. My head was sure Joseph would spend a lot of time in that section though it would probably still upset my heart.

"Act as if you belong so we don't have to deal with any kind of snobs. I have experience in this department," I whispered to Miss Lacey. In dealing with Grandmother's gang, Dad would always say if you act like you belong then you do. Miss Lacey's expression told me she didn't know who would be stranger in that situation, unfamiliar with the word snob.

While Joseph registered, we waited in the elegant yet flammable lobby. Everything was a tinderbox in this time period with wood everywhere – the walls, displays, stairs, and counter. I considered asking if we might stay on a lower floor then remembered it wouldn't catch on fire for some time yet, not until the early 1960's, when it burned to the ground. Not wanting to change history was a struggle when I wasn't ever sure I hadn't already done that just by being here.

The richness of the furnishings explained why it was considered the finest hotel in the city at that time. All the display cases were made of mahogany. One had displays of silver and fine jewelry that could be purchased at Calhoun Jeweler's Store inside the hotel. Glistening many-tiered chandeliers competed with bright gilded mirrors. Shiny brass was everywhere from the hotel desk to light fixtures to door knobs and knockers.

Our rooms were as grand as the main entrance. Miss Lacey couldn't get over the fact there was a bathroom on each floor. If I hadn't spent so much time in the outdoors lately I might be upset there wasn't one in our room. How my perspective had changed in so little time. I never thought of myself as spoiled because I never needed much, not a high maintenance kind of chick. But here I felt very spoiled and newly appreciative of the advantages of my time.

We freshened up a bit and had a light lunch in our room. Joseph was determined to give us a tour of the city that afternoon though I would have preferred to hang out in the room in my undergarments. So many layers of clothing in the middle of summer was something I would never get used to. The only consolation was wearing lighter material.

Joseph had hired a carriage for our afternoon's endeavors, most of his business on Market Street, toward the river. The buildings along the way, whether basic or grandiose, were impressive. Dry goods, shoes, hardware, and jewelers were all in simple brick buildings of three or four floors with windows shaped from standard rectangular to curve topped and the occasional bay style jutting from the building. The court house, customs house, banks, insurance and publishing companies were ornate buildings with huge columns and lavish towers of every architectural style. Churches ranged from simple box style with modest bell towers to elaborate sanctuaries with delicate stain glass windows, ornamental slender steeples, decorative parapets, tall arched doorways, and elaborate towers.

As we got closer, it was obvious the wealthy had begun their flight to the suburbs. There might have been a business and then a residence on some streets, but for the most part the well-to-do were closer to the Capitol and away from the river and for good reason.

The market was a place for farmers to sell produce, but further down the street it turned into a mixture of shops and residences filled with different nationalities, races, and economic levels. Some included a family atmosphere and others were distinctly of vice. Joseph's eyes lit up when we reached the seedy end of the street, making an off-hand remark about how easy these people were to sell product to. That might have been so, but I believed it was more how easily he could talk anyone into anything.

The overnight storm had made the dirt streets muddy and the few streets that had pavement of crushed rock or brick were reeking and slimy from the mixture of manure and urine ground in from the horses' hooves or wagon wheels. The closer we came to the water the worse the odor became, the streets a garbage dump from unwanted trash, ashes, animal carcasses, and the contents of slop jars all awaiting the final destination of being dumped in the river.

It's no wonder typhoid and diphtheria along with a host of other diseases flourished in such an atmosphere. A little air pollution of our day seemed mild in comparison until Joseph pointed out they had that too. The limestone streets made choking dust when it was dry and, he said, in the winter burning coal caused black smoke all over the city, probably a high incidence of lung disease in addition to all the others. If this weren't enough, a little further north waste from meat slaughtering and packing houses was also dumped in adding to the stench that was the Cumberland River at that time. Miss Lacey reminded me of the problems Memphis had, and as she had said before that all cities of any size, on a river, had the same problems.

We turned back to make a loop of the city when she politely asked if we could see the rest tomorrow for she wasn't feeling well after witnessing all the filth. I agreed thinking a bath sounded wonderful about now.

"Mr. Mulholland, if you would be so kind as to take us back to the hotel, we might rest a bit before dinner time." It really tweaked him when I imitated the lady from the shop in retaliation for his being over anxious to get back to Second Avenue as he probably did in my day with Drew Foster, partying and picking up girls. Two peas in a nasty pod.

"Of course, Miss Manning. It would be my utmost pleasure to escort you." Bad attempt at an English accent but I got it. Equal opportunity jealousy and jabbing.

CHAPTER 41

The Art of Persuasion

It was a gorgeous coat with colors so vibrant you knew nothing bad could possibly happen while in this coat. I felt safe and good wearing it. Teal, orange, purple and brown all striped on the ivory background. Strong, dynamic shades lead me out of the valley of the shadow of death. The music was so sweet I couldn't help but skip and dance. Someone's hand grabbed mine to run across a beautiful meadow of daisies and sweet green grass. Side by side we ran, equally delighted, and equally satisfied in each other's company. I couldn't remember when I had felt so happy. His hand was warm in mine and his voice soft and kind. I tried to see him but I couldn't, I could only feel his loving presence. Suddenly, I found myself sprawled out on the ground where I had tripped. As I began to laugh, so did my phantom friend. We continued laughing as he pulled me up. Again I gazed into the tranquil windows of his soul.

Was it the sun waking me or the wonderful knowledge of having another calm and peaceful dream? The bed was so comfortable and I felt truly rested. The warm and fluid maple syrup eyes poured into my memory, and I wondered where they were now. Was he having thoughts about me?

Since she had remained in the room last night, I was concerned for Miss Lacey since I had never seen her sick. I agreed to have dinner with Joseph in the dining room if I could return soon after. We discussed our plans for the next several days including getting more suitable clothing for the appointments he had scheduled. He said we had been very fortunate to receive an invitation to a dance in the ballroom next week. We would definitely need different dresses for that. The whole time we were talking I felt as if he were trying to talk me into something. I finally called him on it.

"What is your problem?"

"What do you mean my problem?" he questioned my question.

"I've noticed recently you are trying harder than usual to get my attention. It's very annoying."

"What's wrong with wanting the person you are with to pay attention to you?"

"I generally try to look at someone who is talking to me but you seem to want me to look right at you the whole time, into your eyes. Why?"

"Because I think you have the most fascinating eyes I've ever seen, sometimes they seem greener and sometimes even blue-gray…with your mood."

"Okay, okay but I don't think that is exactly it."

"What other possible reason could I have than to want the person I care so much about look at me when I talk?"

It made me uncomfortable when he mentioned he cared for me. I couldn't let him go, needing desperately for him to go to my time. That was probably a cruel thing to do to someone, but he hadn't been exactly true to me either.

We had many errands and appointments today so I was thankful Miss Lacey felt better. Our first stop was the fitting. She did not want to go to the dance, but Joseph would not hear of it. He had a true regard for her, and I was glad for her company as well.

On the way, we talked of her last trip here, a couple of years ago when her husband was still living. They had come to see Buffalo Bill's Wild West and to take care of some business pertaining to the farm. Unable to get a word in edgewise the first night when we talked, she made up for lost time, animatedly speaking of the grand spectacle and all the animals, the Indians, the stagecoach, and her favorite, Annie Oakley. I was careful of my reactions having been to the museum in Cody, Wyoming when we performed at a rodeo in the area.

"You ladies have been carrying on for at least five minutes without taking a breath. We are almost to Market Street again." Joseph sounded jealous I was talking to anyone but him. We looked up in time to see a pair of clocks mounted to the front of a building with a side sign reading "watches and jewelry." It was an effective advertisement for entertainment or in case someone couldn't read.

We waited in the carriage while Joseph spoke to several farmers. Our conversation continued about the show long after he returned to drive down to some of the other establishments.

The whistle of a steamboat arriving could be heard for some distance, a dirty, rather small vessel used much like a barge. Not anything like the well-known Delta Queen, now a hotel docked in Chattanooga on the Tennessee River, with its grand staterooms and parlors sailing the Mississippi and other rivers for over seventy five years.

We had just pulled in front of a dry goods store ready to enter when a motley crew rounded the hill looking as if they were ready to incite a riot. A lady opened the door and waved us in with a warning.

"Since Captain Ryman got religion and closed down the saloons on his steamboats we have to put up with the angry lot of them once they get here and then the drunken heathens after they've been here a day. If it's not the raft riders, it's the coal barges coming in. Why, you can barely see their faces but you better get out of their way when they are takin' the town."

She looked pretty rough herself, and I was confused over who she was angry with though glad to be inside. I whispered to Joseph, "Is she talking about the Ryman of the Grand Ole Opry? Can we go by Fifth Avenue on the way back? I want to see the auditorium."

He nodded but continued to browse the store before making his pitch to the owner. Long and narrow shelves filled a long wall with what I thought of as "dry goods" – blankets, bed linens, table cloths, towels, wash cloths, dish cloths, and some clothes but mostly underwear and night clothes. On the opposite side, kitchen ware was everywhere with rolling pins, pots, pans, stoneware jugs, pitchers, dishes and a counter in the middle with some shelving forming a square. It contained toiletries such as soap, toothpaste, toothbrushes, toilette water, and some kind of hair ointment. The creak-creak of the boards on the wood floor, as we walked across from front to back and back again, was the only sound before Joseph spoke in his usual flirty yet condescending tone to the lady.

"May I please speak with the owner of the store?" Not using exactly the same tone as Miss Conceited from the dress shop, but I guessed it was because this woman was about twenty years older.

"You're lookin' at her." She popped back with great confidence. "What can I do for you?"

"You mean your husband and you own this store." He countered.

"No. I mean I own this store. You must not come to the city much. Now what do you want?" Her voice was rather gravely, like someone who smoked Camels without filters.

"That's wonderful ma'am. I am well acquainted with women in business." I bet you are, I thought to myself. "Why, here is the lady that owns the boarding house where I live and this lady is a business associate of mine."

"Glad to meet you. There are several women who own stores, mostly war widows. Didn't come from no plantation but my little old house was burned up just the same. Came to the city, worked hard, own a pistol, take care of business." I wouldn't want to meet her on a dark alley.

Miss Lacey spoke up with details I didn't know. "Yes, I know how you feel. My father was killed at Shiloh, and my husband was wounded at Murfreesboro. It was a miracle our house wasn't burned when they left out after living in it for a spell." I immediately thought of the clothes and food I took from her house when it was occupied. What extraordinary women they were to have lived through that.

Joseph cleared his throat. I could see he was trying to change the subject without being a heel. "Miss Lacey, I believe you could use one of these lovely pitchers for that ice tea you make that is so wonderful on a hot day like today. Let me get that for you."

It took her by surprise he was offering to buy her something. I knew it was just one of his many ploys to get the owner to buy his wares. As she was taking his money, he commented on what a great idea it was to sell scented water. "Not only does it smell nice it is so soothing to the ladies. Had you ever considered something else that is soothing to the ladies? I have a nice elixir that relaxes and calms. It can even settle an upset stomach." His voice was soothing as well, the serpent trying to get Eve to eat the fruit. He didn't pause for a second. "The farmers at the City Market wanted more than a dozen bottles to sell there but I said no. Do you know why I said no? Because I didn't think it was the appropriate place to sell this calming elixir. But your store, now, this is the place. Right here next to this lilac scented toilette water."

The elixir had not been appropriate for the market, but the tonic had. He took several orders to be delivered in a couple of weeks. I was pleased to find out he had also secured orders for produce from Mr. Monroe's farm. His thinking was to begin now with corn or beans and then totally take over the strawberry market next May. Evidently Joseph's first stay over a year ago in Nashville had been very educational. He had learned how things worked, and it wouldn't be long before he was a businessman in every sense of the word.

Explaining later, the river was good for both the city and areas north. Rural areas sent produce, meat, eggs, tobacco, and furs and received hardware, shoes, farm implements and stoves. Once Joseph saw how the produce worked out, he would jump in somewhere else. It was strange to think how useful that river was when before I thought about it only when it flooded in 2010.

Before we were out of the store, he had bought a bottle of the lilac water for me and wrote up an order for two dozen bottles of elixir. We went out to the carriage and waited while he finished up the details.

"Do you believe him? I always said he could sell water to a drowning man."

"You knew him before, didn't you?"

"Before what? I just meant since I've worked with him I've noticed his sales ability." Goodness, she was observant, and I wondered if he had picked up on that as well.

Depending on the clientele, for elixir or tonic, we spent several hours taking orders on Market Street alone. Sometimes we would be used in the sales pitch and other times we didn't even go in the store. Finally, we all had enough of the stench of the river and headed back.

The next several days were much the same. In the morning we spent several hours calling on businesses and in the afternoon we took mini-tours of the city. The Ryman had not begun construction yet, so we chose to tour the Tennessee State Capitol. In pictures from the 1860's, Federal artillery pointed from the new building. Sitting atop the highest point, it could still be seen all over town with the front entrance illuminated by gas lamps at the gates. The carriage drive, shaded by a variety of trees, wound up around the grounds used as a public park. Massive fast growing poplars, the state tree, stood along the front and sides as windbreakers, although today it did no good. On a mild day, it would seem windy on this hill.

On the east side was the stunning bronze likeness of Andrew Jackson on a raring horse, exhibiting the take charge kind of person he was. "He isn't thought of as kindly in my day because he owned slaves and ran Native Americans west, but I would challenge anyone to try and survive his upbringing. The British weren't exactly kind," I whispered to Joseph. "He expected the same of horses as he did himself, all or nothing."

The wind was gusting so hard we could hardly stand up. Joseph had hold of Miss Lacey's arm as we ran back to the carriage. A storm was building and we decided it was better to get off this hill when it hit. The horses were spooked and difficult to manage, but Joseph came through again with unfamiliar maturity. By the time we made it back to the hotel, the sky was egg-like, equally cracking and pouring. He let us out at the door and went to take care of the carriage. How take-charge he was in life and irresponsible in relationships, ours anyway, mystified me.

CHAPTER 42

Haunted

"Makenna, Makenna, what is wrong? Oh my goodness, what can I do?" The voice was screaming at me to wake up while my body was on one of those weight reducing machines with the belt. Over and over again, I was shaken until I could finally focus. It was Miss Lacey who was visibly horrified from watching me.

"I'm okay, I'm okay." I was still in my wet clothes, on the floor, leaning up against the wall.

"What on earth was that? I've never seen anything like that! Are you sick?" She had already changed for dinner so it must have been some time I was out. She was holding a cool washcloth to my forehead. "At first I thought you had seen a ghost! Rumors are that it's haunted…you know they used this as a hospital during the war. It wasn't even finished and some soldiers got killed when the stairs collapsed on them. Feel better now?"

"Oooh, really? How awful! No, I'm fine. I, I don't really know… I've been having these weird dreams lately. I thought I was changing clothes but I must have drifted off…it's nothing. I'm so sorry I scared you." A blanket was on the floor next to the chair. I must have started out there before I had another episode about those creepy kids and their ice cream. This time they were burying me in it. "Another building used during the war…is there one around here that wasn't?"

"Not many, if they survived anyway. You sure you're okay?" I nodded. "Okay, let me help you get dressed."

Later, when we met Joseph in the dining room she began to tell him all about it. Things were weird enough without adding this to the picture, so I cut her off and talked about the gorgeous building we were in as we walked to the dining room.

We sat at a larger table tonight with some gentlemen Joseph had met earlier in the men's parlor. Because of their dress they looked eerily similar to people in my dream although I hadn't seen their faces. Thankfully, no children. I suspected from the turn of the conversation they were local men beginning their night out, and I was also pretty certain Joseph would be with them.

Because Miss Lacey and I had little to contribute to the conversation we resumed our conversation about Buffalo Bill's Wild West. It wasn't long until the men decided our conversation was more interesting.

"Yes, it was spectacular. It was of particular amazement to me they could bring so many animals. It was the same at the show I saw recently when traveling on business in New York City." A middle aged man spoke with an accent similar to Charles, Scarlett's first husband in *Gone with the Wind*. He was the first Southerner I ever heard that had the sound and inflection of one of those characters.

"The show is in New York now?" I could hardly contain my excitement.

"Why yes," he drawled "in the area of Staten Island. Have you seen the show?"

"No, but I really want to. It's been a secret dream of mine to perform in it!" They all laughed because they thought I was joking.

"Yes and I want to be the announcer," they laughed at Joseph as well.

"No, I think you would be better at telling stories on the street corner out front." Another man referred to something unfamiliar to the rest of us. "Have you heard Mr. Mulholland's tale of a disappearance? They were having some kind of liar's contest in the barroom across the street, and he won, hands down! Begging your pardon ladies." He was speaking more to the gentlemen but, of course, I wasn't going to let this one go.

"By all means Mr. Mulholland, let us hear it. I'm familiar with…your methods of persuasion, this should be a treat." Miss Lacey blushed, not used to such boldness in the company of several men.

"I'll be glad to take you to the scene of the crime when we get back." He looked toward the gentlemen and winked and looked back at me. "I never said the story was a lie. I just told what happened. Just like this…

It was September, I believe it was, a few years ago. Now you all know what a beautiful area this is we call home – rolling hills, greenest grass, and the best pasture land for farming. A Mr. David Lang owned just such a farm with not only those attributes but beautiful horses to ride, as well as breed to sell. On that warm afternoon in September he was riding, expecting some visitors who wanted to look over his fine horses. One was his brother-in-law and the other was a local judge. Peck was his name. He had gotten off his horse to walk across that beautiful pasture land to meet them as their carriage came through the gate. Mr. Lang called out to his guests. They answered back with a wave. Right after they acknowledged him, he totally vanished into thin air. He was there…and then he wasn't.

Now his children had been playing in the front yard and his wife was on the porch, so when they heard the visitors arriving, naturally, they got up and came to the fence. The children saw their father and the wife saw her husband. They both saw him wave to the others, and they both saw him disappear. Right in the middle of that beautiful pasture, in those rolling hills, in front of one of those prize horses that he was known for. The children cried for their daddy and the wife ran over to see where he had fallen but he hadn't fallen because he wasn't there. Judge Peck declared he had vanished and called for a search party. Neighbors came to help but he was not to be found. Why, they even brought in some high-fallutin' scientists to study the ground. They proclaimed no holes or caves or such were there he could have fallen into.

Yes, it was a pitiful sight. It got even more pitiful a few months later when the kids were out playing where their Mama had told them specifically not to go. She didn't know if it might happen again. They had noticed something strange about that area. The grass was burnt up, yessir, dead and not anything living would go near it, not an ant, not a cow. One of them youngun's ventured right into the middle of the area, you know how kids do things they are told not to – tellin' em' no makes them want to do it that much more. That kid heard a moaning and got down on the ground. He jumped up and squealed and ran to get his Mama. He had heard his Daddy's voice down there, faint mind you, but it was his Daddy all the same. Mama then heard it too but there was nothing they could do.

A few years after that happened, those poor children had to go through something else. One of the girls, named Sara, I believe that's what it was, anyway, she got a letter in the mail. It was her father's handwriting. All it said was help…help…help.

No one knows to this day what happened. That poor tormented family has had to live with that for some time now."

Everyone sat still and quiet for a few minutes trying to wrap their heads around it. The men who had heard it were quietly chuckling at what a masterful delivery Joseph had. Miss Lacey ooohed and ahhhed. She ate it up with a bowl and spoon while another laughed and clapped. "Good story, my man, excellent story."

"I can see why you won that contest," I added.

Basically, it was the same local legend that had been told over and over. The same one my history teacher mentioned. The one my mom and Pa knew with a few minor differences. Joseph was the salesman that made it up in a contest. Made up something essentially happening to three people, maybe more, who's to say? Different circumstances but we did disappear.

He gave me that sly wink only Joe could give and said, "Remember mood eyes, I will take you there when we get back."

CHAPTER 43

Harmony

We had been in Nashville almost two weeks. Joseph had been extremely successful in selling his wares and stories. The Lang Legend had even been told in the ladies' parlor so it was already making the rounds. It was a useful tool in the saloons to draw in customers, elixir or tonic, who might own a business or maybe buy from him on a corner. He was not particular about where or how he sold it just as long as it sold.

Usually gone most afternoons, Joseph left us with nothing to do but shop. Normally, that would have been at the bottom of my list, but here I had become quite fond of the jewelry store in the hotel since it had several things matching the dresses Joseph had ordered. They had arrived that morning and put us both in a panic since two of them were ball gowns for a dance the next evening. Neither of us were party girls, so we were a little nervous to say the least. We had agreed to help each other though I was sure she was going to get the short end of the stick since I knew absolutely nothing about dressing up in any time period. The amount of lace, buttons, and hooks on the dresses assured me it would be a daunting task.

Still needing a few things to complete the ensemble, we hired a carriage to continue our shopping in town. However, when I got in I completely changed my mind, something I did a lot of lately, feeling the urge to head back to the Capitol. Miss Lacey agreed to procrastinate with the weather better than our last attempt. It was another warm day as summer usually is though a bit overcast. The shade and the nice breeze were welcomed for reclining on the lawn and then strolling the pathways, circling back and forth in front of the statue of Andrew Jackson. As we stood there having a trivial conversation about Rachel and Andrew, I felt his presence. Coming down the Capitol steps in a brown suit and bowler hat carrying some kind of brief case was Christian, Gabriel Christian looking very Bond, James Bond-like.

"What on earth are you doing here?" I said with way too much astonishment in my voice. He hadn't seen me at all until I spoke.

"Miss Manning, Miss Lacey," tipping his hat. "I am about business, but nothing, I am sure, that would be of any interest on such a summer's day. Shall you be about business as well?"

"No, just enjoying the grounds and thinking about going inside. I'm interested to see if it lives up to its reputation."

"Permit me to accompany you," he offered with a gesture of both arms.

"Oh no, I couldn't, y'all go on ahead. Outside's more tolerable than in." She practically pushed us up the stairs.

"We could not leave you unattended…" I objected.

"Yes, you will. I'll be fine." Obviously, she was not going to take no for an answer but he still hesitated.

"If you insist then, we shall return soon." Christian took my elbow to escort me. I appreciated the gesture not having quite got the hang of the skirt *and* steps. Of course, the hair on my arms and neck stood up, and I tried to think of something that might keep me from acting the complete idiot, if that was even possible. We were halfway up the steps when he asked if I needed to rest.

"Wow, you have such manners. I'm fine. Not used to these clothes yet." I let go of my skirt and smoothed my hair. A definite chuckle escaped his lips when I started but stepped on the hem again. Glaring, I swallowed my pride. "I needed some exercise. The time in town has made me soft." I was winded but not from the steps. "I've missed riding since we've been here."

"Yes, I remember…wow…peculiar word." He mumbled to himself. "Soft, would that not be a desirable thing?" I glanced away, ignoring the question.

At the entrance, we passed men in lighter weight summer suits some wearing straw hats. The massive doors were open to keep things cooler with the marble floors and walls assisting in the endeavor. It was an impressive building, but I hadn't been here in either time so I had nothing to compare. A different kind of chandelier hung from the ceiling in between the frescoes. Instead of tinkling crystal, white globes circled a molded iron base reminding me of an upside down vase of puffy dandelions about to be blown away.

"Guess you know it wasn't my idea to come to Nashville early. We left the very next day after I talked to you. In my time, I could have called, emailed, text, or driven over to let you know I couldn't come. I couldn't do anything to let you know. By the time I could have gotten there you would have been gone." I was still feeling a little uncomfortable but my mouth had taken over anyway.

Of course, he didn't know what I was talking about, but he didn't ask. Neither did the frumpy little lady in a charcoal gray dress with high neck and enormous bustle, frowning at me, like I was a nuisance. The antennae attachment on her hat completed the bug-like appearance, adding to my annoyance, and I had a sudden desire to squash it. I was perturbed, unable to read anyone anymore.

We continued downstairs toward the basement, unlike any I had ever seen, housing courtrooms instead of junk. Walking through the hallway of this elegant building, among spittoons similar to the county courthouse, amused me. Manners were lacking in this time period as well for a hand written sign read "DO NOT SPIT on the FLOOR OR STEPS."

Trying to even my breathing by speaking I managed, "How did your trip go, by the way?"

"It was successful for business. Although not the way I would have liked for much has changed." I sensed a familiar ache.

"What did you find out, I mean about your relatives and . . . your girl?"

He was shocked I had keyed in on that immediately rather than the business. Why wouldn't I? I knew about change, too much change, and a world of hurt. The intensity of his pain was evident as I pulled him to a bench out of the way of passersby in quite a hurry. Clasping hands, I shared his hurt.

"The opportunity presented itself to research their fate…the present owners of the land and records. It seems the Revolutionary War was devastating. My uncle was killed in battle. His wife and one daughter perished in a fire set to their house while he was away. My intended had already wed but died in childbirth."

"I'm so sorry." Unsure of his expression, I guessed correctly, "Are you thinking it would have been different had you been there?"

"Pray what difference would I have made? My parents and sister passed, and I could do nothing to save not one of them. If I could return, would I not perish as well? If so, then what purpose is served?"

"But she was…" Curious to know his feelings, he interrupted.

"My intended, yes. I loved her, indeed… I loved all my cousins. Had I married her I would have inherited the estate since there were no sons. I am heartily sorry all their lives ended. But you must understand I did not love her in the way I want to love a wife. I did not, I do not want to be married to someone for what her family is or has." He looked past me, out into space somewhere, and in a low voice said, "Rather someone in harmony with my being."

A proclamation I was embarrassed to hear, a violation of privacy. A confession to someone special he saw in a vision. Did he know he said it out loud? Not knowing what to say, my feet were suddenly very interesting to look at.

"Shall we continue our walk then?" He said, regaining his composure as quickly as it had left. I smiled hoping he would share his feelings, but he didn't.

We walked slowly around and back up to the legislative floors while he told me about other adventures back home. The horse business was alive and well. The owners had made several purchases upon his recommendations. He had enjoyed the process although it was confusing sometimes to understand new terms and equipment. I agreed reminding him change was inevitable even when you hadn't travelled in time.

The chandelier on this level was double tiered with a chain running from the wall to the fixture. As delicate as it was, it was also operated with gas. Christian pointed out the chain stabilized the gasolier from the breezes with the doors and windows open. Even that was ornate. He might have felt left behind by new inventions, but I was amazed at how well he adapted and learned in another time.

When we returned to the front steps I still had so much more to tell him.

"Joseph has been telling a story around town." He didn't let me finish before he hit back at me.

"Think you I would be surprised by that revelation? Nothing you would say about him would be of interest to me." I didn't know how to reply.

Since I was a step away from rolling down the steps, the mental picture of me at the bottom with my dress around my ears horrified me. I grabbed tightly onto his arm causing him to jerk and witness the look of panic on my face.

"Sorry, there, I really didn't want to fall in this clown suit."

"I see." He tried much too hard not to laugh.

Miss Lacey jumped up from the bench and crossed to us. He apologized for keeping her out in the heat.

"There's a dance tomorrow night at our hotel. I thought you might come since you're in town," she countered.

"How kind you are. An invitation has been given me by an acquaintance." He looked down as he spoke. Who did he know in town?

We said our goodbyes. She would have thought he was the best thing since sliced bread if they had had it then. He took her hand and kissed it with a promise to dance with her and left me standing there without a kiss my foot or anything.

All the way back, I watched her rub her hand. She knew he was much too young for her, but it had been some time since a man had paid special attention to her. I was happy for her to feel appreciated. In a strange turn of events, my angry, confused feelings for him were taken away and replaced with a warm place in my heart for being so good to someone I cared for.

Another pointless feeling hanging out there with nowhere to go.

CHAPTER 44

The Ball

Miss Lacey and I made our grand entrance, floating down the stairs into the ballroom to soft music. Additional pearly white Corinthian columns, top-gilded with a marble base, adorned both ends of the rectangular shaped room. From the orchestra end to the other, filled with ornaments and people, the heady scent of jasmine permeated the air. Except for the elegantly dressed attendees, it resembled a garden party. Four arched windows on the opposite side had huge plants in between. A large round table held a silver punch bowl equally as large with overflowing scented baskets of jasmine on either side.

A rather important looking crowd with their jewels and tuxes, I didn't have the faintest idea who any of them were with the exception of two. It was obviously not a sock hop with the swaying of tails and swishing of bustles of which I was not a fan.

Joseph waited at the bottom of the stairs, not surprisingly, surrounded by a group of young ladies. He briefly looked up, pretending to be gaga over our beauty, but we were no more special than any of the other girls he had been talking to. Truth be told, I was glad because my feelings for him had evaporated with each passing minute.

"How does it feel to have men adore you?" Miss Lacey whispered to me as she grabbed my arm feeling out-of-place, the country bumpkin at the ball.

"I wouldn't know. You're the one who was married. I just don't care – not one whit."

"Pfft. You know, you clean up pretty good. Everyone is looking at you."

"Thanks, I tried. What makes you think they aren't looking at you? Besides, you know how society people are. They don't want to overlook anyone important."

"Well, okay then. They are looking at the both of us, and it's a complete waste of time." She found that pretty funny and laughed a soft, warm laugh. I was glad to call her my friend.

She really did look stunning. We were both wearing off the shoulder bustled gowns. Her peach colored gown accented her upswept auburn hair, and the lower cut, close fitting bodice with the draping in the front showed off her curvy figure, perfect for this time. Mine, on the other hand, displayed my thin but muscular body with the bodice fitting close, gradually into drapes and then down to the stiff ruffled bottom, the blue grey silk complimenting the white ruffles. I was a scare crow in this garden. My light brown hair was wound in a cinnamon roll, ringlets below tickling my neck while I fidgeted with my fan wondering if I would need it to smack a cawing crow.

"Sorry to disappoint you but there's one in the corner with his back to us, your friend Mr. Christian," I observed. He was standing closer to the flowers looking out one of the windows.

"Why that varmint…what do you mean my friend? He's more your friend than mine but I wouldn't mind too much if it was the other way around." She was too funny.

Joseph winked at me and went right on talking to a young lady with many jewels and a bent feather sticking out of the back of her hair. It must be the latest thing, the room dotted with similar ridiculous accoutrements.

"I suppose that conversation is way more important than anything we could say." I nodded my head towards Joseph, continuing to walk toward the back corner.

"He is the ladies' man. But he usually seems so struck on you. I'm surprised by that." What I could tell her. "Mr. Christian?" The sing-song accent warmed my heart wishing Tennesseans had retained the softness of their spoken heritage.

Slowly, uncertain who had addressed him, he turned displaying the tux, so becoming as were all the other clothes I'd seen him in. His eyes darted past me to Miss Lacey.

"Why ladies...what a surprise."

"Do tell. Where is your acquaintance?" He looked to answer but his eyes fell to the sapphire necklace clasped around my neck.

"Is that not one of the many gifts you have acquired during this trip?" Another insinuation meant for me but right over Miss Lacey and she responded.

"Yes, Mr. Mulholland has been so kind to us. He said we had made the trip a success and also it is our last night." Her pearl necklace was perfect with the style of her dress. Joseph either knew style or the right jewelers, either way it was a homerun.

"You were not of assistance at the Southern Turf, I hope." Miss Lacey's worried expression didn't faze him. "Is he not also quite popular in the saloons toward Broad Street – I believe they call them dives – with a peculiar story?"

"Mr. Christian, you know ladies would not go in such places. Gentlemen shouldn't either, I expect. Are you trying to say Mr. Mulholland has been in there?" she questioned.

"Would it not be an improvement rather than keeping the company of the prattling hussies surrounding him now?" he countered.

"Thought you weren't interested in that story," I said, purposely keeping my back turned on him. "Hey girlfriend, don't you worry yourself about that, let's get some punch." We left him standing where we found him.

She was shocked at how bitter he was until I explained the unfortunate situation his sister had gotten into, leaving out the detail it happened over 100 years ago. Of course, she was touched he cared so much for his sister and liked him even more.

Making our way around the room, the buzzing of different projects was louder than the orchestra. The dance for businessmen could be considered a failure since they weren't interested in dancing but networking and showing off their expensive clothes.

Before long, Joseph was in my face. Miss Lacey embarrassed, excused herself, and walked back over to Christian. It was an informative evening for her to say the least.

"What did he want? What's he doing here?" Joseph inquired.

"What did who want?" I asked.

"Don't play with me Makenna. You know very well who I'm talking about." When I didn't answer he gave up. "Come on let's dance."

"You know how to dance here? I figured you could only jitterbug."

"Very funny but now you mention it, I am pretty good. Bet I could throw you up and down a few times." Mischievous eyes dared me but with no reaction from me he continued. "I've been to a couple of these things and girls have been very obliging to teach me."

"Really? What a shock." Yeah, I bet you taught them a few things, too, I thought nastily.

Miss Lacey and I had taken a few lessons on the afternoons we weren't touring the town, but I didn't let on. I found out quickly I couldn't step-ball-change fake this waltz as I could when dancing with an old movie. The spinning jenny, an early machine, gave this dance its name because of the spinning wheel type motion made. Joseph couldn't possibly have learned it at a dance with all the fancy footwork. I can still hear the instructor in his nasal monotone, "Right, left, right, ah, left, pivvvv-ot."

The orchestra began to play louder, and the conductor motioned for everyone to come and dance – to the polka! Could I hop in this dress? Would my hair stay up? He bowed. I bowed. He closed his arm around my waist, and we made it around the room with my clothes intact. The music wasn't exactly sensual but in my time the touch of his hand would instantly set my cheeks ablaze. Today, nothing.

Surprisingly, he was very chatty and not winded at all. I figured anyone who dabbled in moonshine wouldn't be able to dance and talk. He pointed out all the important men in the room: retail merchants, other salesmen, wholesalers in dry goods who were not opposed to scratching backs, and, of course, attorneys to give the impression of legality. Every word he spoke reminded me why I didn't love him anymore.

"We have made a hefty sum of money the last couple of weeks. I've even made some deals that paid for our stay. What do you think about that?"

"Oh, is that why you were at the Southern Turf? Isn't that a gambling spot?"

"Now I know what he told you. He was there too, did he tell you that?"

"No, but I'm not stupid. How else would he know? Why do either of you think I care you were there?"

"That hurts."

"Why should it? If you cared that it mattered you wouldn't have gone if it isn't a socially acceptable thing to do in this time. So why should it hurt you?"

"It's all about him then."

"What are you talking about? He would rather be in outer space, if he knew what that was, than be around me. He actually thinks I gave you something in return for this necklace. So there." I pushed myself away from him and left the room to get some air and catch my breath.

The lobby wasn't much cooler, and I was thankful to find the fan wasn't just for decoration after all, jerking it back and forth to stir a breeze until I thought I could go back in. I didn't want to leave Miss Lacey by herself if Christian had tired of her. He was usually polite to her, but I couldn't bet on anything or anyone.

Still swaying to the music in the gorgeous ballroom, everyone seemed to be having a great time but me. All the stupid thoughts roaming aimlessly inside my head were killing my joy. I sipped a rather plain punch and watched Miss Lacey dragging Christian, the new puppy, around the room into several conversations. It was rather comical until she grabbed my cup and shoved us together on the dance floor. Neither of us knew what had happened until another tune had begun.

The room seemed to slow down and blur all around us. Swaying and winding around the room, his hand on my hand in the protective hold, a top in slow motion, we waltzed. It was so natural I didn't even think about which foot went where and when to turn. Dreamily, his eyes looked deeply into mine then at the sapphires adorning my ears and again into my eyes with a wealth of emotion, locking mine there.

Gently touching my neck as he cradled my ear in his hand, warmth against my skin brought a mist I blinked away. The music flowed sweetly along, unrecognizable to my modern ears, yet I was sure I would never forget the tune. Though it seemed we were dancing closer than anyone else in the room, our bodies barely touched yet with each encounter, I felt the blush of my cheeks and the tenderness in his expression.

Not knowing how to respond, I was a tangled mass of raw emotion. There was no one else in the room, only Gabriel and Makenna, until the music stopped, jarring us back to reality. Awkwardly I stared. What else could I do? He responded by pressing his lips to my hand. Bowing, he turned and walked away.

CHAPTER 45

Mud

"What a crazy year this has been for weather! We got all that snow in February – almost 10 inches – and then that horrible wind and storm when we were trying to go to the Capitol that day. Thank the Lord we survived it. Were you praying for us Preacher Man?"

"Yes, Miss Lacey, I prayed for us both the whole time. I never saw so many women come out of the woodwork in my life…wanting to cook every meal for me, even darn my socks. It was more than one man could deal with!" I thought of Pa and smiled.

"Well, now, everything is back to normal. You have what you need, and we got a much needed rest. Thank you ever so much."

They had been talking about their adventures for some time when I came down to breakfast. Joseph had already gone to Mr. Monroe's with word for me to be ready mid-morning to go on a ride. His famous story had made the rounds, here and in the future, and now he was going to show me where it all happened. He wanted to go, then he didn't, now he does. Who knew what was in his head, but I was relieved we were on again.

Then there was the trip. It had taken care of one problem but created another. I knew for sure I didn't care for Joseph but what was going on with Gabriel? There were some feelings out there all tangled up with my dreams. Preacher Watson interrupted, eerily knowing my thoughts.

"Miss Manning, you had a visitor looking for you while you were away, that Mr. Christian, such a nice man. He said something about a missed appointment, so I told him where you had gone. I have to admit I didn't fix the roof. He stayed awhile and did it…some other things too."

Miss Lacey and I looked at each other equally baffled. Whatever this piece was to the bigger puzzle, all of it was driving me crazy. He hadn't mentioned coming here only that he had business, and someone had invited him to the dance.

"What do you think about Mr. Christian? I mean, what he said to us in Nashville?" Straightening out the wrinkled, freshly washed clothes and hanging them on the line, Miss Lacey and I tried to figure it out.

"Makenna, I wasn't going to say anything but both your young gentlemen have me baffled. Don't get me wrong now. Joseph is a good man and all but he doesn't do right by you – nice to you but nice to other ladies, too. Guess he wants it both ways. You could have fried an egg on his head when he saw you dancing with Mr. Christian. Speaking of him, he is lovely to me but rather hateful to you sometimes except, of course, last night. When I saw y'all dancing I could have sworn …that he knew you…a lot better than he claims."

"First of all, neither are my young gentlemen. I know Joseph says he cares but he doesn't really. For exactly the reason you said. Now, you got me with the other one. Crazy mixed up dude."

"You and your talk! Why I never heard the like of things you say." She turned muttering, "Makes me laugh."

"Thanks, I'm glad I'm good for a laugh, at least." We grinned, glad to be friends and done with the enormous washing from the trip.

By the time Joseph got back, we were finished and sitting on the front porch drinking coffee. He jumped across the rail and jerked me out of my chair.

"Come on sugar pie. Time to get this show on the road."

"Uh, okay but cool it with the sugar pie. You'll make me blush."

"Joseph, you get her back soon, ya hear? We have a lot to do."

"What on earth could you two have to do?"

"Never you mind. Just get her back soon." A worried tone in her voice caused me to double-take and mouth "It's okay, thank you."

Once in the wagon, we rode towards the area Christian and I had come in on that first day into town, passing where we had pulled off to camp. On the road to the farmhouse and the big bull brought back so many memories of Leoia and her grandfather.

"Yep, it's the same place. Where did your car run off?"

"That bank, but there was a ditch there." He pointed to a now grassy yard but the same small house, with only a few differences, the fence for one. It wasn't elaborate but the split-rail surrounded a smaller yard. How many years would it take before the road would be improved so there was a ditch?

"Any ideas about how to get back?"

"Nope. I told you I don't want to go. I just wanted to ride out here with you so we could talk."

"Well, I know it rains and then storms before we shoot through to the other side. Do you think it would work if we were here on a stormy day?"

"I told you sweetie, I don't want to go. I don't care. Let's talk about something else." He had stopped the wagon and was nuzzling on my neck.

"Joseph, stop. What did you want to talk to me about?"

"This." He tried to kiss me, but I would have none of it.

"Wait. You need to hear me out."

"Hear you out?" I could feel his anger, the "I'm not getting my way" anger. "This sounds serious. Don't bother. I know what you're going to say. It's him. You even invited him to Nashville, didn't you?"

"Of course, I didn't. You keep saying it's about him. I have a connection to him because of time travel. That's it."

"You wouldn't mind it to be more though. Don't kid me, Makenna. I saw how you both were looking at each other." His words slapped me as hard as if he had really done it.

Grabbing the reins surprised him, and I turned the wagon around to head back, screaming at him. "Quit putting words in my mouth. I'm tired of it. What I think or don't think is none of your business. Let it go." I was matching emotion for emotion. "Look Joseph, I care *about* you but not *for* you. You admire too many girls and would not give them up even if I was madly in love with you. I know that about you. I've always known that about you."

Gradually calming down, he seemed puzzled as we rode into town in silence. The wagon was mine to take back when I got done, he informed me and would show up later. No sooner had I gotten out of the wagon and watched him disappear around the corner did Miss Conceited with the fake accent come walking by.

"Why, if it isn't Mr. Joseph's hired girl. That's what he calls you, did you know that?"

"No, but I really don't care what he calls me."

"Then there's Gabriel. What a man he is. Guess you know he doesn't even mention you when we're together."

"When you're together? What did you call him?" As funny as he was about first names, I couldn't believe he would allow that. What was her game? Did she want either or both of them? I must threaten whatever her goal is, or she wouldn't be telling me all this.

"Yes, honey. We spent a very nice afternoon together at the race. That English accent is so divine. Couldn't you just melt?"

"Look, I'm not sure why you feel the need to tell me this but I only work for Mr. Mulholland. Nothing else. He bought clothes for my job. I do not care for him in that way. He's all yours. Now about Mr. Christian…"

"Why, who cares about Joseph when there's Gabriel?" She said it again!

"Okay, you have about ten seconds to get out of my face before I beat the tar out of you for even using his name so carelessly. I don't think you want your new dress muddied by me." That is if I can even get a good swing at her with all these layers of clothes and this growth off my backside.

"How coarse and rough you are. It's no wonder you couldn't catch either of those men." She was really pushing my buttons. I had seen her twice and spoken to her once. If she wasn't into Joseph then why did she care?

"Ain't nobody gonna mess on me and call it apple butter." Giving as good as I'd got, I shoved her into one of the few large mud holes and walked off. It was too easy.

"AAAAHHHH, just who do you think you are? My daddy will get you for this!"

"Well, I'll tell you. I'm Audra Makenna Manning, my Pa's best girl, and don't you forget it!" I said, over my shoulder, walking and flinging my hands to rid myself of her. The big chicken called me out, saying her daddy would get me. Ha!

With all the excitement, I completely forgot what I needed in town. But I knew what I was going to buy now. These clothes had seen their last days if I could help it. Into the dry goods store I went and bought jeans, a long jacket, a cotton shirt, boots, socks, and even men's underwear. It was better than what I had. After paying, I asked the lady clerk about a room to freshen up in and received the familiar odd look – what else is new – and she pointed, muttering in French. Carrying my dress, I left behind several surprised clerks. "Hey, stop staring. People dress this way where I come from."

No one saw me later when I climbed the stairs of the boarding house to spend the rest of the night in my room, weary of trying to explain or not explain. Maybe I would have fit in fine if I had been raised in this time, but I wasn't, and it was beginning to suffocate me. There was no choice for me. I had to try to get back home.

CHAPTER 46

A Visit

The sun was just coming up the next morning when I left in my new clothes. Mr. Monroe's work for me had steadily declined, and I wasn't ever working for Joseph again. He had left a little before me for Nashville to fill the orders, having loaded the wagon the night before. The noise kept me awake for some time with Miss Lacey's voice doing nothing to quieten him. He must have been pretty angry or drunk. Pick one, it didn't really matter.

Riding through the early morning on Quasar felt good. Here, on a horse, I was myself, the wind tangling my longer hair. I refused to put it up today. How I missed the no fuss, shaggy look. My thoughts, like my hair, were a jumble of decisions that needed straightening out. Gabriel's feelings weren't clear – after the dance I hadn't seen him at all. It might be awkward, but if he could help me find some answers I would try. So that's where I went. Still early, I found him out on the back patio having breakfast. He seemed amused to see me and, stifling a laugh, offered me a seat.

"I am all astonishment to find the new prize fighter in the latest fashion. To what do I owe this privilege?" He poured coffee and handed me some kind of roll.

"Cut it out. She was asking for it. Lucky for her I just pushed her. Besides, who could fight in those clothes?" Hungrily, I devoured the bread.

"Have you no concern about your lack of recommendation?"

"Not especially. What about you? You're the one that was at the racetrack with Miss Hot to Trot."

"I shall never become accustomed to your manner of speaking although I suspect she is just as you say. If that was the cause of her muddying, it was all in vain. She spoke falsely, for although she may have stood near, my acquaintances were closer and interested. I was not."

"Remember the day you punched Joseph out in town? It was the same kind of situation. She talked about you in too familiar a way for your time."

"Ah, defending my honor?" he chuckled. "It does concern me you have no care for the perception of others."

"I've pretty much always felt like a square peg in a round hole, or is it a round peg in a square hole? You know what I mean. I don't exactly fit in with others, and the thing that kept my sanity — what I know how to do — isn't exactly accepted here, in this time."

"Pray, what exactly is it that you do? You have alluded to it on more than one occasion, but I have yet to see it."

"Uh, are the owners here?"

"No, they are still in Williamsburg...I came back early for business, if you recall." I didn't know if he was referring to our appointment or whatever business he had at the Capitol.

"I'm not sure Quasar will be the best. Do you have a slower, gentler mare?"

The coppery colored mare he brought out stood calmly nosing the ground, giving the impression she might just stand and eat grass.

"Okay, hold her a minute. I need something to tie my hair back with. How about your scarf?" He was wearing a long bandana tied loosely around his neck and gladly handed it to me, eager to see me make a fool of myself, I reasoned.

Doing a few stretches and some cartwheels to warm up, I practiced hand stands against the fence. Penny was calm as I took her around the ring a few times doing simple one leg balances, nothing grand. She was easy-going, so I took a chance and stood up on her. Her pace a little faster, unsure of what I was doing, worked out perfectly for me with a quick hand stand, but I needed a little more practice with her to stay on longer. Without a trick saddle that was about all I could do. Trotting over to Christian, I tried to read his face, without success.

"There you go, that's what I do." I patted and soothed the horse.

"Whilst not insulting your efforts, how is that thought of in your time?"

"Depends on who you ask I guess. It's a form of entertainment like a race might be to you."

"Where might one enjoy this form of entertainment?"

"A rodeo and sometimes a circus. Oh, and I would think the Wild West. Have you heard of that show?"

"I see. No, I have not." He paused for a moment deciding how he felt. "You are quite accomplished at what you do. She was very calm. I did not foresee that."

"Why? Does she usually buck or something?" Surely, he didn't set me up.

"No, no, that was not my meaning. I was in amazement she was agreeable in such a small amount of time."

"I actually have a saddle that helps with a few more tricks. I've thought a lot lately maybe I would find my place if I joined some kind of a show."

One eyebrow flicked up considering what I said. Then he walked inside leaving me wondering what to do. The man was confusing with a hint of infuriating. I never knew at any time which would win out. After a few minutes, he returned, grabbed the reins and said, "I shall be but a moment." Sipping another cup of coffee, I thought about his status here, most likely considered an elite trainer. It was a grand place to live with no reason I could see for him to want to go back.

Soon, a thin man in a dark suit came out on the patio and handed me a large pouch. Although smiling pleasantly, he said nothing, and went inside. I thanked him though I didn't know what for.

Two gorgeous thoroughbreds, dark and sleek snorted behind me.

"Ah, our food. Excellent. Would it please you to ride this beauty?"

"Are you crazy? Of course, it would please me." I handed him the pouch and jumped up on the gorgeous animal. "I don't think he's exactly a trail riding kind of horse is he?"

"No, we shall travel mostly on level land, unlike what we saw in my time."

Side by side, we rode off over the gently rolling land. Mid-morning and relatively cool for August, it was easy to let everything go and just ride. My head cleared, and I had no problem keeping up.

It had been a huge plantation of almost two thousand acres. A shady area along the river invited us over. With the gentle wind lapping the waves, it made for a very peaceful setting. We dismounted, and I pulled his scarf out of my hair, fluffing it in the breeze then tying it back around his neck. Flicking pieces of grass and swatting the occasional bug, we sat in silence for some time before I mentioned the story Joseph had told. Gabriel had heard it now, as well, and decided he told it to advance the theory of disappearance and eventually time travel – to make money, of course.

"The ramifications of this travel…it is perplexing to consider what might be changed at any time. Would he not hurt you, in your time, if he remained here?"

"Yes, I have thought of that," I said softly. "But then I would not have been upset by his friend at the barn who caused me to ride off angry…" Once again, I left it up to him to fill in the blanks after I told him of the Drew fiasco. Talk about perplexing, if he understood my meaning he didn't say so, grabbing the pouch and inhaling some of its contents.

As he watched me stuff myself, he played a rowdy version of Funiculi, Funicula on the harmonica. "What don't you play?" I asked. He laughed but didn't answer. "You know Pa played that song too. It got him through many a hard time." He still didn't answer and continued playing. Singing and then humming, I thought about Pa and smiled at the familiar music.

"Some think the world is made for fun and frolic, And so do I! And so do I!

Some think it well to be all melancholic, To pine and sigh! To pine and sigh!"

Funiculi, funicula, funiculi, funicula, Joy is everywhere funiculi, funicula!"

He continued playing. Some I knew as war songs others as hymns.

"They are very musical here with a good selection of music as well as instruments. This one is war, of course." After *When Johnny Comes Marching Home* he segued into *When I Survey the Wondrous* Cross. "The hymns are within," pointing to his head. Softly, I sang along to myself while playing with pieces of grass, making a clover chain.

He had stopped playing and there was an awkward silence while I continued to eat, the laziness of the day and the comfort of the songs were contributing factors to my gluttony.

"I love these rolls. Thanks for telling him to pack these. Much better than squirrel I must say."

"You are very welcome. I am told they are scones though they are unlike any I ever had. Ours were rather flat."

"Whatever they are, they are good," I mumbled again with a mouthful. Half-smiling, his heart was not into a discussion of English tea bread. He was trying to decide how to say something, I guessed, but I charged ahead to avoid awkwardness again.

"I suppose someone explained the rest of the war to you."

"Nay, they have rather an extensive library. It was quite a daunting task, but I have acquainted myself with your Revolution through the Civil War, as they refer to it. A question arose about some involvement with Mexico, but my interest was with England first and, then, the general in connection with Traveller. In desiring knowledge, I have become quite the dull boy."

Anything but, I thought. The silence was deafening. Wanting to be in the moment and making that happen were two different things. The lapping of the waves was hypnotic, and as Gabriel began to play again I fell into a deep sleep.

Bright light, so bright I had to hold my arm up to shield my eyes from it. Fog began to creep in replacing the brightness but I still couldn't see. I could hear giggling and laughing – those kids again. Out of the mist walked the same man as before wearing a white tux with long tails. Stretching out his hand as he approached, our touch set off bolts of lightning that struck all around us, setting him on fire, and nothing I tried put out the fire. All I could do was watch him burn…

"Makenna, are you quite well?" The voice was soft but getting more urgent. Shaking off the horror and coming back to reality was not difficult.

"Nothing, oh nothing," I whispered and angrily wiped the always flowing tears away. Walking over to the water, I grabbed a stick and flung it around, splashing the water back and forth.

"What is the cause of your distress? All seemed so calm and peaceful." He had come to stand beside me, handing me the scarf, this time to dry my face.

"Oh, you know me and the waterworks." I cleared my throat and tried to clear my thoughts as well. "When we were in Nashville, I had a bad dream of some sort and just now I had another."

Explaining my weirdness the best I could, episodes and bad dreams, he listened with full attention and amazement at the details. I wondered at their meanings and told him what I had come up with. He agreed with the roller coaster and train dreams being about death and losing those close to me.

"For the life of me, I don't understand what those kids laughing have to do with anything."

"Do you not? I see it as your innocence being taken from you by death and those you are afraid to trust."

"Okay, then why have you started being in them as some kind of angel?" It embarrassed me to say it, but I had to tell him the truth to understand.

He came over and kneeled next to me, smiling, taking my hand to soothe me.

"I have been a protector. Your childhood, must away for you to behave as an adult."

"Wow, your mother must have known you would be an angel…." I jabbed at his arm trying to lighten the situation only to have him lift me up, standing to face him.

"I must confess the idea of being a heavenly being is appealing but that description belongs to you alone." My breath caught in my throat as his tone took a completely different turn. Looking down at first then reluctantly into my eyes he spoke softly, "I cannot say whether you were lovelier the night of the ball or today, the wind whipping your hair, your carefree manner," turning, he muttered to himself, "… eyes sparkling brighter than any jewel I have ever beheld."

My face flushed, his words startling me. I had to make another joke because I didn't know what else to do. "Why Daniel Boone, how you do go on," I simpered in Southern Belle. He stepped back irritated at my words.

"Gabriel Christian. I have a name, it is Gabriel Christian. Pray, speak it." He spat the words desperately, pacing back and forth raking his hands through his hair. Stopping, he turned and stared, not with persuasion or force, but pleading with sincerity. The effect his eyes had on my soul put any other efforts by Joe or Joseph to shame.

"Okay, Gabriel Christian, it is," Gently, I took his hands in mine. He, in turn, took mine, kissed them, and placed them upon his cheek. After a few moments, he kissed me softly, tucked my hand under his arm, and we walked silently back to the horses.

CHAPTER 47

Not the Itsy Bitsy

What if you loved someone and you feared it might kill them? Would you be selfish and pretend it might not happen? That was the road I chose, ignoring the burning angel of my dream. Mind you, Gabriel chose it for me over all my objections by winking and smiling, knocking my socks off.

Back at the barn, he insisted on accompanying me, switching horses for the journey to Miss Lacey's. Of course, I was happy to spend extra time with him. Along the way, we talked of the possibility of premonitions. Trying to explain to him how much I had already lost and maybe I was the reason they all died. I was the unlucky rabbit's foot or the noose around their necks, whatever. It hadn't ended well for those closest to me, and it occurred to me it wouldn't end well for Gabriel either. But he would hear none of it. According to him at most he would get struck by lightning and recover, thank you very much.

It was an ethereal experience riding through the purples and pinks of twilight as the evening cooled. Lightning bugs flashed and low mists appeared as we made our way up the ridge. Approaching my road, he stopped, gently leaned over, and gave me a very potent kiss. Needless to say, I rode off in a daze, looking back only to see him grinning with self-satisfaction.

It was right at sunset when I rode up to the house where Miss Lacey was on the porch enjoying the evening.

"Oh, thank heavens. I knew you would be all right but seeing is believing." Her eyes widened when she realized I was dressed differently. "What on earth are you a-wearing?"

"Please forgive me but I got used to wearing pants to ride. Ladies that work on ranches have done this for some time, I believe."

"That might be so but you might better change before Preacher Man sees you." She lightened up a bit. "You have had a wonderful day. I can see it. Did you get everything straightened out with Mr. Christian?"

"How did you know I was with him?"

"By the look on your face, silly."

"It shows, huh? Yes. It was one of the best days of my life. Is Joseph here?"

"No. He pulled up about an hour ago and when he saw you weren't here he went to see John Robert. That isn't a good thing at this time of night."

"We already had that talk, but it won't be easy for him to see me with Gabriel." I paused a minute to savor his name on my tongue, feeling delicious and more so since he had asked me to call him that. Not a big deal in my time but in his, or to him, very serious. "Did you know the owners are still in Williamsburg?"

"Why did he come back before the others? Never mind, I'm a silly thing. He came back to see you and when you weren't here he came looking for you here, then to Nashville. He wasn't going to let Mr. Mulholland get ahead of him." She grinned from ear to ear then looked worried. "Oh Makenna, please tell me y'all didn't eat supper before ya' said grace."

"What?" I was baffled by the question then realized she meant had we been intimate. "No, of course not. Oh Miss Lacey, I'm sorry. I didn't think of how that would look. Seriously, he...is a gentleman." It would be too hard to explain how many conversations we'd already had about that subject. "Seems I have broken a lot of rules today. I'll try to be a little more careful for your sake," leaning down, I hugged her.

"Well, I reckon' the Lord asks us to be faithful, not perfect," she said, hugging me back.

Cornbread and buttermilk were the closest snack I could get to cow patties. No sooner had I got into bed, thoroughly stuffed, the wagon came rolling in loudly. I felt bad for the horses when I heard a loud voice stumbling over words while another coaxed trying to get Joseph to come in and go to bed. He didn't listen, obviously drunk on his own concoction, singing loudly, "You're a mean red spider, you been webbing all over town…yeah, you a mean red spider, you been webbing all over town."

As soon as I heard him, I threw on a shawl and ran down. By the time I reached the porch, Preacher Watson and Miss Lacey were shushing him.

"I'll just go get a bucket of water and throw it on you. That's what I'll do."

"You just go do that Preacher Man. But I don't need it. She needs it. There's the mean red spider." He pointed at me and started singing again. "I'm a big black spider, y'all, gonna tear your web all down."

"What in heaven's name is he singing?" Miss Lacey was horrified from the song but didn't seem too bothered by the drunk. She must have seen a lot of drunks in her day with so much to forget.

"Why Mizzzzz Lacey. That's Muddy Waters. Ask Makenna (hiccup) woopsie (hiccup) her …Miss Manning there about Muddy Waters. She knows all 'bout the blues. Don't ya sugar?"

"Yep. I sure do. Mostly inflicted from the likes of you," I could have been as easily speaking Japanese from the looks they all gave me so I added, "gettin' your corn from a jar."

"Joseph, I am just shocked. That's what I am just shocked that you would come here, of all places, in this here condition. In front of these ladies…what were you thinkin'? You have some pretty powerful repentin' to do come mornin'." The preacher was red faced to the point I thought he might have a heart attack, and I did not want to explain CPR.

"Come on Joseph, get around back." Pulling and tugging, we got him up and around to the back of the house all the while Miss Lacey gave him a tongue lashing. "If brains were leather, you wouldn't have enough to saddle a June bug. What are we going to do with you now?"

"Where's that bucket?" I looked around ready to drown him.

"Nah, you wouldn't do that, you too busy spinnin' that web." He grinned and got right up in my face, trying to kiss me. Miss Lacey wasn't having any of that so she let him have it.

He screamed and blubbered. "All right, I get it. Just let me be."

"I'll let you be but you just remember if you don't straighten up you won't have a pot to…" She caught herself and then added, "…or a window to throw it out of, ever."

CHAPTER 48

A Date

I did not enjoy it all but I put the dress back on, mainly for Gabriel, not wanting to embarrass him. It had been too sudden a change, and I wanted him to get used to my habits gradually. When I was presentable I made my way downstairs.

Joseph was still sleeping it off when we sat down to breakfast. Preacher Watson was still appalled at his behavior, talking to himself while scooping out a double helping of gravy. I tried to smooth it over a bit by explaining the situation and my choice of suitors, causing him to be a little more sympathetic. A knock at the door made me jump to my feet in anticipation of what the day might bring.

There he was, the English gentleman, grinning and melting me with those eyes.

"Good morning, Miss Manning. These were begging to be plucked from alongside yon road. I believe you said they were friendly." He presented the daisy bouquet with a bow.

"Why thank you, Mr. Christian." Taking them, I curtsied in return.

"Do show the gentleman into the parlor." The preacher was excited to see him for some reason. He had that effect on a lot of people, not just me.

"It is nice to see you again, sir, ma'am."

"Have some breakfast or a cup of coffee? It's the least I can do after you mended the roof." Miss Lacey had always loved him.

"No, thank you. It was a pleasure after the delicious meal you prepared for me. Miss Manning and I have commitments for the day. Will you be ready then?"

"Of course. Since I have no idea what those commitments are, am I dressed properly?"

"Yes, of course, lovely as always." Unaccustomed to such compliments, I blushed. He turned toward the others. "It would be my pleasure if you would accompany us tomorrow evening for the assembly in town. I believe it is called the Opera House, although there is no opera."

"Mr. Christian that would be lovely." Her face flushed with excitement.

"By the way, Makenna, you do remember you work for me. We need to get started early today," growled Joseph, coming into the room unshaven with tousled hair.

"Excuse me everyone. I need to speak with Joseph alone." I urged him out to the porch.

"You know very well you are in no shape to sell anything. I wouldn't want to be around you while you still stink of drink. Besides I have other plans," pouncing on him immediately.

"If you refuse to work today, then you can consider yourself out of a job."

"No, I don't refuse to work, I quit."

"Makenna, you are making a huge mistake. How do you plan on paying Miss Lacey for board?"

"That isn't your concern anymore." I went back inside to let them know I was ready to go.

Joseph seethed as he watched us walk to the carriage Gabriel had for us, obviously more elegant than the wagon he drove around.

"Remember what I told you Makenna."

"Sir, I prefer you address her as Miss Manning from now on." Gabriel said matter-of-factly as he whisked me onto my seat and jumped in next to me.

He hadn't given him the opportunity to answer and pick a fight, driving away hurriedly.

"I'm sorry he is such a jerk."

"Jerk? You must be very fond of that word since you use it often. Once you said I was a jerk. Pray tell me do you still feel the same?"

"That doesn't apply to you so much anymore, just him." He grinned back at me happily being upgraded from jerk status. "But you'd better watch it."

"Think not of it today. Today is ours. What is it that you would do on a fine day such as this?" He winked and grinned, making me incredibly happy to be there.

"Can't think of a thing other than being with you." I winked back.

Everywhere was the scenic route and we took it. Not in any hurry, we told stories and laughed about our time together in 1772. There were so many things that seemed comical now that were terrifying at the time. We found a pleasant area close to where the salt lick had been and spread out a picnic, happy to be alone together although he was afraid it would not be good for my reputation. I asked him what difference that made if that was not one of my customs.

"Are not men forward when alone with young women in your time?"

"Sometimes. It can be a tricky situation if they don't take no for an answer."

"Seems all the better to bring along another."

"Lately I'm beginning to agree."

"In this time," he paused searching for words, "young women are forward with men."

"What? Who would we know fitting that description?"

"You know of whom I speak. It is not enough she accompanies Joseph, she insists on letting it be known she is readily available to others. You are aware, I am sure."

"Well aware." My stomach had knotted, waiting for the other shoe to drop.

"I only speak of it to assure you of my desire." He paused for what seemed another eternity. "It is my desire, whatever the dimension we find ourselves, you and I are not separated."

I cried, of course.

CHAPTER 49

Revenge

Why did I continue to have this ominous feeling I couldn't shake? All the light was being turned down low as I sank inside myself into a dark pit of nothingness. I had promised to go with him to a show tonight in town, but that was the last place I wanted to be. Matter-of-fact, I didn't want him to be with me. I must be dangerous to him. We had avoided that dream or whatever you want to call it of lightning striking him for one wonderful day. I had even considered sharing the letter with him thinking he might shed some light on it. But today it was back, and I knew that wasn't good. The odds were astounding, but what had started as harmless diversions had become too real and I was truly frightened they would be right, somehow. He ignored my pleadings when he came to pick me up that afternoon, saying the feeling he had was nothing more than wanting to be near me.

Miss Lacey and Preacher Watson would not go with us either. I thought they might weaken whatever power I had to hurt him, but they wouldn't budge. She wanted us to be alone, and he did not believe those shows appropriate although he didn't know much about Shakespeare except he was sure it was bad. I would have found it funny if I had not been so preoccupied.

Not able to resist this new easy going manner, I couldn't stay upset around Gabriel for long. He was trying to learn "my language" and said some pretty funny things. Of course, the flowers and compliments didn't hurt either. He "found me carefree in jeans and charming in a dress," while I secretly thought he looked hot in the "breeches" he worked in but absolutely sizzling in a suit and hat. Then he spoke of the enchanting hue of my eyes when his could melt an iceberg in two seconds flat.

We rode to town in what he referred to as a curricle. There were so many different kinds of carriages and often with the same name it was confusing. He confided his friends razzed him about bringing the very private one out, but he had chosen it so he couldn't possibly give anyone a ride and, besides, it had a hood in case it rained. Evidently, it was the sports car of the time. I told him it was fine as long as we didn't gallop through town at break neck speed knowing he wouldn't get my reference to Willoughby in *Sense and Sensibility* – his time in England was before Jane Austen.

Pulling closer to the Opera House, there was a man I didn't recognize selling Joseph's elixir and tonic. Joseph must have been waiting to be sure I knew about it, for no sooner had we gotten out of the carriage then he and Miss Conceited were in our faces.

"Why, fancy meeting you here, Miss Manning." She made me want to throw up every time I heard her talk. Nobody else sounded quite that nauseating, around here or in my time, only in really bad movies that didn't bother to research regional dialects. I did not answer her.

"Mr. Mulholland, you will pardon us," Gabriel smoothly asked and tried to maneuver us.

"Makenna, I guess you noticed I hired someone to take your place already," completely ignoring Gabriel's polite request.

Peering at me with those crystal blues, causing most girls to drop in their tracks, I knew for sure he meant less than nothing to me because all the life and good had been sucked out of them and replaced with contempt.

"Yes, and that's fine since I already quit. Have a nice evening." I shuddered, trying to shake off the bad vibes.

Already angry, it didn't help matters when the usher announced he had our balcony reserved as requested. I could feel Joseph's anger through coughs and impatient remarks, "We don't have all night" and "Move along, please" and the kicker "When did the entire balcony become available?"

His comments met with deaf ears, both of us determined to have a beautiful evening. Though we had met with one storm and another was threatening, it wasn't worth it to acknowledge his brewing tantrum.

The simplicity of the theatre made it perfect for local and smaller traveling groups. Small compared to venues of my time but quaint topped big any day. The tan carpeting with rich red swirls complimented the similar tan of the wall paper. In the entrance way hung a small gasolier similar to the ones we saw in both court houses. What it lacked in beauty it made up for in practicality. We took the stairs to the balcony and sat towards the back.

Gabriel decided the less attention we called to ourselves the better. However, Joseph kept turning in his seat and glaring our way trying to make everyone else turn to look. It worked reasonably well but wouldn't matter once the show started, and we were alone in the balcony. PDA's were definitely a no-no, but we could hold hands here without causing too much of a disturbance. He might even put his arm around me when the lights went down.

"People of this day continue to enjoy Hamlet," he said with a note of amusement. "I do not recognize but a few of this crowd." Looking around, he comfortably took his hand in mine. "You must forgive me my choice of entertainment. This is a play by an Englishman, William Shakespeare, before my time, as well, but still very popular. Many of his plays are of an historical nature…concerning kings and countries…"

"Ghost stories, too," I interrupted.

"Shakespeare is alive and well in your future?" He was astounded.

"It's amazing isn't it how great works of art and history survive? Shakespeare has been read and performed in some of the unlikeliest places." I tried to explain the Hamlet musical on the old television show "Gilligan's Island." It got a little complicated to explain when I realized Carmen, the opera, hadn't been around in his time and maybe twenty years or so in the time we were now in. He pretended to laugh at "I ask to be, or not to be," but he didn't have a clue what I was trying to tell him. The lights went down and saved me from more explanation. Some things were just beyond translation.

It was a small production with props and scenery that had seen a lot of wear and tear. The audience, though small, seemed anxious for it to begin. I leaned over and whispered in his ear, "I'm surprised this many people know Shakespeare with so many farmers and few that can read."

He whispered back, "I care not what you say, but put your lips to my ear once more."

I tickled his ears with, "To thine own self be true..." and then watched for his reaction.

He looked directly this time and added, "And it must follow, as the night the day, Thou canst not then be false to any man." Suffice it to say, we were both distracted at that point, staring at each other rather than the stage.

Somewhere around Ophelia's madness I wished for an intermission, still a little on edge. Trying to shake the bad, I considered the good. He was amazing. Not only could he fend for himself in the woods and against Natives, he could quote Shakespeare too. His command of a horse was something to behold as well as his tenderness in caring for them. I smiled to myself, knowing we had fallen hard with our declarations yesterday.

"What is in that brain of yours? Is it this Hamlet?" His husky voice sounded a bit jealous.

"Well, he's good but he's no Laurence Olivier...or you," I said as sweetly as I knew how, not having much experience with this kind of conversation.

A loud pop and crash made everyone jump, probably just a pop-up storm. From our vantage point, it was easy to see Joseph and the real spider get up and leave. Gradually, it became clear something was wrong. Hamlet was arguing with Ophelia's brother at her grave when she began coughing and stood up. The king and his wife began to snatch up what scenery they could, the skull and the gravedigger's shovels, and left the stage as smoke began to barrel.

Audience members screamed, pushed and shoved, as panic struck. The building was on fire, yet we had not heard any mention of it. Since we didn't know where it had hit, we ran down the stairs into a huge problem. The door to the balcony was locked shut and would not budge with all of Gabriel's might thrust against it. Back to the front of the balcony, we witnessed the floor cleared with the audience out the front door, and the actors escaping from the stage door.

Flames were ripping up the stage curtain and one side of the auditorium. Before I could fully comprehend our dire circumstances, Gabriel had flung himself over the side, hanging on tightly before dropping to the floor below. Looking up with confidence, he motioned for me to jump. There was no other choice. I grabbed the bustle of the ridiculous dress the best I could and managed to climb over and fall, on top of him, knocking us both to the floor from the force of my impact.

Smoke made it difficult to breathe as we scrambled to our feet, trying to get to the door. It would have made it easier for breathing to crawl but slower to get out of the line of danger. By the time we had finally made our way to the lobby, part of the ceiling was falling and, just as in my dream, caught Gabriel on fire. Struggling to douse the flames and get out the door at the same time, I screamed to stop, drop, and roll. He never questioned why, he just did it with me. We must have appeared mad to those watching when we hit the ground and rolled to put out the fire. Our clothes were torn and skin was scraped, but we had made it out alive.

The place had ignited quickly. Just as quickly, wagons had come from down the street and men were already throwing buckets of water from all directions. Evidently they had begun to put the fire out before we had even escaped. Around the back stage door the fire was contained.

Most of the patrons remained in the pouring rain that aided in putting out the fire, watching the horror that could have been – except for one couple. They were nowhere to be seen. Even his man that sold tonic had packed up and gone leaving lots of shocked people without means of solace. Joseph would have never missed such a money-maker unless something much bigger was to happen – the tragic death of his former employee, me. "Though this be madness, yet there is method in't." The words from the second act screamed at me.

We stood, as well, in the rain-shocked silence for a few moments and then left when it was under control. Slowly, we got into the carriage and headed back. Neither of us spoke for some time. When he finally broke the silence, I could not answer.

"Makenna, think you then he locked the door?" When I didn't answer he continued, "Were it certain he did such, he will have much to answer for." More silence. "You had nothing to do with this. Nature alone is at fault. Nature answers not to reason."

We drove out of the rain watching the storm off in the distance, charging up for another attack on the unsuspecting land. He wrapped his arms around me, and I leaned my head against him, my tears strangely dried up. When we arrived at the boarding house, I knew what I had to do. Not long after we had said our goodbyes, I had saddled Quasar and was on my way.

CHAPTER 50

The Real Big Daddy

When I rode past the gates of the fine old plantation house of Joseph's girlfriend, ready to let him have it, he was on his horse about to leave. Miss Conceited waved from the porch.

"Stop Joseph, I mean to talk to you," I yelled.

"Now what could little ole' Makenna say I would care about?" he slurred back, having consumed way too much of his own product.

"I know what you tried to do tonight and it didn't work. But you're going to pay for it. I'm going to the sheriff right now and tell him what you did. I don't know what the laws are about that tonic of yours, but I'm sure they will be interested to know it's all a front for moonshine."

"And just how do you think you are going to accomplish that?" laughing at me, turning his horse around and raring up ready for a rodeo. "Girl, you don't know your history. It's a while yet before prohibition!"

"What are y'all talking about?" Since she was being ignored, she brought out the big guns. "How dare you think you can come on my property and talk to my guest in that manner!" she stomped her foot resembling a two year old and continued with "I'll just go get my Daddy." She huffed inside.

"Well whatever, the people you've tried to fool need to know what you've been doing." I accused. He continued to laugh. "Honey, they know what they've been drinking!"

I felt ridiculous and changed the subject back to tonight. "What about attempted murder?"

It had started to rain again making my hair stick to my face but through the mess I saw, Gabriel riding up in the carriage about the time "Daddy" stepped out on the porch with his spoiled brat.

"What's all this nonsense going on out here?" he boomed, looking back and forth for an answer.

Gabriel stepped out to approach Joseph, who by this time realized his explanations might not fly, instead choosing to take off. Although I didn't know what I was going to do with him exactly, I was not going to let him get away, taking off after him, slowing for Gabriel to grab on. It was awkward for a bit trying to get in rhythm but Quasar, even with the extra load, soon had us close enough to spot him in the distance.

Erratic as his behavior, twisting and turning through the trees and bushes, he rode on trying to lose us in the woods. Maybe he would, the weather having become foul again making it hard to see in the downpour, but we kept our pace. Lightning was cracking all around us causing Quasar to suddenly stop and rare up, emitting sounds I didn't know could come from a horse. Ahead of us, echoing Quasar, his horse suddenly skidded to a stop, throwing Joseph into the air, encapsulated in fire, shooting sparks. Time seemed to freeze with the too familiar tone filling the air and then he was gone. His horse had not been transported and trotted over to us, nuzzling Quasar, unsure as all of us at what we had witnessed.

Gabriel jumped off and grabbed the reins, but the horse would not follow him over to the site. I held them both while he investigated the charred ground. A sense of foreboding had come upon me, a portent of a coming storm, worse than what we had seen.

"It appears the same. It is the same place, the same order of events — save the horse and the shooting fire." It hadn't taken him long to draw his conclusion and tromp back over through the mud. Staring at me he queried, "What think you of it?" Twitching his head, he was obviously bothered by what he had seen as well.

"I don't know! Each time we travel this horrible stinging happens and instantly a feeling of some kind of possession. We didn't travel tonight but don't you feel it anyway? Is it coming through that crater, making evil everywhere, in every time? Did that happen to Joseph? Was he not able to shake off the bad vibes when he traveled here and he just got worse and worse?" Placing my hands on my head, trying to think, I continued to babble, "I have a horrible connection to that man and it causes bad things to happen to people around me. Now, you have been snatched up into this, not of your own will!" I screamed at him for no good reason still trying to shake off whatever had taken over.

"You did not will any of this either! Had I listened to you and gotten here earlier instead of finding him departing the house of that wretched woman, I could have detained him from riding away from his part of our misfortune." He could see he was only making matters worse for me and tried another tactic. "How, say you, could he possibly out ride Daniel Boone? Only by being in league with those from the outer reaches of the sky or the depths of Hades!" His timing was uncanny, attempting a joke, but speaking more truth than he realized, and I grinned wickedly at the absurdity.

After some time we calmed each other, Gabriel humming a familiar hymn until we could quietly get the carriage, hitching the horses, without disturbing our friends at the plantation. Soaked to the bone, we drove back. Even though it had stopped raining, he wouldn't hear of me riding back by myself nor would he take Joseph's room for the night.

When we said goodnight, I tried to seal his eyes in my memory, kissing him desperately in a way I had refrained for so long. His eyes were concerned and questioning, brows knit together, not able to read me. I kissed him again briefly and then whispered, "Gabriel Christian…"

I wanted to say "I love you as dearly as my Pa. That's as much as I have loved anyone. Take care of yourself." But it wouldn't come out. Saying those words would only hurt him more in the future.

"Makenna, why behave you in this manner? Is it that evil?" His hand was in my hair, tightening as though he could get answers from me if he squeezed hard enough, then loosening, petting me as a child.

His eyes, though soft, bore a hole into me, searching my soul. As I touched his cheek I gazed at him for the last time, knowing I was ignoring the letter, and my heart, but I had to. As I saw it, I had no choice.

September 1886

Dear Makenna,

Thank you for the note telling me where you are! Oh how we miss you here on the farm. Doesn't a day go by I don't hear somebody ask where that girl is? Mr. Monroe is sure short-handed now both you and Joseph ran off. Most folks think you two went and got married or something including that girl in town that is sweet on anybody that looks at her twice. I tell them all to hush up for as long as I've known you there have been folks somewhere that left you or you left them.

You know I don't have occasion to read the paper much but Preacher Man brought this to me before he left. The man that wrote the story must have only talked to her...

Here I stopped reading, fumbled to find and scan through it quickly to find what she meant.

Man Disappears after fire, feared dead in blaze

Lightning struck the Opera House on Saturday... players...dashed from the stage...daughter of prominent businessman...described the scene. "It was horrible...loud bang...everyone was rushing all over the place. My companion...Mr. Joseph Mulholland rushed back in to save someone... never came out...Miss Makenna Manning is missing as well."...broke down inconsolably...deepest sympathies go to those families.

The rest was praise for the Fire Department for saving the south side of Main Street and it was believed the Opera House could be restored eventually. The nerve of that girl! I paused for a moment before getting back to Miss Lacey's letter, anger washing over me.

...That other man of yours came by and demanded to know where you were. I told him I didn't know but he begged me so I said I'd put his letter with mine when I ever heard from you. Forgive me reading it but I didn't want him saying anything ugly. He said some strange things I don't understand but nothing that was bad, I guess.

It's been a long time since I had a true friend. We had such a time in Nashville. I will treasure that always. Come on here when you get tired of traveling. There's always something here to do.

Lacey

P.S. Quasar is doing just fine.

I turned it over catching sight of the swirly writing on the next letter. Without thinking, my hand instinctively ran across the beautiful penmanship trying to feel and communicate with the one who penned the words to me.

September 1886

My dearest Makenna,

    Your destination is unknown to me. Although your devoted Miss Lacey would not divulge your whereabouts, she agreed to send this to you. She knew not whether it would reach you.
    My love, our time together was of a short duration yet what we felt had transcended time and would continue to do so. Did I not procure your affections for mine own? Why should I not come to you and return you to what I think of now as home? But wherever you are, home will be for me.
    He has not returned so I feel certain he is gone to another place in time. Is it possible he is now in your time? If so, I wish not for an easier time for you then. Is that horrid? No, it is not for it was his behavior and that of his acquaintance that brought you to me. A blessed day indeed though I knew it not for some time.
    If you are concerned for my safety, pray think not of it. Think you that your existence brought death to your family, but did I not as well to mine? Think me selfish, but I desire the risk of greater joy. Our journey has been as turbulent as the sea but drown me in that sea for your love in return.

Most faithfully yours,
Gabriel

CHAPTER 51

Another New Life

When I received the letters, it had been only two weeks since I left carrying a horrible, gut-wrenching pain. It was best for him though his letter had been agonizing to read – add that to the list of things he did well. Once again my heart was broken, but this was not about me. I had to endure.

The clickety-clack rhythm of the train was the soundtrack to the movie I watched through the big windows. Watching the landscape roll by, I thought of how all creatures led such different lives in any time. I passed through country where black and white cattle moved on gently sloping hills, chess pieces on a velvety green crayon colored board. Tall, spiky trees lined the railroad tracks, and occasionally a break would reveal weather-worn farmers moving about tending their crops. Deer scampered away from the charging bull spitting cinders at them. A change of scene would reveal cheerful towns/sad towns/dirty towns with small water towers and depots.

When we stopped, people would scurry about to gather their belongings and find loved ones. Sometimes hugs and kisses, other times a look of despair as they left to go home, wherever that was. Large brick houses with dormers and manicured lawns turned into neighborhoods of wooden cracker boxes with barely a twig of grass. Ruffled skirted women with feathered hats scurried absent mindedly into a variety of stores and shops around a square downtown. Streets crowded with mule-pulled wagons were driven lazily by dungaree clad men smoking corn cob pipes. Erect, puffing stacks from factories, maybe ice or coal companies, stretched to the outskirts. Thrown-up shacks and muddy streets existed on the edge as well, next to the tracks. Then more trees, more fields, more towns, more people, more scurry and hurry, more happiness, more disappointments, more sorrow…

The train trip had given me plenty of time to think about Joseph. Specifically, to that horrible night and the realization Joseph had tried to kill us. He was so angry things didn't go his way, not really anything to do with losing me to Gabriel, just losing. If he had really loved me, when he arrived in 2007 he would have found a way to make it work or a way to prevent me from traveling. Instead, he introduced cruelty to a young girl's heart, revenge dumped me, and spread the story around.

Joseph wasn't always bad to me, or I wouldn't have cared for him at all. Sure he hadn't had the best of upbringings but lots of people didn't and turned out fine. Did traveling have anything to do with it? I felt horrible after being shocked into another time and prayed for release. Was it possible an evil had been waiting for a host to travel through the portal, jumped on board with Joseph twice sucking it all up and spreading it? Modern times must have then been his fool's paradise.

Then there was Miss Conceited. I hadn't considered the story would wind up in the paper, however, I was not shocked it was inaccurate. To save face she had to make others wonder if we had died in the fire but the implication was stronger that we had run off together. Either way she came out as the injured party. Just as in my time, everyone had an agenda. Was it Napoleon who said history is the version of past events people have decided to agree upon?

Miss Lacey didn't understand why I felt the need to go. Of course, I couldn't explain it in full but the gist of it was I needed to be away from both Joseph and Gabriel. In her mind, I had given her a huge gift when I asked her to keep Quasar for me. She wouldn't take any money for his upkeep but assured me she wouldn't sell him unless times were hard. I couldn't ask for a better friend in any time.

It had taken over three days to get to New York City. First class was worth it, but eating would have to be a luxury after I arrived since I spent extra on the ticket. They provided water but prohibited tobacco. That was a very big deal in this time. Second class was a rough bunch of men, tobacco juice spit, smoke, and vulgar talk, as Ma would say. I did need sleep sometime and didn't expect that to be possible in the atmosphere of second class with its low ceilings and hard benches, basically the baggage car with a partition. That was wishful thinking. Once I switched trains for the last leg of the journey, it didn't matter what car I was in. We stopped at almost every town of any size, and I got no rest.

Not knowing what to expect hadn't helped. Although I had been to New York City to visit my Dad's parents several times, certain landmarks were familiar but most weren't. The problem, I decided later, was not recognizing buildings but most of the ones I knew weren't even there yet – the Flat Iron Building, the Empire State Building, and Madison Square Gardens, to name a few.

When we pulled into Grand Central, I was dumbfounded. This was not the building I had seen in so many movies too numerous to count. Nor the one my father showed me the backward zodiac on the ceiling and the four-faced clock of opal. Huge, as so many buildings were in this time and place, and elaborate but not quite as ornate as some others, its different sections spread all over the place from what I could tell.

The train shed was magnificent to look at it in its own right with archways for different tracks and then archways over them for decoration. A mixture of glass and iron made a sky light that dazzled then electrocuted from the sheer pandemonium of passengers getting off and getting on at the same place, pushing and shoving. The Nashville station had been a walk in the park compared to this. The smoke and soot from the coal-burning trains made it hard to breathe, and the noise was deafening. I rushed inside as soon as possible.

There wasn't much improvement when I entered the passenger area. My bag and I were bumped and knocked without even a measly "sorry." The only way I could catch my breath and keep my balance was to stand over to the side and let all the traffic get by. I kept hoping it would die down soon, yet one train after another left and came in, so there was a constant stream of people. Since I hadn't really planned much other than getting here, I found a bench against the office area wall and sat down to plot out my life from here. It took all my energy to calm down, to think what to do next. How could I find what I was looking for? How could I have been so stupid to come without any assurance? No, I wasn't stupid. I had to leave before Gabriel tried to stop me, before something else happened to him.

And then a sign appeared. An Indian in full dress on horseback with the caption "Buffalo Bill's Wild West" was there, directly in my line of vision, what I had hoped to find. Chills of excitement ran down my back and into my toes, as I remembered the conversation I had with Miss Lacy and the businessmen. That's what a girl in 1886 does if she can ride! The relief I felt quickly turned into fear again. How on earth would I get Buffalo Bill to hire me?

The front of the building was right at street level with black carriage taxis for hire. The smell of manure mixed with the smoke made me light-headed having not eaten. Despite saving money, I had no desire to find the elevated trains and trudged on, hiring a taxi instead to take me to Staten Island. The driver, standing next to his horse, hesitated at my request so I said again, more distinctly, "Buffalo Bill's." I wasn't sure from the look on his face if he could understand English even though my 2000 era Southern accent wasn't nearly as thick as the 1800's one, due to television and the invasion from everywhere. "Oh, Erastina, yes."

I stumbled, of course, as he helped me get into the carriage, my bags stowed on the back under where the driver would ride. He walked forward and leaned down to check the feet of his horse, lovingly speaking to her as a family member. In this rough and tumble environment, I admired the man for taking time to care for his horse.

Small boys were all around the building screaming something about an earthquake, holding up a paper, but I couldn't make it out. "What happened?" I mouthed. "South Car-lina, uh, Chas-ton, bad." He responded and grabbed a paper for me. Since it was doubtful he could read if he could barely speak English, I offered to help.

The story said it happened last night, August 31, lasting just under a minute. Of course, the destruction was horrific to imagine even without pictures. At that count it was over sixty dead but I knew it would be closer to a hundred. One of my favorite places, St. Michael's church on the Four Corners of Law, had completely fallen off into the street. Every building had cracks in it if some part of it hadn't collapsed. Chimneys fell in heaps. Railroad tracks were bent in all directions. Fires lit up the sky, waterlines and wells ruptured. It was a mystery why it occurred since there was very little seismic activity in the area.

After reading the article, I was dazed but the world kept turning. The driver tried to pull out from the building with no luck, heavy traffic forcing me to notice my surroundings again. A clock adorning the top of one section looked down upon me reminding me of time – this time, that time, any time. Different sections of the building made a giant L shape screaming "lost." It seemed arched windows were a dominant theme of this building, so many eyebrows arched in question over peering eyes. What were you doing? Where were you going? Just who did you think you were? Okay, I got it. I'm lost in time and mass confusion.

Charleston and I had a connection of death and starting over, many times. This was just one of the many things devastating that beautiful city. Holding its Southern head up proudly through hurricanes, war, fire, and disease gave me courage.

Mom and Dad promised to walk instead of bike when we were on a trip there some years ago. We hunted for all the various cracks in the buildings, caused by that long ago earthquake, from Rainbow Row around to the Battery where the Ashley and Cooper Rivers met. I remembered the grand old houses throughout the town with their earthquake bolts in the shape of stars or circles with some having crosses on their outer walls. Rods ran through to the other side of the house to give it stability in the event of another major earthquake though it was doubtful if they would work but they had to do something. Just like this trip for me. It was an earthquake bolt. My whole life had been ripped apart and I was trying to do something to keep it from being ripped apart again.

Our way through the noisy, congested city took some time. Lots of new construction crowded the streets as people rushed to get around it. Traveling further south took us into a more commercial district cluttered with telephone and electrical lines, looking like a spider playing tic-tac-toe. It terrified me riding under the maze of lines crisscrossing in every direction. All I could think of was a thunderstorm striking and burning the whole city but it must not have happened. It was not something that stuck out in my education of the city. Relieved as I was to get through the tangled mess I traded that nervousness with not knowing how any of my efforts at a new life would work out.

Many times I thought I recognized a building or thought I knew what street I was on only to find out I was wrong. The streets themselves were familiar, comparable to those I had witnessed in Nashville, a mixture of stone, gravel, and sand ground down with water, urine, and manure – similar problems from horse traffic that didn't change no matter what else around us did. We ran off and on cobbled roads jerking the carriage and me in it like a sack of potatoes. There was a dull roar from the many individuals selling their goods on the side of the road, and in some cases into the road. More young boys screamed the day's headlines, and others wore signs advertising all sorts of things to buy or see.

When traffic began to move, the carriage suddenly took a fast leap to the side. My head pounded along with the jerking of the carriage as we traveled into unknown territory running under an elevated train. In its shadow several factories angrily spouted smoke and soot while other sad buildings obviously cried tenement housing. Though neither were an ideal place to live, slave houses were bigger than these and Grandmother had nothing to be proud of. I was sure this had to be another city until I saw the Brooklyn Bridge in the distance.

When we finally made it to the Battery area, a fort to protect the harbor at one time, a large round stone building caught my eye for it was quite busy. Trees and bushes lined the walkway while a steady stream of people came from the building with suitcases, suggesting this was an earlier immigration center. The slumped postures and shuffling steps caught my attention, as I was accustomed to the look of the country folk back home during this time, how the elements showed in their faces – deep lines and a rough texture from working in the sun, heat, cold, and having little heat in their homes. However, the harshness on the faces in town and those just off this steamer docked behind were totally different. Coarseness etched in the deep lines of their faces along with pock marks but more importantly, the dead look in their eyes, from living in cramped quarters and crowded streets with constant exposure to disease and filth leaving many walking corpses. The stench around some made me consider whether they had died already but their bodies were so used to pushing on to do the impossible and hadn't gotten the message. The curse of city life in this day and age was an unwelcome sight.

"Cas-ell Clin-ton," the driver said, mistaking my curiosity as he held out his hand for a chunk of my dwindling funds. Another hand requested a dime for the ferry after I made my way up the walkway onto the boat dock. The air had become stagnant as I wound through the clumps of people looking for a space. Hopefully, a spot around the outside would enable me to catch my breath, and I finagled my way there.

The breeze hit me full in the face when the boat pulled away from the dock. Hanging off the bars enjoying the fresh air, we passed an island with some kind of grown over, dilapidated fort causing concern in several passengers. Two men behind me with matching moustaches were terribly upset. One couldn't believe they had left munitions there, and the other knew the southern tip of Manhattan would be blown to bits any day because of it. Why they hadn't done something about it after the Civil War was a mystery to both of them. We were looking at Ellis Island before more land and the well-known red building had been added.

Another island came into view with a functioning fort garrison and a great deal of construction going on. Conversation turned to it and how appalled they were it took so long to raise the money for the pedestal while she sat in pieces on the island. It was certain it would not be finished by the time of the dedication in a month. Witnessing workers hanging off a partially constructed Statue of Liberty was beyond awesome. The skeleton of the arm and head rose out of the already constructed robe part. Gleaming, it was a shiny new penny before the elements had a chance to cause patina. But in my mind it was holding hostage the magnificent lady whose greenish hue gave rise to ethereal beauty in my day.

Again, someone from behind commented on how strange the hand and torch had looked in Madison Square Park. Another seemed proud New York got the statue instead of Philadelphia who thought it should belong there. That made better sense to me, too, except that in this time more immigrants came through New York.

Of course, the New York skyline was nothing yet – no skyscrapers or jet trails in the sky, no Flat Iron Building or Empire State. My favorite, the Chrysler Building, was still fifty years from being built. The Brooklyn Bridge, however, could be seen in the distance. And of course, you could buy it since there were many crooks out there willing to sell a piece of it.

The ride had bolstered my spirits somewhat, my own personal Scarlett O'Hara whispering to think about eating or train fare later. Instead, I concentrated on the St. George Terminal in Staten Island with a completely different feel that of a grand old barn. Heavy on the grand because it was brick with a two-tiered roof. Its size allowed doubling as shed and passenger area combined. Since there wasn't as much rail traffic here it didn't have the same safety issues as Grand Central. Come to find out, the train was free, built for the show, leaving a nickel in my pocket. I was truly thankful to have that much.

Staten Island had neighborhoods of impressive Victorian style houses and sidewalks tending to be nicer than the functional board houses that were not in any particular style. Some neighborhoods had dirt streets mixed with sand. Others had cobblestone roads. None of them close to the tracks, I could still get a pretty good view from my seat on the train.

Before long, an Erastina Woods sign appeared indicating I had reached my destination. The three o'clock show had just let out, and the next wasn't until eight leaving a little over two hours, maybe, to do some persuading. People were everywhere, so I chose to stand off to the side by the ticket wagon to let them all pass or risk being knocked down. The enclosed white wagon was embellished with large gold lettering on the side reading "Buffalo Bill's Wild West" and on one end smaller letters read "Ticket Office."

The main entrance was covered with a large canopy made out of the same canvas tent material as everything else with the words "Main Entrance Buffalo Bill's Wild West." Just inside to the right was a display of "rarities" – a sale of souvenirs. On the left were concessions, wafting the smell of popcorn and peanuts reminding me how hungry I was.

A man with a handlebar moustache picking up litter from the earlier show hollered at me, "Hey lady, the show's over 'less you're ready to pay your quarter for the next. The village is 'round the back of the big horseshoe if you want to see them Injun teepees."

"I have an appointment right here. Thanks anyway, though." I dropped my bag at the door and slipped inside the next tent with my nickel, not enough for anything.

"Excuse me, sir." A very dapper looking individual with a full beard and moustache sat behind a desk in the small room. His manner of dress told me he was someone important, busy going over books, not bothering to look up.

"Yes, what is it?" A deep impatient voice questioned.

"Well, er, I'm here to speak to the hiring manager for the show." That was the most confident voice I could muster after almost four days of travel.

"You've found him, but we don't need anyone right at this time." His voice indicated impatience.

"Hello, I'm Makenna Manning. What is your name sir...sir?" I held out my hand to shake his. Reluctantly, he got up and shook my hand.

"Nate Salsbury. Now if you don't mind..."

"I can't believe I've come all this way, and you won't even talk to me about the show. I've heard so much about it, and I think I could really contribute something to it. I've performed at rodeos and fairs. My partners and I tried a circus once but they never quite pay what they say they will." I was becoming impatient now.

"Well, young lady, that's an impressive history, and you're right about circus life. What is it you do?" Curious, his tone changed somewhat surprised by the resume.

"Whatever you need me to do, as long as it isn't immoral or indecent." He grabbed the lapels of his jacket and chuckled a little.

"Okay, you have my attention. Specifically, what is it you are able to do for the Wild West?"

"Well, I can ride, trick ride, shoot some, take care of animals, that sort of thing."

"Hmm, that's interesting. A woman trick rider?"

"Yes, sir, I've ridden for several years. I can do lots of tricks, but I would have to show you for you to understand what I do." About that time, I became dizzy from hunger. He ran over to catch me.

"Are you sure you aren't just looking for a meal, young lady?"

"No, sir, well, yes sir. I mean that would be helpful. I haven't eaten today because I was saving my money to make sure I had enough to get here. I should probably eat before I show you what I can do, unless you want me to fall off the horse."

"No, that wouldn't do at all. Let me show you to the dining tent. I have a few things to take care of then I'll meet you in the ring with a horse ...not afraid of which one?"

"Nope. That would be great."

Before I had the chance to go with him, the big man himself strode into the room. Over six feet for sure, his personality bigger, and he hadn't even said a word yet. About the same age Dad was, his already graying long hair fell past his shoulders slicked back from his receding hairline. The constant wear of the Stetson hat he carried probably didn't help. Of course, he had a moustache – everyone had a moustache – and his chin beard did complement his hair. He swaggered in wearing leather hip riding boots and a belt with a buckle so large I wondered if his pants were really difficult to hold up. That air of confidence telling you he knew exactly what he was doing at all times reminded me of Gabriel.

"My, my, who is this you have here Nate? I don't believe we've been introduced?" He took my hand and looked at me with large almond shaped eyes, speaking through the thick moustache. Part Paul McCartney, part Confucius, and part Joseph Mulholland.

"Cody, this is Miss Manning. She has come here to join the show as a trick rider. Has quite a background in the rodeo and circus."

"Why Nate, you know our entertainment don't want to smack of a circus, it must be on a high toned basis."

"Well, I didn't stay long. Clowns and monkeys terrify me."

After they chuckled at that for a few minutes, Cody turned to Salsbury. "Remember what P.T. Barnum said when he was here, "take this show to Europe they will astonish the Old World?" Well, I've been thinking a lot about that. Think we ought to do just that. Will be quite a feat but the other side of the world should know about the American West. You being the principle owner will make the decision, of course… if you agree, then let's make arrangements."

"You act is if money grew on trees," Salsbury countered.

"Now Nate, if you can leave the Army $20,000 richer from draw poker, you can make this happen."

They were conducting business as if I wasn't even in the tent with them. "Ahem."

"Oh, yes, Salsbury, why on earth would you even consider another female star when two right now hardly get along?" It wouldn't be the first time I didn't get along with other girls. "My dear, you are welcome to stay for the show but then you need to just go on home."

"Don't have one."

"I'm sure you didn't come here all by yourself. Where are your companions?"

"I did come here alone. My parents are dead. I was living with Pa and he's gone too."

"Well, now, that's a shame." He stroked his short beard and moustache. "And you say you came here all alone. Where did you come from?"

"Tennessee, sir. I boarded the train on Sunday out of Nashville and arrived this afternoon. The taxi, the ferry, and another train brought me here."

"You are in good company young lady. Half of that million people living on these islands have sailed past the new statue and onto our trains." He wasn't impressed. I hadn't done anything others hadn't done as well.

"But I came from Tennessee, not from Manhattan. My pockets are almost empty." I didn't want to sound desperate but I was broke and had to play the sympathy card. Determination would do that to you.

"You don't exactly sound Southern." He hooked his thumb into his oversized belt and leaned back twiddling his moustache. With a nonchalant pose, I wasn't sure if he was making an observation or a criticism.

"Well, sir, my dad was a Yankee and that's another subject altogether. All I'm asking for is a chance to ride for you. If you can't use me, then I'll go away. Don't particularly know where, but I'll leave." I threw that out there thinking it was a long shot.

"Well…," a long pause, "all right then. Go over to the dining tent and get yourself something to eat first. Rest a few minutes and we'll take a look-see."

"I'm very grateful, sir." I was actually shocked.

They walked out of the room complaining they really didn't have a place for anyone else in the show already costing around $4,000 a day now to put it on. For some reason, they were going to give me an audition anyway. They continued mumbling about a lady that was in the family way. In other words, she was pregnant and they couldn't keep her if she couldn't ride. Everyone in the show had to do multiple tasks. That turn in the conversation sounded favorable for me.

The dining tent was not far from the manager's office and closer to the arena. They pointed the direction of the ladies' tent where I could change and meet them at that side of the arena in about a half hour.

The dining tent was quite crowded with all the performers trying to eat before the next show. I shoved my bag under an edge to hide it as stealthily as possible in an attempt to avoid explanations. The smell of the food made my head swim, so I didn't waste any time getting a plate full of bread and vegetables. Not wanting to eat too much before my ride,

I wrapped the rolls in a napkin for later in case things didn't work out. Everything was grand for what was essentially a traveling restaurant. Sugar bowls and pitchers were etched with the Buffalo Bill logo as well as the flatware. No paper plates or Styrofoam here, everything had to be washed and someone had to do it. No machines. It was mind boggling how much work had to be done in this tent alone.

A few ladies dashed in and out of the tent I was told to change in, but most were still in costume from the previous show and mingling in the dining tent. It had been a good idea to bring my original set of clothes even though it had not occurred to me I would need them for this. Those were the only clothes I could wear to show what I could do on a horse. I shoved my old hat down over my hair, put my newer jacket on, and went to find them.

Before they had a chance to say anything I explained a dress would not be appropriate for the moves I could do. The gorgeous horse they had brought around was a white thoroughbred, much too grand for my stunts, but I didn't argue and jumped on. A couple of times around the ring to warm up and get used to this beauty should be enough. It was a giant horseshoe of an arena with canvas covered grandstands. Surprisingly, electric light poles stood around each section. At the open end of the horseshoe was a giant painting of the western landscape of mountains and plains.

The men were leaning against a tent pole obviously fatigued from the earlier show, talking to each other, barely noticing what I was doing. My aim was to wow them, but I didn't want to scare them with something no one else was doing. I rode faster to show my ability to handle the horse, and once I was sure of myself, I flipped myself around to ride backwards in the saddle. His gait was easy enough so I turned back, and then stood up. Their interest was now piqued, so I did a handstand. Stands with one foot in the stirrup would be enough since I didn't have a trick saddle. They weren't made yet anyway. The finale was to mount the horse while he was moving. All in all, it was a pretty good audition.

They were arguing back and forth whether it would cause more competition and jealousy. Cody thought it would be great and would distance the two sharpshooters from each other. Salsbury said it would be disastrous if I was more entertaining. He feared the other two would quit. Before they went any further I had to know if I even had a job.

"Listen, gentleman, it would be nice to know if you plan on hiring me. This may help you to decide. The idea of toning down my stunts because I have to wear a dress doesn't sit well with me. Since there are a few more I definitely can't do in a skirt, I am perfectly willing to dress as a man to continue to do what I love." I paused a minute while they stared at me – nothing new there. "So, what'll it be? Am I hired?"

Salsbury spoke nervously, "Miss Manning that would certainly take care of things. We could use another hand, in general. But some of our patrons may not approve of this plan."

Cody interrupted, "It could work, her dressing as a man. She is rather tall and has strength for a woman. They aren't likely to know. My concern is the attitude of the cowboys. They are a rough bunch and may not want to work with her."

"I'm not planning on working with anyone for my stunts. It wouldn't be a problem for me to dress as a woman for the rest of the show. I could do lots of things."

"She's right Cody. She could fill in *wherever* she is needed."

"Absolutely, Mr. Salsbury. As long as I get to trick ride sometime, I will do whatever I have to the rest of the time."

They walked off for a few minutes to discuss it again. When they returned, I had a job.

CHAPTER 52

The Show not to be called a Show

From the beginning I was treated well. Both Cody and Salsbury made sure I understood everyone pulled their weight. The rules were no laziness or frivolity on the job suiting me fine since I was pretty much raised that way with a time and place for everything. But I was curious how this huge traveling themed show managed to keep it all together.

Having changed back into my dress, Mr. Salsbury walked with me to the village explaining along the way how he had conceived the idea of the show. He considered himself the brains of the organization but conceded he could not have pulled it off without Mr. Cody seizing the reins, using his past as a springboard. Essentially, showmanship and a desire to tell the story of the west now allowed us to see "Injuns" playing cards in front of their teepees in show clothes that were, of course, their everyday clothes.

Rows of walled tents hid behind the Indian village peeking out at the curious eyes of paying customers. Home was canvas for this motley crue, and I gladly accepted my spot. An empty tent welcomed me while the middle cot and trunk received the contents of my bag. Then I was off to explore the 'hood with Mr. Brains.

The entourage took up a lot of acreage. We continued walking for some time, stopping occasionally to introduce me to someone in the show or someone that worked behind the scenes. Most times it was both from what I had witnessed. There was not a lot of down time, and

I was already thankful for that, needing to be busy and glad to report to practice the next day.

Several of the women's tents were homier with cots pushed to one side to give room for chairs or a small table. A curtain might be hung between the sides and on the wall a picture or other personal memento. Others, like mine, were functional only with two or three cots and the same amount of trunks for personal storage.

Cowboy and laborers' tents were plain with the occasional gun display or risqué picture bringing character to an otherwise gloomy existence. Most were empty of men now with many in the dining tent or seeing to their animals for the next show. A few were occupied by workers chopping the massive amounts of wood needed to fuel the fires for the large kettle stoves. Others were prep cooks, of sorts, that peeled potatoes and onions used in the cast and crew's food. One man, wearing a long-sleeved striped cotton shirt tucked into dusty britches, stood outside his tent thumbs hooked behind his suspenders rocking back on his heels, thoughtfully examining me, the new addition to the zoo.

The many service tents were adjacent to the village. Evidently, it was considered a modern establishment with its own electricity and fire department proudly demonstrated by the comment, "Have you ever seen such?" I refrained from responding, "You have no idea." Wheelwrights and blacksmiths were closer to the tents serving as stables where many of the show horses stood in front drinking from a trough to hydrate for the strenuous show ahead. The barbers and seamstresses were up ahead closer to the many dressing tents.

In that direction, we headed to a tent crowded with tables of stacked clothes and lines strung with more apparel. Busily working and humming, the seamstress seemed surprised when interrupted by the type of order and time of day, yet she smiled and agreed. Salsbury cautioned her to keep it to herself, tipped his bowler hat at me, and left with an air of sophistication that didn't exactly fit the surroundings. Stripped down to my undergarments, she skillfully got measurements for dresses, pants, shirts, and even shoes. Without a cobbler, I assumed they must go into the city for those. While she worked, her hunched shoulders and scuffling feet indicated her weariness. I asked if she was always so busy. She mumbled back the only time a performance didn't create mounds of work was after a parade. The cowboys had to be clean and their clothes immaculate, unlike the show where everyone was filthy and tore their clothes frequently. Whatever Mr. Cody said was what she did. I felt guilty for causing this poor woman more work. Feeling my eyes on her, she realized her ravings, smiled and patted my hand in a gesture of apology. "There now, we all need to eat don't we?" she reasoned.

Crowd noise became louder when I came out of the tent and realized it was show time. People were milling around outside of the arena but rushed in when the noise increased. Someone was speaking but I couldn't understand until I was actually inside the grandstands. A man standing on a wooden platform, with no public address system, shouted with a deep booming voice, "Now a song about our country, The Star Spangled Banner, played by Buffalo Bill's Wild West Cowboy Band." He described the song like it had just been brought to his attention and might be a hit. After listening and observing the crowd I realized most wouldn't have heard the song since there was no place to hear it. No amateur or professional sports and, if I had to guess, the country had not yet adopted a song for the National Anthem. I had already found out everything had to pass Mr. Cody's inspection so it stood to reason if William F. Cody thought it was good enough to begin his show about the American West, then it must be good enough for the country... eventually.

The patriotic mood continued when The Cowboy Band played a variety of marches that had everyone clapping along to the beat of the tuba and bass drum. Laughing at the antics of the slide trombone and baritones, the audience attention then turned back to the man as he left the podium. The level of excitement heightened when he strode in front of the stands similar to a matador ready to conquer a bull, removed the white sombrero with a sweeping gesture ending in a bow directed at the crowd and announced, "This is an exhibition of skill, tact, and endurance by men who gained their livelihood on the plains."

The Grand Procession began. Cowboys, vaqueros, and cowgirls rode in single file followed by the Indians in full dress, wagons with mules, and the stagecoach. The platoons formed squares to the change of the music. The celebrities of the evening were announced with a lot of hoopla. They were the rock stars of the day, all exceptional marksmen – Annie Oakley, Lillian Smith, Buck Taylor, and last of all the Honorable William F. Cody. Buffalo Bill, in thigh boots and tasseled buckskin coat, charged out to the front, doffed his white Stetson hat, and shouted, "Are you ready? Go!"

The crack of carbines, war whoops, and the neighs of bucking horses filled the air. Feathers flew behind Indians wearing heavy war paint alongside brightly attired Mexican vaqueros whose pants were so tight they could split at any moment. Cowboys wearing chaps raced and chased the fringed cowgirls around the ring. Some jumped off their mounts to expose double belted holsters, drew their pistols, fired at each other, and then into the sky.

Nothing I had ever seen compared to this. Yes, I had been to rodeos, circuses, stadium rock shows, westerns, Dixie Stampede, and Medieval Knights. Everything that had been exciting about them was in this show. Since I had participated in some of these, I had witnessed bucking broncos, lassoing, shooting, calf roping, trick riding, and racing at close range. It was all here but with even more of a dramatic flair. All those shows owed Buffalo Bill for including showmanship in his history of the American west. I would argue with P.T. Barnum *this* was indeed "the greatest show on earth."

The spectacle was grand on so many levels. Amazingly, the twenty piece band played marches, ragtime, waltz, and what I assumed to be the popular music of the day mixing it up with opera tunes. It was insane how this pistol and instrument carrying pack of cowboy professional musicians would react with the change of events or the enthusiasm of the audience.

Buffalo, elk, deer, horses, mules, donkeys, and steer were all actors, as well, herded around on this crazy horseshoe shaped stage. Cowboys, Mexicans, and Indians swerved in and out of each other's stories battling themselves and each other. Women on horseback were racing and shooting, then being captured and saved.

"Little Sure Shot" Annie Oakley's choice of weapon was a shotgun. She shot with both hands, behind her with a mirror, and so many glass balls it was hard to count. As gritty and gutsy as Barbara Stanwyck played her in the movie "Annie Oakley," she didn't hold a candle to the real thing. Young Lillian Smith was impressive with a rifle while a man, whose name I missed, stood on his head to shoot.

By the time the show was over, I knew two things. First, it was unmistakable where the cowboy culture came from in my day. You could put on a Stetson, boots, and a fringed jacket and be a cowboy whether you owned horses or did any ranching. My time was all about feeling and emotion whether it was grounded in fact or not.

Secondly, I should have known it was my destiny as many times as this show had popped up in my life from Sharon and Hank to Miss Lacey. I was in the right place and had never wanted to be a part of anything so much in my life. Tomorrow must be the beginning of the life I was supposed to live.

September 1886

Dear Miss Lacey,

It was so good to get your letters. Say hello to Mr. Morgan and just tell the others I'm up North. Haven't found my relatives yet, but I will have more time soon when the show closes on Staten Island. It reopens at Madison Square Garden right before Thanksgiving. I will send you my new address as soon as I'm sure what it will be.

We get three hot meals a day and a tent I share with two cowgirl sisters who are pretty tough. Nobody bothers us. Mr. Cody is a combination of Santa Claus and prison warden. He lost his parents when he was young and two of his children to illness. Annie Oakley had to provide for her large family to keep from being farmed out. We are all a sad bunch of misfits, but you better work hard no matter whether you are Indians or cowboys, men or women, or even Annie Oakley.

We perform for thousands of people. Cowgirl and barrel racing is fun, but the reenactments are the best. I get captured by Indians and saved by cowboys. Other times I get to ride on the Deadwood stagecoach and get robbed. Sometimes I'm one of the cowboys that save the day. Even though I'm from Tennessee and the girls are mostly from Ohio, we do have to pretend sometimes to be from the "real" west to make a living.

Thank you for taking care of Quasar and everything you have done for me. He is a special horse and you are a great friend to do that for me. I miss you so much.

Your friend,
Makenna

CHAPTER 53

A New Prediction

When the show closed at the end of September, I didn't know exactly what to do with a week before we had to leave the tent city. For a month, I had been performing twice a day and taking care of horses. All day I kept myself so busy I didn't have time to think about Gabriel, but it was a different story at night. No matter how tired I was, the minute my head hit the pillow I dreamed about him, vividly, in color. Different scenarios but he was in every one of them. Some were comforting where he would be there to tell me everything was going to be okay, and in others he demanded I come back to him, his life was nothing without mine. My tent mates didn't care much for this one because I woke up sobbing and begging forgiveness.

Packing up and taking care of the horses was a welcome distraction, always a source of comfort and grounding to me. One day I thought too hard while brushing down Charlie, one of Mr. Cody's favorites, a dark beauty that pranced magnificently around the ring to every command. My brain took off and suddenly, I was on him, out in some random field. I could feel his sweat as we rode along with the sweat running down my neck as well. We were galloping and I knew, as sure as shootin', I shouldn't be riding Cody's horse so I pulled up. "Whoa," I commanded and dismounted.

An odd collection of horses, paints, thoroughbreds, quarter horses, walking horses, and Arabians cantered by. I wanted so desperately to ride but I couldn't catch them. No matter how fast I ran, they accelerated to a full gallop. When I stopped to rest against the fence, a paint came and nuzzled against my arm allowing me to get on.

Charlie was nuzzling my side when I realized I was in the stall, still brushing with something new to contemplate. The end of the show and a new set of stressors gave way to wishing for what I couldn't have and more heartache. Now, I had a dull headache and a sore jaw as well.

"What on earth are you mumbling about?" Lily and Jean, the sisters I shared a tent with, came from out of nowhere, making me jump ten feet. "Sounded like a horse cribbin'," Jean joked in her usual direct manner. I stretched my mouth open wide rubbing along the jaw line to release the tension.

"Well, she'd need a fence to do that, silly." Lily softens it a little. "You okay there?" She elbowed me clicking her tongue but didn't give me a chance to respond. "We have good news."

"Yeah? I could use some of that." The change of subject allowed me to relax and put the tack away.

"You want to rent a room with us through the next show? We've saved up some money, and we know you have 'cause you don't go anywhere or do anything. Just can't stand the thought of living in the tents any longer, especially through the winter, if we don't have to." Again, she didn't wait for a response but continued trying to convince me it was a deal. "This man we met in Salsbury's tent has been to our show several times. Do you believe it? We just can't imagine why anyone would want to see it more than once. Anyway, when he heard the show was moving to the city, he mentioned knowing of several boarding houses in the area we might be interested in."

If it had been anyone else, I would have asked what exactly he wanted in return. But these girls were no-nonsense and didn't put up with that kind of thing unless it was their idea first. Before I could comment Jean jumped in. "Makenna, he's a serious businessman. Mr. Salsbury told me he and his wife are involved with variety shows, you know actors and singers."

"I thought it was mandatory to stay in the tents…besides aren't you the tough girls that loved life on the road? You would actually have to be civilized, somewhat, to live in a house!" They scoffed and made faces at me.

I thought out loud, "Well, we are show people...but what I don't understand is why he would care where we stay, unless of course he is thinking of using us in one of his shows sometime. Is that what you're thinking?"

"You're crazy. Whatever we could do without a horse would have to be up in the Tenderloin." Lily noticed the confused look on my face. "You know what I'm talking about, all those dance halls and joints up closer to Five Points. Name it and you can probably do it there...it's under Tammany protection." She whispered the last part indicating some kind of conspiracy, but I didn't have a clue what she meant.

"Lily, remember, she's never been here before this show. Southern girl – but I must say you don't have much accent."

"My father was from here," and I left it at that. "How do you guys know so much about this area? Thought you were from out west somewhere."

"Absolutely, the great plains of Ohio, same place as Annie. But we've been here longer than you, since before June when we opened here. Had plenty of time to explore some pretty nice places and some just plain disgusting. Saw a lot of cowboys there."

"Yeah and that other shooter girl, Lillian Smith." They were talking on top of each other, so I didn't know who was saying what.

"She's pretty young to be bar hopping isn't she?" I managed to squeeze that in not able to believe it since I had heard she was 15 years old.

"Bar, what, ha...that's a funny way to say that. Who cares about that with all the characters we see? But anyway... you got me off track here. It's a decent enough place to live. Besides we already told him we needed a room."

I didn't really have another option and agreed. Maybe that wasn't the smartest move I'd ever made, but it sounded entertaining at least.

CHAPTER 54

A Tour of the Town

Lily and Jean were all excitement and enthusiasm when we moved into the house on East 18th not too far from Stuyvesant Square. According to Jean, who knew quite a bit about the place for someone who had supposedly been invited to live there, it was about thirty years old. She grabbed the "Room to let" sign from off the front entrance as we went through the loosely landscaped small yard, under a trellis of tired clematis, up a flight of steps to the cast-iron veranda. It must have been a grand home at one time now embarrassed by the many repairs that needed to be made. The outside walls cried with peeling paint and begged for a new coat or at least a good scraping of the textured stucco. It brought to mind something seen in a New Orleans neighborhood, to my eye, seeming out of place here in this city. The covered porch seemed to be an afterthought, maybe a last ditch effort to be unique in this area of brownstones. However, on a rainy day it was a useful place to shake off the cold and wet.

The scraggly peach colored house was a bowl of jambalaya. The tenants were from varying backgrounds each with their own eccentricities creating a unique blend. A very outspoken writer was on the main floor, as well as Mrs. Rochester, a big-boned, rather tall and loud caretaker who reminded me of Ma Kettle. She and her daughter cooked and took care of the place, never batting an eye at the lively discussions over dinner and in the parlor. Their small rooms, as well as the kitchen, were along the back of the house behind the large open room that served as living and dining room. On the lower floor were two large rooms housing a couple of female vocalists who practiced most every afternoon. An artist, who spent most of his time either sitting on the front stoop sketching or in the park painting, was on the upper floor in a tiny room across the hall from our medium sized one, barely holding us, two beds and all our stuff. Mrs. Rochester's daughter Goldie pronounced us "a not very feminine, rowdy sort," and so she thought we would do just fine on top of each other. In fact, it could have been much worse.

The first weeks we were busy settling in. Finding a place to put all our things took some finagling, but we finally agreed on assignments of drawers in the one bureau. James Lee, the artist from North Carolina, heard of our dilemma, being all our activities were of great interest in the house for some reason, and offered use of some rope, which we promptly strung through our room to hang extra clothes on. It was very handy with the laundry as well, even though it was a bit striped from the usual artistic endeavors.

Getting used to everyone's schedule was a challenge when sharing one bathroom. I was surprised and thrilled there even was one, and they took my enthusiasm for being a country bumpkin. According to my roommates, nice homes had them for about ten years, and we were fortunate to board in one. It was primitive yet functional, located on the lower floor. I wasn't complaining since I had no desire to be on the floor below if there was a problem with plumbing of any sort. The toilet was a very large, rather high bowl with a wooden seat attached to the cabinet behind that held the workings. A pipe ran from there to another small cabinet attached to the wall at the ceiling. The tall, stilted porcelain sink was on the same wall, and on the other side was a large claw-footed tub, the cause of many an argument when someone had overspent their time soaking.

By our invitation, we had taken peaceful strolls around the neighborhood with James, not stopping to chat with anyone but to observe from an artist's perspective. He was a rather quiet man, and my roommates had taken it upon themselves to bring him out a bit. He, in turn, agreed with Goldie's opinion proclaiming my roommates as boisterous as "Sherman marching through Georgia." Suspecting he was sweet on Mrs. Rochester's daughter, we invited her along as well. A small, shapely girl, typical for her time, she was the exact opposite of the tall, thin James. A surprisingly soft voice, she spoke her mind advising us this trip was to spend time with Mr. James Lee, not us, without the peering eyes of her mother albeit I suspicioned a teensy-weensy bit of curiosity about us.

A walk south on Second Avenue brought us through the park where on either side were tall cast iron fences enclosing garden areas. Late blooming flowers and bushes surrounded each fountain. Quiet walkways wound around through the trees. Out of the garden on the right rose the massive, most impressive gothic spires of St. George's church. Mr. Lee stopped to explain its burning twenty years before, damaging the upper parts. He felt they should be removed as they were quite frightening in a heavy wind though the matching clock towers should remain. Goldie's whisper, "Attempting to paint them must be dangerous," brought a smile to his face. Lily, shrugged her shoulders, while Jean preferred the less extravagant building of the Friends Meeting House past St. George's though neither really cared. I was just happy to be out and around with people, even for a short while.

Needless to say, Lili and Jean left for other pursuits as soon as a serious conversation ensued. With a bit of resentment, Goldie had returned to help her mother with dinner, and I took the opportunity to learn more about the time period. "What brings you this far north Mr. Lee?"

"Oh, the South is still a rather bleak place for creative people. Everyone still thinks they can make a go of it by farming." Nervously, he ran one hand over his sandy cropped hair and propped his foot up on the stoop out front, popping his pipe in his hand.

"The farm I worked on wasn't exactly prosperous, but it provided jobs," I added, taking a seat across from him, with Joseph and his side-business crowding into my mind.

"They are up against a wall with all the regulations and will continue to be. The only way out is with Northern business and capital."

"Surely you don't think the South should just remake itself in the image of the North do you?"

"No, that would be a lot to ask of those who fought so hard to keep their land. But constitutional issues were settled, albeit in a rather horrible way, and it is time to move on. For the sake of future generations, there has to be industry as well." Putting the pipe in his mouth and taking it out, he considered his own words.

"How did you put all this behind you and move on? And how are you treated?"

"The same way you did, I expect. You weren't old enough to experience it but you grew up with the results, all the same. It does no good to wallow in the mire, you get no further ahead." He scratched his neck and took a seat on the stoop, finally lighting his pipe. "New York City is dog-eat-dog... more about money than your birthplace. I try to focus on how I treat others alone. The other is not worth the anxiety."

I recognized the truth in his words – the power of money and forgiveness. I ruefully voiced what he took prophetically, "Whether it is now or 150 years from now, there will be repercussions."

"To be sure, but I am hopeful 150 years from now our governments will be more honest and able to work things out and keep it from happening again. At present, it is a sad and mournful place to be." Honesty from government was unfortunately still a pipe dream.

A week later, one of the writers asked permission to give us a tour of the city on a clear and bright, robin's egg blue, perfect fall day. The crispness made the others shiver drawing their shawls closer to them but with all the layers of dress women were expected to wear, I was bordering on hot. Working in a barn my whole life hardened me to weather but events of last year topped even barn experience for dealing with the elements.

The neighborhood was a hodgepodge of structures and nationalities. Several Italian families lived in the newly built row houses across the street and one street over lived a block of Jewish immigrants, their country unknown to me. In the brownstones down from us lived several German families including a couple of bachelors. Our Mrs. Rochester, a widow, warned us to be careful, pretending fear when in fact she fancied knowledge.

"Myee, myee! "ow are awll ov you on theese fine ewtumn day?" Our neighbor stood at the bottom of his steps sweeping leaves from the large trees at the corner stopping only to reach out and roughly shake Mr. Bentley's hand. They were about the same size, and hysterically, the image of them sumo wrestling came to mind.

"Uh, Mr. Rohmann, hello. May I introduce Miss Makenna, Miss Lily, and Miss Jean? They have a room at Mrs. Rochester's as well. Mr. Rohman is in the restaurant business." Bentley sounded uninterested in making conversation yet trying not to be rude. "Everything going well there?" He took a few steps trying to move us along.

"Oh, fine, fine. Vat lauvlee frauline you haf in your halbhausen, Mr. Bentley." He stroked his gray beard with his left hand while positioning the broom and his other arm on the right. "Not aunly her but ter seengers and vee must not forget Mrs. Rochester. Does she cauk as lauvely as she looks?"

"Of course, she does Mr. Rohmann. We had a wonderful corn beef and cabbage only last night." Mrs. Rochester was not Irish, but attempted to cook a variety of meals, grateful to have the opportunity to run the house and do what she could to make it pleasant for her boarders. The philanthropist friend of my roommates had chosen her to oversee, until he decided what to do with the property.

"Ah, she makes a gute cabbage, red cabbage? Vould dass not be grande vith viener schnitzel and spatzle? Vun can aunly vonder," he stroked his beard some more while he pondered.

"You will just have to find out for yourself some time by having dinner with us." Lily, unable to understand him, was bored by this conversation and was trying to find a way to end it. Mr. Bentley just wanted to get away.

"Tat vould be lauvlee but eet must caume fraum Mrs. Rochester. Gute day my frients."

As we left the neighborhood and the park area, I couldn't help notice the disparity. We walked along a pleasant row of houses, a few still with some semblance of a yard, turned the corner into muddy streets and a mass of dilapidated buildings used for multiple purposes over the years. Afterwards a few small businesses, pleasant to look at with large windows and signs etched in gold or black wired to the ledges, would come into view and once again a shock of unkempt property, broken windows and mud-caked steps. From our area and onto 14th Street, the tightness of space and change of scene was a back and forth aesthetic jolt to the senses. I wondered aloud at how Grandmother would explain this since she had a ready explanation for New York but anything Southern was trash, any time.

"Your Grandmother lives here? Why we must go at once to visit! What is her address?" Mr. Bentley was very insistent.

"Oh, I'm sorry to have confused you. I have some relatives here, but I don't know where they live. Um, Grandmother used to live here…some time." Well, that was as close to the truth as I could get.

"That's quite all right. I gather you are not close?" He leaned in waiting for some juicy gossip but my friends woke up and jumped right in.

"That's putting it mildly. Every time we bring up anything related to family, she turns green," Jean challenged.

"That's not true and you know it…I love my Pa, but I recently lost my parents and it has been difficult. Now it is true I'm not especially fond of my father's family, but Dad wasn't like them."

"Dad?" Bentley was baffled by the expression and miffed by my withholding information. Evidently, he was someone who wanted to be in everyone else's business, and I had confused and annoyed them all.

Very impatiently I snapped, "Can we change the subject now please?" The girls gave him an I-told-you-so look, shutting him up for the moment.

While passing a type of market that doubled as a bar, Mr. Bentley made an attempt to lighten the souring mood or even the score. I wasn't sure which. He pointed down the next alley way. "If your next endeavor is a flop, you might always apply to the pickpocket school that meets behind the grocery. I understand there is a booming business on the Third Avenue Railroad." He laughed alone at his joke.

It was a curious remark. I replied, "Which should I be more concerned about, your opinion of our work or having my pocket picked?"

He didn't have a chance to respond. Lily piped up snidely, "We'll be sure not to wave to you from our carriages when you're taking the train."

"Ah, hem..," he cleared his throat suddenly aware his foot should go there and returned to being the knowledgeable tour guide. He gazed down the street past several large buildings. "Mr. Rohmnann is employed there at Luchow's, one of the finest German restaurants in the City. Well, for that matter, any type of restaurant. Not only can you be seen, you can enjoy the atmosphere while you dine on the most delicious of food – wild game, knackwurst, sauerbraten." His eyes lit up with the importance the place held for him as he turned to garner our approval.

Politely, I smiled, my mind turning over and over with stories from Dad and Grandmother as we walked past. Grandmother vowed they would never go to the once upscale restaurant again after a visit in the 70's when Dad was young. When the theater district gradually moved further uptown over the years, it left few businesses that could survive and a lot of crumbling buildings. Dad remembered a "full out bloody brawl" between two crazed drunks right there on the sidewalk of 14th Street. Now, NYU undergrads and moms pushing strollers made their way to Trader Joe's and Whole Foods.

Charles Bentley was rather short and his emotions affected his stance. When he began his animated history of the area, the excitement caused him to rock back and forth from heel to toe then side to side flinging his arms right to left to point something out. He was explaining to us at one time or another all the inhabitants of the boarding house had performed at the Academy of Music or Tammany Hall. This fact made him especially proud as a charter member of a prestigious club.

The Academy was large, boxy, and unimpressive with those arched windows on all sides that I was beginning to detest. The covered entranceways did little for its appearance. The original building had burned not long after the war and Charles understood it to be very elegant. Tammany, on the other hand, was not an elaborate building and blended in with buildings on either side. The arched windows were not as offensive, only seen on the façade of the building, and topped with a white marble statue of Chief Tamenend, lover of peace and friendship. In an unfriendly gesture, I had to burst his too proud bubble.

"Wait, I understand about the singers but what could you and the others do?"

"Of course, I didn't mean Mrs. Rochester and her daughter but James, our artist, has displayed his work in the lobby while Michael and I have done recitations of famous works."

Yep, I had decided he would fit right in with Grandmother. He had the same conceit that screamed my way or the highway. There was no way to put them in their place and it only made them angry if you happened to know something. Mr. Bentley grimaced when I lamely pointed out the Steinway building was famous for pianos. Painted on the windows, it was not hard to surmise although famous in my day. Even so, he took offense I offered anything.

As we continued to walk along, he waved his arms wildly. I half-expected him to dart up and away like a dragon fly. He obviously suffered from short man syndrome and therefore, didn't have an humble opinion in his short little body, which explained why he went on and on about things. It was only interesting to me because I was from a different time but bored the socks off Lily and Jean.

The neighborhood, in Bentley's opinion, seemed to be a source of energy for the whole area. His benefactors were part of an upper class that had lots of new money yet didn't understand or care two wits about the arts. In an attempt to fit in with the old established society, they tried anything to get noticed with the end result being invited to a social function with the in-crowd. They supported artists who, they thought, might do something great and thereby make them somehow connected to that. Or they just had so much wealth they didn't quite know what to do with it all.

When I asked if I had read any of his published works, he replied, "No, my dear girl, of course not. I write for my own amusement, not theirs. Besides the fact, it isn't necessary. They only ask me to read at dinner parties. Sometimes it isn't even my own composition, but they wouldn't know the difference."

As we continued walking, he expounded on why the Metropolitan Opera was built. It seems the newly rich weren't admitted to the Academy by the old, something about not making new boxes. It was the only place in town for the more refined entertainment of Italian Opera. The Vanderbilt family took care of that problem, along with others, and built their own. After a while the stuffy old members begged admittance to the new. He lost me when he went off on a tangent about the cost of box seats and the wrong choice of colors in the entrance area.

Lily kept trying to walk faster. It was obvious she had in mind a certain destination. Although Bentley took short, quick steps he made little ground while continuing to speak, oblivious to her wishes. Jean tried to interrupt what she felt was rambling to suggest a different route, but he continued on with his pleasant albeit rather dull speech. It never occurred to him we might be aware of what he was telling us nor uninterested in what he had to say. He resembled the drawing of Fezziwig in *A Christmas Carol* with his round belly and rosy red cheeks, yet Fezziwig was jovial, in contrast.

"Even though the opera recently moved to the Metropolitan, Broadway at 39th, built some three years ago," he continued, "theater and other upper class entertainments do well at the Academy. Now Tammany Hall contains a rather nice theater used for variety shows. As you see here…Tony Pastor's…" He began to whisper at this point, "But it is more well-known as the house of the political machine with its domination and corruption…but that is a story for another day." Everybody whispered when they spoke of Tammany. Evidently, the statue of Chief Tamenend, the peace lover, had been ambitious on the part of the builder since the principle inhabitants were corrupt, back-stabbers. I noticed my friends suddenly paying attention.

He raised his voice to its former volume and went right on. "The variety shows appeal to a more sophisticated audience than your regular beer hall crowd. One night you might hear a beautiful young soprano, our own Miss Martha Chambers, and the next a reading from some great work of art of which I have been privileged to participate, as well… as I said, quite sophisticated. Ladies, you must accompany us some evening. " They rolled their eyes at his opinion of beer halls and shrugged when he spoke of more tame entertainment.

By this time, we had passed several more theaters and arrived at a big open area that I recognized as Union Square from the gorgeous statue of a victorious George Washington on his horse. Having caused the British to flee Manhattan during the Revolutionary War was a major accomplishment, one of which the horse had a part. Around the statue was a busy area of shoppers patronizing businesses. We walked through the dirt road then by horses hitched to posts. Mr. Bentley escorted us to a bench in a small grassy area near the statue. He cleared his throat and renewed his diatribe on the *nouveau riche* in New York City prompting me to ask,

"So, who were the old rich?" You would have thought I nailed a stake into his heart by the expression of shock on his face.

"My dear, I thought you were merely being polite in conversation, but you obviously know nothing of the history of this wonderful city!" I wanted to respond, "Not this history but if you want to know anything about Grandmother's social crowd or their arch-enemies, I could fill you in." Of course, I didn't and meekly shook my head.

"From the old Dutch Knickerbocker families mostly, the Schermerhorns, Brevoorts, Stuyvesants…and then the newly old, the Astors…"

"And who was it they wanted to exclude?"

"Mostly the Vanderbilts…from Cornelius, because of his well-known vulgarity, but his sons as well for success on their own terms, I suppose." This seemed exactly the opposite of the way things are in New York City and the whole country now, where vulgarity is celebrated.

He continued, "The Morgans, Rockefellers, Whitneys and then there were the Belmonts and a few other families who were excluded because they were Jewish." They were all familiar names of public buildings or donors who were celebrated in my day.

"Oh, there goes the omnibus!" Lily jumped up but since no one else moved she sat back down. It resembled a stagecoach, maybe a little longer. Through the windows you could see the seats lined all around the inside with the door in the back while the driver sat on a pad at the front of the top.

A lull in the conversation made me, once more, aware of the glorious statue nearby. Bentley, noticing my attention, began to tell the story of the statue, and I knew we would then be subjected to one of Lily's off-color remarks, never making it any further as a group if I did not step in.

"Yes, yes, this is a wonderful statue of George Washington…he was a wonderful man, in my opinion…a decent person, God-fearing, loved the country he fought so hard to start. Did you know you mostly see him in paintings with a white horse, who was actually grayish and named Blue Skin but his favorite horse, in battle anyway, was Nelson. He didn't try to throw him or run during battle." I took a quick breath and rattled off some more horse knowledge. "It's particularly ironic to me he turned them out to pasture as a reward for service and poor Old Onzie – that's what he called Nelson – lived to be almost thirty when he was accidentally shot and killed. Don't you think that's sad?" The girls chuckled knowing I was trying to head him off, but I really thought it was an unfortunate thing. Charles Bentley, though obviously frustrated, did not give up his job of tour guide easily, clearing his throat. I had to interrupt.

"Now, Mr. Bentley, surely you recognize we ladies enjoy a different sort of tour. You have been most kind but is there no place we might shop? If we are to attend the variety show we must have something appropriate to wear." I almost gagged at the idea but it was a better choice.

"My apologies, we shall be at the Ladies Mile directly. Allow me." Angrily, he took my arm as he stood and trotted off at an odd pace. I tried to keep up the pace, despite the giggling and commenting behind me, trotting worse than a pony. A head taller with much longer legs, my effort was awkward to say the least. Throwing menacing glares at my roommates was useless for they were a tough lot and didn't threaten easily.

As soon as we reached Broadway, it was mass confusion, the same as the day I first arrived. A white-gloved policeman wearing a tall helmet attempted to direct traffic. Carriages of different types and sizes rattled by or waited at the curb of the many different kinds of stores. People crowded around the low windows, leaning on polished brass bars enclosing each, straining to see. In my time it would be television or possibly a computer.

You could hardly move without someone handing out an advertisement for a confectioner or jewelry store. A young boy wore a board advertising a new liniment. A bearded man with a worn out hat and suit stood next to a doorway trying to convince anyone going in to buy something, anything, from him first from the crate on the sidewalk beside him. Mr. Bentley noticed some tooth polish and pulled me closer to warn, "It will remove the enamel off the teeth causing them to rot instead of whitening them." I smiled to myself about teeth whitening when bathing would be more helpful if the aim was to attract. A woman with a faded dress and a fluttering scarf tied under her chin carried a basket of apples pacing back and forth trying not to miss the eyes of anyone, imploring everyone to buy just one apple. I gave her a penny and told her to keep the apple.

We continued to push ourselves northward, but I fared no better. I had gotten loose from Mr. Bentley's arm once only to have him put his entire arm around my waist to guide me through the traffic. Lily and Jean finally came to my rescue when they spotted a horse-pulled wooden trolley stopped to let some passengers on. Much longer than the bus we had seen in Union Square, not attached but on a rail, it only needed one horse to do the job this way. The girls squirmed around a few ladies that insisted on moving at a snail's pace to show off their maroon dresses. We managed to get around them, placed a nickel each in the tin fare box, and took a seat on one of the benches along the side of the bus. It was a relief to get out of the crowd until I realized the crowd was coming with us. Not unusual for New York City in any time.

Facial hair was everywhere. Men with wild, untamed beards and propeller-like moustaches wore bowler hats and derbies. An older woman, one of the few that would be considered heavy, had a bit of a moustache as well. Small pox was still a problem as evidenced by the scars on some faces, so hair grew strangely around some odd spots.

The worst thing about public transportation, I would find over the next few weeks, is the smell. Bathing habits had not progressed yet and most people bathed once a week, if that often. It wasn't so bad in the country because everyone was out in the open or washed up when coming in from the fields. But in a crowded city, body odor was horrific. Different segments of the population had their own distinct odor coming from their particular bathing habits, type of food consumption, and employment. Getting on a crowded bus or el with someone who worked at the slaughterhouse or stables was a totally different experience than with a shop keeper or office worker.

Tobacco was an odd smell to my nose since it was not widely used in public anymore, but here it was everywhere. Same as back home, if not in smoking form, it was being chewed. The problems caused by this were almost as bad as body odor. Spit was everywhere on the streets and even on the floor of this bus. It didn't matter if there was a cuspidor at the entrance of the bus, tobacco juice flowed freely. Your footsteps always stuck a bit.

Mr. Bentley dabbed his face with a handkerchief and then held it to his mouth and nose. He leaned over and whispered to us. "Ladies, I am not at all sure why you chose this mode of transportation, especially when we were within such a short distance of our destination. Here it is now." He elbowed me up with him and said aloud, "Let us experience the el on our return trip."

We got off at 20th Street to shop at Lord and Taylor. The only thing this store had in common with the one on Fifth Avenue Grandmother patronized was large display windows. Surprisingly a department store full of clothes and carpets, it reminded me instead of the palace of a proud Viking. The impressive cast iron building rose up off the corner like the shield of a warrior knocking back his opponents' right and left, standing tall in its four stories up to the sloping roof and dormers.

A black beauty of a horse stood at a trough near the curb, attached to a glamorous vehicle, bright yellow with shiny black fenders and wheels, parked outside and guarded by a serious-looking gentleman with a matching yellow silver-buttoned outer coat buttoned back over white pants. The top hat and polished boots he wore equaled the shiny black of the carriage. His finch-like appearance made me want to laugh especially when Bentley informed me, excitedly, the infamous Minnie Byrd, evidently a rock star of her day because of her wealth and eccentricity, must be inside. Intrigued, I began to climb the four stone steps leading to the entrance and, once again, forgot to lift my dress. Lift it too much and you were considered a hussy. Lift it too little and you still ended up on your face as I was now.

"My word, Makenna. I know we have been in costume a lot lately, but you would think you had never worn a dress as clumsy as you are on steps." Jean had no idea I could count on one hand the times I had worn a dress in my time.

"Thank you Mr. Bentley. You may let go my waist now." Even though he was trying to be helpful getting me to my feet, his hands were a little too familiar for my liking, even if he wasn't the most masculine specimen on earth.

"My apologies Miss Manning. However, we need to move quickly if you are to receive an introduction."

"Wait…is she old rich or new rich? Would she even want to speak to me?" Not that I really cared but I was not into awkward at all.

"A bit of both, really, but she doesn't care about that. Now we must go."

Inside the huge store, Charles Bentley pulled me over to a section I thought might be embarrassing for him. He wove in and out of display tables of corsets and other undergarments to a sales counter with displays of gloves and some items I had no idea what they were. This man could have easily worked in Victoria Secret selling push-up bras to tweens and never bat an eye. Green velvet seats lined the counter where a lady sat, in a dress of many yards of material with a large plumed hat, obviously a familiar face. I instantly thought of a fat robin.

"Mrs. Alfred Byrd, Miss Makenna Manning."

I turned for him to mention Jean and Lily to find they were nowhere in sight. Mr. Bentley elbowed me as she began to speak in a low, monotone pitch clipping short the word at the end of every sentence.

"Hello. Why, I believe I recognize you. You're one of the cowgirls in Buffalo Bill's Wild West."

"Yes, ma'am. How kind of you to notice...and remember."

"Charles, have you seen this lady's performance? It is really quite spectacular. Why, it was the thing to do this summer. I cannot believe you didn't attend." She leaned in and quietly added, "She is also the rider who performs stunts on horseback but that will be between us." Winking at us, I immediately liked her.

Mr. Bentley coughed and replied, "Ahem." I guessed a code between the two of them inasmuch as the context of the conversation gave me no clue to the meaning.

"You must bring her to Tony's opening of the season," Mrs. Byrd demanded.

"Why, of course. That is why we are here. She has need of the appropriate clothing to wear."

"No, no, no. Nothing here will do. Only black and other depressing colors in clothes equally boring and dependable. We aren't in mourning. We need color! I will send something over that will do."

"Mrs. Byrd, that isn't necessary, although I do appreciate the offer. I'm sure I can find something. It's just I have been so busy performing..." I protested.

"Precisely, the reason I want to help. You go ahead and see the parks today and rest. Let me take care of that for you."

"Minnie, I didn't realize you shopped here." I was surprised to hear him speak informally to her. Maybe she was the meal ticket he spoke of earlier.

"Of course not, you know very well I have my own dressmaker. I'm here for the entertainment."

"Entertainment?" I didn't get the joke if it was one.

Again, she leaned forward, whispering loudly. "Mrs. Van Buren shoplifts here on Thursdays. They have recently hired a woman detective to catch her. It will create a huge commotion as she is questioned and the manager will back down for fear of publicity that would do damage to the store. Yes, quite an entertaining scenario. I saw this happen in Macy's, but in the end the manager ended up apologizing for offending her and the family, and their position in society, all the while she had the stolen goods in her purse! I do wish she would hurry though. I am now more interested in speaking with my dressmaker for Miss Manning."

"You don't mean it. Impossible! I haven't read about this in Town Topics." I thought Mr. Bentley might just pop a button on his waist coat already too snug. "She's a wealthy woman…why?"

"Probably the same reason you read to us from Whitman." Her eyes danced as she caught him in his deception. "Don't worry though, Charlie, my boy. I'm probably the only one who recognized it. And you absolutely know why you didn't read about it." She pinched his cheek.

"Ah, the pay-off…" he nodded.

"My heavens Charles, a dead clock is right twice a day. Of course, Mr. Van Buren has paid dearly to keep that out of the paper. Now off with you both before I am recognized."

We crossed the room as the elevator doors opened. He whispered, "That would be the lady of which Minnie spoke." The blonde-headed lady with an impish face proudly exited swishing her skirts and clicking her heels as she marched into battle, head held high. Boredom causes people to do some wild things.

"I suppose you know her," was all I could manage to say.

"Yes, both of them, quite well."

Seeing that I had no idea where my so-called friends had gone, we left the store. Bentley urged me out quickly saying we should take the el instead of that horrible omnibus. After we crossed the street and continued on to Sixth Street, I turned to look at that magnificent building once more, more enticing from that direction.

Using assets to your best advantage was a good lesson for any time.

September 1886

Dearest Makenna,

Time and again I ask myself what I might write that would persuade you to return. Nothing comes to mind I have not already conveyed to you in person and in writing. Yet I will say again, you are mistaken! Your being does not cause pain to others. The opposite is true. You bring such joy! Please believe it as fact. Your absence is the cause of pain, more specifically, my pain. I pray you have seen me in your dreams again. If so, you could not deny my deepest affection for you.

With all my love,
Gabriel

The next day I received his letter, forwarded from the show. It came with a brief note from Miss Lacey.

Makenna –

All is well with us but he is a might miserable. He has gone to find you, I 'spect, on accounta' no one's seen him in weeks. You take care. Lacey

CHAPTER 55

Roller Coaster

What was I supposed to do with that? His emotional roller coaster was equal to mine. By this point, hadn't he moved on? It had been weeks since I had dreamed of him.

Was that even him? His language was so different, unfamiliar. Now full of despair and not at all that strong, confident man of the frontier I called Daniel Boone. It was hard for me to believe I had that effect on anyone. It was best for him to move on even if it wasn't for me. I just had to keep on, keeping on…

Lily and Jean knew something was wrong at breakfast. They laughed and poked at me trying to get me to tell them.

"So Makenna, how was the rest of your shopping yesterday?" Lily cut her eyes over at me.

"Just fine. I'm sure you had a great time, too, after you two ran off and left me with Charles Bentley!"

The others had already eaten. We were late and Mrs. Rochester stopped pouring coffee to direct her comments to them. "We need to have an understanding here. You were allowed to stay here on the recommendation of the owner. However, he has given me charge to do what is best for all our tenants.

First of all, you two do not leave a young lady unattended, without a chaperone. Second, you are aware of the dinner hour and must notify me if you have other plans. Third, it is not acceptable to come in that door after twelve o'clock at night unless there is an emergency or you have permission from me in advance. Ladies, do we understand one another?"

"Yes ma'am." Lily said through a half-giggle.

"We don't need pestilence in this house because you choose to associate with vermin from the tenements spending all their pay packets on drinks and cigars in those dance halls instead of getting a more decent place to live. More often than not they will end up in a brothel and you will bring their filth in on us." We speculated if she had experience in any of the above because she was so adamant. Jean's mouth was wide open in surprise that Mrs. Rochester even knew what any of that was. Quickly, she brought up our walk from yesterday.

"We saw your Mr. Rohmann yesterday and invited him to dinner."

Her face went white and we thought she might faint. She was still so angry. "Mr. Rohmann? How could you possibly do that? You know I warned you of him and his brother." She smoothed the front of her dress and took a deep breath, turning away from us.

We looked at each other and silently decided it was best to finish our breakfast. A few minutes later Mrs. Rochester added a curious note. "What did he say?"

"Who…oh, he said you would have to invite him. Guess he didn't believe us. But he did say you were lovely and wanted to know if you could cook." For a second she was pleased but caught herself.

"There aren't many decent rooms available and you will find yourselves at the Wetmore Home for Fallen and Friendless Women with that kind of behavior. Imagine saying that to a gentleman…a German man." She was flustered all right but thankfully had calmed down from her earlier outburst.

"Considering you brought it up ma'am, I am having dinner later this week with Mr. Bentley and several of his acquaintances. I believe some of the other ladies may be coming as well but they will have to tell you seeing that I can't tell you if all are." Their faces soured. "Oh, and Mrs. Rochester, I'm unclear how this is going to happen but I'm expecting a dress to be delivered. I don't know how, when, or where but I wanted you to know it's for me so you wouldn't be confused."

"Of course, Miss Manning." She spoke pleasantly with me considering I wasn't the source of her anger. Giving the other two the stink eye, she left for the kitchen.

"You're kidding! You really are going somewhere with...him?" Jean whispered the last part incredulously. "We thought you had a gentleman, uh, at one time. You don't mention him much anymore."

"Jean, hush. That's none of our business."

"It's okay. I talk in my sleep sometimes, I know. No, there isn't anyone special anymore. That's over. And no, I'm not going with Mr. Bentley especially. Are you kidding? His friend invited us, and if you had stayed you would have had an invitation as well."

"Believe me, I'm fine with that. We had a very interesting evening in a concert saloon not far from where we were yesterday. But how did she know what we were up to? Very curious." Jean picked at the remains of her food while trying to figure out Mrs. Rochester.

"Seems every time we are in town, they get closer and easier to find. I bet we passed four dance halls, didn't we Jean, before we found this one? They had the funniest knockabout skit. That man fell down a hundred times."

"Yeah, and we didn't have to get a new dress to go either. Everybody gets to sing along, too."

"Yeah, and everybody gets a shot at a bottle to the head," I added wearily.

Lily guffawed and Jean slapped her leg forgetting she was wearing a dress and not chaps.

"I'm glad you had a nice time but remember what she said. Not only that, but I would be sad if anything happened to you or... you chose to do something you regretted." I meant it. They bordered on the wild side and it worried me. But they had become dear friends as well.

"What's going to happen to us? Anybody mess with us and they'll get a right hook for sure. Besides that, my conscience is clear."

They looked at each other and started sniggering again. The slyness in Lily's expression told me there was probably more to the story I didn't want to know. Pa always said a clear conscience is usually the sign of a bad memory.

CHAPTER 56

Maroon Morocco

The next few weeks were spent exploring the city, sometimes on my own, sometimes with James and Goldie but mostly with Lily and Jean. Sometimes we took a taxi, the horse-pulled kind, or the el but I preferred to walk if it wasn't raining. Even though the pollution caused by the trains made breathing difficult, the smells in enclosed spaces were still unpleasant to me to the point I avoided them if at all possible. Lily couldn't quite figure out why, after all I mucked stalls frequently. I couldn't very well explain horse manure was a familiar smell in any time, but constant body odor was not common to mine. Jean told her to leave me alone and let me be odd if I wanted to be.

On this particular day, we headed out for Central Park and all my arguments for walking made no sense, even to me. It would be an all day trip even taking the el so there was no time to walk all the way. I did, however, convince them to walk to 14th Street and over to the Sixth Avenue Station. It wouldn't be strange to them that I didn't know my way but I preferred, for my own safety, to stay as much as possible in areas I had become familiar with.

Sidewalks to the station were crowded with the usual hustle and bustle of a crisp fall morning. The pungent odor of pickles and garlic filled the air along with the shouts of market owners. Shop owners swept their stoops. The sleepy and unmotivated leaned against the already overburdened electric poles. The train station, itself, had a platform on either side of the tracks with covered stairs leading up to each side, entrance and exit. From the street, the style of the structure put me in mind of a chalet or a Buddhist temple, I couldn't decide which. A giant, maybe an Asian from a video game, could have worn it for a hat. The little people running around inside would give him a massive headache for it was quite busy – calm compared to an hour earlier.

Along the way, newsies cried out from around most every corner about the latest earthquake in Charleston and Summerville. It was considered an aftershock of the one in August causing damage – "75 chimneys have to come down", "doors hard to open all over town." Thirty more seconds of suffering was coming, but I could do nothing about it.

Inside, we walked across floorboards worn from the scurry to purchase our tickets at the booth window and return to the ladies waiting room. We leaned against tongue-and-groove walls that had felt the hands of many a passenger and custodian then looked out a bay window to the street below. A tin-covered ceiling lamp caused the room to smell of kerosene. Tired and sleepy workers on their way to jobs explained why very little laughter or conversation could be heard as they made their way to the train. It had chugged down the tracks with a well-then-let's-get-on-with-it-HUFF-HUFF-WHEW and stopped, all the while spewing steam from its sides and spitting the occasional red spark from the stack on top.

I thought of the frustrating day I had ridden with Charles Bentley, forced to take in two settings at one time. He was a non-stop chatterbox and the information might have been helpful had it not been so confusing. Whenever I noticed something, he talked over top of me, such as when I admired the way the dark heavy carpeting set off the beautiful oak and mahogany woodwork. The conversation thereby turned to the mahogany used in Mrs. Byrd's chateau on 5th Avenue.

"Of course, her house on the Hudson or the mansion at Newport doesn't compare. She almost drove her architect mad but, of course, he wouldn't say no. Who could say no, that marble wouldn't do or you would not combine Oriental flourishes with, say, French Louise's when you are staring at Benjamin Franklins?

Of course, I was left to wonder just how many Benjamins an architect, in 1886, would get paid to be gaudy. I refocused and ran my hands over the soft maroon seats. He had to say something about that, too.

"I was very surprised they used morocco on these seats, you know that is goatskin. Minnie thought about using maroon but opted for heavy red velvet and dark satin drapes. They do go nicely with the covering she chose..."

I had to interrupt when the connection of maroon morocco to drapes irritated me. "What on earth are those pointy things on the buildings? We've passed several."

He glanced out the window and rattled off, "Oh, Miss Manning, those are water towers." I must have had a blank look on my face when he added impatiently, "to prevent high pressure that could burst pipes." He continued talking down to me, "In buildings higher than six stories. They do look atrocious, completely spoil the allure of many an expensive edifice. Minnie was concerned with one ruining the refinement of her chateau so they decided on five stories." Everything was about Minnie.

"She has decorated each of her houses in a completely different style. I adore her mansion in town. She uses so many great masterpieces throughout. James Lee was amazed when he visited saying one need not go to Italy to study the renaissance – Mrs. Byrd's house would suffice!" He chuckled, considering himself an authority on all things of an artistic nature, not only literature.

"What is different about the style of the other houses? I would think she would have the same sort of things."

"Oh, each has a completely different feel because of the season of the year and the type of entertaining. In town, she holds balls and formal dinners. On the Hudson, she presents comfort with gardens, strolls, and buffets. There's a portrait of the family painted by John Singer Sargent. At the beach, there is a carefree, almost adventurous spirit with light heartedness and games. She has picnics and hires entertainers."

"I thought she was big on society from the reaction to the woman in the store."

"No, not at all. That is a game to her. She actually ridicules her position. Who and what has she done to be so important? She is great at nothing with a lot of other nobodies, she often says."

My grandmother came to my mind as the opposite. A perfect example of nobody who thought she was somebody because she had always been told so. Therefore, being somebody, she had to make sure everyone else knew it and took hers as the last word on everything.

"Charles, where did you learn all this about design and decorating?"

Hesitating, a bit flustered, he informed me of his keen eye for the finer things in life. Evidently, that was true. My stomach growled and I realized I was either nauseous or hungry.

Lily and Jean had been chatting about their usual adventures and didn't seem to notice I had no idea what they were talking about. My mind had become cluttered, tired of being jostled about, we had been riding for a much longer time than I imagined it would take due to the stops at every station.

They were giggling and pointing at a building with a flag on top reading Koster &Bial's. The building was a familiar style, similar to Tammany. They mentioned something about a concert hall.

"You should have been there Makenna."

"She wouldn't like that…it's burlesque." Several women turned around to stare at my friends and whisper to each other. Burlesque was, I presumed, provocative.

"You are going to get yourselves arrested. Your elevator definitely doesn't go to the top." I worried as soon as it came out of my mouth if they knew what an elevator was.

"What? AHHHHHHH, that's funny! You know Jean won't even get on one of them…says they make her sick and if we were meant to go up fast we would have wings." Jean elbowed Lily, furious to be thought of as a scaredy-cat. "But how would you know what that is country girl?" Lily challenged.

"What on earth does that even mean?" she questioned loudly, before slapping her head. "Oh, I get it!"

"He who laughs last thinks slowest." She didn't notice my evasion in view of the fact we had arrived at the 58th Street station, the end of the line, where we grabbed the mass of baskets and wraps we needed for our lunch in the park.

CHAPTER 57

First Names

It had been a long morning of walking and riding, worth it if only for seeing the huge difference in the park of the 1880's. The roads were recognizable, if you could call them that, only because of the bridges and arches that crossed. Flowering bushes and trees had opened up small nooks when someone had the bright idea to make faster roadways and chop them down. Many were deeply rutted, winding around into muddy paths, often surrounded by any remaining unattended shrubbery and flower gardens, in or out of season. Recent rains must have helped the dry, dustiness of the open spaces. Every now and then I would be pleasantly surprised by a fountain or stream.

It seems this park was similar to the climate – cyclical in nature and greatly affected by political winds. As I looked at it now, it was mostly neglected. Jean mentioned, again with a whisper, Tammany didn't care two hoots about the park. Grandmother remembered the removal of the sheep during the Depression so they wouldn't be eaten. In an off-hand comment she tossed out once, candidates used the park for campaigns when they needed an issue. That was only when citizens weren't absorbed with other cares like jobs and war.

According to my father, it became a place to protest, first war, and then civilized society in general, becoming unkempt and dangerous in the 1970's. He was saddened to see those who were troubled use the park to hide their destructive behaviors and even sadder when it became acceptable to do so. After another wave of political maneuvering, the park was cleaned up and Grandmother became a member of the Conservancy as well as adopting benches and endowing trees. That was a good thing to do out of love for the city but Dad doubted her sincerity, chalking it up to political correctness when he caught her admiring her name all over the park – her nose up so high she could drown in a rainstorm.

The day was beautiful, and I was glad to walk. We strolled along the sandstone balustrade of Driprock Arch, as gentlemen on their sleek horses maneuvered against the red brick façade, on to the bridle path. Every day had the feel of an old movie, from the baby carriages of the wealthy pushed by nurses in stiffly starched uniforms to all kinds of carriages driven by coachmen in long, stiff overcoats with shiny top hats. Despite the landscaping, everything else was just so.

We were discussing the Dairy, in the distance, as a possible picnic site when one such beautiful carriage, a shiny black, two-seater with the hood back, drove by and stopped. An even more beautiful Cleveland Bay, out in front, was anxious to continue the journey, snorting and stomping. The coachman pulled down hard and calmed him in low, soothing tones.

"Why, my lands! It's Miss Manning. Allow me to introduce you to my daughter. Miss Manning, this is my daughter, Victoria Genevieve Byrd. Genevieve, this is Miss Makenna Manning," an excited Mrs. Alfred Byrd cuckooed.

"Audra Makenna Manning, seeing that we are using our full names. How nice to meet you and how nice to see you again, Mrs. Byrd." I reached to shake the hand of her daughter while rattling off my information. Evidently, that wasn't much of a custom then considering they both looked at me oddly, but shook it anyway. They would really be freaked out by all the hugging people do in place of handshakes in the 21st century. Once again, I turned to introduce Lily and Jean, but they were already off in the distance.

"Out and about, have to be seen in this ridiculous society. Out with Victoria in our Victoria! Ha!" Mrs. Byrd snorted and her daughter rolled her eyes. I got that was the kind of carriage, but I was more interested in the gorgeous creature pulling them. The smooth reddish shoulder twitched under my hands as I rubbed and patted. Another sign of prestige, if one was needed. In the not too distant future, Queen Elizabeth would use Cleveland Bays in her entourage.

"This young lady is with the Wild West and she certainly knows horses. You should see the tricks she does. The show has closed at Erastina Woods – why on earth you didn't go – but I have it on good authority they will play at the Gardens." She said this to her daughter, in one breath, took a quick one and continued on, speaking in crisp syllables. "Miss Manning, you must see my stables at Newport sometime…more splendid than my house there, to be sure. We have Arabians and Thoroughbreds as well."

"It would be a pleasure. I'm quite fond of these bays, though." It was about to be awkward so I jumped in with a question of my own. "Do you ride, Miss Byrd?"

"Why, yes, when we are in the country." She was a soft-spoken, delicate sort with strawberry red curls swept up behind the satin cap pinned to the crown of her head. Complimenting her pale, slightly freckled skin and bright green eyes was a matching green satin dress. It was fashionable to be without a tan, so they each held a fringed parasol, of sorts. If they used the hood, they wouldn't need the parasols, but I supposed the hood would keep them from being seen and that, after all, was the purpose of being out in the park.

Mrs. Byrd looked over at Genevieve who was hunting through a large leather case attached to the inside front, matching the deep blue interior of the carriage. From where I stood, it looked to have a clock on the outside and several compartments inside with cards and note pads. She handed her what I guessed was a schedule.

"Oh, I see. Yes, yes. We must be on our way…taking the leisurely route up to Harlem Lane…wouldn't miss seeing," she leaned in, talking behind her hand, "or being seen, by gentlemen in their sulkies getting ready to race." She sat up and continued, "Are those your friends there? I certainly wouldn't want to leave you alone."

"Yes, they are with the show and for some reason they disappear whenever I am about to introduce them to someone."

"I'd say they are a wild sort, in the Wild West, ha!" She snorted a bit and waved her handkerchief, "See you… tomorrow evening!" she called as they drove off.

Lily and Jean were outside the Dairy with our lunch things spread out on the lawn. I said nothing to them when I sat down and helped myself to a piece of bread.

"Don't be mad. You didn't really expect us to stand around and talk to them did you?" Jean whined.

"I don't see why. I wasn't asking you to go to dinner."

"Yeah, but she might have. She is a peculiar one, they say. Why she has dress up parties with animals and such! Not for me." Jean had a mouth full of something, continuing to protest. It suddenly sounded a lot more interesting to me.

CHAPTER 58

Ambush

On Sunday evening Charles Bentley escorted me to Tony Pastor's Fourteenth Street Theatre. Lily and Jean had laughed for about an hour, on and off, on Friday when they found out I was actually going with him. I had the last laugh, though, in the gorgeous blue chiffon dress courtesy of Mrs. Alfred Byrd to meet a group of people at the theatre and later have dinner at Luchow's. They informed me there wasn't enough money or clothes to entice them to walk out the front door with that windbag instead headed to Coney Island for a night of "fun and frivolity." The laughing began again when I was trying to understand exactly what they would do at an amusement park this late in the season.

"What do you think we are going to do?" Lily could hardly speak for laughing so hard, Jean had to explain the plan.

"We aren't going to The Gut if that's what you're thinking. There are some decent hotels with shows…and other amusements…you can climb up to the top of this giant elephant. Last time we went Lily looked out of the eyes and saw Paris! There's a new racetrack and we're staying through the weekend. Maybe make ourselves a buck here and there."

I had no idea what The Gut was but found out later from Charles it was a pretty shady area of cabarets and flea bag hotels ripe with prostitution. Lily and Jean would probably be gambling on something and finding trouble somewhere but pretty good at handling themselves. They had already told Mrs. Rochester a wild story of meeting friends from the show there, so I wouldn't have to worry about being questioned by her.

"Well, I thank you for not involving me but please try and behave yourselves a little." I would not lie for them, but if they needed me I would do what I could. Although their friendship was the total opposite of Miss Lacey's, it had become important to me and I could count on them just the same.

"What's the use in that? Make hay while the sun shines, I say. It won't be much longer before snow and then the show starts again." Lily turned to me while shoving some things in a bag, wrinkling them as I cringed.

"Folks that sew wild oats had better pray for a crop failure," quoting that fond saying again, I then added, "Seems pretty sensible to me."

"You don't have any fun do you?" Jean said in the most pitying tone.

"Not lately but I don't think our definition of fun is the same one." I couldn't begin to explain how much I loved trail riding or watching old movies – things they couldn't comprehend. But I was willing to settle for live theater of the time period I had been placed in and hoped it might be a substitute for the things I loved in mine.

A typical season opener according to Charles, sold out with standing room only left. Flowers were everywhere, as we entered, and the scent permeated every pore. Only the gorgeous colors of the ladies' gowns, including my own, rivaled the aesthetic quality. We crossed the red carpet of the lobby and were greeted by two gentlemen.

"Ah, Mr. Bentley, so glad you were able to attend our little event tonight and bring a guest. Is this the lady that performs with the Wild West?" I looked down, only slightly, at the stocky man but was immediately grabbed by the expression in his eyes, reminding me of Pa. Blinking the sadness away, my eyes caught onto something else, big gold buttons with diamonds, twinkling brighter than his eyes, in the shape of the letter P fastening his sleeves.

"Mr. Tony Pastor, I have the pleasure of introducing you to Miss Makenna Manning. Miss Manning, Mr. Pastor. Miss Manning is indeed a member of the show." Charles had changed his tone from condescending to authoritative, now the expert on me.

I smiled the half-nod, remembering to keep my hand to myself this time. "How very nice to meet you…" I knew his name from somewhere, a tune running around in my head, but I couldn't quite place where.

Something of a ringmaster, he stood in this grand lobby with his swallowtail coat and riding boots briefly twisting the corner of his salt and pepper moustache. All he needed was a silk hat.

"Are you quite comfortable at Mrs. Rochester's?" Rather than gazing around the room at everyone coming in, he kept his attention on me and the question at hand, confusing me.

"Why yes, just fine...why do you ask?"

"Mr. Pastor owns the house, of course. It is such a grand gesture to artists," Charles said in his best imitation of Grandmother yet.

"Well, I wasn't aware but I thank you for your kindness."

"Please, enjoy the show." He turned away. As far as I could see, he tried to greet each guest, giving them the same personal attention. While I was contemplating the impressive man I had met, my elbow was used as the rudder on a boat to cross the lobby and ascend the staircase, to find Mrs. Alfred Byrd. There, along with her daughter, in plush box seats she waited impatiently.

"My goodness Charles, what took you so long? There's always something exciting at Tony Pastor's!" Mrs. Byrd sparkled with anticipation. "Hello, my dear. You remember my daughter, Genevieve?"

"We'll join the Astors at Tony Pastor's...that's it!" I blurted out, relieved I remembered his name from a song in "Hello Dolly."

"I don't know which Astors you are speaking of, but *the* Mrs. Astor would not be caught dead here. She only left the Academy because the opera went to the Metropolitan. It was rather fun watching her grovel for a box there." Mrs. Byrd loved a good story on someone who took themselves too seriously.

Charles Bentley was staring at me, angrily. "Why you said nothing of New York society when I showed you the City that day. You acted as if you had never heard of them."

Before I had the chance to defend myself, Genevieve cut in. "My goodness Charles, it wasn't as if Caroline Astor snubbed you for a party. Miss Manning overheard something...probably a laughing song from Jolly Nash. Anyway, why would you expect someone from Tennessee to know about our social society?"

"Why, I wasn't aware, I assumed you were from Ohio..."

"You're liable to swallow a fly if you don't close your mouth soon," I teased.

"Charles enjoys pretending he knows all of high society," Genevieve whispered to me, "Don't take him too seriously." She then turned to her mother excitedly, "Are the gentlemen with Mr. Belmont those we dined with? I'm sure they are Mother!"

"Genevieve has to know the identity of any man of consequence... for potential matrimony," Mrs. Byrd tittered. By the time we turned to look, our vision was blocked by a rather large woman with an equally large hat. "Oh well, I do not know but I will before the night is through," she said assuredly.

The scent continued to swirl from the floral arrangements on the stage and around our box where velvety draping hung with Mr. Pastor's initials on them. All the colors of the room from the luxurious drop curtain to the swirled walls competed for finest. My fingers felt the elegant material covering my legs.

"Mrs. Byrd, thank you so much for this lovely dress." Shortly after we met, she had sent a seamstress over with nothing but a measuring tape and swatches. It fit me perfectly.

"Peacock blue is a good color for you...call me Minnie." She, evidently, got pleasure out of doing things for people but didn't want to dwell on it. "You met Tony downstairs. He and his lovely wife are going to join us to dine later. What a couple, they are. She is such a support to him even though she was an actress in her own right before they married...and he, why, you have to ask to get anything out of him, all modesty...good horse sense though...I like a man with good hard horse sense...not all dandified airs you see in most of these theater folk."

Applause erupted as the show began and continued enthusiastically for every act then rewarded with an encore. Variety definitely described the acts beginning with a ballroom dancing couple and a serious song from a female singer. The comedians surprised me, one after another, with songs, skits, or rhymes poking fun at the odd or peculiar of every different culture in the city at that time. The PC police of my time would have shut this down, yet here it was understood we all have things that are funny or peculiar to others. You might as well laugh knowing you were next and just as bizarre. Several acrobats accompanied a comedian and another dubbed "high wire antics" but it didn't seem particularly high to me, of course. When Tony Pastor came on stage for his "Rhymes for the Times" act, he was cheered for several minutes before he began and several encores were the result of the reluctance of the crowd to let him go.

All in all, it was very entertaining and the audience demanded a speech from the Master of Ceremonies himself. A modest man, he brought out the entire company and took bows together, leaving the stage singing and dancing. It had been a fun evening, and the audience didn't want it to end evidenced by the time it took for the theater to clear.

It was late, the norm here, when we got to Luchow's. No one in fashionable circles ate earlier than eight o'clock, and no one called it supper either. Intending to embarrass, Charles instructed me that eating earlier was what the old fashion was. It was one of many times when he looked at me like I had two heads when I asked, "Old-fashioned? Don't you ever consider your digestion? We ate earlier so Pa wouldn't get indigestion."

The beautiful restaurant reminded me of something right out of the *Sound of Music* with rectangular windows, for a change, painted meringue-white tinged in regal gold. The middle set of the upper level was boxed as if royalty might step out to view its subjects. As we entered the canopied doorway, I could hear a Viennese waltz with the smells of what you would expect in a German restaurant. High ceilings and the beautiful dark wood of the paneling, bar, and archways made all the mirrors and crystal fixtures pop with the shiny excitement of white lights on a modern Christmas tree.

Luchow's was packed, but we were escorted directly to our private room a bit before Mr. and Mrs. Pastor and a few others whose names I did not recognize would arrive. The murmur of voices around us as we walked through the main dining hall and past the band, questioned my association with the group. If you were in the company of Minnie Byrd, doors opened. The ticket to Minnie's company was being interesting. Seeing that I wasn't sure how that had happened, I didn't know how to keep it up. The best bet was to be myself, although not exactly my 21st century self.

We were seated and tried to engage in small talk, discussing the menu for the evening, the weather, and Genevieve's new dress. Charles seemed frustrated by something and suddenly let it all out.

"Mrs. Byrd, I do believe the patrons of this establishment are concerned we have a Southerner with us," Charles said in a low voice having only recently learned this information himself.

"Charles Bentley...she doesn't have some sort of disease...she's a new guest. Besides, it's been over twenty years since the war. Why should they care? We won."

"Cornelius Vanderbilt married a woman from Alabama, not a Knickerbocker, but his mistress was Tennessee something or other," Minnie Byrd mumbled some odd information to herself loudly while the buzzing between them continued.

"Yes, you are correct on the second marriage, but the mistress was from Ohio," Charles said condescendingly then added, "where I thought Miss Manning was from."

"Hmm, was she a suffragette?" Genevieve contemplated.

I was incensed over how flippant they were. Minnie looked at me, I assumed, waiting for my response. Inasmuch as she left the opening, I took it.

"With respect for my companions, I don't think anyone won. We all lost loved ones." I did my best to keep a civil tone.

"The South had slaves, starting the whole thing." Charles fumed with as much indignation as one of the Tarlton twins in *Gone with the Wind*, wrong side, though.

"You cannot blame the South alone, or its people, for the evils of this century. Most people didn't even own slaves. Have you forgotten your own New York, as well as other states in the North, had slaves – the Irish, then the Africans?"

"That was a long time ago. It was stopped nigh-on eighty years," he huffed. His holier-than-thou attitude tripped my switch.

"But it happened here, too, didn't it? And when they stopped, they weren't freed here but exported for cold cash. Why, New York continued to make money from the trade until just before the war, in shipping slaves to other places. How do you think the industrial base got its money?" Breathing deeply, I made myself stop.

"Charles Bentley, you know Miss Manning is considered a curiosity because she is from the South. She will probably be at the top of the list to be invited to the next Old South party," Genevieve added trying to downplay what she had started. Oddly enough, it was a new fad to have garden parties imitating the look of a plantation and things Southern. Poor Sherman found the fascination New Yorker's had for Dixie during this time period repugnant after his efforts to snuff it out. Wryly, I smiled to myself at the irony.

"Please forgive me if I have insulted you but that is not my intention. I think we can agree that slavery was and continues to be wrong, but most of the issues were the same as in the War for Independence – unequal taxation, driving up prices on goods for ordinary people, the dishonesty of government." Shuddering, I realized I was describing what was happening over a hundred years from now. With every word I knew it was bound to happen again. "You went through a lot in this city, rioting and lynching…the mishandling of the whole thing still angers me. I distrust any government, of any time period. True freedom is freedom from interfering governments." I was surprised they were still listening and not shouting me down.

"Touché," Minnie quipped lightly.

Charles Bentley piped up again, clearly miffed at me. "You must admit the Northern populace is superior in every way." Grandmother couldn't have phrased it any better from her high horse. Even so, Charles was only stepping on me to elevate himself. Incredulously, Minnie motioned with her hand for me to carry on.

"Well of course, Confederate deaths were 3:1 leaving lots of starving war widows. Thanks to those that robbed many of those widows and their children – not plantation owners – the Federals came back from the war pretty wealthy. There was no money for education since any tax money collected went to pay down the debt the carpetbagger governments had created. So, now, what is your point?" I was addressing Bentley's tactlessness, but I could tell Genevieve still felt guilty.

"Makenna, he was speaking of now," Genevieve said as she turned to Charles, "although I will say in a very rude and conceited manner."

"Oh well, let's see…what has the Union Army accomplished after mowing down the South? I believe they have been busy mowing down the Indians in the west." I took a sip of water challenging him to continue but seeing Genevieve's face as she turned back to me, I thought better of it.

She was stunned and questioned, "How do you know all this?" I wanted to answer I decided a long time ago if I was going to be blamed for something I might as well know what it was I had done.

"Forgive me Genevieve. I don't normally bring it up but it grieves me to have such opinions hurled at my home." I wanted to add, "And I had the opportunity to change things and failed." Hoping she hadn't noticed the unanswered question, I left them all to wonder about my knowledge.

"Being you are so informed, may I ask your opinion of Mr. Roosevelt's nomination?" Charles refused to be one-upped about anything and changed tactics.

"Nomination?" I knew it wasn't for President yet. What else had he been involved in before?

"Why yes…how could such an opinionated young lady be in this city and not know Theodore Roosevelt had been nominated for Mayor?" He sat back smugly, crossing his arms across his chest.

"Just busy, I guess," I retorted. Charles Bentley knew something was not right about me but couldn't put his finger on it. Wouldn't it be hilarious if I told him? He wouldn't think of that in a million years… unless he was in a thunderstorm and stumbled upon a time warp crater.

Minnie cleared her throat to speak. "I see no purpose for this conversation at all although I do admire Miss Manning for having the courage of her convictions. This should be a pleasant evening. Can we not find more amiable conversation?"

The maître d' announced Mr. Pastor had arrived and would be in shortly.

"My, my, my Miss Josephine…it is so good to see you. Didn't you think Tony's show was just marvelous? Well, of course you did! Here now, have you met Miss Manning?" The couple and their friends made it to our table, and Charles was forced to retreat.

While we went through the tedious set of introductions, he continued to look at me. Mr. Pastor nudged his wife, and whispered something.

"Why, yes I do. I do see the resemblance," she answered.

"Let's not keep it to ourselves now, Tony," Minnie cackled.

"I noticed earlier in the evening how much young Miss Manning reminds me of Lillian."

"Why, yes…I do see it when she was younger. What fresh complexions they both have."

They couldn't possibly be talking about me, the girl who couldn't so much as sip a carbonated beverage without breaking out.

"I disagree. Miss Manning is much too tall and thin, nothing compared to Lillian. It's a shame Miss Russell couldn't open the season this year. She always brings the house down." Charles, nasally whining, spoke as the authority.

"We all care for her, of course, but she is in San Francisco with *The Mikado* and, if I'm not mistaken, won't return until April." Mr. Pastor didn't acknowledge him. "In the meantime, I have some ideas for the spring."

"You can't keep your stars forever, any more than you can keep children from growing up. I'm hearing of all kinds of new acts. Any new protégés you are considering?" Minnie loved to be in on things or just stir the pot.

"Yes, but Mrs. Alfred Byrd, if you so much as tell anyone, I will not attend your next party, even if you weren't going to invite me." His eyes were so warm, like Gabriel's, they drew everyone in.

"All right, already, do tell."

"We had worked with Helen and Jeremiah some years ago but they have added their son in the act. It's quite charming. He's so precocious at nine."

"Do you mean the Cohan's?" Minnie asked delightedly.

"Cohan, you mean George M. Cohan?" Suddenly I began to choke and spit the sip of water. The whole story of *Yankee Doodle Dandy*, with the awesome Jimmy Cagney playing George M. Cohan, was about to unfold. Tony Pastor was hiring George M. Cohan!

"You don't mean you know – what was his name, Cohan? – but you don't have a clue about Lillian Russell?" In the same smug way my grandparents shamed me for my faith, Charles made a clicking sound with his mouth then chugged his beer with satisfaction and ordered another. "Wurzburger is only imported here. You really should try some Miss Manning. When in Rome..." He was really after me.

"I'm also considering something with a more Western feel to it. Not with horses or shooting, but singing and maybe a bit of those stunts you do, Miss Manning, if you are interested." Mr. Pastor was such a kind man and his wife's eyes sparkled with enthusiasm at his idea.

"That sounds exciting, but I must say I'm committed to the Wild West through February at least. Thank you for considering me though."

"Speaking of horses, Mother, have you told Makenna about the wonderful new thoroughbreds you are buying?" Genevieve's eyes sparkled with excitement.

"Pshaw, she isn't interested in the horses. It's the gentlemen handling the arrangements for us. They were highly recommended by Belmont and are wonderful, dividing their time between my three stables. We spent several evenings with them and Genevieve is entranced."

Genevieve leaned over, her face flushed with excitement, and whispered she would tell me all the details later.

CHAPTER 59

Lady Liberty

It was October 28, 1886. Not the best of weather for a dedication, it had been drizzling since daybreak. The Statue of Liberty stood ready at Bedloe's Island, draped in the flag of France, ready to be introduced to the crowds invading the city the day before. All the hotels were at capacity from the influx of patriotic Frenchmen and curious onlookers coming anyway they could but mostly by trains from every direction.

A clear reason for time travel had not presented itself yet, but if for no other reason I would not miss historic events such as this despite the fact I didn't care for crowds. There were going to be people everywhere whether I joined the throngs outside or not. Mrs. Rochester had agreed to house guests of all the boarders so even inside it was packed that morning. Wearing the darkest dress and overcoat I owned, along with a dark bonnet, Lily, Jean, and I set off to see and celebrate. Minnie would be disgusted at my lack of color but a wet, dark dress was better than the alternative. My roommates didn't mind my dress, but thought a bonnet was a bit matronly. I wished for jeans, sweatshirt, and a poncho instead of another heavy layer of bustle.

Much of the rest of the day was a blur. Mist, mud, and crowds of people were at every turn. "People, people, people everywhere swarmed over the face of the earth," is how *The Sun* reported it the next day. Lily suggested we catch a ride wherever we could and watch from the top of the reservoir on 42nd Street, after all the parade began on 5th Avenue near

Madison Square Park. We left early, but it was useless. All the trolleys, buses, and hired cabs were either full or not moving anywhere. Moving with the crowd was our only option and they were headed for the Battery.

Others were disappointed President Grover Cleveland reviewed the parade from the stands near the Worth Monument but didn't join the parade. After his duties there were over, he and the other dignitaries headed over to what would be called in future years Liberty Island, to make his acceptance speech. *The Sun* noted he spoke "in a voice so clear and his articulations so good that all his words were heard 200 feet away." His impressive words: "We will not forget that Liberty has here made her home; nor shall her chosen altar be neglected…a stream of light shall pierce the darkness of ignorance and man's oppression until liberty enlightens the world…" pricked my heart knowing in my day we were giving away liberty faster than you could say socialism.

Sometime in the afternoon, we began to hear the *Marseillaise* and *The Star Spangled Banner*. All the buildings in the business district, and all along the parade route, had been decorated with the tri-color flag of the French Republic or the Stars and Stripes. Everyone was waving small flags or handkerchiefs. As the parade came nearer, anyone in uniform pushed the crowds back to the curbs of the sidewalks. The crowds, in turn, pushed each other for a glimpse of what was coming.

We tried to hang on to each other the best we could, but it was impossible. By the time the bands blared their way past us, streams of ticker tape were hurled from the upper windows down onto the crowd. Shouting and singing, pushing and shoving, it was wildly out of control. Cannon fire boomed nearby. Out of the din, as loud as the sound a mouse might make, I heard him say my name. Only once before I felt a dull thud to my head. Liquid oozing into my eyes made his appearance distorted, but I was sure those were his arms around me.

No one was at the house when he carried me in, all celebrating out in the streets. I vaguely remember Lily explaining where we lived, and his worried voice asking me if this was the right block or street. How he got me up the stairs and found what he needed to clean my wound was beyond me. In the haze were his words, soothing and gentle, over and over, "Makenna, my love" and the occasional, "my horse girl."

At some point, he kissed my bandaged forehead and held my hands to his cheek. When he sat me up to check the back of my head, I had a weak moment and pressed my lips to his and held him tightly. I heard him say it was true when you stopped looking for someone they would appear. Searching everywhere, he had finally given up, but now I was here. Crying, I told him it was no good and wouldn't end well for him but he kissed my hands again, assuring me all would be fine. Making a joke, something about being in London again with all the fog, he cradled me while I fell into deep slumber not knowing when he left.

If Mrs. Rochester hadn't had issues with Lily and Jean before, I think we could have worked it out. But this time, she would not listen to their explanation of the crowds and the fact that I knew the man who carried me home.

"Girls, there was no reason to be out late. They couldn't even light the torch of the statue nor have the fireworks because of the deteriorating weather. It wasn't proper. I returned home and found Miss Manning alone with a young man – very nice looking young man – attending her wound. It is a miracle he was available and she is well today. You still should have accompanied them." The subject was closed in her book.

Having taken one look at Gabriel, they knew he was the person in my dreams and thought I was in really good hands. But they couldn't exactly tell Mrs. Rochester that. It didn't seem right to me they should lose their room because of me, so we all packed up that day and moved to our new "Tent City" inside Madison Square Gardens.

Lily and Jean chattered on the whole day about my mysterious gentleman. Not only was he exceptionally good looking, but he was dressed in grand style with the narrow lapels and tie complementing his tight fitting, high buttoned dark suit. They wanted to know all about how I met him, and why I wouldn't be with him when it was obvious to them he wanted me.

"It's a long story and I don't want to share it. Maybe someday I will but I can't now." Stuffing clothes into bags was not an issue when you had to get away quickly. Besides, the pounding in my head couldn't match my aching heart, and I tried to ignore both as I shoved essentials in.

We finished and made our way downstairs for quick goodbyes to our new friends who promised to come and see the show. Mrs. Rochester agreed to keep the matter to herself, being mindful of my reputation, and to store my extra things for a week. She was given strict instructions I did not want to be found by the gentleman, and it wasn't any of Charles Bentley's concern either.

"What is his business? He fit right in with the 5th Avenue bunch but why on earth would he have been in the street crowd?" Jean didn't miss a beat, questioning me as we walked to catch a ride on whatever was available today.

"I don't know," I said weakly as I adjusted the bandage around my head. "I didn't know he was in town."

"You know you don't have to move out. You aren't well enough. Mrs. Rochester is right. We should have come back to see about you. But when a gorgeous gentleman sweeps a lady off her feet, we didn't want to interfere with that in any little way!"

"It's all good. You know you had a blast out in the middle of all that, and I'm glad I didn't spoil it. If I had been along the whole night it would have been a drag. How many different bars did you end up in anyway? Catch any fish?"

"Ha…yeah we did meet some fine ones…" they both giggled "but we had to throw them back. Very rarely do any of them have money and we get tired of buying." Jean leaned back in her seat on the omnibus, satisfied for the rest of the trip she had a captive audience to hear their escapades.

November 1886

Dear Miss Lacey,

Since I wrote last, I was introduced me to a wealthy lady and her daughter who have taken me under their wing, going to shows and restaurants that make our time in Nashville seem small, though I much preferred your company! I have just received an invitation to a ball for the end of December. Ha!

You wouldn't believe what women wear here. The stores sell a lot of dark brown and black but you see tailor made dresses of maroon, bottle-green, and blue. What amazes me the most are hats! Some of them are so tall I don't see how they keep them on, and the other day I saw bonnets piled high with the entire stuffed bodies of bluebirds and red-headed woodpeckers. Another had parts of an owl on it. I don't get that at all. My friend Genevieve said she had seen a necklace made out of toads. I figured you would wonder why they waste food.

A few days ago, they had a big celebration to unveil the Statue of Liberty, a huge statue of a woman that stands in the harbor of New York City It was in this huge parade of about a million people (that's what the paper said and I believe it) that I hit my head. Out of nowhere, Mr. Christian appeared and took care of me. Our rehearsals started today anyway, so I moved back with the show. NYC is a big place so maybe he won't find me again.

I miss you like crazy and even Preacher Man, too. Have you found any more boarders? I wouldn't want everybody to start talking about you two again!

Love, Makenna

CHAPTER 60

An Unscheduled Visit

We were scheduled to open Thanksgiving week and Madison Square Gardens was already in the beginning stages of being transformed into the Wild West. This was the original building, actually located at Madison Square at 26th Street, not the one where Dad saw the Concert for Bangladesh. After asking a lot of questions, as is my usual nature, I found out it used to be the old depot of the New York and Harlem Railroad.

None other than P.T. Barnum bought and converted the terminal when the depot was moved to the Grand Central Depot, the one I arrived at months ago. Barnum turned it into a hippodrome, uncovered arena, to show off his circus animals, particularly the elephants that were always prominent in his shows. When he either tired of staying put or had played to everyone in the city, I don't know, but he chose to rent it. First, to a band leader who filled all the space with flowers and fountains and called it Gilmore's Garden. Then one of the Vanderbilt's bought it, named it Madison Square Gardens, put in a roof, banked the curves and used it mostly for a bicycle track. That, apparently, was a big thing for a while until our own W.F. Cody showed interest in using what was being called a velodrome.

The next several weeks would be a gradual transformation to the forest and plains of a Buffalo Bill extravaganza. Over two hundred people were in the show not to mention the oxen, burros, mules, deer, elk, buffalo, and horses. It was some feat to take care of that bunch while they cared for the set and the animals. Tents in the main hall were open to the curious after the performance and later more were erected nightly in the plains area for the Indians. Bunks were erected on the other floors for the cowboys and Mexicans. There were fewer women in this show so we counted ourselves fortunate to be a part of it and to have bunks in the dressing areas.

Madison Square Garden had regular watchmen and, in addition, Cody set up cowboy patrols, a guard at each entrance and two Indian policemen chosen by the Chief. The patrols were all night long being that the camp was over 200 people.

Six a.m. came pretty early with inspections, breakfast, more inspections by Mr. Cody and then, for me, taking care of animals. After what was called dinner, the big meal of the day at noon, we got down to rehearsals. Supper was a light meal at six p.m. and until the show began its run, my evenings were free.

Rehearsals went well considering everything, but I continued to feel diagonally parked in a parallel universe. My mind wanted to go back, seeing his face again and, oh, the softness of his lips, but I refused to let it. If I had learned nothing else from the misfortune in my life I knew if I concentrated on the present, the future would work itself out, somehow.

Would the somehow include the friends I had made along the way? Not only did I miss those from the boarding house, but I missed Minnie Byrd. Genevieve was my age, and I didn't mind her company, but Minnie was just a hoot. You never knew what would come out of her mouth, or what compelling situation she would involve you in next. The only minus was it usually included Charles Bentley because either he was with her, or I needed an escort to meet her. Their friendship was odd. Not of a romantic nature, it was still obvious he was jealous of any attention she gave anyone else, mostly me. Maybe Genevieve would explain it to me.

On a whim, I decided to pay a visit and find out if Minnie really didn't stand on ceremony. According to Charles, who seemed to always be there, Minnie's house wasn't quite as ostentatious as any of the Vanderbilt houses. I didn't see how that could be possible as I removed my coat in the marble foyer. It actually did remind me of Biltmore, one of the Vanderbilt's mansions in North Carolina. I didn't imagine there would be an indoor swimming pool or bowling alley at Minnie's, but it wasn't out of the question with her personality. None of the remaining plantation houses or mansions in Charleston or Savannah I had been to was anywhere near this grand. Yet, it was New York City and there would be no condemnation of the poorly paid immigrants who cut the stone for these grand houses, in addition to digging the ditches and laying cable for projects all over the city.

"Alfred Byrd died two years ago but you would think it was yesterday the way people think I should act. From all that nonsense about wearing black to taking care of my horses, one would think they had nothing else to occupy themselves with but my affairs." Managing the fortune her husband had made with the railroad and the few dollars she had brought to the marriage had not been difficult. From the looks of it, she was doing fine.

"Now Minnie, you know we all just want the best for you. It's a miracle you didn't catch cold on the yacht. We could have all stayed at the chateau and had a marvelous party after the parade went by. I never saw so many marvelous costumes though I do believe the mansions could have decorated a little more maybe a banner draped from the upstairs windows or some garland wrapped at the door, in addition to the costumes and flag waving." Charles was rocking back and forth as he spoke.

"It should have been a wonderful day, Makenna. Genevieve expected to meet her gentlemen friend, but the fog was so thick in the harbor they were separated. Wasn't it a fine thing we had to sail out to see the dedication to this grand lady when there were very few ladies invited onto Bedloe's Island? Granted, I was much more comfortable than any of them, to be sure, but it's the principle of the thing."

It had been several weeks since I had seen them, and we were all catching up. Charles was dying to know what was really behind the story of us moving out of the boarding house. He tried several tactics to get me to tell it, and I finally lost patience with his nosy ways.

"Charles, the girls stayed out too late, again, and got kicked out of the house. We weren't going to be able to stay when the show started anyway. Mr. Cody and Mr. Burke, our other manager, were the only ones allowed out of camp once rehearsals started. You know how Jean and Lily are. They thought they could get a special favor. Now can we drop it? Tell me what y'all have been doing the last few weeks."

"Well, now, Charles, I would say she gave as good, or better, than she got." Minnie found humor in everything. "The only thing that has happened of interest since the Dedication is President Arthur's death. Poor man, sorrow and ill-health have marked his presidency and then he died. His funeral is on Monday morning."

"Oh my, the parade for the opening is Monday morning and the performance that night." It seemed unthinkable the funeral for a former president would be at the same time as a parade. However, there wouldn't be television cameras everywhere for the world to see and New York City was a big place.

"Not to worry, the funeral will be over and he will be on to his final resting place in Albany before you step out from the Gardens." Charles was always to-the-point. It still seemed so wrong but I had to remember only a small percentage of the population even knew he had died, or been president. Many did not have access to newspapers, the only source of information, where in my time many ignored political information unless it merged with pop culture or got half the facts from the media.

Genevieve was not her usual self. She seemed preoccupied and not interested in small talk at all. Due to being in rehearsals, the plans we had made had gone by the wayside. I don't think she minded at all on account of having better things to do with her time.

"I'm very sorry to have to leave your company, but I must go and ready myself for my guest," she said casually, as if she were checking items on her calendar.

"Victoria Genevieve Byrd, how very rude of you." Mother Byrd was having none of that behavior.

"It's quite all right. My social skills are a bit rusty, and I wasn't invited. I'm rather tired and need to get back anyway," I reasoned.

"My dear, you never need an invitation here. I suspect you could hold your own with the Duke."

"Why did you say that? Mother, you know I wasn't referring to him." Genevieve was smitten with her new gentleman friend but obviously not through with the Duke of Whatever.

"No, I haven't heard so. Don't worry…I wasn't going to make a match I was only saying she has a strong personality and so does he."

Minnie reminded Charles that I was tired and insisted he see me back on his way home, much to his chagrin. He pretended to be happy at this suggestion although it was obvious to me he had not planned to be on his way for some time yet.

"Look Charles, it isn't that far and I don't mind to walk. You don't have to do this on my account," I said, standing in the marble hallway once again, this time struggling with my coat. Having told the butler we would see ourselves out, he could ignore courtesies of the day with no witnesses.

"Nonsense, dear girl, Minnie would have both our heads if I let you go in this manner. It won't take two minutes to get you there in her cabriolet. See it is ready."

As we trotted down the street I decided to find out for myself what was with his dislike of me.

"Charles, I know you don't care for me, and I can't believe it's the Southern thing."

"Oh dear, you are very direct aren't you? But it's really none of your business."

"Well, yes, I am but how is it not my business? I'm very sorry if I have offended you but you must know by now if you insult my friends or my home, you insult me. I will stand up for us both. I know women don't do that much around here…except for Minnie…and she can afford to."

"If you want the long and short of it, you will have to find out from someone else. Good evening."

He left me standing at the entrance way with the cowboy patrol and he was gone.

CHAPTER 61

The Mirror

The ad in the paper called it a "Monster Free Parade," making me wonder if there were ever monster parades or monsters in parades. Was it a notice to parents this wouldn't be scary? Whatever it meant, the parade and the "inauguration" had been postponed until Wednesday, and I was grateful for whatever reason – funeral of a president or too much work needing to be done on the set.

By the time Tuesday came around, things were smoother, and I had some time off. Genevieve had wanted to speak to me whenever I had the chance so I dropped by to see her that afternoon.

"Makenna, whatever am I to do? Maybe you could speak to Mother. It's just impossible."

There was no trace of her usually cheerful self. I'd never seen her so miserable and all because Minnie wanted her to marry the Duke of Whatever in England. She had been keen on the idea until she met one of the men that bought the new horses. Minnie liked him fine. Even so, he had no money and neither did the Duke, only the title. Genevieve wrongly thought I had some persuasive powers. Although I had no idea what to say, I promised I would try when I had the time. Someone I used to know had that ability. I only knew how to ride a horse. Who doesn't know how to do that?

It seemed no time until we were marching up Madison Avenue to 42nd and on to 5th past the Alfred Byrd residence, all of whom were out waving and clapping, servants and residents alike. It was surprising how many were out and about on a Wednesday morning at 10:30 a.m. Businessmen and boys, women and families were wrapped and ready for the parade. The girls and I were sandwiched between the rows of cowboys in hats and chaps along with the highly painted, feathered Indians. On a beautiful paint, something else to remind me of Gabriel, the wind whipped at the fringe on my blouse as I waved. My cowboy hat was more a cross between that and a sombrero, tall yet wide and rounded. Even though I had to wear a skirt, it was ankle length and thankfully, no bustle. The only thing similar to the Christmas parades I rode in as a child was that I was on a horse. It was a street of people for the crowds didn't stand on the curb and watch but walked along side us at many points, excited to be part of something. Advertising "Buffalo Bill's Wild West," a large arch, decorated in garlands and flags, awaited us as we made our way down Broadway.

All week, Lily and Jean thought attendance might be low due to the draftiness of the building and, being the winter season, the possible travel complications. Instead, I thought it would be that half of New York had already seen the Staten Island shows. The locals quickly put both theories to rest proving New Yorkers are a hardy and determined bunch when entertainment is involved. More than 5,000 turned out for opening night. The advertisement for the New York Tribune had certainly set the bar high.

"Inauguration of the most stupendous and in every respect, grandest, most unique, thrilling, sensational, perfect and superbly artistic and realistic exhibition ever seen or attempted in the metropolis of America."

If anyone could live up to that billing, it was William F. Cody, and anyone associated with the Wild West had sure better try. On opening night, with whoops and yells, the mass of Indians, cowboys, vaqueros, and girl riders entered and gave it their best shot. Forming lines then crossing into circles, each group rode with the precision only years of experience and weeks of practice could demonstrate. Stage lights electrified everything in the Garden and such a spectacle had not been seen since the illuminating of the State of Liberty a month before.

It was during our section's performance we locked eyes. Flipping side to side on horseback, I felt his gaze. It burned across the seats, across the prairie, and burned another hole in my heart. When I stood, when I flipped, when I was right side up and upside down, I could not release the hold of his eyes.

As we left the arena, Buffalo Bill and Annie Oakley each came out performing to the roar of the crowd. It was a show unlike any other even though Mr. Cody did not like to refer to the Wild West as a show. Nevertheless, I think he could have made an exception this time. The "Dawn of Civilization" was much more theater than anything else as the arena was transformed into primeval forests then windswept plains. The four acts were narrated in such a way that the scene changes were as exciting and tempestuous as the final scene – a tornado created with elaborate special effects.

How I tried not to look at anyone but Buffalo Bill when I came back on in the cattle ranch scene. I even pulled my hat down further over my eyes, something that wasn't out of character for a cowboy trying to round up attacking Indians. It made me crazy and with each beat of my heart I heard, "Look-look, look-look…" until I couldn't stand it. Jerking my head around to see him talking to the red-headed beauty Victoria Genevieve Byrd, I lost my balance and tumbled into the dirt.

The crowd gasped to see me rolling around in the dirt then rolling over and back up to my feet. Grabbing to secure my hat, I whistled for the paint, and, thankfully, he obeyed my cue despite the noise and confusion of the scene. A quick side stunt and I was back in the saddle again, *a la* Gene Autry. The applauding audience wasn't sure if that was part of the act or not. Had I lost my hat, it would have caused a myriad of problems the least of which was whether I had fallen.

When the final scene of the mining camp came around, I was in a stagecoach screaming for my life as the helpless female. It was much more fun to play the demanding, vicious robbers, but I was glad after the performance that it had been my turn to play the prairie Madonna. When the tornado flattened the town, I escaped to my bunk to alleviate the agony that had welled up in every part of my body.

"Makenna, there you are. Oh my goodness, you have to get a hold of yourself. They are downstairs asking for you to come down. Mr. Cody is talking to them and everything." Lily and Jean were in shock seeing me cry my eyes out.

"Here, wipe your face and put your dress back on. Lily, go tell them she's on her way. Stop it, don't you dare let them see you like that. Do you hear? No man is worth that kind of agony…I don't care what happened or whose fault it is. You straighten up here. Come on now, it'll be okay."

Jean's harsh words could have easily been my Mom's. The same meaning but with a "hush now" or a "Shhhh, sweetie." They were both right. I couldn't let them see me this way, and I couldn't refuse to come down. Honking my nose like a semi, I threw on a dress and tried to fix my eyes, not very convincingly. Nonetheless, it was the best I could do.

Mr. Salsbury grabbed me first, introducing me to some businessmen, one of whom owned the racetrack where the Belmont Stakes were run. At any other time, this would have thrilled me, but tonight all I could manage to do was thank him for his kind words and promise to come watch the horses sometime.

Before I reached Minnie's clan, Goldie and James Lee from the boarding house caught up with me. Their congratulations and excitement at being out together gave me the extra boost I needed. They were so sweet together, yet the real shocker was Mr. Rohman accompanying Mrs. Rochester.

"Mr. Rohmann, I am so glad to see you here. If I ever make it to Luchow's again, you must come and speak to me!"

"Ah, Miss Manning, tat vouldn't be a guut ting to do but I know you mean vell. Vee must go now…and get teese sweet ladies ter home."

James Lee, my friend from North Carolina, leaned over and whispered, "Remember, it was horrible. Still and all, we have to move on." Goldie looked suspiciously while he shook my hand then took my hand as well. Before I had finished goodbyes to my friends, Charles Bentley had my elbow turning me to meet someone.

"Miss Manning, I would like to introduce you to an admirer of yours, General William Tecumseh Sherman. General Sherman…Miss Makenna Manning." Charles practically pushed other admirers away to get my reaction at what he thought to be a great nemesis.

It was definitely Uncle Billy, as his men called him, not imposing at all though tall. Dressed in typical black-tie formal wear for the times, he was thin and rather stiff. Sporting a white beard, he had surprisingly dark hair just slightly edged in gray. The many wrinkles on his face moved with the motion of speaking, and only then did he give off any air of command, his light hazel eyes penetrating my way. Constricted from the many years of asthma, his voice was hoarse, yet it didn't matter. I didn't comprehend any meaning. Oddly, all I could think of was how trapped he was by fame, for the people all around us were trying to get close to him.

Everywhere he went someone wanted something from him, whether it was a donation for a fellow soldier's statue or one of his soldiers, down on his luck. In numerous articles and books, he not only had to defend his actions to those that suffered needlessly at his hands but to other generals that contradicted his memories. Never able to get the tune of *Marching through Georgia* out of his head, it was played at countless dinners and ceremonies.

Bentley stood, eager to see me explode but I seriously disappointed him. Another well-researched yet misplaced paper I wrote came flooding back to me. Whether he was jilted by a Southern belle or not is debated but not long after his return from military duty in South Carolina he married a girl he grew up with, a supposedly, deeply religious Catholic girl that made his life miserable. Comfortable in Ohio with her wealthy father's connections, he trekked miserably across the country searching for a career, at her insistence, until war and a rank happened.

Ineffective in battle, the family tendency for depression took hold until her connections came through. He gained favor once again, yet it wasn't until the death of a favorite son due to typhoid that brought out the plan to mow down anyone in his path. Blaming the outnumbered Rebels for tainting the water rather than himself for bringing the child to camp or his wife for ignoring the illness, he turned a blind eye to suffering. Making a name for himself – or his wife – he won the war for the condoning Lincoln but at a high price. So-called heroes always pay.

Chapter 62

Sneaky

The next morning in my bunk, I waited for the sounds of others waking up. After performing to a capacity crowd, it had been a fitful night. Thanking Sherman for his kind words, I excused myself declining an invitation to Delmonico's. Charles Bentley was in heaven, I'm sure, but followed me anyway and demanded an explanation.

"What is wrong with you? Mr. Cody is quite upset with you for not dining with General Sherman and greeting Mrs. Byrd's guests. Mr. Lawrence Jerome was there… *the* Mr. Jerome…Jerome Park Racetrack." He was trying to make some point I just couldn't grasp.

"Well, for one I'm quite tired from a grueling performance, but I suppose you mean why didn't I take the bait?"

"Bait… I don't know what you mean."

"Cheer up Charles. He already has a tree named after him, Atlanta will be thrilled when he gives them a donation to the Cotton Expo, and he will have grand statues, one will be in Central Park, all for taking food and shelter from defenseless women and children including slaves that starved or died following him. Now you run along and have a nice dinner with Attila the Hun."

It was his plan all along to take me down and score points with Minnie. What he didn't realize was she would support me, and I could care less who was upset. General Sherman was liable to cause me to blow my cover, but there was no way I would have dinner with Genevieve making over Gabriel. All the pieces fit together during the show last night causing me to lose focus and fall off my horse. It was Gabriel that was one of the trainers. It was Gabriel she wanted me to talk to Minnie about. It was Gabriel she was crazy about. But it was Gabriel who had rescued and argued with me. It was Gabriel I had rescued and endangered. It was Gabriel I loved.

The next few weeks were tough. Mr. Cody had dinner with all of us on Thanksgiving on account of having a show to do. While we were riding, shooting, and screaming Tuesday, Thursday, and Saturday matinees and everyday but Sunday, my friends, including Gabriel, were seen at variety shows across town and again twice at ours. Despite Minnie's aversion to the opera, she and her entourage went to the Metropolitan to see Faust as well as Tristan and Isolde in the space of a few days.

Of course, Mrs. Alfred Byrd left a card at the front inviting me to several dinner parties and reminding me of the ball that was later the talk of the town. Due to work, thankfully, it was impossible. On Sundays, not only was I exhausted, I was not ready to be one of the gang although I would have given anything to know why Gabriel was still in town.

Genevieve showed up one Sunday afternoon, before Christmas, and told the patrol to fetch me, or she was coming in herself. Not wanting to cause a scene, I went down unsure of whom I would find. She was alone, dying to talk to me about her new beau. Trying to make excuses why I couldn't talk wasn't working, she talked over me. As a result, I found out in addition to Minnie, Gabriel had taken a position with an important horse-breeder and would be travelling overseas with other agents to markets in England, Germany and France. They had excellent reputations, regarded as some of the finest authority on horses in New York. Mrs. Byrd was paying him a pretty penny alone for his horse services.

Everything was going so well for them it seemed. All I had to offer to the conversation was that we had several buffalo with lung trouble and two had died. When I mentioned the buffalo, I thought of Gabriel and the herds we hunted. Everything reminded me of him.

Then she asked to speak to Mr. Cody but wouldn't tell me why. The patrol said it was okay if I escorted her to his office seeing that he was in with Mr. Salsbury. Genevieve begged me to wait and was in there at least fifteen minutes when the door opened allowing me to hear her coquettishly ask, "All set then?" Satisfied with the results of her mission, she shut it behind her. "Mother will be so pleased!"

"About what?" I demanded.

"You are spending Christmas with us…you don't have to work Christmas Eve or Christmas Day!" Pleased as punch, she grabbed my hands, emphasizing every phrase with them.

"Wait a minute…I'll have to think about that." I let go, trying to figure out how that would work, pacing like a polar bear and nervously twisting my hair.

"Can't you be spontaneous for once and do something for fun?"

"How about I plan to be spontaneous tomorrow?" I stopped, feeling very caged. "Seriously, I need to think this over."

"All right then, but you already have it off whether you come to our house or not!" She put her gloves on, meticulously pushing every finger into place.

"Are you having other guests?" I asked as innocently as possible.

"Of course, the usual will all be there: Charles, Mother, and James Lee from your boarding house with his sweetheart Goldie – you know Mother, loves to have artists around her – and me." No Gabriel, my heart sank although I should have been relieved. "Oh, and Martha Chambers, the singer, and then, of course, darling, Mr. Christian," she cooed causing it to hit bottom.

CHAPTER 63

It's the Holiday Season

Christmas had been difficult for several years anyway, but this year had to take the cake. I knew in my heart Pa was in heaven rejoicing with the angels, so there was no one missing me. My other grandparents probably never looked for me and were probably glad to be done with me. Now, being without family was painfully obvious.

Mrs. Alfred Byrd had been keenly aware of my situation and insisted I stay with them through New Year's. I couldn't possibly stay that long, so it was settled that tonight we would dine out with friends and spend Christmas Day at home with all the others Minnie found herself surrounded. It was nothing compared to my home, rather like living in the Grand Hotel where John Barrymore and Greta Garbo might actually show up. Of course, 5th Avenue, as well as Madison and Park Avenues, were lined with the magnificent mansions of the movers and shakers of the time, and Minnie's didn't disappoint. The room I was given for my stay was larger than the whole upper floor at Pa's, the home Ma had thought lavish as a girl.

"Oh, it will be wonderful at Tony's on Christmas night to see a pantomime called the 3 Phoites. Then there will be an eccentric dance group, the Julians, and a woman who flies like a bird." Minnie, excited with the season, tried to convince me.

It didn't sound wonderful or very traditional. Even so, I appreciated her attempt at giving me a happy holiday season. Thoughtful of everyone around her, I was sure she had guaranteed many filled seats to get Mr. Cody to break the rules for me. In doing so, others had predictable reactions, namely Lily, Jean, and Charles Bentley.

Explaining the situation to Lily and Jean had been tricky. They didn't mind a bit I was going but my stated reasons didn't fly. Giggling, Jean shoved me playfully, "If it's Christmas that has you all sad, why just come on down with us to the Tenderloin…we'll find you some fun!"

"Mac, you don't like her that much, thanks to courting your old beau. Why on earth would you want to watch the two of them together?" Lily could see right through me, knitting her brows together in disbelief.

"I know it seems weird to y'all but I stayed away from him to protect him. Too many people I love get hurt by me. He's with her now, so it should be okay." I reasoned since I hadn't had any more bad feelings or dreams about him.

"Speaking of Christmas," I changed the subject as skillfully as I could. "I thought you might like these," handing them each a present, "although, I'll probably be the one needing to read some verses while I'm at Minnie's." Their New Testaments were leather bound, two of several I bought for presents at a small book shop. Jean's eyes gave her away, not caring what was in the package. The thought someone cared enough to give her something had touched her as she slowly untied the green string.

Opening hers Lily quipped, "Guess this means you won't be going to the Tenderloin…you'll be sitting up there reading about envy." She joked, hugging me tightly. "Maybe it's a good thing you aren't coming with us…if you're that dangerous."

Now Charles, who had no feelings for anyone but himself, had been a different story. The thought of me living in the Mrs. Alfred Byrd home enraged him to a different level, as Genevieve forewarned me. Minnie had not found him so interesting since I came on the scene, and he had never forgiven himself for introducing us in the first place. When I arrived early that morning with my few belongings, shown in by the very English butler, he was there having breakfast.

"Ah, you see you are not the only one invited to spend the holidays here," he said snidely, roughly wiping the butter off his mouth from one of many pieces of something he had devoured, leaving only crusts. Crumbs were still everywhere proving how relaxed he was in this atmosphere, as if he owned the place.

"Charles, I have no idea why my mother puts up with you." Genevieve put down her cup and jumped up to greet me.

"Why Miss Genevieve, haven't you heard that contention is better than loneliness?" He ostentatiously snapped for the footman to pour him another cup.

"Have some breakfast, Makenna. It's the only meal of the day that slightly resembles American food, the rest of the day we have French cuisine. That is if you can keep it down with this kind of company." She referred to the sumptuous buffet, rather astounding for breakfast, and then to Mr. Know-it-all.

"No, thank you. I've eaten. Where's Minnie?" I was finally allowed to get a word in edgewise.

"Mrs. Byrd always has her breakfast in her room." His aloofness only made him look foolish, I decided.

"Good, you can come and help me with my fitting then." She ran off, motioning me to follow her upstairs.

Up in her equally enormous room, a Victorian nightmare with something in every nook and cranny, the seamstress who had taken my measurements months ago was now waiting to make alterations on a beautiful gown.

"Hello… it's Ruth right? You did such a nice job on my dress," I said to the woman waiting patiently for the lady's maid to help Genevieve into her dress.

She looked surprised that I had spoken to her, as was Genevieve, and nodded her head to me in thanks.

"Ooh, those pins, Pauline," Genevieve complained.

"Oh, forgeeve me ma'moiselle," the French maid apologized quickly, adjusting the dress.

"Please hurry Ruth, he will be here soon. How does it look Makenna? Do you think Gabriel will find me attractive in this dress on New Year's Eve?" While my ears burned at the mention of his name, my eyes misted as she examined herself in the elaborately carved stand-alone mirror.

"It's lovely, but I can't speak for Mr. Christian." In truth, I saw only sparkles. "What do you think Pauline?" She smiled politely while they all looked curiously at me.

"You think the Duke likes me better. I think so too, but I haven't made up my mind yet." She said matter-of-factly as if either of them had a choice. While she changed, I tried to make small talk with Ruth. Incredibly talented with the needle, I was fascinated watching the quick motion of her hands. She said nothing. I couldn't tell if she would get in trouble, or she didn't want to talk to me.

"Why do you try to engage them in conversation?" Genevieve wanted to know.

Surprised, I answered, "Trying to make friends." It hadn't occurred to me not to.

"I understand the situation with Charles, but it really isn't necessary," Perplexed, my skin crawled as she patted my arm. The friction between them was easily seen, and I didn't want to dig up something that might be better left alone.

By the time she was done putting the finishing touches to her ensemble, I had headed down the stairs to the drawing room. A familiar tune from *Ball of Fire* with Gary Cooper and Barbara Stanwyck wafted up, plucking at my heartstrings, and I smiled, remembering how many times I watched it with Pa.

"Oh, who knows this song? It's so precious!" I said excitedly, stepping off the last step half-running into the drawing room. Too late to take it back, all those happy feelings came crashing into the realization that the name of the song was "Sweet Genevieve" when I recognized the person behind the piano. Gabriel continued playing, though stopping the words briefly, surprised by my entrance. The so-called sweet one took long strides into the room, demurely batting her eyes, as he resumed, singing softly. Charles, of all people, stood and loudly sang the chorus. Minnie motioned for me to come over and sit with her on the divan while the serenaded one stood beside him, dreamily watching. Instantly nauseous though trying to disguise my misery as an intense admiration of what I presumed were Turkish furnishings, I couldn't drown out the quality and tone of his voice:

"O Genevieve, sweet Genevieve,
The days may come the days may go,
But still the hands of mem'ry weave
The blissful dreams of long ago."

As soon as Charles took a breath to begin the next verse, Genevieve interrupted him to make introductions. Motioning me over to the piano, a rosewood Steinway grand, polished to a beautiful glossy richness matching the depth of sound, it held its own in the center of another immense room with rugs and wall hangings. I was sure Gabriel delighted in playing it, if he had ever played a grand.

"Miss Makenna Manning, may I present Mr. Gabriel Christian. Mr. Christian, Miss Manning." I didn't want to look at him. She continued rambling while I fought for self-control. "Gabriel, this is my friend from the Wild West. We missed her after opening night…and many nights after, she is such a busy one! " He didn't utter a sound but stood, half-bowing, and then sat when she asked for him to play a seasonal song, turning into several, while the rest of Minnie's guests arrived and joined in. Incredibly, no one noticed except me that we had meant anything to each other. How pathetic of me to want him to still care knowing I couldn't have it both ways. Excusing myself not long after Charles did, my throat was dry and parched as well, and I was not in the Christmas mood at all.

There in the foyer stood Charles and Ruth, having some kind of a disagreement. When he saw me, he lashed out.

"Was she rude to you?" he demanded.

"No, no not at all," she said softly, looking away.

"Why would I be rude to her? Matter-of-fact, I thanked her for doing such a good job on my dress. She is very talented. How is that your business?" Knowing his personality, I would be at fault for some reason. Why would he care about her though? He didn't care about anyone else. "Is there something I can do to help you Ruth?" I asked.

"No," she said looking to Charles for permission to speak. "I am fine…a misunderstanding."

"Charles, now it's my turn…have you mistreated this lady?" I stepped to her, linking arms.

"Lady? *You* call her a lady?" The question seemed incredulous to him, raising his voice he spoke contemptuously to me. "I cannot believe what I am seeing."

"She seems perfectly respectable to me. Lower your voice or all the guests will be out here." He did not take to shushing very kindly.

"Of course, she is a lady and much too fine for the likes of you to dare call her one," he continued, loudly.

"Bartley… that is enough. I have no quarrel with her and neither should you. The past is the past and I can't see how she had anything to do with it." The woman was obviously miserable but had some kind of connection to Charles.

"Who is Bartley?" I wondered aloud.

"Minnie has her blinders on, for some reason." Charles seemed to have an opinion about everyone's life whether it was his business or not.

She patted my arm, smiling slightly. "I am sorry." Turning and out the door, she was gone in a flash.

"Who is Bartley?" I repeated.

"She meant to say Bentley..." he snapped and pushed past me, passing Minnie on the way.

"What is all the commotion out here?" Minnie had pushed open the doors, and the sound from the piano floated through the hallway.

"Bartley will have to explain. I'm sure I don't know," I shrugged and made my way back into the merriment.

CHAPTER 64

Coincidence

Feeling like a piñata, I knew I couldn't continue being hit on all sides without letting all the hurt go. From one odd situation to another, the rest of the afternoon was torture being around the now nonchalant Gabriel and listening to Genevieve go on and on as I had never heard her talk before. What was it about him, or any man, that made her squawk like a parrot when she was normally reserved? All I had heard from Minnie about the Duke indicated he didn't seem to mind the chatter, and Gabriel who had definitely been angry at the thought of marrying his preening Virginia cousin was now perched on his seat seemingly rapt at every chirp. Even Charles was on the receiving end of her clucking albeit he quacked back with a bite. Over the course of the afternoon they must have heard coos, twitters, and trills from a bonny bluebird instead of the noisy blue jay in my ear.

After the tremendous spread called lunch, the ladies, apart from me, chose to rest while the men went to the study. I couldn't rest in the middle of the afternoon if my life depended on it rather itching to be in the stable to ride off the frustrations of the morning. Something to wear presented a problem, and I gave up searching. Everything I found was for side saddle, and I desperately needed a romp, requiring a pair of jeans and a good, free-spirited horse. Trying to figure out what to do, I was spied by Minnie.

"Come in here this instant and stop that incessant wandering." Why she had left her door open when she had servants at her beck and call was puzzling, but then again, Minnie liked to be in the know. Contrary to her constitution, she was lounging on a fainting couch. "What in heaven's name are you doing?" She patted for me to sit next to her on the elegant chaise longue.

"Trying to figure out what to do with myself...I have a bit too much energy to rest." Unable to sit down, I wandered about the room instead.

"Yes, I see that. Well maybe we will have some time to clear the air." She propped herself up on massive pillows, ready to talk.

"Clear the air? I didn't know there was anything wrong between us. You have been incredibly kind and good to me." I was shocked.

"Don't worry child, that isn't what I meant. I have enjoyed your company immensely, but I had ulterior motives in bringing you here." Stopping me from protesting, she raised her hand, and cleared her throat. "Dear heart, in the beginning Charles enjoyed your company. I dare say he found you attractive, at first, that is. It occurred to me that continuing to include you and bring you here, with your energy and wit, would enable him to get over this tremendous grudge he has. It is understandable if you knew his background though it serves no purpose other than to make him miserable." Again, she motioned me over, and I complied.

"An Irish man named Honor McMurray built many a stone fence all over the South before he came here and met his wife, Mary. A black family worked here already when they were hired, and though it was said that the Irish, who came here to keep from starving, were treated worse than blacks and hated by most of them, got along well with Ruth and her family. They were decent God-fearing people, and we loved them both.

"And then the war came. You see, it was legal for a man of wealth and position, such as my husband, to pay a fee for someone to go on his behalf. I did not think this right, but I also did not want to lose my husband as we were newly married. If I recall correctly, Bartley, was about two when Honor was drafted midway through the war."

"Bartley...is that Charles?" I interrupted.

"Yes. He was such a cute little boy, pudgy cheeks. But it was an ugly time – the city turned on itself – and as a result Ruth's husband was killed in a riot while Mr. McMurray, one of many Irish, fought and died in the war. Then Mary and her next child died in birth. Oh, the pity of it all.

"Of course, we felt so bad, maybe somehow to blame…having an advantage, yet we always did our best for him. Ruth brought her sister here. They raised the boy until he was school aged and went to a private boarding school, but he was always here when school wasn't in session. When he began his writing career several years ago, he moved to the boarding house."

"He always knew so much about your houses…" I thought of the very long conversation on the train.

"Well his aunts are both excellent seamstresses and sew everything we need, from clothing to curtains. They have a natural talent, and Charles always took an interest in their work. Though I will say, he is a very good writer when he puts his mind to it."

"Why does he go by Charles Bentley?"

"That was Ruth's idea – such a prejudice about the Irish."

"What a sad story," I thought out loud, "and he blames me for what happened to his parents..."

"…and Ruth's husband. When he got older and learned, he was angry with us, feeling somehow that absolved him of doing anything but criticize until he came upon the realization that Mr. Byrd worked many, hard hours, too many we know now, and how much we gave away to this city…and to him. He knows there is truth in what you say, and that you don't want to be held responsible."

"I try to get along." Well, not so much with Grandmother. "I just can't listen to falsehoods continue to be told, no matter how many years go by."

"I do understand and hope he will at least meet you halfway, but we cannot worry about those who insist on criticizing. Try to love them anyway and move on." Though from totally different walks of life and times, her words were eerily similar to Pa's bringing warmth to my heart.

"Thank you so much for sharing," I whispered, "and for caring." Hugging her tightly, my dress caught on the broach she was wearing.

"So sorry, Minnie," I sincerely apologized feeling very foolish. Trying hard to get it separated from me, I pulled it off into my hand. The hair on the back of my neck stood straight up as I looked at the familiar ornamentation.

CHAPTER 65

Dashing through the Snow

Christmas should have been wonderful from all the festive decorations to the elegant dinner that evening, Christmas Eve, at Luchow's. Dad reminisced about the scads of electric candles on the magnificent twenty-five foot tree trimmed with carved German toys, under a holy village. Were these the same ornaments and the same menu? Minnie declared that the singing of Christmas carols along with the orchestra, as the lights turned low, was a tradition she would not miss even if we had to arrive before six p.m., earlier than we ever had. The December Goose Feast, or a hundred ways to eat a goose, would take several hours to enjoy anyway.

It was a season of beads and baubles, gingerbread men and marzipan candies, glass angels on top of tall trees, and "Angels We Have Heard on High." I tried to get involved in the festivities, but I thought of Christmas past, my past, a *Tender Tennessee Christmas* and *Christmas in Dixie*. I was in Christmas limbo.

All the happy faces laughing with holiday joy shared the special time not seeming at that moment to have a care in the world. I knew for several of my acquaintances it wasn't true, just a brief respite from thinking and acting on what they felt was a life that had betrayed them somehow. Minnie and Genevieve were the only ones of our group that might fit the category of happy, but that would not last long if I didn't keep my emotions and suspicions in check.

Later that evening, all of the occupants on the glorious sleigh ride into Central Park were bedazzled with the evening including me, tossing off the anxieties of the day to enjoy myself briefly. It was everything *Jingle Bells* described except we had two horses and a larger sleigh. As yellow as a goldfinch, the carved sleigh was bedecked with brightly woven tassels and set atop highly polished runners while plush velvet seats and buffalo lap robes carried us comfortably as we dashed through the snow. The part Arabian trotters were all decked out, their harnesses ornamented with rows of brass bells, their mains adorned with feathery multi-colored aigrettes, and their bob-tails entwined with red velvet bows. The jingle-jangle of the reins and harnesses assured us we had nothing to dread, but I didn't believe that for a minute.

Normally, a servant would have taken on this job but Gabriel had insisted and Minnie, being the non-conformist she was, consented and immediately chatted on for a while about some of her other horses competing in some race in Massachusetts later in the year. While I was mesmerized by the synchronized movements of their legs, I could faintly hear Genevieve ask if he had ever worked with trotters. It didn't matter what the answer was. She hung on his every word.

Laughing all the way through the curves and banks, Gabriel masterfully handled the sleigh sending glittering spray through the frosty air. Seeing how excited he was had a dual effect on me, first warm and loving, then supreme frustration when Genevieve giggled at some comment he made, turning my stomach. Like Quasar I missed him terribly, but he wasn't mine. How many times would I enter his life, altering his plans for the future? Another knee-jerk reaction to circumstances would make him hate me this time, I feared.

While we took in the surroundings, I made an effort to talk to Charles Bentley who was once again seated next to me. It wouldn't do any good to further the history lesson, giving him a more rounded picture of events, as he would have to research and decide for himself about that. But I could give him sympathy, knowing how it felt to lose people around you that you cherished more than anything else and trying to move past the grief, to find a new life.

"Tell me about what you are writing now, Charles. Is it something that you might read for us tomorrow, on Christmas Day?"

Flabbergasted, he answered, "Of course not, who would possibly be interested in what I have to say?"

"Reading has always taken me from a place I don't want to be to one that forces me into the lives of others and their circumstances. I'm just beginning to be interested in poetry, so I would find it a particular favor to me if you might pen some verses from the heart and share them with us." Afraid my sincerity might be taken as a joke, I reached over and squeezed his hand causing his face to flush, then held onto his arm as we got out of the carriage. Into the church service we walked, my hand resting lightly on his arm, unbalanced as a couple but calling a truce on the war of words and lands.

Church buildings have always fascinated me from the small plain congregations with an occasional baptistry painting to the large cathedrals with stain glass windows of celestial figures. Believers are the Church, but the building has always required reverence, and it was no different for me on this night. The monastic entryway echoed with our footsteps as we found our seats, then filled in splendor with all the thankful voices. The children's choir, as well as everyone in attendance, were accompanied note for note by the glorious tones of the magnificent organ rising from earth up to heaven through the simplicity of stone that reached to the vaulted ceiling and arches. Adding to this, the richness of details in the carvings of its reredos and woodwork expressed the simple invitation to come to the Savior and marvel in the richness of His love. Like faith itself, there was something permanent and abiding about the Gothic structure, comforting and awe inspiring. Overcome by the beauty of the place and the angelic voices around me, I joined in singing as I had never sung before. Recognizing one in particular, Gabriel was close by singing and praying, like the calming dream of the angel. It was everything a service should have, Christmas or not, and I left revived.

After everyone said goodnight, I went up to my room and roamed around, pulling out the much perused yellowing letter, smiling at the amount of money compared to the place I was staying. Opening it, instead of words I saw Gabriel's face smiling and laughing at Genevieve, leaving me cold and confused contemplating how, and even if, the broach fit in the narrative somehow. Where did Grandmother get hers? Unlikely that there were two ruby and diamond swallow bird pins, I couldn't imagine her picking it up at an estate sale as proud as she was of her ancestors and heritage – yet denying anyone else theirs. Not able to turn my brain off or come up with an answer that wasn't too bizarre, I tried counting sheep.

Before long, the restless night turned the fuzzy white beasts into the faces of those I loved instead of bringing the sleep I so desperately wished for. Wandering over to look out the massive window, I wrapped my robe tighter around me to watch the swirling flakes and think how this must seem the perfect Christmas to anyone outside of Hotel Byrd. Thinking of the few times I had seen snow on Christmas Day, I grinned at Mom telling me it always snowed when I said it would. Whatever snow power I supposedly had as a child had long gone, but now as I sat in a foreign land and time, I conjured up the images of those special times, bringing them as close to my heart as Pa's howling at the Big Mouth Billy Bass Mom gave him, or the way Ma's jam cake spiced up the whole house while Dad swiped at the icing.

At last, feeling assured and peaceful, I crawled back into my own magnificent manger and slept soundly, floating on billowy clouds while the voice of the angel soothed me once again.

CHAPTER 66

Byrds

Minnie came into my room early that morning bearing gifts. She had noticed how I had been mesmerized by the broach yesterday and wanted me to have it. That was impossible. It had to be given to Genevieve and passed down to her descendant, meaning my grandmother, Genevieve Alice Manning. Had I gone crazy? Did I really believe what seemed to be true?

"My heavens child, you look as though I had just given you the key to my house! It's just a broach, no harm if you don't like it, but I could have sworn from the look on your face yesterday you had a particular fascination with it."

"Oh Minnie, its lovely, truly lovely, but I can't accept it. That's something that needs to be passed down through the generations through Genevieve. You don't need to give me anything, but if it isn't too much to ask could I see your other bird pins?"

She wondered why I would be interested in those not nearly as grand. Confirming what I thought, these were Grandmother's broaches, most of them anyway. Lovely and delicate, an assortment of cameos meticulously painted with bluebirds, love birds, or doves and individual pieces of a peacock and cardinal glittering with bright reds and blues all rested in a bird shaped jeweled box. My favorites weren't here yet. The parrots in paradise and the other gold swallows came from England, not yet purchased by the Duke for Victoria Genevieve.

The large and exquisite meal, complete with polished silver and gold services, china, and crystal was laid by the handsome and well-dressed footmen who waited on us assisted by the well-mannered butler. The rest of the day was spent awkwardly moving around Gabriel and Genevieve, trying to fill up the time before we went to the theater. If they were in the drawing room socializing, I would be in the library or the enormous ballroom, anywhere but watching them. Maneuvering into the stables for fresh air, despite the weather, I ran right into the man I wanted to avoid the most.

"Oh, so sorry." Face-to-face with Gabriel, mine red with the immediacy of the situation, I quickly stepped back. Brushing the snow from my arms, fluffing it out of my hair, I tried to recover adding, "Where's Genevieve?"

"Resting I would suppose...the principle occupation of a lady of means." He stepped back as well, running a hand nervously through his hair, his sleeves rolled up to the elbows, obviously working at something.

"Yes, that and dressing. Aren't you cold out here? Uh, dumb question, I'm sure you've been a lot colder than this." Horse heads were poking out of the stalls, and I grabbed the first one, rubbing the smooth nose.

"I might inquire the same of you, but I know as well we are both accustomed to the elements. Sitting near the fire..." he trailed off, frustrated at our conversation that might as well have been about the weather.

"It's very odd to be staying in such a big house with stables and all. In my Grandmother's time it's all skyscrapers and traffic. I don't belong in either place." I rested my head on the horse's neck trying to figure out a way to say what I knew had to be said.

"I would agree. Perhaps you have heard..." He pulled the heavy doors shut and stepped over to me.

"Before you tell me any of this, I have something to tell you. Something I only found out myself yesterday, something you will have to decide for yourself what to do about, if anything, but I thought it right to tell you." Puzzled, he stepped back wondering what bomb I was going to drop on him this time.

"No, I will not hear it. My plans will not be altered whatever you say. I will marry." Assertive as usual yet this time the stoic expression both surprised and shattered my feeble heart though, in his estimation, I'm sure I deserved it.

"I figured as much. She's a beautiful girl. What man wouldn't want to marry her? But understand, and I don't say this for myself but for Pa, if you do you will be marrying my great-great-grandmother…Victoria Genevieve Byrd." My voice shaking, I explained the broaches and how Grandmother always mentioned the Duke, her grandfather. "I know I keep interfering in your life but I didn't ask for any of this. Think about what I have said, the implications. I'm so sorry, really, I am so, so sorry." The tears streamed down my face.

Before he had the chance to say anything else, I ran out of the stables, inside and up the steps. Gasping for air and afraid of changing my mind, I slammed the door behind me, frantically grabbing deep inside my undergarments where I carried it close to my heart. The note from Pa and the money would be mine forever, but the hauntingly old, still mysterious letter would no longer have me under its power, nor would I be able to use its contents in any way. It quickly turned to ashes in the fireplace.

Chapter 67

Intermission

The poem was lucid and affecting, describing his life as a challenge to honor the past without smothering under its weight, struggling to realize future dreams through that spectrum. Charles Bentley had written for both of us, and delivered a passionate reading that made even Genevieve sit up and take notice. When he was done, the fire crackled behind him while everyone sifted the information through their own sieve.

Minnie jumped to her feet crying, "Well done!" and the rest of the room murmured in applause and admiration, James Lee in particular.

"Poetry suits you Charles, you should continue in that vein." Shaking his hand and slapping him on the back with hearty congratulations, James demonstrated sincere appreciation. He had found a way to make peace with the Charles Bentleys of the world. I had to find a way to forgive. History teaches us to never forget.

Later that evening we entered the theatre, hastily taking our seats at the moment the music started. On a holiday, seats were scarce as hen's teeth, and I was happy to be in Minnie's box singing carols and winter songs with the crowd. This time it wasn't so bad sitting next to Charles.

"Your poem said a lot. Christmas is a good time for looking inwardly," offering another olive branch when the music ended.

"Don't misunderstand. I don't agree with everything you say, but certain considerations should have been made. I will say you have a working brain." Charles conceded, taking one step at a time.

"It would seem I am always recovering your combs," a person whispered from behind me, after pulling the comb from my hair, much as a schoolboy would. Handing it to me but not letting go until he had added, "I have considered what we spoke of earlier, and I think it would be most horrible to deny life in one so vibrant," I thanked him, excusing myself to find a mirror. Pushing the unruly hair back into its place, I was relieved at his words yet at the same time felt sad for him. What would he do now he had made this tremendous sacrifice for my life?

"But only on one condition, Miss Manning," said a low voice. Surprised, I jumped back into the arms of the smiling perpetrator. The music stopped suddenly leaving only the hum of conversation in the background waiting for the next act.

"What would that be?" I said trying to put some distance between us.

"You must marry me," he answered, amused with me for whatever reason I couldn't guess.

No sooner did he utter the words, than did our party, along with others for intermission, come bursting out of the doors, laughing and talking with no idea the effect his words would have on everyone.

"Uh, uh," I managed to grunt, stunned he still considered me in that way.

Genevieve had not heard what he said but could read the language on our faces though pretending otherwise. Looping her arm in his, she whisked him down the wide corridor, purring, "There you are my sweet. Charles had the insane idea you had gone to check on Makenna when that would have been his responsibility as her escort, after all." This time she was the cat instead of the canary.

Squeezing my hand, Minnie smiled and we walked slowly for some time before she asked, "Do you mind very much that we miss the bird girl? She chuckled at the thought of it. "I'm sure the others have returned by now."

"Of course not, I hope I haven't offended you in some way."

"Offended me? No, no, I hope you aren't hurting yourself."

Squinting, I questioned her comment, hoping it wasn't what I thought it was.

"Do not be angry with Charles or me but we both know the story of why you are no longer at the boarding house. Let me finish." She placed her hand on my arm and continued. "It was only a matter of time before he would find out, as curious a soul as he is, and you know I want to be in on things as well. He told me about the mysterious gentleman who we both know is not so mysterious to you."

"Oh Minnie, I don't know what to say." My eyes watered with emotion despite my best effort to keep it together. "I wouldn't hurt your daughter for the world."

"You think I haven't noticed how melancholy you are when he is around? What in heaven's name is wrong with you? Go after the man. I certainly would if I was your age. Genevieve loves the man of the moment, and it will soon be the Duke again, with my blessing."

Dumbfounded though grateful I wouldn't lose her friendship over the mess I had made, it still didn't help my situation at all. Someone would be hurt no matter what. Little did I know when I told Miss Lacey I was looking for relatives up north I would actually find them and be responsible for the unhappiness of a great-great-grandmother.

CHAPTER 68

The Jubilee

It was good to get back to work again. The days off had helped in some ways and in others had made things worse. Lily and Jean were anxious to know all the details of what we did and what we ate, but I couldn't share more than that. It was either too personal or too painful.

Gabriel had left for Europe the next day without a word to me. Mixed up six ways from Sunday, I was angry at him for not giving me the chance to answer him, as if I knew what the answer would be, and at the gall of him keeping Genevieve on a string. It was an impossible situation.

New Year's came and I stayed close to the show, begging off invitations, one from Minnie and the standing one by my roommates, and a few from new acquaintances met through the show. No way did I want to encourage anyone into this mess that was my life. The Wild West continued to keep me busy, and the few days I had off were in new amusements. The Eden Musee, a new wax museum close by entertained all my friends but particularly Lily and Jean who, having a fondness for the macabre, attended the Chamber of Horrors. Never a fan of horror movies, even of Vincent Price, I enjoyed the Winter Garden with its music and refreshments while they went below to "The Crypt."

Minnie insisted that I accompany her to see Ajeeb, a 10-foot turban wearing papier-mâché-and-wax robot play chess. It was curious to be sure, but we both came to the same conclusion. Someone was inside who knew what they were doing. Though bizarre, I didn't have to be told why

Genevieve wasn't along. She had not spoken to me since the day Gabriel left, unloading on me with both barrels, "Did you think I wouldn't notice how you managed to sit next to him at every gathering? Did you not think I would put two and two together, that you knew each other from the way you kept looking at him? You played with his heart one too many times, dangling him on a string, and now he doesn't want you, you want him! Well, you can't have him!" Her face resembled a strawberry, and she stomped her elegantly booted foot, emphasizing, "I'm going to England soon and will be married whether you like it or not."

Funny, but I had thought she was the one on the string. She pointed her finger directly in my face, fueling my ire, and I cautioned her, "You know, you might just draw back a stump if you don't get it out of my face…" I regretted saying it as soon as it came out of my mouth.

Cutting me off, she chilled me, "I was nothing but a friend to you, mostly because my mother thought so highly of you, but it appears to me that you are nothing." She sucked in another breath and plunged the sickening addendum in my heart, "Not only you, but all your kind… Southerners…you backwoods ignorant hicks!"

Unlike Ajeeb the robot, I didn't have a clue in my head what I was doing. Contemplating how to change her mind was as futile as the war had been. I knew she would always resent me, and the South by proxy, enough to cause some mighty nasty resentments that were passed on to her daughter. I took some wise advice and moved on.

It was no surprise when Minnie told me they were sailing to England at the beginning of February. In my mind, I saw the two of them, Genevieve and Gabriel, marrying and contemplated how that would work out for me. Did I just disappear into the cosmos somehow? Genevieve felt certain to be marrying Gabriel. However, Minnie assured me her daughter would become a Duchess instead, leaving her to come back alone in a few months. I would miss her terribly no matter what happened and told her so.

"Ah Makenna, I have known you for such a short time but admire you mightily." Half-grinning, she snickered, "It must be this penchant we have of thinking for ourselves."

"Pa always said if everybody is thinking alike, then somebody isn't thinking." I smiled, sorry to have to tell her of my plans. "Well, keeping in that tradition I have signed with Mr. Cody to do the Wild West in

England for Queen Victoria's Golden Jubilee. We sail sometime around the end of March, I believe."

"It's doubtful we will return before you sail but I'm sure we could work something out with Mr. Cody to get you to the wedding." I grimaced and she explained, "Once I get Mr. Christian out of her head, we move on to the Duke. The wedding will take some months to plan. Heaven forbid, I should bring her back here to marry." She paused and patted my arm. "Makenna, my dear, you have the opportunity, now take it."

CHAPTER 67

Angels and More Angels

Washington's Birthday came before long, and the show closed. Both of the runs at Erastina and Madison Square Gardens had been very successful. I'm sure I would have been sad to see the time end if I wasn't going overseas, too. Now the task at hand was packing away scenery and costumes, procuring food for the long trip then seeing to all the animals. With the large crew, it would get done with the last big push later in the month when all the supplies for those people would be packed, mostly dining supplies and tents.

Lily and Jean were going as well and talked of nothing for at least a week of what all they were going to do in London – Big Ben, Tower of London, the cathedrals, and, of course, pubs – until they realized there were still things they hadn't seen or done in New York City. Every free day had us in a museum, store, or park. At night I had Charles as my escort, instructed by Minnie to take me to the finer places I cared to attend. Although sincere and generous to a tee, I couldn't take her up on it until he would come and insist, himself out of sorts with them gone.

With our newfound truce, we began to test those limits. I agreed to a dinner party Sherman attended, and Bentley attended a most bizarre Old South party, until we both decided it was tacky and left. I enjoyed getting to know Ruth, and he saw I genuinely cared about others.

Genevieve was angry she had not heard a word from Gabriel before they left and wasn't exactly sure where he was staying in London.

Of course, Minnie found out in a heartbeat as soon as they arrived in Liverpool. It wasn't long before Charles received a wire informing of their safe passage and that Gabriel had returned to the states, no location mentioned. Genevieve wasn't one to be toyed with and to save face had immediately notified the Duke of their arrival. Charles expected a wedding announcement soon.

"So Makenna, it's your turn. It's our last day off before we leave, what do you want to do?" We had just left Sunday services with Lily and Jean staying close to me as they usually did these days with departure time getting close. March had gone as fast as February, and we would be boarding the boat on Thursday to sail on Friday. There was so much to do, but this afternoon was free.

"Too bad it isn't summer. I really wanted to see the Belmont Stakes before I left New York City." It was hard to imagine that the race started here, and the track would be a reservoir in a few more years.

"We can still go to Jerome Park. It's too late for skating, or sleighing but I'm sure there is something going on." Lily would have gone anywhere just to be going.

"Do you believe her? Our last day off for who knows how long, and she wants to watch the horses?" Jean threw her hands up in disbelief adding a little tisk to her comments.

"Okay, okay. It's a beautiful day…let's go to the park," I wanted to walk the six blocks north but was quickly vetoed by Jean. "I need the energy to walk in the park once I get there silly," she grabbed my arm, pulling me into a carriage.

Looking around for what I felt sure would be the last time, I felt the wonder of time travel, taking it all in, every detail, sight, and sound. It was an early spring, and the blue skies made everything cheerful including the monstrous mansions of the wealthy to the poorest looking person on the street. Flowers were beginning to bloom and birds were chirping. There was every reason in the world to be upbeat, but instead I felt akin to the weeping cherry. As we got out at 72nd Street, a bee buzzed by my head but I hardly flinched, not really caring if it took it off to parts unknown.

"Makenna, if you're going to be this way all afternoon we might as well tie you to a bench somewhere and come for you later," Jean fussed. I thought I was going to be okay, yet here it was, down to the wire, and what I had said all along I wanted was happening. He wasn't coming, and I should be glad for his safety sake but it was a lie. I wasn't glad at all.

My dreams were all of him, waking and sleeping. I was an anxious cat, at any moment hanging from a ceiling or teetering on a limb not knowing what my next move should be. I was miserable and stupid and longing for as much as a second of time with him. Memories haunted me – hunting with Daniel Boone, watching him train thoroughbreds, transfixing me with those eyes, quoting Shakespeare. I was going insane!

Couples strolled by, and I wanted to stick my foot out and trip somebody. Maybe I should trip myself going down the staircase to the fountain instead. Anything to get even with this pain I had inflicted on myself. Walking across the terrace, I marveled at the size and height of the fountain and the powerful effect the Angel of the Waters had on me. Its hand was outstretched blessing the water all around while the four small cherubim represented health, purity, temperance, and peace. Of course, I should have done this much sooner.

Closing my eyes, I prayed for the blessing of peace, that whatever happened from now on I could accept. I had accepted the death of my family, the strange travels, giving up Gabriel to keep him safe, but really, no, I couldn't do that anymore. Denying myself love again was insane when I knew life in any time was short. I instead began praying for peace with that decision and that somehow I would find him to let him know how stupid I had been. Over and over, I prayed for what seemed an eternity.

My friends had vanished when I opened my eyes, and another angel stood next to me, mystifying me with his presence, warming me with his eyes. Though my mouth was open I couldn't speak, didn't know what would come out if I could, but I didn't have to because his words were more than sufficient.

"You have no more power to influence the future than I – that is the Almighty's." Waiting for my reaction, all I could do was blink back the avalanche that was coming. "No one is guaranteed a tomorrow and if I only have a few – as you fear, you do not know – then I am content as I desire to spend them with you." Gently, I took his hands in mine. He, in turn, took mine, kissed them, and placed them upon his cheek. After a few moments, he kissed me softly, tucked my hand under his arm, and we walked away silently.

In the best old movies, all was resolved and everything turned out fine. It wasn't the ending of a swashbuckler, Errol Flynn and Olivia de Havilland in *Captain Blood,* the pirate and his lady love together at last but pretty close with Daniel Boone and the horse girl sailing away on Buffalo Bill's ark to begin whatever our lives together held in store.

EPILOGUE

Our life together began in London, continuing to several towns in England before traveling on to Europe. The show was well received everywhere we went. Royalty from every country attended and were fascinated with what they saw of the American West.

Ready to settle down to anonymity after the command performance of Queen Elizabeth in 1892, we bought an older seaside place overlooking a bay. It was a very comfortable home, reminding me of *The Ghost and Mrs. Muir*, for it had belonged to an old seaman. There was enough available land for a small barn as we found ourselves still drawn to caring for horses. Often, we rode on the beach, exploring the coast.

It was beautiful to watch the years pass there with the sea breezes and ocean sounds often making us forget the outside world although inevitably, tragedies came. Sometimes, we changed things without realizing, yet we did not interfere in events of the world. No one we knew got on the *Titanic*, but we did not look at passenger lists to connect dots. Although the War to End All Wars would not really be that, we found a way to help, working at a clinic or at dances to raise money. Learning the extremely popular Castle Walk – played by Fred and Ginger in one of their dance movies – was a blast, especially when you consider Gabriel knew how to do the Virginia reel.

In between the horrific years of war, Gabriel often went to London to marvel at the changes taking place. He particularly liked Leicester Square and the theatre district where we had gone several times when touring with Cody's show. In 1926, Fred and his sister Adele Astaire were playing at the Empire in *Lady Be Good!* The audience seemed to favor the playful and graceful Adele but I was, of course, mesmerized by Fred, especially his solo number *The Half of It, Dearie, Blues*. With a turn of phrase, his interpretation of George and Ira Gershwin songs made you forget he didn't sing nearly as well as he danced. *Fascinating Rhythm* was catchy, and I sang it long after the show was over.

Many of the royal family were in attendance on that particular night: Prince Albert, Duke of York (future King George VI and father to the present day Queen Elizabeth, recently born), Prince of Wales (later King Edward VIII who abdicated his throne), and Prince George (younger brother to the other two). Even then, royals were captivated by entertainers, inviting Fred and Adele to visit their box during intermission.

As others did during the Great Depression, we went to the movies, first to see the silent movies with Buster Keaton then through the fantastic thirties with Norma Shearer, Cary Grant, Jimmy Stewart, and Irene Dunn, just to name a few. Debra Kerr, Humphrey Bogart, Lauren Bacall, and Robert Mitchum were still to come! Although I had seen them all before, I was as fascinated as Gabriel.

Although we were beginning to show our age, we frequented dance halls to experience the Big Band music of Glenn Miller, Benny Goodman, and Tommy Dorsey that I had only dreamed of all those years ago. Youngsters laughed at the old couple out on the dance floor to "cut a rug." As much as we enjoyed the times, it was hard because we knew what was next.

Although in our eighties, we were healthy and answered the call to help with the war effort. We had to, though many laughed at our determination, calling us mad to come to a place that endured constant bombing, temporarily trading our home with a family fleeing their small apartment in London. Our work began with greeting the incoming and outgoing service men.

It was inside the train station in early 1944 I saw him, a tall, thin good-looking young man with thick, wavy red hair. He had a good-natured way with the other servicemen, telling one of his many stories with that oh-so-familiar sheepish grin causing them to walk away laughing at whatever fantastic tale he had told.

"Young man, care for a cup of coffee?" I asked, searching to see those eyes I was so fond of.

"Oh, yes, that'd be right nice, ma'am. It's been a long day," he answered with the same, maybe a bit clearer, Southern country accent.

He took the coffee, with a spoon of sugar, drinking it like it was his last. Thankfully, I knew better.

"My name is Makenna Christian, and this is my husband Gabriel. Where are you from?"

"My name's Will Ross…from Tennessee. Jest outside a' Nashville. You been there? I mean, you don't sound English." Grabbing Gabriel's hand to shake and then mine, I was warmed to my toes. "This coffee is jest how I like it."

"I know. I'm American and from Tennessee though I haven't been there in some time. Tell me about it, how things are there."

"Oh, ma'am I'd love to but we're 'bout to leave – duty, of course, shippin' out soon." With youthful exuberance, he peered closely with his bright green eyes. "You know, you 'mind me of someone. Same color of my girl's eyes, hazel, well, not all time, they change a lot dependin', she's a bit moody. I dunno why I told you that. Homefolk, I guess. Anyway, it's been a real pleasure to meet you ma'am, sir."

Expressing the joy I felt, I grabbed and hugged him for dear life, feeling the familiar embrace returned. Embarrassed, he turned up that aw-shucks grin of his and turned toward Gabriel, hand out-stretched.

"It was wonderful to finally meet you sir," Gabriel said, sincerely, shaking his hand again, taking a couple of steps back to look at the both of us together for the first and last time.

Confused and surprised by the show of familiarity and respect, Will Ross hesitated to say something but instead turned to leave. As he climbed the stairs at the train, he waved goodbye. My heart was heavy, aware of what he would have to experience, though through it all he persevered.

The train wasn't scheduled to leave for another five minutes and knowing exactly what to say, I hastily wrote a note and gave it to a nearby officer, asking him to make sure he received it. The atmosphere was charged with emotion, the smoke encircling couples crying their final farewells when we stepped upon the crowded platform joining all the others waving to the wonderful heroic young men. As the train pulled away, Pa's astonished face appeared in the window, and then leaned out. I blew him a final kiss, smiling through the tears puddling on my cheeks.

The stuff good movies are made of.

April 1944

Dear Mr. Ross,

Everything will be just fine as you will come out of this war in one piece and live to marry Miss Audra from back home. Though you will have a precious daughter and many happy years together sometimes life will have its tragedies. You are a wonderful husband, father, father-in-law, and best of all, grandfather.

Although I still do not understand fully what happened to me, know that I am okay. I had to leave to meet Gabriel, the man I have been married to for over fifty years. What wonderful men you both are. There must be a special place in heaven for you to have put up with me!

I will always love you very much, Pa.

Your granddaughter,
Audra Makenna Manning Christian